First Hardback Edition, October 2021

Cover Design: www.getcovers.com

Map designs: www.startwithadoodle.co.uk

Hardback ISBN: 9798763915976
Paperback ISBN: 9798763914958

About the Author

Jacqueline Florence is originally from the East End of London. Blue Star Rising was her debut novel and the first in the Kelan Series. She achieved her dream of joining the Woman's Royal Naval Service before eventually gaining an MA(Hons) in Psychology at the University of Aberdeen and a Postgraduate MSc in Urban and Regional Planning at Herriot Watt, Edinburgh. She has two grown up children who, over time, have made various attempts to leave home, but so far, only one has been ousted successfully. She now lives in Aberdeenshire with her husband and various other animals.

Also by Jacqueline Florence

The Kelan Sagas

Blue Star Rising
Sapphire Tree

For Bill

Acknowledgements

To Emily Florence, Carolyn Forrest, Jemma Body and Barbara Forbes for your invaluable input and critique. But especially to my husband Bill, who has listened and encouraged even my most fanciful imaginings without judgment; though the odd sideways glance has been known. To GetCovers Design, for their fabulous work and patience; and to Gail Armstrong of Startwithadoodle for bringing Kelan to life with her amazing maps and family tree. In particular, a thank you to Andy Lawrence, who won the competition to be a character within Sapphire Tree. Also, to David Scott and Ian Hammond for their help in military defensive planning.

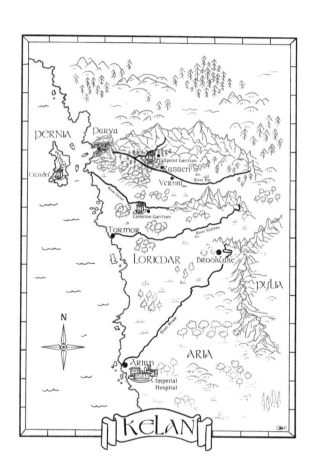

KELAN

Sapphire Tree

Prologue

His screams echoed around the darkened chamber, eyes bulging in terror, muscles rigid from the agony and tension of torture. Until finally, in an all too brief lull to his misery, he collapsed back onto the stone surface to which he was bound by wrist and ankle. Barely able to catch his breath, the hot, stale atmosphere burned at his lungs; instinct forcing the searing air inside.

The stench of his own sweat filled his nostrils. His insides had loosened long ago, though his pain confused mind couldn't recall when. The irony, that despite everything else,

1

of the pain and the horror, it is the embarrassment of losing control of his bowels that concerns him most.

He had no idea how long he has been in this living hell, whether he had been conscious throughout it all, or, if he'd even had a blissful respite of oblivion. Having given up begging his tormentors to tell him what they wanted, he had already succumbed to the madness; he was never going to escape this waking nightmare alive. Anger, horror and confusion were slowly, and terribly, being consumed by agonising pain, its measured advance lumbered towards the inevitability of death.

The creature administrating his living hell, had moved away from his side, but somewhere in the shadows he knew there were others.

Were there two of them?

There was slight movement in the shadows, where light from the few sconces set into the walls couldn't penetrate. When they finally came into view, he was sure he should have recognised the two men, but his exhausted and pain wracked brain was failing him. All he could see now were their dead eyes, wide with pleasure as they relished his dying moments before they returned to the darkness.

The creature brought its hideous body back to his side, he flinched; its greyish green skin oozing with a noxious liquid that shimmered in the dim light. A misshapen, bulbous head with boney triangular spines protruding from its skull, contained a muzzle of broken, pointed teeth. A long grey tongue hung from its drooling jaws, as hunger filled its insane eyes.

2

In the few times it moved away from its victim, the creature walked awkwardly on two legs, like an animal that was used to walking on four rather than upright. Wiry, strong arms with long thin, sharp fingers on gnarled hands, were already glistening with the man's blood. Its tongue licking at the thick, hot red fluid.

His body shivered uncontrollably, crisscrossed with cuts that had been sliced into his flesh; deep enough to cause pain, but not so deep he could bleed to death.

Not yet.

Arrogant and callous, he was a man who had spent most of his life dominating those who were desperate enough to enter his. He had never believed in any gods, he'd created his own fate and didn't owe anyone anything. But now he begged any spirit willing to listen, to purge his soul of this agony and let him die.

The creature watched with hungry eyes, the man knew it had finished playing with its toy, now it meant to finish its work.

Closing his eyes, he uttered a silent invocation.

The creature stood before the pathetic form. It wasn't concerned with the foul stench of the excrement and vomit that pooled around its victim's body; all it wanted was to taste the pure pleasure of his misery. Fed for so long on small, helpless creatures that barely satisfied its cravings; at last, its masters had been generous and brought it food that would sate it. Ready to gorge, hungrily, on the latest feast it had so lovingly prepared. Not flesh and bone, but the essence of pain and agony.

As a unique creature, created to perform the tortures that were such pleasures to its masters, it had no name. Why should it need a name? Those it met would never have the chance to tell of their final tormented encounters.

Stretching its arms up, breathing in the hot fetid air, it closed its wicked black eyes, before eventually opening them onto the delicious sight laid out before. It had no worries that its victim would fall unconscious before it had finished its feast, the toxic liquid that covered its body ensured that he would stay awake. It wouldn't want him to miss a thing.

Lowering its arms, it placed its sharp fingers against the skin, just above each of the man's knees, and thrust downward, piercing flesh, until it reached the hard bones of his thighs. The throat wrenching screams of the man reverberated around the chamber again, while the creature lifted its head, feeding on the sweet morsels of the man's agony.

Following the line of bone up the desperate man's legs, towards his groin, two lines were cut bone deep, the flesh slowly separating as its fingers sliced through skin and muscle.

Delight danced across its features while the victim's agony grew. Fingers, almost tenderly, encircled the flesh of the man's genitals. The creature, encouraged by his heightened pain, savoured the moment, taking precious time to slice through the soft, delicate tissue.

As the genitalia fell to the floor, the creature began its slow, sweet journey again, up to the fleshy torso. The man begging once more for oblivion; but he would just have to wait. The creature had yet to finis its feast.

4

Now, using both hands, the creature ran its razor sharp nails over his quivering stomach, lightly caressing his body before sending its sharp fingers down, digging deep into the flabby innards. The creature swayed slightly, feeling giddy as it gorged, slowly and lovingly it moved from his groin to throat, pulling the bloated body apart in its progress.

Drenched in its victim's blood, almost sated on his agony, the creature knew the feast was near its end. Laying its gore covered hands on the horror stricken features of its quarry's face, it dug its fingers about the flesh until they grated against solid bone. Then with a final wrench, the man's flesh was ripped from his skull; the creature crying out in ecstasy.

Rapturous in its pleasure, the creature absorbed the final throes of his agony, lapping up lingering morsels, before shredding the man's throat, allowing, at last, the sweet surrender of death.

Silence fell once more.

The man's body laid upon the stone slab, virtually pulled inside out. The creature surveyed its work with pride, before making its way, unsteadily, back into the shadows; intoxicated by the fruits of its endeavours.

Within the darkest corners, Gellan glanced at Duran, his eyes burned with manic delight. Their recent plans for that bastard Nathan may have been frustrated, but an unexpected opportunity had recently arisen. So, for now, they relished in their pet's work.

Only one more of their pawns to go, and soon they would unleash a hell that Nathan could only imagine in his most darkest nightmares.

Part one:

New

Beginnings

1

nici

There was an air of regret as the back door to the Retreat was closed behind them. Eight figures made their way along the overgrown path to the gazebo at the other end of the garden; the only point within the Retreat that they could translocate from. One woman, Jean Carter, walked amongst the group of seven men. She was looking particularly pleased with herself, having managed to convince the two Knights, Simon and John, that they should take their newly acquired food with them on their latest venture.

The sun was high in the sky over the Imperial City of Parva, its heat warmed their faces as they walked, their pace unhurried and relaxed. In passing they may have looked like a group of friends hoping to enjoy a picnic in the sun. Eight figures, strolling through the abundant, if overgrown, greenery of a garden that wouldn't look out of place around a stately home.

The truth was, a gentle stroll was about all any of them could manage at the moment, having fought a vicious battle only a few hours previously. Their adversaries had been Kaimiren, psychopathic soldiers genetically modified to withstand extreme situations. Highly trained to hunt and kill, their owners demanding vast amounts of money for their services.

The battle had required an adrenalin hit so high to defeat the Kaimiren, that it wasn't until sometime later, their bodies finally felt the full effects of the battering they had taken. Bruises were already blooming, and several ribs were feeling a little tender.

Paul was limping noticeably since the damage to his hip had left him almost lame; an injury that would have left any normal human unable to walk for some considerable time. But with Jean's intervention to help ease his pain and Stephen's ministrations as a surgeon, he hobbled along with the others, trying to ignore the looks of concern on their faces.

However, one advantage they all had, was that they would heal ten times faster than was normal for anyone else. Of course, the inevitable disadvantage was that the pain would be ten times worse. But with Stephen's expertise, a surgeon with a particular restorative talent for manipulating energy to heal the body, they were all able to continue. Only

8

the occasional wince indicated that they were not completely comfortable.

When they had made their way through the overgrown garden of the Retreat earlier, it had been more of a hack through a jungle. Fortunately, as some semblance of a path had now been cleared, the going was much easier, and far quicker.

The Retreat itself was created by the Knights as their home. The house and its gardens were beautiful havens where they could relax and unwind, forgetting the worlds outside, at least for a while. However, after Nathan had ensured the house and its grounds had been shut up and off limits for the past five years, the flora and fauna had run riot. Now brambles and weeds choked the pathways, and young sapling trees and bushes sprouted unchecked, as seeds took root and ran rampant through the garden.

Walking across the long grass of the once manicured lawns Nathan, Emperor of the Prime Worlds of the Seven Sectors, had a lot to think about. He was still unclear as to who these *Kaimiren* were and where they had come from. As well as finally consolidating the impact Ephea, his thoroughly disagreeable wife whom he'd been forced to marry under extreme circumstances, had on the public's perception of the Knights and the Order. The past five years had created suspicion and mistrust of the authorities by those within the Empire, and Nathan didn't blame them at all. It was going to take a lot of work to fully gain their trust again, if that was at all possible.

Instructions had been given to the High Council to begin the process of regaining order within the cities and areas

9

most affected by Ephea's Patrols. It was a start to a long journey, but for now, they had work to do elsewhere.

He considered Jean and the impact of her actions over the last few hours. A fellow Guardian, whom the Knights had only just met prior to the battle, yet she had provided the key to bringing down the final vestiges of Ephea's chaos. While they walked, Jean was discussing with the others how she had spent her time in Kelan over the past four months. Having first encountered Nathan, and several of the other Knights in Rassen, she was unaware at the time of the significance of who they were and the predicament the Empire had found itself in.

Stephen had been pleased to hear that Niall was still doing well on the farm with his prosthetic leg. An unfortunate legacy from his time as a knight in the Order, while serving as an engineer on Earth. Jean had spoken of their encounters with Captain Karen Johnson within Ephea's patrols, including her unknown whereabouts since her defeat at Jean's hands. She had been pleased to find out that PC Croft, an ally in solving a series of murders in the city, had been promoted to Sergeant. The Knights heard, with some amusement, how she had met Captain Ty Coniston, along with Colonel Anna Priestly, partners of Damien and Paul respectively.

Nathan noted that Jean still looked uncomfortable around Damien. She had seen Ty fall prey to the Kaimiren and was, for a while, convinced that he was dead. A fact that his cousin considered something Jean had no right to keep to herself, despite the impending battle that lay ahead. But it appeared Ty's death was very much over exaggerated and

10

luck was on his side, escaping with nothing more than some cracked ribs and a badly bruised arm.

Nathan fell in line with Jean as they continued along the garden path, observing that she spoke to the group as a whole and not any one person in particular. She still seemed to be smarting over their disagreement earlier concerning the fate of the decimated town of Belby, and to be fair, he wasn't exactly over the moon with her actions either. She had justified her behaviour by declaring that she had spent the last several thousand years making decisions alone, and that she didn't have the luxury of six other people to rely on. In turn he had pointed out that, whilst her isolation had been unfortunate, she was now no longer on her own.

He found himself sighing quietly to himself. Even though they had encountered each other some four months previously, it was less than twenty-four hours since they had finally met and talked; albeit briefly. And only this morning the eight of them had come together to fight the Kaimiren that had been sent to kill him.

Until a few days ago, Jean had believed that she was one of a kind; alone in the vastness of the universe. She was surprised when they had still expected her to stay with them, but the truth of the matter was, she was one of them, a Guardian. Irrespective of how long she had spent alone, she had a right to be part of their little coterie. She had a right to come home, whether she, or they, liked it. However, Nathan couldn't shift the feeling that life wasn't going to be quite the same again.

Reaching the gazebo, Nathan reflected on how Jean's presence had affected the other Knights. Damien was still fairly distant, his relationship with Ty had been difficult over the past five years, and Nathan got the impression that the speed in which Ty and Jean had become close had unsettled him. Simon, however, was just looking forward to going to Jean's spaceship and Nathan could only picture a giant child promised a special present on his birthday. He found himself chuckling quietly, which earned him a few odd looks from the others. He ignored them.

Paul was broody and quiet, nothing new there, but it probably didn't help he was still limping in pain from his injury.

His musings were interrupted as Stephen and Daniel shared a joke. Jean, still walking beside him, also started to laugh. Nathan felt a pang of something uncomfortable in the pit of his stomach. It was a strange sensation, one he hadn't felt before, but for some reason it was focussed mainly on Daniel. He frowned and tried to brush it aside, feeling ridiculous, why should it concern him if Daniel and Jean became friends? Of course it shouldn't.

But it did.

Looking up, he watched as Simon and John placed the box of food they were carrying on the ground under the gazebo some way ahead. Jean may have managed to persuade them to bring their coveted rations onto her spaceship, but it would only be under their watchful eye. Woe betide anyone who came between Simon, John and their food. A slight grumble from his own stomach reminded him that a decent meal was due soon, he hoped Jean knew what she was doing.

He glanced at the woman walking next to him, she seemed contented and relaxed and he found himself pleased to see her so.

'So Miss Carter, what exactly is this plan of yours?'

'Please call me Jean, Miss Carter sounds like an old school teacher.'

Nathan inclined his head but his face still remained impassive.

'Very well, Jean, what are we going to do when we get to your spaceship?'

He couldn't hide the exasperation in his voice and Jean frowned.

'You don't have to come you know. I can do this on my own, I'll let you know when it's all over and finished with.'

'And what the hell is that supposed to mean?'

He stopped and glared at her. How the hell did this woman manage to get under his skin? He noted the concerned glances that passed between the others. Jean didn't seem to care. She glared back.

'I don't know what your problem is with me, but I've had better mornings too. I'm sorry if you didn't like what happened to Belby, but a decision had to be made and I made it.'

She held up her hand as he tried to say something, he felt himself bristle at the gesture.

'Can we at least agree that while it wasn't the best solution it was one that worked. I promise that next time I will make sure everyone is kept in the loop, then you can do whatever you damn well like.'

13

Nathan clenched his jaw in frustration and took a while to answer. He calmed his breathing and closed his eyes, taking a moment before opening them again.

'Very well. What happened at Belby was unfortunate. But, considering the circumstances, we can't do anything about it now.'

He took another moment while he studied Jean. Putting his hands in his pockets, he forced himself to relax. His features softening, he concentrated his gaze onto her own. Jean gulped and looked as if she had to force herself from taking a step back. He presumed her reaction was a show that she was backing down. Feeling a brief moment of satisfaction he immediately dismissed it as childish, and looked away feeling guilty.

'As for leaving you to deal with everything else on your own, we both know that is not going to happen. I'm sorry if I was offhand earlier, I can assure you I'm as intent on getting to the bottom of this situation as you are.' He took his hands out of his pockets and indicated the gazebo. 'Shall we continue? And, I really would like to know what your plan is once we get to your ship.'

Jean hesitated before turning and making her way to the gazebo, Nathan falling in step beside her.

'It's NiCI, I call her NiCI after the computer that runs her. It stands for Neurological Cognitive Interface. But NiCI is not such a mouthful I find.'

Nathan raised an eyebrow and smiled. Jean's cheeks reddened and she lowered her gaze, stabbing the toe of her boot at the overgrown slabs that lined the area under the gazebo, clearing her throat before replying.

'NiCI is currently sitting behind Saturn's rings in Earth's solar system. She is out of range of any sensors that Earth may or may not have. She is programmed to keep up to date on all system processing within range, which is basically Earth.

'Unfortunately, the information we need is on the other side of the Seventh Sector, so all of the data we have seen so far is about twenty-four hours out of date. Therefore, we need to get back to her base where she can search for the information we need.'

Nathan frowned. 'That is the bit I'm stuck on. What information, and why do we need it?'

'Obviously, we need to find out who instigated this whole situation. We have assumed that it is Gellan and Duran that are ultimately responsible for everything that has happened, but we know that they can't directly interfere with the workings of the universe. So they had to have subtly set a string of events in order for all of this to happen.'

She waved her hands to emphasise her point.

'They would have had to organise the cleric from the monastery to finally make his way to Kelan, then persuade Royston Morecroft to play his part. They would have had to make sure the Kaimiren were here, ready to strike when the situation within Parva and the Empire was sufficiently rebellious and that you were vulnerable. That takes a lot of planning, involving a considerable amount of time and energy. And we've just put the kibosh on it all. They won't be best pleased, and by the sound of it, the information that NiCI has come up with would suggest they're already trying to cover their tracks.'

15

Nathan considered this a moment. 'I have to admit that having my head on a spike doesn't hold much appeal, but it wouldn't have made that much of a difference to the Empire. Other than the security barriers and links that I have created, in the long term there may have been some upheaval, but it would hardly be the end of the world, or the universe.'

Jean looked at him questioningly but he continued. 'Tell me more about these Kaimiren and what is the significance of the information we are looking for?'

'Well, the Kaimiren or Ren as they are more commonly known as, are genetically enhanced soldiers that go under further adaptations to make them strong, fast and difficult to beat.'

'Mercenaries then?'

Jean shook her head. 'No, they are not soldiers of fortune. They don't receive any payment for their services. They are owned by a very few powerful and highly dangerous people, who hire them out to those who have ridiculous amounts of money to pay for their services. To be honest you'll be lucky to find more than two or three Kairmiren working together as they are so expensive. The time and effort that goes into creating them is huge, so to lose one is extremely costly.'

Nathan looked at her questioningly. 'But you just said there were nearer to seventy of them here on Kelan.'

'Exactly. To have that many Kaimiren together would require hiring from more than one owner, and the expense alone would probably buy you a good M class planet.'

Nathan didn't actually say anything but mouthed something that Jean could only agree the sentiments of.

She nodded and said. 'Someone really wanted to make sure you were dead.'

Nathan shrugged. 'But that's the point, it wouldn't have made that much difference.'

'But you are the Emperor. Don't you run things around here.'

Behind them Jean heard quiet chuckles and looked back and saw a sea of amused faces.

'What have I said that's so funny?'

Nathan looked at her wryly.

'Yes, I hold the title of Emperor, and *we* effectively are the ultimate power within the Empire. But no, we do not run it as such.'

Jean just looked on confused and Nathan explained.

'Here, within Parva, we have a High Council. A large body of members who are democratically elected by the people of the Empire. There are, however, no Political Parties and no one, single General Election. Those who are elected have to be capable and must be completely trustworthy to represent their people. Only the leader of the High Council is appointed by me. If they fail to comply they are removed from office.'

'By whom?'

'By me! The Council have the responsibility of ensuring the efficient running of the Empire, but we make sure that it maintains the standards required to govern. Every six weeks, two of us sit over a Council meeting and any issues raised that need our attention, which we then work to gather to reconcile a solution. Every six months there is a full Council meeting where we are all present.

'Of course that is if we are still within the Empire and haven't been sent somewhere within the universe on a mission.'

Again Jean heard muttering behind her. She understood what he meant.

They had all assembled under the gazebo that Nathan had created within the gardens, allowing them to translocate elsewhere, and now she was aware of it Jean felt the subtle change when they entered the small area. Sending her thoughts to NiCI, Jean took the eight of them back to her ship. Within a moment they were all standing on her bridge deck, somewhere in space behind Saturn's rings.

They had arrived in the centre of a large circular area within NiCI's bridge. Sensing their presence, NiCI activated life support and lighting, though there was a brief moment until clean air was soon circulating around. The lights were dimmed, and consoles with flickering lights lined the hull and bulkheads. To one side there was a large viewing screen which showed views of the Gas Giant, Saturn; its surface of orangey/yellow gas clouds, consisting mainly of hydrogen and helium. Its rings of rock and ice glowed in the distant Sun's light.

Jean momentarily forgot that the Knights had never been into space before. The other six Sectors would not support a man-made spacecraft, so this view of a planet and space was a first for them. They stood for a while, transfixed, temporarily stunned into silence by the sight. Simon broke the spell by walking over to the viewing screen and reading

18

the information that constantly passed across it, before inspecting the consoles around the room.

The other Knights were shocked at his manners, and were quick to tell him to not be so rude. But Jean just laughed. She has had so few visitors over the years, and few of them are usually so intrigued by NiCI's workings.

'Well, as beautiful as Saturn is from this angle, I think it's about time we took NiCI back home, she can search for updates on our people of interest from there.'

They watched the viewing screen as Saturn disappeared and the image of a rock face came into view. Jean was met by looks of confusion.

'I thought we were supposed to be in space?' Nathan said.

'We are still in space, only we're inside an asteroid that is floating around in space.'

John perked up instantly. 'That is the inside of an asteroid?'

Daniel rolled his eyes. 'Fabulous, that's both of them off now. Simon with his toy spaceship and John with his rocks in space.'

By now, Jean had set NiCI to search for the information update needed, when she spied the large box that John and Simon had abandoned in the centre of the bridge floor.

'I don't know about all of you, but I'm starving.'

The suggestion of food seemed to do the trick. John and Simon retrieved the forgotten food box, and with Jean leading the way, they all followed her off the bridge and through a set of sliding doors. They were now within a long corridor lined with other doors. The lights were also dimmed here and Simon asked why it should be.

19

Jean shrugged. 'Simple fuel consumption. Everything in space has to be produced artificially, whether it's food, water, heat, light or air. So, if you don't need it, you don't waste it.'

'Fair enough. Quite an ominous thought when you put it like that.'

'Yep, you learn your priorities pretty quick out here.'

Jean then stopped them outside a set of doors which opened into a large room, where another viewing screen ran the full length of one bulkhead. A small kitchen had been created at the far end, with space made for a dining table and an arrangement of occasional chairs and sofas.

She spread her arms. 'This is basically my living space. I can keep an eye on what is going on via the screen and, when I actually have food around, I cook.'

Simon and John placed the food box on the kitchen counter, when they noticed the bowl Jean used to keep the mountain of crystals she had collected.

'Nathan, look at these. Are they what I think they are?'

Making his way over to the kitchen counter, Nathan eyed the crystals. He was intrigued.

'Surely not.'

He exchanged glances with Simon and John as he picked up a crystal and turned to Jean.

'Where did you get these from?'

He passed the crystal to the other Knights. They also looked enquiringly at Jean. She just shrugged her shoulders unconcerned by the interest.

'Bloody things are a pain in the arse. I've been dragged all over the Sector looking for them and bringing them back here. They've been causing chaos everywhere. The ones I didn't get to in time have been responsible for horrendous damage to people. There are even those that have disappeared altogether. To be honest, it is usually assumed that they have been vaporised. But personally, I've not seen evidence of this. Vaporisation at least leaves some genetic imprint, but in these cases, however, there is nothing left at all.'

Nathan looked shocked. 'You really have no idea what these are?'

Jean narrowed her eyes, she was suddenly far more interested in the crystals. The Knights watched as she made her way over to the bowl and picked one up.

'I have absolutely no idea. But you obviously do.'

Nathan opened his left hand and showed her an empty hand. Then from seemingly nothing, a crystal exactly like the ones in the bowl, formed in his palm. Jean was stunned. Taking the new crystal he now passed to her, she looked up at him, her eyebrows furrowed.

He grinned. 'I'm the one who's produced all of these crystals. They are actually part of me. I make them so that other people can move from one part of the Empire to the other without the necessity of using the official portals.'

Jean suddenly remembered Niall ordering her to run back to the farm from the picnic site, telling her to find the crystal in their kitchen when George was injured by Johnson.

'Right. So if you make them for people to use within the Empire, how the hell did they end up out here in the Seventh Sector?'

Nathan shrugged again. 'I have no idea. As I create them from pure energy, it is possible that the crystals that have

21

been unused and forgotten about over the centuries, have been absorbed by the universe. Only to appear again in another place, even another Sector. I have to admit it isn't something I have ever considered before.'

Jean pointed to the bowl. 'So, what do we do with these now?'

'Oh that's the easy part.' He grinned.

Placing his hand into the bowl, a gentle blue glow appeared around his hand, and slowly the crystals began to disappear. Soon the bowl was empty and seeing the look of confusion on Jean's face he explained.

'Just as I created them, I can reabsorb them.'

Jean began to walk around the room, playing with her bottom lip as she thought. She stopped and looked up at the Knights who were watching her.

'Does this mean that those people who have disappeared over the centuries, have in fact just been relocated to a different part of the universe? If so, there are some pretty unsavoury characters currently setting up business in places completely unprepared for them.'

The implications of her words were not lost on the Knights.

'Out of curiosity, how did you know where to find them?' Nathan asked.

'To be honest, I didn't actively go looking for them. I often find that now and again I would be drawn to a specific part of the universe, and inevitably one of these little critters is lurking around somewhere causing trouble.'

Damien sat down heavily in one of the sofas. 'Well, that would definitely answer a few questions about some of the

22

situations we've had to deal with over the years, and all because of Nathan's crystals. Talk about creating work for yourself.'

Everyone looked at Nathan and he just shrugged.

'Well there's nothing I can do about it right now. We'll just have to sort it when we get back home.'

But despite his attempt at indifference he looked concerned, this was quite a lot to deal with and the possible damage already done made him feel slightly sick.

By now Paul had started rummaging about the kitchen and unpacking the food box. Jean joined him at the counter, with Daniel following. Nathan watched them but said nothing.

Jean was looking at Paul with concern. 'You don't need to do that you know.'

Daniel laughed. 'When it comes to cooking Paul is your man. You'll never starve with him around. However, don't let Stephen near the kitchen. He can burn water. A genius on the operating table, a disaster at the kitchen table.'

'Bloody cheek. I'm not that bad.'

Stephen seemed put out, but the looks from the other Knights convinced Jean that maybe she should keep him away from the kitchen in future.

Turning to Paul she asked, 'Are you feeling any better now?'

He looked up and nodded, before carrying on with his endeavours.

'Still a bit tender, but a lot better now Stephen has sorted me out.'

He paused for a moment, then looked at her.

'I haven't thanked you for what you did for me back in Parva.'

Jean blushed slightly. It wasn't often she was thanked for the work she did. She looked down at her fingers, studying her nails.

'Not a problem. Anytime.'

He returned a smile and looked as awkward as Jean felt. Daniel grinned at them both and filled the uncomfortable silence.

'So, what are we having for dinner then?'

Paul seemed to recompose himself and grunted.

'You'll have to wait and see.'

Daniel was still grinning when he explained to Jean.

'Not exactly the life and soul of the party is our Paul.'

He received a dark look for his comments.

'You still want feeding I assume?'

Daniel held up his hands and grinned, saying nothing.

Nathan sat down hard next Damien and tried to make himself comfortable.

'I thought your computer, NiCI, said that the information would only take three minutes to gather. It seems more like twenty now.'

Jean agreed. 'You're right. NiCI, what's the status on getting through the Galactic Police encryption?'

The calm, female, disconnected voice of the onboard computer answered.

'There has been another layer of encryption added to the security protocols referring to this data. It is taking time to work through the various algorithms to break down the coding.'

24

Jean sighed in frustration. 'How long before you can get through?'

'Fifty-seven minutes.'

Jean started to pace again and played with her bottom lip. Nathan watched, this was obviously Jean's default thinking mode. As she paced, Jean looked up at the viewing screen and asked another question.

'NiCI, who is the Officer in Charge of this investigation?'

'Current data indicates Superintendent Atiko Ramboss.'

Jean groaned and placed her hands onto the back of an empty chair.

'Well, that explains a lot.'

'It does?' Nathan asked.

'Ramboss and I don't exactly see eye to eye. He's probably added the extra encryption in order to put me off. Well that's not going to happen. NiCI, is Peyton Chi involved with the case?'

'Inspector Chi is the lead investigator.'

Jean grinned. 'Excellent, Now we're getting somewhere. NiCI, use the following code to bypass Ramboss' encryption.'

She then conveyed several numbers and random words. NiCI's voice then confirmed that access to the previously hidden files was now possible. Immediately, file names and data began to fill the whole viewing screen, followed by a dozen or so vivid pictures of crime scenes.

The pictures were graphic to say the least. They were of, presumably, once living beings that looked as if they had been turned inside out. Flesh ripped from bones, entrails strewn around the crime scene.

'SHIT'

Damien and Nathan stood up and joined the general consensus of shock around the room. Even Paul stopped his chopping of vegetables to take in the data now displayed on the screen. Jean studied the information before speaking.

'NiCI, these are four of the people you have identified as owners of Kaimiren. What about the other two?'

Two more pictures appeared, though this time they were of people still living, NiCI replied.

'Deimi Ka has been identified as missing. No information is available as yet. Franco Choi was last located on his ship, the StarBird.'

There was a pause then NiCI continued.

'Reports have suggested that Franco has been gathering reinforcements to his security over the past several days.'

Jean raised an eyebrow and shared a look with Nathan.

'He's obviously spooked after all the other deaths. NiCI, make a flight plan and take us to the last known position of Franco's StarBird. But stay out of range.'

'Understood. Estimated time to arrival, one hour fifty-five minutes.' Then the computer went silent.

Stephen was studying the pictures of the bodies on the screen. Paul had joined him, he seemed to be frowning more than usual.

'I have to admit I can't see any animal causing this kind of damage. The wounds to the skin and flesh edges look as if they are incisions by a very sharp knife. But I don't see any damage to the bones which would suggest the flesh had been pared with a metal implement, or chewed by teeth. It seems more likely it's been physically pulled away from the bone.'

Stephen nodded.

'I agree. The flesh was possibly cut down to the bone with something extremely sharp, but then ripped apart with considerable brute strength.'

He demonstrated with in hands in the air. Everyone got the point.

Daniel joined them. 'Were they alive when this happened?'

Stephen and Paul shrugged and Stephen turned to Daniel.

'That's impossible to say from these pictures. But to cause this much damage you would hope it was done post mortem. If not, it soon would be.'

Jean shook her head. 'Unless someone knows what they are doing and managed to keep them alive until the end.'

Everyone looked at her in horror.

Jean shrugged. 'Welcome to the Seventh Sector.'

'This StarBird we are going to now. Are you sure Franco Choi will still be there?' Nathan asked.

'No, of course I can't be absolutely sure. But he's probably terrified like all bullies who find themselves at the wrong end of a punch. His natural reaction is more than likely to run to a bolthole, putting as many people he can find between him and possible danger.'

'So you know this Franco then?'

Jean snorted. 'Oh yes. In fact all of these people…' She indicated the viewing screen. '…are known villains, who have enough wealth and dubious friends in high places to make sure they stay, legally, squeaky clean. You don't own Kaimiren for hire as a public service.'

Nathan sighed and put his hands in his pockets.

'Sounds like the usual people we meet in this line of work. Well, if we have a couple of hours to kill I suppose Paul, you can finish whatever you are doing in the kitchen.'

His stomach made some loud growling noises to prove a point. 'I have to admit to feeling a bit hungry.'

There was a lot of nodding heads from everyone else and Paul gave a smile before continuing with his chopping, eventually making some particularly mouthwatering smells in the kitchen.

2

A Gruesome Scene

Peyton Chi grabbed hold of the handle above her seat.

'For fuck's sake Boyles.'

Boyles glanced at his passenger sitting next to him, her knuckles were white from where she had held on so tightly. He had barely slowed down as he made a hard left onto the main road. Peyton did miss his half hearted attempts to hide a smirk.

'Sorry Boss. I thought you wanted to get to the scene quickly.'

She wasn't fooled by the smarmy little git. 'Quickly, and in one piece.' Chi barely got the words out through her gritted teeth. 'Now, slow the fuck down.'

Boyles rolled his eyes and slammed the brakes on hard. Peyton was ready for it and braced herself with feet planted firmly against the floor of the police vehicle. Its velocity was almost instantly reduced from breakneck speed to a sedate walking pace in the middle of Downtown Beida traffic. It may not look pretty but it was better than being hurled against the windscreen and covered in impact foam. All around, the angry blasts of vehicles' horns rang out as people tried to avoid the, almost stationary, police vehicle.

Satisfied that Boyles wasn't going to kill her, or anyone else on the road anytime soon, Peyton resumed scrolling through the police files on her hand held screen in front of her. They were on their way to a piece of wasteland on the outskirts of the city limits. A body had been found by a couple of lads making their way back home, after a prank left them naked and dumped by their friends in the early hours of the morning. They had literally fallen across the body as they both went for a pee behind some bushes on the side of the road.

Peyton grinned. *Bet that sobered them up pretty quickly.*

Details of the crime scene were sketchy, but there were marked similarities to the other four bodies they'd found throughout the city in the past two weeks. Apart from the horrendous ways the victims had died, it was *who they were* that had the top brass panicking upstairs. These weren't just big chiefs in the underworld, these were the biggest and baddest of the lot. Men and women who terrorised the galaxy, but through the slick work of some expensive lawyers, and letting others get their hands dirty, they were virtually untouchable by the law, anybody's law. Or so everybody thought. Someone however, was able to get past some highly sophisticated heavy security. Not caring if every lethal hitman available in the Galaxy was employed to hunt them down, as those still left alive panicked and ran for cover. What concerned Peyton the most however, was that for some reason, all the bodies ended up dead here, in Beida — hardly crime central for the underworld.

She looked up as Boyles slowed down, pulling the police vehicle over to the brown, heat blasted grass verge. Leaving the city behind they were now in amongst dried grass, stunted bushes and some very resilient trees. Not the most welcoming place to visit. Not a bad place to dump a body though, no cameras and traffic would be light, particularly in the early hours of the morning.

It was already threatening to be another hot day, and the thought of a festering dead body bloating in the heat didn't appeal to Peyton at all. Just as she was about leave the vehicle, an alert flashed across her screen. She told Boyles to go ahead and she would join him in a minute. Settling back into her seat, the vehicle door left open to allow a breeze in. The rapidly warming air around her barely moved and her shirt was already stuck to her back with sweat under her jacket.

She checked her screen again, noting with satisfaction that someone had accessed the encrypted police files with her own code number. Peyton sighed. There was only one person she knew who would be able to do that. Jean Carter and her pet computer NiCI. Wryly she reflected that, while Carter may have a particular knack for bringing chaos wherever she went, she ultimately got the job done. Ramboss was going to be furious but to hell with him. Right now Peyton was beginning to feel quite relieved and positive about Jean's interest in the case. Though she was damned if she was going to tell Carter that.

Peyton joined Boyles, who was talking to one of the forensic team. As she approached the pair, she was hard pushed to decide whether the scientist was either male or female, the all in one suits did nothing to help to decipher the usual lumpy bits of the anonymous person. The Inspector just nodded to the stranger as she joined them, and the Detective thanked the innominate individual as they went off to continue their work.

He turned to Chi. 'It's as we thought. Same as before, bits of them all over the place. Looks as if the wildlife has been busy as well.'

'Oh how wonderful.' Peyton grimaced at the thought of what was about to greet them.

'Pathology isn't pleased either. Apparently the two lads who found the body weren't too bothered where they threw up. Seems there's going to be a fair bit of last night's bar snacks and alcohol to clear out before the body can be dealt with properly.'

'Yuck. Who's the duty doc on site?'

'Dr Jules Cain.' She didn't bother to hide her grin as Boyles could barely contain his disappointment. Cain always managed to make him feel like a six year old child.

'Never mind Boyles. So where are these party boys then?'

The Detective inclined his head towards a paramedic vehicle where two young men sat wrapped in blankets, shivering despite the increasing heat. They didn't look at all well.

'Ok, make sure we have their statements and get them home as soon as possible. They look as if they could do with a good bed right now. In the meantime let's take a look at the body so the paramedics can clear it away and out of this heat.'

They donned their own protective suits handed out by a young police woman. She didn't look too well and Boyles noticed Peyton's glance.

'First murder. At least she had the sense to chuck up away from the body.'

Peyton nodded. 'That's a start. She could go far with brains like that.'

Boyles looked at her sharply, sensing a jibe in there somewhere, but Peyton's face was a mask of innocence.

'Right, let's get this over and done with.'

They made their way to the body, following a path laid out by forensics. The smell hit them before the sight, and Peyton was satisfied to see Boyles struggling to keep his own stomach contents down.

'Over there Boyles, don't want any of that crap you eat and drink contaminating the scene anymore than it is.'

He scowled and mumbled something about being perfectly alright. They finally caught up with the source of the smell, and no matter how much she braced herself, Peyton reeled at the sight. Internal organs were strewn around the ground and caught up within the branches of bushes and trees; chunks of meat beginning to dry in the increasing heat and wind. It looked as if someone had thrown them haphazardly around after they had dumped the body.

Now Peyton had to look at the body whether she liked it or not. It appeared to be a male by its build and fine hair covering, but Peyton knew that wasn't necessarily an indication of gender; though there was a gaping hole where his genitals should have been. However, there was evidence that it was once a human being; its skeleton for one thing. Broken white bones were open to the air, while flesh was pulled back and flattened against the ground, barely attached by tendons and torn skin. She found herself forcing down her own breakfast. A slice of toast grabbed on her way out of her apartment to meet Boyles in the waiting car earlier.

The grinning skull lay at an odd angle to the rest of the body, eyes and tongue already scavenged by wildlife, the face and scalp pulled back and fanning out on the ground behind it. Her stomach lurched again at the sight and she clenched her teeth tightly. Unfortunately, this meant she had to breathe through her nose which wasn't helping at all.

Standing over the remains was the pathologist, Dr Jules Cain, directing one of her assistants to take various photographs of a point of interest to her. Hearing Peyton and Boyles approach, the doctor looked up and gave a cursory greeting, before barking that they should stay right they were.

'There's an eyeball at the bottom of that bush, obviously dropped by some animal but it needs to be collected anyway.'

Both police officers stopped dead and looked down at their feet, spotting the bloody sphere just inches away from Boyles' right foot. One of Cain's assistants rushed over and picked up the eye and dropped it into a forensic bag. Peyton heard Boyles give a slow quiet groan, but said nothing herself. She knew exactly how he felt.

When she was ready, Dr Cain made her way over to the two police officers. She was a tiny woman who looked as if a breath of wind would knock her over. Peyton wasn't fooled however, this woman had been in the business for over thirty years, she was heaving dead bodies around when Peyton was still dodging bullies in the school playground. Her assistants were terrified of her, but all loyal to every last one.

'So what can you tell me Jules?'

'Well, he's definitely dead. That much I can confirm.'

'Thanks for that. Even in my limited capacity as a lowly police officer I could have figured that out.'

Cain scowled and rolled her eyes.

'If you insist. He didn't die here. This is a dump site.'

Boyles looked up from his notebook. 'How do you know?'

Cain narrowed her eyes at him, he tried not to flinch.

Peyton shook her head. 'Sorry Jules, we haven't found out how to turn off the idiot button yet.'

A red glow rose up his neck and coloured his cheeks. Jules ignored his discomfort.

'Hmmm. Well, young man, I can tell he didn't die here because, despite various bits of him littered everywhere, there is hardly any blood. Whoever is responsible for this...' she waved her left hand to the twisted remains. '...did it elsewhere until the body bled out. Then they moved it.'

Trying to claw back some self-respect Boyles replied.

'So there should be a kill site somewhere and a means of moving the body?'

Cain nodded. 'Correct, and the kill site will be absolutely swimming with blood. Even if they try to clean it up its likely there'll be traces.'

Peyton felt frustrated.

'Can't you tell us anything new? I'm assuming this is the same as all of the previous ones?'

Cain gave one of her usual scowls.

'I am not going to confirm either way until I've examined the body properly.'

Peyton sighed loudly and gave Cain one of her own glares back. The pathologist shrugged.

'Indications suggest there are many similarities. But that is not a confirmation.'

'Fair enough. When can you get him, or her, onto the slab?'

'Oh its definitely a him. Even without his essential equipment available.'

Cain glanced at Boyles who looked confused.

'Balls young man.'

'I beg your pardon?' Boyles was shocked.

To her credit Peyton did try not to laugh.

Cain explained further.

'His genitals. His meat and two veg. Do I need to expand further?'

Boyles held his hands up. 'No, I get the drift. It's a guy.'

Cain and Peyton glanced at each other before looking away with grins on their faces. It was Peyton who composed

36

herself first while Boyles looked murderously at the pair of them.

'So, how exactly do you know this is a man?'

'Oh that's easy Inspector Chi, I've seen this man before, we both have.'

Cain moved over to the body and raised the remains of his left arm. A tattoo of a dragon eating its own tail was still visible. Peyton let out a gasp.

'Deimi Ka.'

'The one and the same.'

Peyton turned to Boyles.

'Franco Choi must be shitting himself. See if you can get an exact location for him right now. We seriously need to speak to him before he gets butchered too.'

Boyles nodded and left the crime scene, quickly. Peyton was sure he was probably just as relieved to get away from the horrendous smell and sight, as well as the two female nemeses.

Nathan, Jean and the rest of the Knights had just finished the lunch that Paul had created. Apparently it was a traditional dish in Pylia, Paul's original home, made from fish and vegetables highly seasoned with herbs and spices. It was similar to the food created in his newly adopted home on Earth. Unlike the rest of the Knights who had set up homes within Britain, Paul had opted for the warmer climes of the South of France. Jean made a mental note to ensure an invite to visit the exotic climes of the Mediterranean was forthcoming quite soon.

Clearing the dishes away, the eight of them were now sitting down, feeling full and satisfied, a welcome change after the trouble of the previous twelve hours. Moments later the disembodied voice of NiCI cut through the peace.

'A body has been found on Tandor outside the city limits of Beida.'

'That's where all the other bodies were found.' said Jean.

Everyone looked up and saw a file appear and open on the viewing screen, Jean stood up to investigate, Nathan joined her.

'Details of the crime scene are limited, but there are enough similarities to the others that warrant further investigation.' Jean continued.

Nathan agreed. 'Though perhaps for all of us to descend on the area might not be appreciated. I suggest you and I, along with Stephen and Damien, should go.'

Jean hesitated for a moment.

'Is there a problem?' He asked.

She bit her lip and still didn't answer.

'You weren't thinking of going alone surely?' Nathan studied her while she considered how to answer. In the end, she seemed resigned and shrugged her shoulders.

'No, of course not. Are we ready to go then?' She turned away with the excuse of picking up her jacket, while Nathan turned a serious look on the other Knights, in particular to Simon.

'Is there any chance there will still be a spaceship in one piece when we get back?'

Simon gave a look of hurt innocence. 'I don't know what you are suggesting.'

'Hmmmmm.'

Jean winked at Simon from behind Nathan's back.

'NiCI, make all your schematics are available for analysis by our guests.'

Nathan looked at her sharply. 'Are you mad? You want him to know how this thing works?'

'Of course. I'm always thankful for a bit of help with changing the old spark plugs. Besides, it'll keep him busy for a while.'

Nathan looked back at Simon, who barely had time to remove his grin and replace it with his innocent face.

He just shook his head. 'Shall we go?'

Jean, Damien and Stephen followed Nathan out of the room and they made their way to the bridge. When they arrived Jean called out. 'NiCI, all stop.' When the ship had come to a standstill Jean continued. 'Once we have left the bridge continue the course to the StarBird. How long now until ETA?'

'Forty-seven minutes.'

'Fair enough, that should be plenty of time to get the information we need.'

Then, Jean set out her mind and the four of them found themselves on the side of the road leading into Beida. There were police, paramedics and forensic scientists busily going about their business. The sun was getting high in the sky and the four of them were wishing they had left their outer coats behind on NiCI. Looking around they made their way to the centre of the activity that was set away from the road and amongst the sparse undergrowth and trees. People glanced their way questioningly, but when they saw Jean they quickly looked away and carried on with their work. Nathan eyed the woman at his side curiously.

'No one seems concerned that we have just suddenly arrived. They seem to know you too.'

Jean shrugged. 'I've had cause to work with the Galactic police before. I wouldn't say that no one is concerned. More likely trying to keep as far out of the way as possible.'

Damien chuckled. 'A notorious reputation? I'm beginning to see why Ty got on so well with you.'

She shared a glance with him. 'If that is the case what does that say about you?'

Damien said nothing, but a suggestion of an evil grin began to spread across his face.

'What the fuck are you doing here?'

The four of them stopped short and stared at the man who was glaring at them with undisguised animosity on his face.

Rolling her eyes she greeted the man as if he was a long lost friend she wished was still lost.

'Boyles, how lovely to see you. We were wondering where we can find Peyton. You know, the one with the brains.'

'If Ramboss finds out you're here he'll have you run off the planet.'

She didn't look impressed.

'Now we both know he wouldn't have much luck doing that, and the only way he'll find out is if someone tells him. Which of course, you wouldn't dream of doing, would you Boyles?'

The threat was undisguised, and Boyles didn't say anything. He balled his fists in anger and turned and stormed off to his police vehicle.

'Well, good to see you know how to keep the locals happy.' Nathan gibed.

'There's no love lost on either side I can assure you.' She looked uncomfortable under the scrutiny of the Knights and turned, making her way towards the crime scene. The Knights looked at each other before following, with Nathan in deep thought while they made their way along the marked out pathway. They wrinkled their noses at the smell as they approached the body, Jean groaned and turned to Nathan.

'How's your luck with difficult women?'

He looked at her with a well practiced straight face.

'Well, so far with today's experience, it can be a bit hit or miss.'

'Cheeky bastard.' Scowling at him, she stomped off to talk to the Inspector, mumbling under her breath.

Damien raised an eyebrow to Nathan. 'You do know how to press the right buttons to piss her off.'

'Hmm, it's quite mutual I can assure you.' He growled.

Nathan followed Jean down the path and Damien shared a grin with Stephen. By the time Jean had caught up with Peyton and Cain, she had made sure a smile was fixed firmly on her face.

'Inspector Chi, how the devil are you? And Dr Cain, wonderful to see you as ever.'

Peyton spun round and Cain looked up sharply.

'Oh for fuck's sake. What are you doing here?'

Nathan caught up with Jean in time to see the smile momentarily slip. *Did this woman annoy everyone she met?*

'Same thing as you I suppose, looking at dead bodies. Who's this then?'

Cain tried her best scowl, but she soon gave up. It was pointless in trying to intimidate Jean, bloody woman was tougher than she was. She glanced again at the men following and tried to regain some authority on her patch.

'Are you determined to contaminate my crime scene?'

Jean held up her hands. 'It's ok, we'll not come any further. So, is it Deimi Ka?'

Both Cain and Peyton looked at each other and then back at Jean. The Inspector stood with her hands on her hips and confronted Jean, who was quite a few inches taller than her, but she made a good effort anyway.

'Now how the hell do you know that?

Jean sighed. 'Long story.'

'I'm listening.'

'Not here.' Jean shook her head and gave the Inspector a look that suggested the subject was ended. Peyton took the hint and instead she looked at the men standing beside her.

'You decided the solitary maverick look not to your liking anymore?'

Jean forced out a laugh, the Knights were giving her a curious look as she made the introductions.

'Gentlemen, this is Inspector Peyton Chi and Dr Jules Cain. Peyton, Jules, this is Nathan and Damien L'guire and Stephen D'Arian.' Indicating the body still lying on the ground, the smell not made any better with the rising heat and puddles of vomit lying around. 'Interested parties shall we say?'

The five strangers acknowledged each other.

Peyton was cautious. 'Interested in what?'

'All those found dead so far, as well as the missing Franco Choi, have all hired out Kaimiren to one party in the last few months.'

Peyton looked shocked.

'Why don't I know about this?' Jean said nothing. 'How many Kaimiren are we talking about?'

'Somewhere in the region of seventy.'

'Shit. No way. Who the hell can afford that many Kaimiren?'

'Someone willing to cover their tracks by killing Kaimiren owners.'

'So, where are these Kaimiren now? Has someone else taken over their ownership contracts? Shit, have we got rogue Ren roaming the Galaxy now?'

Jean raised her hands to calm Chi.

'It's ok. None of the bastards are around anymore. That little problem has been sorted. We're just here to tie up a few loose ends.'

'Dead?' Peyton shared a shocked look with Cain. 'All of them?'

Jean glanced at Nathan who raised an eyebrow.

'Er yes.'

'You?'

'No, not entirely. I did have a little bit of help.' Nathan gave Jean a hard look, he still let her lead the conversation but he was getting impatient. She grinned back before adding. 'Well, quite a lot of help actually.'

Peyton looked as if she wasn't sure what to say, but her interest in the three men seemed to be growing.

Jean continued. 'Jules, would you mind if Stephen here had a look at the body? He's a surgeon and an experienced pathologist.'

Jules looked at Stephen and seemed about to object but changed her mind.

'Please, help yourself.'

One of her young assistants approached Stephen with an all in one suit and held it out to him. He looked at her as if it was a filthy rag. She flinched and looked to Cain for support.

Jules put her hands on her hips and studied Stephen. 'If you want to view the body, you suit up.'

Stephen was about to object when Nathan cleared his throat.

'Just put the bloody thing on or we'll be here all day.' He took the suit from the assistant and held it out to Stephen who snatched it out of his hand.

It didn't help that Stephen was a big man, and that the people of Tamar were not particularly tall. By the time he managed to get into the suit it was far too short in the arms and legs, and was threatening to burst at the seams. He looked at Nathan in disgust, who, despite his attempt at indifference, couldn't help the corners of his mouth twitching. Behind him, Nathan heard strangled noises from Damien which suggested he was having a harder time controlling his amusement. A few of Cain's assistants were watching with grins on their faces until the pathologist threw a dark look in their direction and they made sure they looked busy elsewhere.

Stephen glowered mutinously, but made his way over to the body, appearing to have problems walking. Nathan had to look away quickly, Damien now had his back to the scene and his shoulders were shaking.

'For heaven's sakes Damien, try to control yourself.'

Damien turned and Nathan had to look away to avoid making eye contact. He saw Jean looking at them both curiously and he made a valiant effort to turn back to the scene with a straight face. Damien joined him with a fixed frown on his face, while Stephen was talking with Cain.

'I gather you've had a few of these over the past few weeks.' He asked Jules.

'Bloody awful. All the same, flesh stripped to the bone and virtually pulled inside out. And all while they were conscious enough to watch and feel every minute of it all.'

Stephen bent down to study the body further, he visibly winced as the suit cut into places he rather wished it didn't. There was a brief ripping sound as if one or two seams had given up under the strain.

Jules continued. 'Toxicology has shown a high level of steroids similar to fludrocortison acetate. We know it wasn't taken orally, more likely directly into the blood stream. All the victims were very much awake during the process.'

She pointed to the body's wrists and ankles. 'They fought their bindings. Even to the point where one of them dislocated their wrist trying to get free. Pointless though.'

Stephen nodded as he heard Jule's findings. He couldn't fault her work.

45

Nathan, Damien, Jean and Peyton listened in silence, suddenly they couldn't remember what was so funny earlier.

'Any evidence of who did this?' Stephen asked.

Jules shook her head.

'We received some DNA from all of the bodies but it's been impossible to find anything conclusive. The DNA was incomplete and no living thing could exist with the data we found.'

'Can I get a copy of the pathology reports? Including a copy of the tests you've done, incomplete or otherwise?'

Jules looked affronted. 'I can assure you my methods are thorough. Are you suggesting I have failed in something?'

Jules gave Stephen her hardest stare and she was pleased to see him flinch. He put his hands up in appeasement.

'No, I can assure you. I have no doubt your investigations have been thorough, let's just say we may have a different perspective on things.'

Jules didn't look convinced and before Jean could say anything, Nathan caught the police officer's attention. 'Please Inspector. We'll let you know if we find anything new.' He hadn't failed to notice the look of annoyance on Jean's face at his intervention.

Peyton took a moment to consider. She was already going to be up to her neck in it with Ramboss when he found out about Jean's involvement. She might as well go the whole way and completely piss him off.

'It's alright Jules. Ramboss is going to go apeshit anyway. We might as well make sure he has a good reason for his impending heart attack.'

Jules sighed and agreed to make sure all documents pertinent to their investigations was made available. Satisfied they had gleaned all the information they could from the site, they made to move away, but Peyton put her hand out to stop Jean.

'So, where are you going now? What do you know about these killings and why they are here in Beida in particular?'

Again Nathan answered first.

'It's something we're just looking into.'

He made to walk away but Peyton wasn't happy.

'Hold on, you can't trample all over my crime scene, demand to have highly confidential information, then just walk away. I'm not some rookie cop. I'm the Senior Investigating Officer and I need all the information available to find out who did this.' She looked hard at Jean.

'Peyton, I'm sorry for Nathan's rudeness.' Nathan looked at her sharply, clearly not happy at being considered rude or requiring to make apologies. Damien and Stephen glanced at each other as the doctor was making a marked effort at trying to wrestle his body out of the ill fitting forensic suit.

Jean continued before Nathan could say anything. 'Look, at the moment NiCI is on her way to Franco Choi's last known location. With any luck he can throw some light on what's been going on; if not confirm what we already suspect.'

'Which is?'

'Jean...' Nathan cut in before she could reply. Jean ignored him.

'Come with us and maybe we can piece together everything we have.'

'You know if Franco finds out you're following him, he'll have every bent lawyer in the galaxy on your tail.'

Jean laughed without humour. I have absolutely no doubt that our Franco will be preoccupied with trying not to be found by others, rather than us, or the police. Now are you coming?'

Peyton didn't think twice, she agreed and marched up the pathway. Jean went to follow but Nathan caught her arm.

'What the hell do you think you are doing?'

'Getting help in finding out what is going on and why someone wants your head on a stick.' She pulled her arm away in irritation.

'Do you really think it's wise to involve other people in this?'

Despite Nathan's height advantage Jean squared up to him, it took all his effort not to step back.

'Let's get something straight. I've worked in this Sector for too many years than I care to remember, and one thing I have learnt along the way is not to turn down help when it's offered. In case you hadn't noticed, I don't have six other experts at my beck and call. So, seeing as you're new around here, the expertise we need are civilians who are professionals all the same. So you get off your high horse and let's get back to NiCI, she's probably at her destination near the StarBird now.'

Jean then turned on her heel and followed Peyton up the path to where the Inspector was talking to Boyles. Behind her, Nathan was trying his best not to grind his teeth in anger as Damien and Stephen joined him.

'Bloody woman is impossible.'

'I thought she had a valid point actually.'

Nathan spun on Stephen beside him. 'Really?'

'Absolutely. Dr Cain seemed very professional and the Inspector and Jean are obviously well acquainted.'

Damien cleared his throat and they both looked at him.

'Nathan, I know it is difficult to have to rely on someone else, but so far we've had every reason to trust Jean. Why change now?'

Nathan raised an eyebrow.

'You didn't think her judgment was so clever earlier when she thought Ty was dead and didn't tell you.'

Damien pursed his lips.

'Well, maybe I've had time to realise that I may have overreacted.'

'You think?'

Stephen stood between the two men.

'Hey, come on. The last thing we need is for you two to have a falling out. I have to admit Nathan, I agree with Damien. Let's see what Inspector Chi has to say, she obviously knows Jean far better than we do.'

Nathan looked at both of them.

'Alright, We'll go along with it. For now'

Satisfied he'd diverted a minor disaster, Stephen made his own way up the pathway to the road to join Jean and Peyton. Nathan and Damien followed in silence, watching in amusement as the man in front seemed to be walking awkwardly before yanking out the material that had been forced between the cheeks of his backside. The pair of them gained disapproving looks from the rest of the investigating team as they both started to laugh, and Stephen muttered something about the legitimacy of their parentage. Then once again, they tried to maintain some decorum before joining Jean who gave them a withering look.

Then without any further delay, Jean took them back to NiCI and the rest of the Knights, waiting out of sensor range of Franco's StarBird.'

3

StarBird

The two armed guards walked along the corridor of the StarBird, one with a tray in hand, the other carrying a rifle across their chest, armed and ready. They passed fellow sentries who stood at their posts, wary of the possibility of a pending threat. It had started out as a joke, all this expense to protect one man, terrified of his own shadow, seeing assassins in every darkened corner. But as information regarding the slaughter of other warlord gang leaders began to surface, their remains butchered beyond recognition, everyone started to take their role very seriously. The news that Deimi Ka was now missing had meant the levels of security were at their highest level. With the unconfirmed reports that a body had been found in similar circumstances as the others, the StarBird was now in virtual lockdown. Only essential ship's company were required to stay onboard, otherwise the rest

51

of the crew were all highly trained armed personnel with only one order; keep Franco Choi alive.

Reaching their destination, the guards were faced with a single locked door with no windows, a keypad and a viewing screen; the only means of communication with the occupant beyond the door. Set in the wall below the keypad was a drawer, about twelve inches square. Balancing his tray in his left hand, one of the guards pressed the call button, then the two stood back and waited in silence.

Eventually, a man's face appeared on the viewing screen. A man that looked far older than his fifty-two years, his unshaven jowls sagging around a face that was once fleshy due to too much food and drink. Now he is wasting away, his skin grey and blemished, his appearance suggesting he hadn't washed for days, and he didn't look as if he had slept for just as long. His bald pate glistened with nervous sweat, while dirty grey hair hung in greasy strands around the back and sides of his head. He was twitchy, eyes darting everywhere, cocking his head as if trying to listen to the slightest noise.

The guards did and said nothing but wait.

Seeming to come to a decision, Franco Choi barked out orders. His voice struggling through misuse.

'Put it in the drawer.'

The guards did as they were told. Opening the drawer beneath the keyboard they saw the cold and congealed remains of the previous meal untouched. They swapped out the old tray for the new one, then looked back to the screen, but it was blank. Pushing the drawer closed, they turned back down the corridor, holding the old stale food at arms length. They considered that at this rate Franco would probably starve himself to death before anyone else got hold of him, but that wasn't their problem, as long as they got paid.

Franco Choi didn't even bother to look at the drawer on his side of the bulkhead, let alone open it, he had lost his appetite a long time ago. Within his panic room he paced the floor, the air was fetid with his own body odour and sense of fear, his bedsheets soiled with sweat, along with some other highly suspicious, foul smelling stains. He didn't care, as long as they didn't get him, his self imposed prison would remain his home. He stopped suddenly, someone was talking but he couldn't make out what they were saying. He cocked his head to try and hear more clearly, but the sound had ceased. Turning round in panic he ran to the corner of the room, determined to keep his back to the wall. Still he couldn't hear the noise anymore. Eventually, convinced the danger had passed, Franco once more began his pacing, then he heard it again. A long low murmur.

Fear gripped at his heart, tears tumbled down his unshaven face when the full horror of the truth finally hit him. The voice he had heard, was his own desperate pleas, a cry for help beyond the reach of his own wealth and power. He was praying.

Arriving on Jean's ship, Nathan and the others made their way back to the room that she used as a living space. Four other men stood up to greet them.

Peyton eyed Jean cautiously. 'How many are there here? At this rate you are coming dangerously close to actually have a crew for NiCI.'

Jean gave her a wry look. 'Pfft, no chance of that I can assure you.' She made the introductions. 'Peyton, this is Daniel, Paul, Simon and John. Gentlemen, this is Detective Inspector Peyton Chi.'

It was Daniel who stepped forward. 'Pleased to meet you Inspector.' He then briefly glanced at Nathan. 'To what do we owe *this* pleasure?'

He replied with just an irritated 'Hmmm.'

Jean ignored him. 'Peyton is here in a professional capacity. She has been investigating the recent murders of our less than salubrious members of society, and she is as interested to speak to Franco as we are. She may also have information that may help us.'

'And who exactly is us?' Peyton asked pointedly.

Jean glanced at the Knights and finally looked to Nathan, who just scowled back. She shrugged and continued.

'Basically, during my last assignment I was on a world called Kelan. While I was there I made quite a significant discovery.' She paused for a moment.

'Which is what?'

'Er. Well you know there is me, and what I do when I'm not doing my *day job*?'

Peyton rolled her eyes. 'Generally causing mayhem from what I've seen during your day job.'

There was general laughter around the room, Jean didn't seem to find it funny and gave Peyton a look that suggested

54

she be careful. Nathan hadn't missed it and added it to the ever growing list of *yet to be answered* questions.

'Yes, well that may be so. But apparently I'm not the only one.'

'What?'

'*They*, are me. Just from a different part of the universe.'

'There are more of you?' Peyton looked around at the grinning faces then back at Jean's worried one. 'Shit. So that's why whoever hired the Kaimiren needed so many?'

'Exactly.'

'But why? What were their orders?'

'Only to put Nathan's head on a pole. Apparently someone has taken a dislike to him. Funny that.'

Daniel laughed. 'Good to see you've made such a good impression Nathan.'

Feigning indifference, Nathan shrugged. 'It's got nothing to do with me.' But still he watched Jean as she ran her fingers through her hair, she looked tired and fed up. Feeling a stab of guilt, remembering that for centuries she'd been on her own whilst also now having to deal with seven Knights intruding into her space. He suggested a cup of tea and was about to make his own way to the kitchen area in search of hot water, when Jean spun on her heel and got there first. Grinding his teeth in frustration, he caught Damien's eye, who shook his head slightly and shrugged his shoulders. Nathan clenched his fists and closed his eyes, all thoughts of guilt evaporating as he considered that it had already been a long day, and he had a feeling it was going to get a lot longer.

While Jean set about the kitchen, everyone else settled down into the sofas at the other end of the room.

'So what are we doing now?' Stephen asked.

Nathan sat in silence, if Jean wanted to call the shots then she can bloody well do so on her own. But to his surprise, Peyton answered.

'We should speak to Franco. Only problem is, the StarBird is heavily fortified. We would need to have a plan to figure out how to get to him.'

Daniel eyed Jean as she moved around her kitchen, there was definitely some tension in the room. He glanced over at Nathan who had a face like thunder, he seemed to be making a point of listening hard to what the Inspector had to say. Daniel was pretty sure that he had nothing to add to the proceedings here, so got up and made his way over to the kitchen area and leaned against the counter.

'Is everything ok? Can I get you something?' She asked.

Daniel smiled and shook his head. 'No, I'm fine thank you. Can I help here in anyway?'

'That's ok thank you. All in hand here.'

It was all very polite and civilised, Daniel was having none of it.

'Good. Then you have nothing to interrupt you while you tell me what is bothering you.'

They had kept their conversation low, and apart from a brief glance from Damien, no-one looked as if they were taking any notice of them as Jean prepared the refreshments. She looked at him with a face that suggested confused innocence, he wasn't fooled for a moment. He had not only spent his very long life as a barrister, but also as a high court judge, having encountered numerous guilty parties trying to look virtuous. She finally gave up and glanced over at Nathan who still glowered in his seat.

Daniel smiled. 'Do I sense a little tension between you and Nathan?'

Pursing her lips, Jean let out a burst of air in frustration. The room went silent and she earned a few raised eyebrows which she ignored. With barely a whisper she replied. 'The man is impossible. Does he think no-one is capable of making decisions other than him?'

Daniel crossed his arms. 'No, of course he doesn't. But making difficult decisions is what he does.' He paused as he considered something and smiled. 'To be fair, we are probably guilty of letting him get on with it. He's damned good at what he does.'

'Well, he may well be, but I've always had to make my own decisions and, despite many peoples efforts, I've managed to stay alive this long.'

Daniel glanced over at Nathan, who hadn't managed to look away in time, he couldn't help himself from smiling.

'It will all work out eventually. We just need to all learn to fit. Once you're at the Retreat I'm sure things will soon settle down.'

Jean failed to hide the look of shock on her face and had to force herself to keep her voice low.

'You still think I'm going to move to the Retreat? On Kelan?'

Daniel put his head to one side as if confused.

'Of course. Why not? It is essentially your home as much as ours after all.'

'That's ridiculous. You don't know a thing about me.'

'That doesn't matter. You have as much right to be at the Retreat as any of us, and if I'm honest, I would say it is probably not before time.'

'I've been alright on my own so far.'

Jean busied herself with finishing off making the tea.

'You may have been alright on your own. But can you honestly say you've been happy about it?'

Daniel put his hand on Jean's arm and stopped her in her tea making, waiting for her to turn and look at him.

'Jean, we are not just anybody who you have met along the way. We have been doing this for even longer than you have.' He looked over to his fellow Knights still talking with Peyton. 'Believe me, we have spent many years not seeing eye to eye with each other. None of us are the easiest of men to get along with. But we all understand the necessity of being there for each other when we need it. None of us is alone, and while we could no doubt happily knock each others' heads off at times, we all have each others' backs. No-one understands what this job is like more than we do. Whether you like to admit it or not, you need to come home.'

She turned away with her back to the rest of the room and Daniel put the tea on trays, allowing her to gather herself. When she faced him again a moment later, she was composed and made an effort to return his smile. Seeming satisfied he then, picked up one of the trays and led the way over to the others, who were discussing how to proceed with the matter in hand. How to get hold of Franco while he was holed up in his own personal fortress.

When they were all seated, Daniel asked. 'So what's the plan?'

It was Peyton who spoke first again and Daniel wasn't the only one who saw the look of irritation cross Nathan's face.

'We know that Franco has a panic room. The man is paranoid to the point of obsession, so the chances are most of those still on board are actually paid protection, with enough crew to keep the ship going and no more.'

'Do we know where this panic room is?' Damien asked.

Jean called NiCI to bring up all available information regarding the layout of the StarBird. Having scanned the ship, NiCI made an assessment of the possibilities of Franco's location.

'Why can't we just translocate onto his ship, inside this panic room and bring Franco straight here?' The other Knights nodded, agreeing with Damien.

Jean and Peyton both shook their heads.

It was Jean who answered. 'Many spaceships nowadays emit a particle ray which is very effective in making translocation nigh on impossible. To get onto the StarBird we will have to actually dock alongside it.'

'What? They can do that? Stop us translocating I mean?' Simon asked.

Everyone looked at Jean but it was Peyton who answered this time.

'Oh yes, most of the defence systems of those who have something to hide, and to be honest those who don't too, are to keep Jean out.'

Nathan glanced over at Jean who now kept her mouth firmly shut. Peyton laughed at the confused look on the Knight's faces and continued.

'Anyone can fire a laser cannon and try to blast each other out of the sky, but that isn't much use if Jean is around. It was figured out centuries ago that if you didn't want to be reduced to a pile of chopped meat you learnt how to defend yourself, without the use of machinery. I guarantee that a majority, if not all, of the guards over on the StarBird, carry a blade of some sort. And they'll make sure they are very good at using them.'

Jean tried not to look at anyone as the Knights studied her, even Nathan had stopped scowling.

Damien asked. 'But why would Franco be afraid of Jean? Surely he doesn't think she is responsible for these murders?'

Peyton laughed again but there was little mirth in her voice.

'No, Franco won't be concerned about Jean, he probably hasn't even considered her. But Jean does have history.'

Jean frowned as Peyton held up her hands. 'I'm just saying the truth. You may be good at seeing off the bad guys, but you also have a knack of bringing some seriously weird shit with you. I remember the Falls of Spar only too well.'

'What happened at the Falls of Spar.'

This time Jean spoke before Peyton could say anything.

'Nothing to worry about now.' She put her empty cup down. 'We had better get going.' Standing up Jean addressed NiCI again. 'NiCI, make sure we are cloaked and set a course for the StarBird and prepare for covert docking.'

NiCI acknowledged her orders and the Knights and Peyton stood up, the Inspector took out her firearm as she would at any other time before entering a likely hostile environment. Then, after a few sideways glances from the

Knights and Jean, she put it away in disgust. Whilst in such company it would only be useful if she threw it at someone.

Based on the information that NiCI had provided regarding the StarBird, it was decided that they should make their way to the nearest room with a comms unit. From there Jean could directly access the security systems and the exact location of Franco's panic room.

They made their way to the corridor and Jean led them towards the ship's docking doors. While waiting for NiCI to confirm their arrival, Jean turned to face everyone.

'Look, I know you have your own way of dealing with things, but this is just about getting Franco out. The men and women who are guarding him, may or may not, spend most of their lives on the right side of the law, but they haven't done anything wrong here.' Jean looked down at her hands as if the words she was searching for were written on them. 'What I'm trying to say is, can you at least try not to kill anyone?'

The Knights looked at each other, then back at Jean.

'Even if they try and kill us?' Damien asked.

'Yes. I would like to think that I…, we should be competent enough to be capable of disabling these people without having to resort to killing. This isn't their battle after all.'

The Knights looked at each other again. Nathan shrugged. 'Agreed. But we can't help it if they lose a limb in the process.'

Jean nodded. 'Fair enough.' Pausing she added. 'I'll be able to sense any guards along the way, if there is trouble, I'll let you know.'

NiCI's voice came over the intercom. 'Covert docking complete. Immediate scans show four armed personal within the immediate vicinity. Nathan put his hand up and stopped everyone, turning to Jean, he looked concerned.

'Will you be able to control that build of emotional energy when the fighting begins?'

The other Knights looked at Jean sharply, she shook her head. 'No problem, just another wall to go up.'

He noted her tone of resignation and paused. 'Fair enough, but that is something we need to discuss later.'

She laughed without humour. 'I'll put it on the list.'

He gave her a brief understanding smile.

'What about internal camera systems?' Peyton asked, cutting into the silence that followed.

'You don't need to worry about anyone being seen via any technology, they will only see a blurred image. The most they will think is their system is on the blink.' Nathan assured her.

She looked at Jean who just shrugged and shook her head.

Once the airlock was opened they made their way cautiously onto the StarBird. Nathan, Damien and Daniel stepped forward first, with Jean following. Once they were all on Franco's ship, they spread out with Peyton between John and Simon. She looked smaller than ever.

As spaceships go, Franco's was a luxurious palace. However, it was still confined to the severe conditions of space. So while its warren of corridors were considered wider and less enclosed, the opportunity for any form of combat was restricted within a limited space. The corridor they found themselves in was quite wide, about two metres across, with access to unknown rooms via doors set into the bulkheads at occasional intervals. It took a moment for Nathan to appreciate that they were only on another spaceship. Where Jean had ensured that NiCI was bright and functional with a few comforts, Franco's StarBird was like walking into a luxury hotel. The lighting was subdued, emitting from expensive looking fixtures set into the walls, alongside expensive artwork, displayed upon bulkheads covered in an expensive looking material. Nathan couldn't make out what it was made of, but there was a golden sheen across its surface. The floor was buffed to a high shine with a deep pile carpet running down the centre length of the corridor in both directions. Franco apparently liked his space travel to be comfortable and extravagant, Nathan wondered if he made his crew walk along the uncarpeted edges. He had to admit to taking a certain delight in stomping along the shag pile. It was childish but he didn't care, it had been a long day already and it didn't look like ending any time soon.

When the encountered the first four of Franco's guards, Jean suddenly pushed past the Knights and headed straight for the startled sentries. Nathan didn't even bother to hide his irritation at her audacity and gave a sharp order for the rest to wait there, before following her himself.

The guards were simple enough to deal with. They were so surprised by the confrontation, a few well aimed hard punches, resulting in a couple of broken noses and some badly loosened teeth, sent them sprawling. Afterwards, using belts and strappings from their own uniforms, the guards were soon bound and gagged by the Knights, before being unceremoniously dumped in an empty room close by. They all gave Jean looks that suggested they were not impressed.

While the Knights worked, Nathan took hold of Jean's arm and held her back. She tried to pull away but he held her fast. She gave him a filthy look but he ignored it. His voice was low but firm, it had been a long day and he was struggling to keep his temper.

'Let's get something straight. Next time we meet someone, don't go off like that again. There are others with you now, and a stunt like that is likely to get someone hurt. We work together as a team, no one is a maverick, do you understand?'

Jean's face was thunderous and he expected to be greeted with a savage retort. But then, after a few moment, her features softened, and the red anger that had passed over her face had now turned to a more contrite pink. She took a long slow breath and closed her eyes. When she opened them again she spoke with a quiet calm voice.

'You're right of course, I'm sorry. That was out of order.'

Nathan blinked, taken completely off guard. Having braced himself for a verbal onslaught, the calm and understanding Jean before him was a complete surprise. He found himself on the back foot, and it was an uncomfortable feeling.

'Well, yes. Thank you.'

Not sure what had just happened he looked around and saw the others further down the corridor waiting outside a closed door. They were watching curiously.

'I think we may have found the room we are looking for.'

Jean followed his gaze, then turning back she grinned, holding out her hand to encourage him to move forward.

'After you.'

He made his way down the corridor towards the others, the look of confusion still on his face. He didn't see the small smile that now slowly spread across Jean's.

Accessing the small comms room they all filed in quickly. It didn't take long for the data pack that Jean carried in her pocket to find the information they needed regarding the location of Franco's panic room once it was plugged into the StarBird's systems. Fortunately it wasn't that far away, but it would still require navigation of a number of corridors before they would get there. Jean instructed NiCI to disable the locks to Franco's room, then it was decided that Simon, John and Peyton would be the ones responsible for retrieving Franco. The rest of them would deal with any guards encountered on the way.

Drawing closer to Franco's panic room they began to confront more guards. This time however, they worked together, and despite a few additional broken noses and a suspected broken arm, sustained by Franco's security team, they progressed smoothly until Jean suddenly grabbed Nathan and Daniel by their coats, dragging them backwards. Before they could argue, she put her fingers to her lips and indicated that they should fall back. Looking confused they followed, along with everyone else, into a recess barely big enough to hold them all.

'What's the matter?' Nathan asked.

Keeping her voice just low enough for them all to hear, she told them her concerns.

'Something is wrong. There are no longer just guards and crew moving around the ship. Someone, or something, has recently boarded.'

Nathan considered this for a moment. 'How do you know? And do you have any idea what we are now dealing with?'

'Being empathic I can sense other people moving around, and as they get closer I can assess how many there are. So far we have just encountered small groups of guards, but now there is something far more sinister onboard. I get the feeling of a hunt.'

Suddenly she stopped, her head cocked as if listening. Nathan was about to speak but she put a hand up and caught his chest.

Nathan could feel his annoyance rise again, but pushed it down when he saw the colour drain from Jean's face. She looked up at him and spoke in voice so quiet the others pushed in even closer to hear.

'Vaupír.'

She was met with blank stares all round. 'What?'

'Also known as vampires, but we are not talking fairytales here. These are real, and they are deadly.'

Paul rolled his eyes. 'Vampires? Really?' He shared a glance with Stephen who just shrugged.

Jean ignored him. 'They are descendants of the Vaupír within Kyawann, but over time have bred with other species of the Seventh Sector. They generally keep to themselves, but you always find those who look for more deadly pursuits. I'm assuming they are here for Franco too, so won't be looking for a general chit chat and catch up.'

66

Peyton looked indignant. 'Well they are not getting him. Come on, what are we waiting for?'

Nathan studied Jean and raised an eyebrow. 'I take it the 'do not kill' notice is off?'

Jean nodded. 'Oh yes. They have already started their killing spree and there is only one way to stop them.'

There was no need for anything else to be said. There was a noticeable change in the atmosphere as the group left the alcove, and once they found their space, the Knights drew their swords. Jean reached behind withdrawing her own two daggers; her first weapons of choice. Inspector Peyton Chi never felt so small and insignificant and found herself falling back. However, John took her arm and moved her forward; whether she liked it or not she was staying with them.

Without warning, the main lights went out and were replaced with a pulsating red glow, and an alarm was blasted throughout the ship. It was unknown if it was the Vaupír or themselves had set off the alarms, but all hopes of a covert mission were gone. Nathan took stock of those around him and the situation they faced. Any personal issues were left behind on NiCI, he knew the Knights around him implicitly, their strengths and determination. Jean he barely knew at all, but she had demonstrated that whatever concerns he may have about her attitude, she could be relied on when it came to a fight. Peyton was a complete enigma, but John seemed to have her under his wing, so that was one problem less to worry about.

While it was obvious that Jean had a huge capacity for empathy, along with a useful ability to recognise anything with a pulse in the vicinity, she wasn't the only one. Nathan had no idea if she had already picked up on his own empathic skills, but he was certainly aware of hers. It was like a bright internal light; he couldn't see it, but he knew it was there. His own skills were no way near as honed as Jean's, but once she had alerted them to the presence of the Vaupír, he too could sense the difference, albeit only subtle, whereas it was more likely a very large signpost to Jean. He really was going to have a good sit down with their latest addition to the group, too much was happening and not enough information being shared to deal with nasty, unexpected surprises.

He made a final analysis of their situation before he and Damien led the way forward. With Jean close behind, he could feel her opening her mind to their surroundings, no doubt also aware of the emotional state of those around her too. Nathan didn't like to admit to himself that the thought made him feel a bit nervous.

As they made their way to the panic room, they encountered two groups of guards that had been slaughtered by the Vaupír; throats ripped out and blood adorning every wall, ceiling and floor. But it was as they turned into the next corridor they finally encountered those responsible for the carnage. Two very tall people stood in their way, the broken and torn bodies of two guards lying at their feet. At first they seemed humanlike, despite the gore covering them from head to foot. But as the Knights, Jean and Peyton looked at the new arrivals, the Vaupír grinned at the prospect of more blood, displaying a frightening array of sharp needle like teeth.

'See, weird shit. Follows her around everywhere.' Peyton muttered to no-one in particular.

Nathan made a quick decision. 'We must be close to Franco now, only a couple of corridors and we are there. Jean, can you tell if there are any more of these Vaupír around?'

Jean nodded. 'Three more, but not as close.'

'Damien, Paul, sort out these two. We'll take Peyton by the next available route, as she will know Franco and get him out of his room. You follow us when you can.'

Immediately Damien and Paul charged at the two Vaupír who raised their own short swords in surprise at the attack. While Paul and Damien made short work of their adversaries, the rest disappeared around the corner into a separate corridor, where they encountered three more Vaupír as they were about to pounce on four unwary guards.

Jean stepped forward and called out. 'Get out of here, now.'

The guards, recognising Jean at once, didn't need telling twice. A final glance at the blood soaked Vaupír and they turned and ran in the opposite direction.

Damien and Paul had soon caught up with them, both covered in blood, Nathan was relieved, but not surprised, that none of it seemed to be their own. The Vaupír were looking at Jean warily and Nathan got the distinct impression they also knew who she was and were coming to a decision. 'John, Simon and Paul, get Peyton to Franco, then make your way back to Jean's ship.'

The tall, thin bloodthirsty Vaupír, raised their short swords and made a charge towards them, in particular at

69

Jean. While the Knights raised their swords in readiness to meet the charge, they were aware of their disadvantage in the confinement of the corridor against the shorter, but still awkward blades of the Vaupír. However, Jean's own twin long knives were deadly, able to pass under the limited swing of the enemies' weapons. She ducked and lunged forward, slicing under the arms of the nearest opponent. He buckled under the first thrust, only to be carried backwards in Jean's charge, causing the other Vaupír to manoeuvre out of their way. As they faltered, Daniel and Damien were on them, raising their swords in a hard downward motion, restricted only by the height of the ceilings; but it was enough to shatter the neck and collar bones of both Vaupír. In a spray of blood and gore, both Knights turned in unison as Jean sprang past the first injured Vaupír, spinning, ready to attack again. But as her pain maddened victim snarled his desperate attempt to counterattack, Stephen charged forward and ran him through; his death mask was of shock and confusion as he slid off the Knight's blade.

Satisfied their task was complete, they heard the running feet of a larger group of guards heading their way. Realising they weren't far from the original comms room near to where they had docked NiCI, Jean urged the Knights to follow her. They ran down several corridors; the walls daubed in blood and gore, evidence that the Vaupír had passed that way too.

Behind them they heard the guards hot on their tails, Nathan was about to call out to Jean to wait while they dealt with their pursuers, when she suddenly stopped. Opening a sliding door to her right, she urged the Knights inside just as the guards turned the corner. She paused and made sure they saw her as she closed the door.

'What are you doing?'

'Now they know I'm here, they will do their best to try and get in. While they are doing that they will stay away from the others trying to get Franco.'

Ensuring the door was in locked mode, she hurried to a console nearby. Nathan watched as she took out the same device she had used earlier, and placed it into the console. He looked around the room, noticing that there was a closed exit on the opposite wall to the door they had entered through. A window looked out into the void of space beyond. He was beginning to feel he wasn't cut out for this space lark.

'Shit.'

Nathan shot Jean a look. 'What's the matter now?'

'It seems that some of the guards that make up Franco's security are not as innocent as the rest. The bastards have given up trying to open the door and are intending to open the airlock instead.'

She glanced at the door that looked out onto space, as her gaze rested back on Nathan, he saw that she at least had the grace to look sheepish. He didn't have the opportunity to enjoy the *I told you so* moment however, because now Jean was looking back at the console and she suddenly shouted out.

'Find something to hold onto, now.'

The airlock door slid open.

Frantically, Nathan reached out and grabbed the edge of a large solid looking control panel. The room had turned into a giant wind tunnel as the air immediately evacuated into space. He suddenly became aware of Jean suddenly being knocked to the side as a chair hit her righthand shoulder, closely followed by the body of Damien with a terrified look upon his face. Nathan could only watch in horror as his best friend looked doomed to disappear into the icy cold grip of outer-space. But instinctively Jean reached out, grabbing at Damien's hand before he followed the chair out of the hatch; his face a mask of terror and confusion.

Nathan's hands turned white with the effort of holding on to the control panel, the thought of disappearing through the airlock forcing him to strengthen his grip. It was with horror he felt his hands begin to sweat. Willing himself to hold on, he looked around him and shared a terrified look with Daniel who was trying to maintain his grip on the edge of console across the room.

The air had almost completely left the compartment, and the main issue they had now was the lack of artificial gravity, which was also disabled when the hatch was opened. Bracing herself against the hatchway, Jean pulled the horror stricken Damien in towards the safety of the ship. The lack of air and freezing temperature of space made their lungs scream with the effort to breathe. But finally, Nathan gasped with relief as Damien was pulled to safety.

Their vision already blurring, Jean reached out and lurched at the close button. The exit hatch slammed shut and immediately, oxygen rich air was blasted into the room and the artificial gravity was activated; followed by a resounding crash as they all hit the floor.

Damien groaned in pain while Jean rubbed at her shoulder where the chair had slammed into her. All of them were desperately trying to suck air into their lungs.

Jean peeled her face off of the none too clean floor and glowered at the prone man lying on the floor next to her. Covered in blood from his clashes with the Vaupír, Damien looked wide eyed and shocked, relief slowly taking over as he realised he was safe. Jean however, wasn't so calm. Speaking through clenched teeth, she brought her face close to his. 'Next time someone tells you to hold on to something, for the love of the gods, make sure it's onto something bolted down.'

Damien had the grace to look embarrassed and inclined his head. 'Non-moving furniture, got it.'

He was still a bit wobbly as he tried to push himself up from the floor. Nathan and Daniel, along with Stephen, had prised themselves up already and came over to help Jean and Damien to their feet.

Nathan looked at his cousin and shook his head. 'For someone who's supposed to be a smart man you can be a complete idiot at times.'

Damien didn't say anything but just grinned as Jean went back to the console, removing NiCI's device, muttering to herself. But as she turned back to the Knights, she took a deep breath as if trying to calm herself. When she spoke her voice was quiet, though Nathan was sure he heard the slightest tremble.

'We need to find the others and get back to the ship. I've disabled the particle field so at least we can translocate now.'

With a final glance around at everyone else ensuring there had been no lasting damage, Nathan hurried with the others to the door to the corridor. When opened, it was to find the guards fighting a losing battle against John, Simon, Paul and Peyton. The last guard losing consciousness as they exited the room.

'Well, that's one problem solved. Let's get back to the ship.' Jean said, giving the nearest guard a sharp kick in the rib cage as she went past.

Peyton was standing with John, who held Franco securely by his left arm. His hands were secured in front of him with, what looked like, a set of irons and chain. Jean looked up at John. 'Where the hell did they come from?'

John grinned. 'You are not the only one to have a little something extra to hand. You have a bow, Simon and I get a set of chains and manacles.'

Jean looked stunned, but as she glanced back at the metalwork holding Franco firmly in place, she noticed the familiar tracery that adorned all the weaponry of the Guardians. She glanced back at John and Simon and gave a brief nod and an impressed look. They both grinned back.

Franco didn't seem so impressed. He wasn't a big man, and he was practically standing on his toes as John seemed to have no intention of compensating for the height difference.

Nathan looked at Franco and then at Jean.

'This man is supposed to be one of the people responsible for the Kaimiren?'

Jean nodded. 'That's him. I know he doesn't look much, and he's probably been starving himself in case someone is trying to poison him, but this snivelling little shit is responsible for an extensive trade in narcotics and arms. There is even evidence, that has been impressively

74

suppressed, that demonstrates various fingers, and probably quite a few toes, in the slave trade. Not exactly your bringer of joy and goodwill to many is our Franco.'

Franco attempted to pull away from John but winced instead as the big man gripped harder. His unshaved, drawn and filthy face took on a look of belligerence.

'You can't prove any of that and I'll sue anyone who suggests it.'

Nathan walked up to the pathetic figure, who winced and attempted to step back, but was still held in place by John.

'Believe me, where you're going, you won't be in any position to sue anyone.'

Franco tried to brazen it out, he'd been threatened by some of the toughest men and women in the business.

'And who the fuck are you?'

Nathan didn't have a chance to answer as a voice boomed somewhere along another corridor. Moments later, a woman with a face of fury, and several guards following in her wake, strode into view.

Franco winced again.

'Mother, what are you doing here?'

Nathan raised an eyebrow at Franco's mother, who blatantly ignored him. While Franco wasn't tall, his mother could be considered tiny, but as she approached her son, she swung her arm back and gave him a resounding slap across the face. Simon grabbed at her arm to pull her away before she should inflict any more blows, but it didn't stop her kicking out and screaming.

'WHAT THE FUCK HAVE YOU DONE NOW FRANCO?'

Nathan turned to Jean.

'It seems we will be having an extra guest.'

Jean raised and eyebrow and nodded in agreement. The next thing they knew, she had translocated them back to NiCI. While onboard the StarBird, a group of Franco's battered and bemused guards, were left looking at each other wondering what the hell had just happened.

4

Deflated

Egos

Once everyone was back onboard NiCI, Nathan suggested that they take Franco, and his mutinous looking mother, back to the living area of the ship. While John, Simon and Peyton escorted them both off the Bridge, Nathan and Jean used their combined blue flames to scour the blood from those left. Everyone was relieved to see that, as after the battle at Parva, all evidence of their bloody encounters were burnt away.

Their entrance into Jean's living space gained a few curious looks from Peyton, Franco and his mother, but no-one said anything. Franco's mother, D'ali Choi, was more interested in glaring at her son. They were both sitting down on the sofas, Franco, still in chains, with wild terror in his eyes and D'ali, unchecked fury emanating from her tiny frame. Nathan wondered if she was possibly going to have a heart attack and considered asking Stephen to check her over.

However, the explosion of venom that D'ali emitted as she gave her son a piece of her mind, suggested that she was quite fit and well and unlikely to keel over anytime soon. For a small elderly lady, she was still a formidable force, and for one brief moment, Nathan felt a small piece of sympathy for her son. He dismissed it immediately.

'You idiot. Who the fuck are they and why the fuck did you bring them here?'

Franco was attempting to explain to his mother, that he had no idea who anyone was, though he eyed Jean warily when she entered the room. Unfortunately, D'ali was not in the mood to listen when she obviously still had much more to say.

'I gave you every opportunity to take over the business and make something of it. What do you do? You're out partying with the fucking police.'

'Actually we're not the police.' Nathan pointed to Peyton who sat in bemused silence in an armchair to one side of the sofa. 'She is, but we're not. Now if you have quite finished, we have business with your son.'

'What business? What's he done? What have you done?' She glared at Franco, who was now sitting like a beaten man with his head in his manacled hands. 'What is the matter with you? You look bloody awful.' She sniffed and wrinkled her nose. 'You smell as if you've been sleeping in your own shit.'

Nathan looked at the man in disgust. Watching Franco, he was reminded of Bales, the one time General of the Order who gained his position of authority by knowing the right people rather than through his own ability. Bales was now on the run somewhere, his wife had hanged herself from a tree in their garden after admitting in a suicide note, that she had murdered their son, Aliex. She had been unable to live with the shame Aliex had brought on the family when he raped his fiancé in a dark alley one night. Nathan was reminded of the uncomfortable feeling of foreboding the last time he had seen Bales leave his own office. He forced his mind back to the present and addressed Franco.

'I really don't have time for all this Franco. You have information that I need, and snivelling about it isn't going to endear me to you, or your mother.'

D'ali gave Nathan a sharp look and narrowed her eyes, but before she could say anything Nathan put his hand up to stall her. There was a coffee table arranged in front of their sofa, and Nathan sat down on it, facing the pair of them. He didn't like the way it shifted under his weight and made a mental note not to move too quickly. He waited until Franco finally looked up, then held his gaze.

'When were you approached regarding the Kaimiren?'

Franco looked shocked by the question, but not, it seemed, as much as his mother.

'What do you mean? Franco gave all that up years ago. I told him it was too risky and he should just get rid of them.'

Nathan raised an eyebrow.

'Well, it seems you haven't been entirely honest with your mother Franco. She doesn't look too pleased.'

Franco just stared at Nathan, determined to ignore his mother, who at that moment looked as if she could quite happily commit infanticide.

'I want an answer Franco.'

He sat in silence, and Nathan saw Jean out of the corner of his eye make her way over to a console and plug in the data device she always carried. Immediately data began to fill the screen. Nathan surmised that when Jean had connected to Franco's ship when looking for his panic room, all of the ships files were also downloaded. Now Franco's business was flashing across the screen for all to see.

'What the fuck do you think you are doing?' D'ali was furious, she tried to stand and make her way over to Jean, but was stopped by a heavy hand on her shoulder. Simon kept hold while she struggled and he bent down, speaking quietly in her ear.

'Sit still and stay quiet and I won't have to put you in chains.'

She stared at him in horror. 'You wouldn't dare.'

There was the sound of metal crunching and he placed a set of irons on the sofa beside her. D'ali gulped involuntarily but said nothing more. Her eyes darting occasionally to the chains.

By the console, Jean was watching the screen while she waited until NiCI had finished downloading the information, before typing instructions on the keyboard. Moments later the details she was looking for appeared and she smiled in satisfaction. Ensuring that all the data was saved into NiCI's memory, Jean removed the device and made her way over to Nathan and Franco. She eyed the table and decided that it was probably safer if she just hunkered down.

'Franco, I have just accessed all of your data files, and amongst them are details of the contract you made regarding the hire of nine Kaimiren. Who did you deal with? And when?'

Franco eyed her suspiciously.

'You're that bitch who keeps poking her nose in business that doesn't concern her. If you found the contract why the hell are you asking me?'

'I believe the names on the contract are false, but that is ok, because we think we know who they really are. We just want you to describe them to us and tell us how they contacted you.'

Franco was silent for a moment. His gaze passed between Jean and Nathan.

'Where are they now? My Kaimiren?'

Jean and Nathan shared a glance.

'Well, along with all the other hired Kaimiren, they are now reduced to dust and scattered to the wind.' She said, and watched with satisfaction the look of horror on Franco and D'ali's faces.

'Other Kaimiren?'

'Oh yes. To be honest, there's a good chance that Kaimiren are almost extinct within the galaxy now. I reckoned on about seventy of them being wiped-out, so that's a fair proportion of the population gone already. If there are any left, then someone owns an absolute fortune. Not you though it seems.'

'Bastards.'

Franco had come out of his self pity stupor and was now looking furious. His mother was eyeing him suspiciously.

'What have you done Franco? Surely who ever hired them paid the expected deposit for a safe return?'

Franco turned an ugly green colour.

'It was just a basic retrieval contract. There wasn't supposed to be any danger to the Kaimiren and I was promised double on completion.'

'You idiot.' D'ali didn't bother to hide the contempt in her voice.

Nathan winced as Franco's mother shrieked in close proximity to his right ear, but Jean ignored her.

'But that's not true is it? Kaimiren will only abide by their contract, and they were employed to seek and kill the Emperor on Kelan.'

'No, it was to retrieve this Nathan guy.' His voice was whining now.

'Franco, I've seen the contract.' She pointed to the console behind her. 'It states clearly it was a seek and kill job.'

Franco looked totally confused and shook his head. Nathan leant forward and asked his question again.

'Who did you discuss this contract with? If it's who we think they are, then it would not have been difficult to deceive you. Also, the fact that all the other owners have been systematically targeted and murdered, would suggest that they are out to cover their tracks.'

'You think they are the ones trying to kill me?'

'Don't you?'

Franco gulped.

'Who did you talk to Franco?'

The man seemed to crumple. He attempted to run his manacled hands through his thinning hair and hung his head down. But when he finally looked up again, he had a look of determination in his eye and he spoke clearly.

'There were two of them. Only one of them did the talking, the other one just sat there, I didn't like him at all. We met in a bar in Bieda, on Tandor, where they said they needed the use of several Kaimiren. They were very businesslike.' Franco faltered. 'Well, at the time they seemed businesslike.'

'You met two men in a bar, who wanted to use some of your most expensive commodities, without any insurance, and you think that is good business?' Jean asked incredulously.

D'ali was looking at her son with utter contempt, nodding her head in complete agreement with Jean. Fortunately she seemed to have finally lost her ability to talk.

Nathan shook his head. 'To be honest Franco, I doubt if you would have had much choice, they have ways of getting what they want.'

He stood up, and the table made some odd noises as it no longer had to take his weight.

'But that is no longer your problem Franco, you are coming with us. I suggest you say goodbye to your mother now, as it will be a while before you have a chance to speak with her again.'

Franco just looked at him and laughed, it was na ugly sound without humour. 'I'm not going anywhere. There isn't a courtroom in the galaxy who'd try to convict me. You've got what you wanted, now fuck off.'

Nathan looked at him and then at John. Before Franco realised what was going on, John had dragged him to his feet. The smaller man was furious, but Nathan got in first before he could start his angry tirade.

'You are not being tried in any court in this galaxy. You are being held for treason against the Empire. Where you are going, they don't care who you are, and I can assure you, it won't be comfortable either.'

'Treason? What Empire? I don't live in an Empire?'

'No, but I do, and seeing as it was me your friends were intending to kill, that makes you an accessory.'

He nodded to John, who almost had to bodily carry him out of the room. Franco seemed to collapse under the realisation that he wasn't going to get out of this problem so easily this time. The only words he managed to say were a pathetic plea to D'ali. 'Mother, do something.'

D'ali just looked away as her son was dragged out of sight. Standing up she stood in front of Nathan where she barely made it to his chest. But when she spoke it was with all the authority that had made her such a formidable mob leader.

'You've got what you came for, get me the fuck out of here.'

Nathan didn't need telling twice. He looked at Jean, who gave the order for NiCI to stop, then she took hold of D'ali's

84

arm, none too gently he noticed, and they disappeared. Moments later she returned.

'That is one very pissed off mother, I wouldn't want to be in her way right now.'

Nathan inclined his head. 'Good. That's one problem sorted for now.'

Jean looked at him and was about to say something when Peyton almost launched herself at Nathan in anger. He noted the look of annoyance that passed across Jean's face.

'What the fuck do you think you are doing? Who do you think you are to take *my* prisoner? Franco has nothing to do with it, yet you practically kidnap him right under his mother's nose. If you're lucky you'll have an hour before his team of lawyers are drawing up a lawsuit, and Ramboss is threatening to nail your bollocks to the office noticeboard. What makes you think Franco is any safer here, compared to where he was before? What's going to stop whoever killed the others from dicing up Franco too?'

Nathan glanced at Jean before answering. 'Now that Franco has started to give us the information we needed to confirm our theory, there's not much point in trying to silence him. But on top of that, Gellan and Duran may be happy enough to send people to do their dirty work, but that takes time and effort to organise. They wouldn't dare try and contact Franco directly now he is at Belan. To enter the Empire while I am still alive would be a step too far even for them.'

'Where the hell is Belan?'

'It's a high security prison on Kelan, it holds some of the most dangerous people in the Empire, and a few others besides. Franco won't be going anywhere.'

Peyton looked totally confused and was about to enter into another tirade, but Nathan just held her gaze, and while she took breath he managed to get a word in edgeways.

'Inspector, I can assure you that I have *kidnapped* no-one, and that when Franco is prosecuted, it will be in a court of law where all procedures will be followed to the letter. Now if you don't mind we have work to do. We will make sure you get back to your station where I will personally explain the situation to this Ramboss, but that is all. I do not have to make excuses or apologies to anyone, and I am absolutely certain that no-one will be removing any of my body parts in the process.'

Peyton laughed and looked as if she was about to tell him exactly what she thought of his legal process. All around them the other Knights were either lounging in seats or relaxed against the bulkheads, happy to watch the floor show. Jean stepped in, and Nathan only now recognised how tired she looked. He found himself sympathising with her; he, like the others hadn't had any sleep for well over twenty-four hours.

With a sigh Jean spoke. 'Peyton, that's enough.'

The Inspector spun run and jabbed a finger in Jean's direction. 'Don't you start. You've caused enough shit with me and Ramboss over the years.'

'To be honest with you I don't give a shit how difficult your job has been. As far as I'm concerned, the least time I spend with the Galactic police the better. But this time you

86

are just going to have accept that there is nothing you can do about it. This is a situation that goes beyond this galaxy's authority, and as such, has nothing to do with you or Ramboss. Deal with it, because I am frankly too tired to put up with any more over inflated, self-important egos.'

Nathan gave her a sharp look and the Knights shifted slightly, but Jean said nothing more. She just glared at Peyton, who silently seethed before finally looking away. A moment later, John appeared, looking around the room. Sensing the tension in the air, his gaze settled on the furious policewoman that looked as if she was about to explode.

'Franco is now being processed at Belan, he'll be ready to be interviewed whenever you want.'

Nathan nodded. 'Daniel, take the Inspector back to her world and wait for us there. I will stay here with Jean while she gathers her things to take back with us. Simon, make sure that any of the food we brought with us is stowed and ready to take back to the Retreat. The rest of you get back to Parva and contact Inchgower at the High Council for an update; we need to know that the Empire hasn't had any lasting effects after recent events.'

He looked at the exhausted Knights and felt a pang of guilt.

'If there is nothing to report then don't worry. Go home and rest, we'll meet up in the morning at Denfield when everyone has had a good night's sleep. I'm sure Anna and Ty will be more than happy to see you.'

Paul and Damien looked at him gratefully, while Simon made his way to the kitchen area and grinned at John as he passed.

'I'm sure Christopher will be pleased too.'

Nathan looked around confused.

'Who's Christopher?'

John was glaring at Simon who made a point of ignoring him. 'It doesn't matter. Are we going or what?'

A few surprised glances passed between the Knights before they all stood up and translocated away. John helped Simon with the box of food, muttering furiously at him, making sure no-one else could hear their exchange. Only Daniel, Peyton, Jean and Nathan remained.

Nathan exchanged a shrug with his Daniel, who looked as bemused as he was, a mischievous grin forming on his face. 'Well, there's an interesting story there somewhere.'

Peyton was still looking murderous when she left with a chuckling Daniel, and Nathan turned to Jean who still hadn't moved.

'Miss Carter, we haven't got all day, and as you pointed out, we are all very tired and would like to get this over and done with as soon as possible.'

When Jean replied, her voice had taken on a whole new persona, one that had gained an extra octave.

'I don't understand. You still want me to come with you?'

'Of course. Unless you want to stay here alone.' Nathan hesitated for a moment. 'I admit that's probably something I should have considered. You don't have to come back if you don't want to. I had assumed that, as one of us, you would want to come back to the Retreat. Then again, that could be my over inflated, self-important ego working overtime.'

He gave her an exhausted grin and Jean flushed, looking away. 'I am sorry, that was uncalled for. And yes, if the offer to come back with you is still available I would be very interested in taking it up. Though how long you'll put up with me will be interesting.'

Nathan gave her a small smile, his face was too tired to cope with anything more energetic. She stood a moment longer before realising he was waiting for her to move. She left quickly, returning to her own quarters to pack a small rucksack with the few possessions that she held dear, along with changes of clothes. She still had some things at Mrs Moore's lodging, but otherwise it was a task that didn't take long. While she packed she gave NiCI instructions to return to her moorings within the asteroid and to power down until she returned. She then met Nathan on the bridge.

He was standing before the viewing screen, his hands in his pockets. NiCI had remained at a standstill, and the view of a nebular cloud in the distance was spectacular. He turned as she entered the room, for a moment he looked as if his thoughts were miles away. Then, just as quickly he brought his attention back to the room and he joined Jean, who gave NiCI a last look over. The two of them finally left the bridge and returned to the world of Tandor, where they emerged from a side alley into glorious sunshine. Then together they climbed the steps into Peyton's police station in Beida.

Once all sign of life had left the ship, NiCI turned off power to life support and lighting. Only the engines were needed to function, and with a course set, the ship made its way home. Ready for the next time Jean would return to its bridge.

5

Ramboss

Superintendent Ramboss pointed a stubby finger at Daniel who was sitting on Peyton's desk, completely at ease, seemingly ignoring the big round man that was currently working himself up into a heart attack.

'What do you mean Franco is under arrest? How can he be under arrest? Under who's orders? And who the fuck is he?'

'Sir…' Inspector Peyton tried to speak, but apparently Ramboss still had plenty to say on the matter.

'It was bad enough when Boyles here informed me that that fucking pain in the arse was at our crime scene. But now you tell me she has taken away Franco too?'

Boyles was sitting at his own desk, a smug grin on his face as he leaned back in his chair. With any luck there was going to be a reshuffle of bodies in the office soon and he might get that promotion he'd been hankering for after all. Peyton looked as if she would have given anything for the legs of his chair to give way and see the little shit sprawled all over the floor.

Ramboss was gearing himself for another outburst, when he caught sight of Jean and Nathan entering the room.

'YOU..!!'

The big man charged towards Jean, his hand up again with his fat index finger stabbing the air as he spoke. Jean felt spittle on her face and wiped it away, though there was little she could do about the barrage of halitosis.

'You have a fucking nerve coming here. Where's Franco? I expect him in this office within the next five minutes, and you had better be on your knees begging his forgiveness. And, for your sake I hope he accepts your apology before he decides to haul-ass his vultures, masquerading as his legal… what the hell?'

Ramboss was cut short in his rage, as a large hand was placed firmly on his chest and he was pushed, with some force, backwards. The rage was momentarily replaced with astonishment, as, in the brief second it took for him to figure out what was going on.

Nathan had stepped forward so that he was just slightly in front of Jean. When he spoke it was quiet and even, though he was sure Jean could sense the anger that bubbled beneath the surface.

91

'That is quite enough. You will lower your tone from now on, and for the sake of clarification, Miss Carter here has nothing to do with the arrest of Franco Choi, other than helping to track him down. He is currently residing in a cell waiting for further questioning. He will eventually face charges in court against him regarding treason under Imperial Law.' Franco's eyes bulged with indignation and opened his mouth to let vent his fury, but Nathan was having none of it and continued with his monologue ensuring there were no interruptions. 'Mr Choi has been complicit, along with other less salubrious members of society who have recently been found deceased. In particular regard to the contracting out of Kaimiren with a specific intent to ensure that my head was paraded on a spike. Since then, these people have been cleaning up after themselves and have littered your city with their victims' remains. Fortunately, we have managed to obtain Franco before he could suffer the same fate. As such, those who wish to see me dead are destined to remain disappointed on two accounts. With regards to any legal teams that may be descending on this station, I can assure you, the only ones you need to be wary of are those from the Empire. I expect you, and your fellow police officers, to offer them the utmost help in their investigations. If, however, you feel you cannot provide this help, I am sure that the cell next to Mr Choi can be made suitably free, and uncomfortable, for your own personal stay. Do we understand each other?'

The colour of Ramboss' face had undergone several changes in hue; from puce to white, then red, then back to puce. His eyes were doing a very strange bulging thing and

Nathan was wondering if he was going to have to catch them if they fell out of their sockets.

'You think I am going to be threatened by you. I have no idea who the hell you are, but I have the entire Galactic police force behind me. I want to see Franco NOW.'

'Sir.'

Jean and Nathan both looked up as Peyton stepped forward. Daniel was still leaning against the desk, relaxed with arms folded. He seemed to be enjoying himself.

Ramboss spun round and Peyton flinched. 'WHAT?'

'Sir. These people are not just anybody. They are like Jean.'

Ramboss looked confused for a moment, then realisation dawned.

'Shit, you mean there are more of them?'

'Well, including Jean, there are eight of them altogether.'

'EIGHT?'

Peyton just nodded and all around the room there was an uncomfortable shifting around amongst her fellow police officers. Up until this point the entertainment had been quite interesting, even a few murmurs of people taking bets as to the outcome, including the fragility of Peyton's rank. But now they seemed uncertain, Jean was not a force to be reckoned with easily, the idea there were more like her was unnerving to say the least.

Ramboss turned back, but this time he focussed on Jean.

'How long have you known about *them*?' He put as much contempt as he could in the word them, but it was ignored by Nathan and Daniel. Jean gave the Superintendent her sweetest smile. 'To be honest, only quiet recently. But I would

93

be careful Ramboss, you may consider me a pain in the arse, but they can be a pain in the arse with a command of a very big army behind them. You'll just have to let Franco go. Besides, I think you should be more worried about his mother, she didn't seem particularly maternal when it came to his arrest. Then there is still the matter of the Choi Empire that needs dealing with.'

Ramboss seemed to deflate before them, which was quite a feat considering his girth. He looked at Peyton, then back at Jean and Nathan, before finally coming to a decision. He spun back to Peyton.

'I expect a full report of everything that has happened on this case on my desk by the end of the day. And you...' He stabbed his finger at Jean again. 'You can just fuck off out of it. And take them with you.'

Jean shrugged and shook her head and made to turn, but Nathan just touched her arm, causing her to stand still while he addressed the furious Superintendent.

'I warned you to keep your tone at a civil level. But it seems you still have a lot to learn. Daniel, please escort the Superintendent back to Kelan where he can sample the delights of Imperial hospitality while he cools his heels.'

Daniel stood up, still relaxed and smiling. But when he caught the arm of Ramboss, his grip was like iron as he escorted the struggling man out of the room.

Boyles was on his feet, annoyed his afternoon's entertainment was ruined. The rest of the people in the room looked confused, unsure what to do. None looked too keen to argue with their unwanted visitors.

'Where are you taking the Boss?'

Nathan eyed the bristling detective. 'He won't be with us long, just enough to educate him on the finer aspects of civility.'

And with that, he and Jean remained only long enough to say their goodbyes to Peyton, before they too turned and left the station. Behind them was a sigh as if the whole room had been holding its breath and was letting it out in unison.

Coming out into the late Tandor sunshine, Jean paused and Nathan stopped to look at her.

'Well, I give you your due. You certainly know how to make an impression.'

Nathan shrugged and gave her a tired smile.

'The man's an idiot, and I can't stand bullies.' He gave her a tired grin. 'It's been a very long day and all I want now is a hot shower, something to eat and a large glass of brandy before hitting my bed.'

She returned his smile. 'You know that sounds like a very good plan.'

'Come on then. I would offer you a cheese and pickle sandwich, but I've run out of pickle and any cheese still residing in the fridge may need to be manhandled into the bin. However, I think I've got a tin of baked beans in the cupboard, if you're lucky the bread might still be edible.'

Jean raised an eyebrow. 'You certainly know how to treat a girl in true gourmet style.'

'Well, if it's gourmet you want, I could be persuaded to toast the bread.'

Nathan wasn't sure if it was just exhaustion, or relief that they were finally getting away from Bieda, but by the time the two of them left Tandor, they were both amiably chuckling to themselves.

6

Bales

Victor Bales lay back against the soft pillows of the bed, while around him five beautiful women attended to his every needs. Their naked bodies, toned and oiled, seemed to move like water as they fed him food and served him goblets of wine. His mind was foggy from the heady aromas of the drink and his eyes felt heavy.

Having no idea when he had entered the bath, its warm waters lapping at his nakedness, he smiled in his pleasure. He felt movement around him and looking up, saw the tall dusky shape of the most beautiful woman he had ever seen. Her body was covered in intricate designs painted in gold, her braided hair hung down her back and across her breasts, hard nipples thrusting through her tresses. Bales felt himself moan in longing. His hands moved to cover his erection but the woman just smiled and moved her hands up his body, her eyes never leaving his. She took his hardness into her own hands and began to tease him with her fingers, his body began to move with hers and it didn't take long before she brought him to his orgasm and he felt the pleasure of his release.

Nearby he could hear the gentle tinkling of water pouring from a jug. He felt its warmth against his skin and the smell of......

Bales' eyes shot open, someone was pissing on him.

His sudden movement made the drunk, standing over him jump back with a start. One of the man's arms had been against the brick wall, holding him up while the other had aimed his flow of recycled lager. Now he staggered, cursing as a trickle of urine ran down the front of his jeans, while he tried to focus on the pile of rags that had started moving amongst the bins. Realising there was, in fact, a man lying there, he started to giggle, and called out to his mates waiting for him on the main road.

'Oi, you lot. There's a bloke 'ere 'aving a wank.'

Trying to hold himself upright whilst he tucked himself in, the happy drunk was still giggling as he apologised to Bales.

'Sorry mate. Didn't see....'

His apology went unfinished as Bales shot a dagger out from under his coat, thrusting at the man's unprotected stomach. He wrenched the blade, tearing through muscle and tissue, disembowelling him; the drunk's eyes opened wide with shock and pain. His hands instinctively moved to

98

the horrendous wound. Staring in horror as his hot, bloodied intestines tumbled thought his fingers.

Bales may have been a useless leader, let alone General, but he was still a highly trained member of the Order — albeit a mediocre one. A final slice towards his throat, and the hapless drunk sunk to his knees before falling into a bloody heap where Bales had been sleeping off his drinking binge.

Bales moved quickly to try and avoid the deluge of blood and guts that exuded onto the ground. But he wasn't as fit as he once was. He had become soft behind his desk, enjoying the finer things in life that Ephea had been willing to pay for. He cursed as he faced away from the body and averted his eyes from the look of shock and pain on the poor man's face. Hurrying up the narrow confines of the alley that he had staggered down previously in his drunken state, he heard the injured man's friends enter the passage behind him. He ducked around the corner just as they found his body.

'Oi, Dave, Dave. Where are you mate?'

'Oh fuck! Shit! No.'

The last thing Bales heard as he ran from the scene, was of vomit hitting the brick wall and someone desperately trying to call the police and an ambulance. Turning down another street, being careful to keep to the shadows, he was furious. Covered in blood, piss and semen, he balled his fists in frustration and anger.

'Fuck.'

He was so angry, he wanted to go back and thrust his dagger into the stupid bastard all over again.

He'd been in London for less than forty-eight hours, leaving his home and family once the police had finally finished with their awful questions. Even dead, his stupid bitch of a wife had caused him trouble. They even had the audacity to suggest he had something to do with her death — *Did they think he had driven her to suicide?* — and, incredulously, that he had helped her kill their son. He had only suggested that Aleix would be better out of the way, but it was she who plunged the knife into his pathetic heart.

He'd come to London in the hope he could hide out, losing himself in the anonymity of Earth's urban sprawl. But first he wanted to get drunk. And he did, spectacularly so it seemed, staggering into the alley for somewhere to sleep off the drink before figuring out his next move. He didn't, however, expect to be pissed on by one of the locals. He sneered at the thought.

They are practically savages.

He was so caught up in his self pity and anger, he didn't hear the two figures approach from behind until it was too late.

Arms seized him and a hand was forced over his mouth and nose. He kicked out, thrashing behind, but whoever had hold of him was much taller and they lifted him off his feet. His body felt like a rag doll. The edges around his vision began to blur, as his brain desperately screamed out for air, but finally his body succumbed and he fell into unconsciousness.

7

A Time for Truths

They arrived at Denfield, Nathan's home within the Devonshire countryside of England, deciding that despite the Retreat having survived the past five years of neglect, it was still going to be some time before everyone could consider it as a home again. So much had happened since Nathan had created the barriers at the Retreat, ensuring that Ephea and her sisters were unable to enter a space the Knights considered private; even if that meant they were unable to access it themselves.

Nathan considered it ironic that, as Ephea hated anything to do with Earth, believing it to be beneath the normal standards of civilised living, that she used members of Earth's criminal fraternity to swell her disreputable band of Patrols. She saw them as nothing more than low life to be exploited. To her, respect and loyalty was something you could buy and bully from other people.

Ephea thought that Nathan and the rest of the Knight's desire to live amongst the people from Earth as a form of madness, grown out of the unnatural longevity of their lives. But the truth was, the Knights enjoyed the anonymity of living with people who had no idea who they were. Of course, there was the added fact that they had been working with various projects on Earth for some years now, and it was far more productive and convenient to be close at hand to their enterprises.

Ephea had always assumed that Nathan was the all powerful Emperor, imposing his will on his people in order to maintain control. In some ways, he had to admit she was right, but instead of dictating his own authority, the Empire was governed by a High Council of publicly elected members. The Knights only ensured that the High Council itself was honest and above reproach. A meeting every six weeks meant the Knights were kept up to date with Imperial Politics; otherwise they remained only as overseers, watching and monitoring, stepping forward to intervene only when they considered it necessary.

As a rule it worked. Apart from the odd occasion, such as with Ephea's father Royston Morecroft and his appalling treatment of his workers and tenants. The Knights considered that the incompetence of the local authorities had allowed the situation to continue for too long. They had finally stepped in, making a few improvements within the local council along the way — deterring members from abusing their position — and encouraging the Imperial High Council to maintain control.

With the closure of the Retreat, the Knights had used the opportunity to create their own homes on Earth; their own personal spaces that would have been difficult to achieve within the rest of the Empire. Their anonymity meant they could express themselves, living as they wanted, without worrying about propriety.

Now there was Jean to consider, their little band was once more eight instead of seven. It had been a long time since they had been effectively at full capacity, and Nathan had to admit that even though he still missed James after all this time, he always felt that the fiercely independent, and often wayward father of Daniel was more of a substitute, a temporary stand in.

Until Jean arrived that is, Nathan had wondered why he should feel that way, but it made more sense as he watched their newest member work. He was under no misapprehension however, it was already becoming apparent that life wasn't going to be as straight forward as it had been previously. The dynamic within the group was already changing. Even now, Jean and Daniel had established a friendship and understanding. Nathan frowned, he wasn't sure how he felt about that. A point in particular was on Jean's ship, the two of them seemed easy in each other's company and he was sure he saw them share a moment.

Now he found himself with thoughts and feelings he had never had to consider before, which made him feel strangely uncomfortable, out of control.

He wasn't entirely sure why he had brought Jean to Denfield. There were plenty of places she could have stayed, including Daniel's home, after all if they were becoming such good friends… But inside a voice told him no, that was not going to happen. He assured himself it was because he had a responsibility to make sure Jean was safe, and of course he had the room to accommodate her, here in his Devonshire home. Though, no matter how much he tried to ignore it, he couldn't dismiss the voice whispering from somewhere around his heart, and every time he tried to evade it, it would give a painful squeeze. More than once he had found himself catching his breath, trying to ease the aching in his chest as he watched Jean and Daniel together.

Feeling angry and quite ridiculous in his thoughts, he was annoyed at his reaction. Daniel was one of his best friends, he should be pleased for him if it meant he could find happiness with Jean.

But now, as Nathan watched Jean make her way across the balcony terrace that ran the length of the house, she looked out at the view, just as he himself had done so many times before. Even though it was the middle of the night, there was a full moon high in the sky, illuminating the landscape of his precious garden and the expanse of Dartmoor beyond. He didn't move as he watched, daring not to break the moment as she closed her eyes and soaked up the atmosphere around her. Clenching his fists, he forced himself into motionless silence, trying not to listen to the voice urging him forward, to move next to her, be part of the space that she experienced. But when she turned to him she had a sadness in her eyes and he couldn't help but go to her, the look of concern etched across his face. He was almost relieved when she finally spoke.

'I've been here before. I know where I am.'

He looked around him, confused. 'Here? At Denfield?'

Jean shook her head and smiled.

'No, not actually here, but this area. This is Devon, we're in England.' It was a statement, not a question. 'We used to come here for our holidays with my parents when I was a child.' She looked back out at the garden and dropped her voice to a low whisper. 'And later, with my own family.'

Nathan looked at her curiously. 'But I thought you said you were seven thousand years old? I can't imagine many people around here holidaying seven thousand years ago.'

Jean looked back at him and laughed. He felt his heart do that squeezing thing again and he found himself reaching out and grasping the wall that ran along the balcony.

Dear gods Nathan, what is the matter with you? Take control of yourself.

'I was born in London in 1966. When I grew up I married and we had two children.' She laughed again. 'I even managed to grow old and die. It was only later that I found myself seven thousand years in the past, somewhere out in the middle of the universe without a clue of what I was doing there. It was also when I met Katherine, who I have only just recently discovered was your sister.'

A moment of pain passed across his face, which didn't go unnoticed by Jean. There was history between Nathan and

Katherine, his twin sister. She had obviously been considering her own thoughts for sometime because Nathan turned his back to the terrace and crossed his arms, he was looking at her intently.

'Are you going to explain that any further?'

He was so close they were almost touching.

Almost.

Jean looked out over the darkened landscape again. 'Eleven years.' She reached out and caught his arm and he felt himself gulp. 'It's been eleven years since I died.'

She seemed to slip. In the moonlight Nathan saw her eyes go slightly out of focus and he was aware of the feelings of pain and confusion that surged around her. He moved and had his arm around her waist, catching her before she fell; his face full of concern, and for a few moments there was silence, the world around them distant and withdrawn.

Then she moved away from him, averting her eyes to the gardens again, catching her breath.

'I'm sorry about that.'

Nathan also turned to look out over the landscape, his face giving nothing away to the emotions that were churning inside. Taking his time to breathe deeply, his heart only moments before swelling with joy, now seemed to constrict harder than ever. He took a while before speaking, trying to fill the awkward silence that had grown between them.

'You have family still living here, in England?'

Jean closed her eyes, nodding silently. He didn't push further, not yet. It was no doubt hard enough to have to process the information that the family she knew, her own children and grandchildren, were still alive. Now was not the time to discuss it.

'You must be as exhausted as I am, and those baked beans are not going to cook themselves. Come in and we'll sit down and eat while we talk further. There are things we need to discuss now but most can wait until tomorrow when everyone else is here.'

He walked towards his house, then waited for Jean to join him. Opening the French windows he stood back and let her enter. As she passed she gasped quietly.

The moment she entered, Jean knew that no matter what, she was safe here. It was a strange feeling, one she hadn't felt for a very long time, if at all. The realisation threatened her exhausted emotions to start flowing again and she bit her lip in annoyance. She felt such an idiot for her dizzy moment, he must have thought her a complete fool. But however much she tried to ignore it, she had to admit that it was her emotions that finally got the better of her. Not a foolish female swoon depicted in story books and fairytales, but a moment when the pain of realising the family she missed so much was still so near, but impossible to see. Briefly, her carefully built walls had crumbled, and a lifetime of hidden emotions had overwhelmed her. Quickly trying to rebuild her barriers, she could not ignore the brief joy of intimacy with Nathan as he held onto her. Mortified to think what he would make of her moment of weakness, she had pulled away, shocked at how much the reaction hurt her.

She gave herself a mental kick, venturing further into what was obviously Nathan's kitchen and general living space. It looked as if, despite the size of the house itself, this was the main area that Nathan spent his time. The kitchen and dining table all had the well used look, scrupulously clean but definitely lived in. As was the comfortable sofas that huddled around a log burning stove at the furthest end of the room. This was the heart of a home, not a show house.

Within the kitchen itself, a large range was pushing out a gloriously warming heat, tempting Jean to curl up on a sofa and drop off to sleep there and then. But a clamouring noise, followed by some pretty impressive swearing from a cupboard, brought her back awake. Nathan popped his head around the door, to what Jean assumed, was a larder.

'Sorry about that. I should have turned the light on in here instead of rummaging around in the dark. I've found the beans, or should I say they found my left foot. Who knew how heavy a tin of beans could be when dropped from a height?'

Jean couldn't help but laugh and Nathan joined in as he returned to the stove with an arm full of food.

'Did you want some help there?'

'No, it's fine. You sit down and I'll have the kettle on and something to eat soon enough.'

Jean didn't argue. Sitting at the dining table, she watched as Nathan took off his coat and busied himself around his kitchen. It gave her time to watch and ponder the man who was playing havoc with her feelings.

Curiously, she considered the strangeness of being with someone who, for the first time, she was unable to read; emotionally anyway. It wasn't that he was completely blank, that he had no emotions that she could sense, it was as if everything was blurred, like looking through an opaque window. It was unnerving and Jean could only put it down to her tiredness and the feelings she herself was experiencing. One thing she was sure of though, was that in some part, Nathan was also an empath; which was both interesting and disconcerting considering her own emotional turmoil at the moment. She just hoped he was as confused as she was.

Watching with some amusement, as this man, who effectively was the most powerful man in a very large Empire — if not the universe — pottered about his kitchen; it was strangely surreal but also quite refreshing, he was confident and happy in his own private space.

A man who could demand the respect and loyalty of an Empire, inspire those around him to listen and act on his every word, yet still manage to infuriate her with his stubbornness.

Finally, having the opportunity to relax, Jean let the creature within raise its head. What was it about Nathan that had her in such a spin? Yes, she appreciated he was a very good looking man. But she had met plenty of men over the centuries that could tick that box, but she'd never had any awkward and embarrassing thoughts about them. On the contrary, she made a point of discouraging any close relationships, mainly because she never found herself attracted to anyone. She had actually got to the point where she believed it was a part of becoming a Guardian, no-one effectively floated her proverbial boat, not even so much as a twinge. No twinges, no boat floating, not even a second glance.

Now, with Nathan, there was many a covert glance and a relative armada of floating ships, with enough twinges to concern a neurologist. She felt so out of her depth she was practically drowning in embarrassment and confusion.

So what was it about Nathan? Well, of course there were those eyes. Pools of blue you could quite easily lose yourself in. Yep, that was definitely a positive factor in his favour.

Giving herself the pleasure of watching him work she considered his finer details while he ran his hand through his mop of black hair as he tackled the baked beans. His face was strong with over a day's growth darkening his jawline. She thought it gave him a particular brooding look when he was especially grumpy.

Like Jean, the Knights had been around for centuries but hadn't aged. It was something to do with their genetics apparently, as well as the fact that the body had to die in order for specific genes to mutate; but she hadn't a clue how it all worked.

If she didn't know better she would have put their ages at around the forties. There were no tell tale signs of ageing, such as greying hair, but Nathan could have looked older despite it. When she considered this, she put it down to the fact that, like her, the Knights had experienced life from the sharp end. No amount of genetic manipulation could take that away. Not having known anyone who knew about the subject of their unique genetic makeup before, she considered a long conversation with Stephen was due at some point in the future.

She caught her own reflection in the glass of the French windows. She had seen that same face for so long she wondered what age someone else would put her now? The way she felt at the moment there was every possibility it could be a lot older than forty. Her hair had been bundled up on top of her head as it always was, stray hairs had come loose and were sticking out at odd angles giving her a slightly manic look. She ran her hands over her tired face, it felt dry and her eyes were sore with exhaustion; her body still ached with the bruises from the battering it had taken against the Kaimiren.

Dear gods she was a wreck. She looked up and Nathan was in the process of breaking eggs into a bowl. He seemed aware that he was being watched and looked up, his brow still furrowed in concentration over the eggs. She smiled to herself.

'Do you mind if I use your loo?'

Away from all the stresses of his everyday life and focusing on the simple chore of scrambling eggs, the years seemed to drop away and he could be any young man making himself something to eat. She felt herself blush as he returned her smile.

'Of course, through the door and across the corridor. The first door on your left as you enter the hall.'

Muttering her thanks, she left quickly, following his directions. The corridor was nothing more than a small passage that led to a set of wooden stairs to her left. The only light was through a window of leaded lights at the height of a small mezzanine landing on the stairs leading upwards to an unseen level. She crossed the passage through another door, which led into the main hall of the house. Again the only light was from the moon outside, but this time it was through an impressive glazed vaulted ceiling that ran almost the whole length of the hall. Jean gasped, she was reminded of the ceiling of the Palace at Parva and its effectiveness as a source of light, which was never more so apparent than demonstrated here. As the sky changed with the weather outside, the ceiling constantly created a new atmosphere in the huge open space.

Despite it being the middle of the night, the details of the hall were still distinctive, and Jean was easily able to navigate her way without resorting to switching on any artificial lights. The hall itself was a large room that rose up to the roof, with the first floor accessible via a grand wooden staircase. Closed doors lined the upper storey, with a terrace that ran around three quarters of the landing overlooking the hall. It reminded Jean of the layout of the hall at the Retreat, and she wondered if Nathan had played a part in designing both the Palace and the Retreat as well as his magnificent home.

There was a sound of pans and plates being moved in the kitchen, reminding her that she should be looking for the loo. As Nathan had said, it was the first door on her left, nestled under the highest part of the staircase. This time she did resort to switching the light on, which, unlike the lighting in the Empire, was good old fashioned electricity. The bright light did nothing to help Jean's mood though as she inspected her reflection in the mirror. At some point she had gained a large bruise on her left cheek, and despite her improved living conditions over the past few months, she was still looking gaunt. Dark circles under her eyes didn't help the image either.

Letting down her hair she attempted to at least run her fingers through the long tresses, she should have brought her pack from the kitchen with her and utilised a brush. Instead she had to try and bundle her hair back up on top of her head, making sure any potential escapees were suitably dealt with.

By the time she made her way back to the kitchen, Jean had achieved all she was going to with what she had. However, the smell of cooking helped to lift her mood a bit and once she had sat down at the table again, Nathan placed a large mug of tea and a plate of scrambled eggs on toast with baked beans in front of her. At that moment it was the best feast in the universe, and she gave Nathan the biggest tired, but grateful, smile she could muster.

Her little tummy monster purred as he returned the gesture, and she gave up trying to push the feelings down this time, it was pointless.

Nathan had happily busied himself around his kitchen. He enjoyed cooking, though it was Paul who was the real expert at creating spectacular dishes. However, his own larder was considerably lacking at the moment to produce anything extravagant, and at this time of night a huge meal was probably not a wise idea anyway.

While Jean went off in search of the toilet, he considered the information that she had revealed so far. He couldn't imagine what it must feel like for her to have not seen or heard anything about her family for seven thousand years, only to find out that they were still alive, believing she had died just a few years ago. Of course, it would be unwise to

113

make contact with them, first of all they would probably find it difficult to reconcile the woman that Jean had become with the mother and grandmother that had she once been. Secondly, there was the issue of security. If anyone found out that Jean had close relatives still living they could use this against her; it was a dangerous option. But at the end of the day, the simple fact was, Jean had family and could she possibly just ignore they existed? A brief image of Katherine, his twin sister, crossed his mind. As the guilt threatened to gnaw at his conscience he quashed it just as quickly.

There was of course the other matter that had occurred on the terrace, which, for a brief moment, everything seemed to fall into place. But then Jean pulled away, ensuring as much space between them as possible, and no matter how much he tried he couldn't fool himself, it hurt like hell.

When Jean returned to the kitchen he made a point of appearing much more relaxed and cheerful. He resigned himself to the fact that he just had to learn to cope with the voice that had made its home around his heart. There were far more important things to deal with, and none of them involved a ten thousand year old love sick Knight who should know better.

Settled at the table, the pair of them tucked into their meal hungrily, not saying anything until they had clean plates before them, along with their second cup of tea. Jean stood and cleared the table, visibly wincing as she stood up. The bruises from their battle with the Kaimiren were definitely showing themselves now. Nathan knew exactly how she felt, his ribcage had taken a battering and his left knee was beginning to throb after one of the Kaimiren had made a concerted effort to try and bring him down with a well aimed kick.

He didn't want to break the amiable silence that existed between them like a warm, soft, comforting blanket; but he had to. He also desperately needed his bed.

'Jean, there are some things we need to discuss, but before we do, you spoke earlier about being with my sister Katherine.' He paused and reached out for his mug of tea. 'What happened? Did she say... anything?' He felt his insides clench, he hadn't heard about Katherine for so long and it suddenly occurred to him that he wasn't sure he wanted to know after all. But it was too late now.

She gave him a tired smile. 'I'll start from the beginning shall I? There isn't a lot to say, but it may make more sense to you if I did.'

Nathan returned her smile without saying anything. He felt exhausted and just let her speak.

'So, eleven years ago I died. It wasn't anything spectacular, it was of old age and quite peaceful if I recall. For most people that would pretty much be it. Where you go from there, if at all, I have no idea. I never got that far.

'Before you ask though, there are many parts of this time in my life, from my timely death to becoming a Guardian, that I can't actually remember; though it's not through want of trying I can assure you. But for some reason, much of the time period after meeting Katherine is a complete blank. Only on occasions when I'm under extreme emotional stress, or a trigger stimulates a memory, do I manage to recall anything. But I can never quite keep a hold onto the thought.

As quickly as it's there, it's suddenly gone, and for the life of me I can't remember any of it.'

Nathan frowned. 'That must be very frustrating. Do you think your memory has been deliberately tampered with?'

Jean nodded and shrugged. 'It seems the most likely explanation, though who and why someone would do that, I have no idea.'

'Could it have been Katherine?'

Jean looked at him sharply. His head was down, giving the impression he was bracing himself for the worst possible answer. She reached out and covered his hand. He glanced at where they touched, she didn't move hers away and neither did he. Jean continued.

'The first thing I recall was an awareness that I was in a quiet home, nestled in a beautiful countryside, within a world I never knew the name of. The house belonged to Katherine, and when I knew her she was a very old woman. In fact, I barely recognised her from her picture in the museum... except for her eyes that is. I suppose thinking back now, I can also see similarities between you and her in your mannerisms. I would have no problem accepting you were brother and sister.'

Nathan gave her a grateful smile.

'She told me of the stone, but not how it was formed. She seemed reluctant to tell it's story.'

Nathan tensed, but said nothing. 'I do know that whatever that monk may have said, the stone didn't stay at his monastery. Apparently, Katherine did try to leave it there in their care at first, but unfortunately for her, whenever she tried to leave the stone, it always found a way to follow.

Wherever she went, the stone went too. Eventually she gave up and admitted defeat, never returning to the monastery, and the stone remained a constant companion.

'She spent years travelling the universe trying to find peace. From what, she never said, but eventually she settled in her little home on the world with no name. Finally, she seemed to find what she was looking for, making a simple life for herself there.

'After a while, the stone left her to her own devices and she discovered that she was beginning to grow older. Ageing still took longer than normal, but over the course of time Katherine had become old, eventually becoming very ill. She was dying. It was something she said she was happy to embrace, and looking back I believe her. The main issue of course was that with Katherine's impending death drawing near, the stone began to wake up again, it seemed to renew its need to secure its heir.

'I have no idea if it was actually the stone that did anything, or the input from a third party, but apparently there were to be no more caretakers of its power. It wanted the rightful heir there and then.'

Jean spread her hands. 'Me. Why me in particular? Who knows, no one has given any explanation, or, if they did, I don't remember it. Anyway, the crux of the matter was, I had died on twenty-first century Earth, and Katherine was dying seven thousand years earlier. Hence the reason I am now seven thousand years old, but I was born just over a century ago.'

Nathan nodded his head. 'Fair enough. Surprisingly it makes more sense.'

'Anyway, I was now with Katherine and found myself nursing her through her last days. Fortunately, despite her illness, she was able to talk, telling me about the stone, and that she had a brother that she missed terribly. Also that she regretted how they had parted, that she had been responsible for many awful things, though she never actually said why or what they were. Only that she wasn't that person at heart.

'The day she died, Katherine was desperate that I tell her brother that she was truly sorry for everything she did, and that she loved him dearly. The only problem being, she never actually told me who her brother was.

'Of course, once she was gone, the stone disappeared but I became the person I am today.'

Jean looked into Nathan's eyes. Their blue undiminished by the sadness of hearing about the death of his twin sister. It wasn't until he placed his other hand over her's that she realised she had caught hold of his again and she had been gripping his fingers.

'She was happy when she finally died?'

Jean smiled gently. 'Yes, she was happy, finally content and at peace. Your parting was her only regret... and Nathan, she really did love you.'

He closed his eyes and remembered his sister, trying to focus on the happier times, but there was always the not so happy times in the background. When he opened them again he stood up and went to a dresser, where he picked up a bottle of amber liquid and set down two brandy glasses on the table before them both. Pouring each of them a good measure, they then raised and touched glasses in a silent toast. Jean sipped at her brandy, drinking slowly as the heat

118

of the liquid made its way down her throat. Nathan, however, had already refilled his own glass, grinning wryly when he saw her watching him.

'It's been a long day.'

After a more adventurous mouthful of brandy and a valiant attempt not to choke as the strong liquid went down, Jean spoke, albeit a bit squeakily.

'You said there was something else you wanted to discuss.'

Nathan nodded as he put his glass down, Jean noting that he had already reduced its contents by half.

'Yes, and then I promise I will show you to your room and you can get some much needed sleep.'

He concentrated on the contents of his glass for a moment before looking back at Jean. The sadness in his eyes had gone and was replaced with a look of purpose.

'First of all, regarding Belby.' Jean frowned and he held up his hands. 'I know, and I'm not going over that again. All I'm suggesting, is that we draw a line under the incident. I know you have been on your own for a very long time, and I understand how difficult that must have been. If it is even half of the kind of difficulties we've had to deal with, then I'm in awe of your patience and steadfastness. You are obviously more than capable of handling a sword as well as your knives, and I have to admit that the archery is a useful addition.'

'You don't have that?'

He shook his head. 'No, the use of the bow is unique to you. Then again, I suppose if you are expected to work alone, then an extra weapon would definitely be useful.'

They both smiled then quickly looked away.

'My point is, being alone does have the very big disadvantage of not needing to be part of a team. Now we, on the other hand, have been doing this for a fair number of years as well, and as such, we have learnt to work together using our strengths to ensure our work is completed. Preferably getting the hell out of whatever particular living nightmare we've been sent to, with as little blood loss and broken bones as possible.'

'And do you?'

'Do we what?'

'Get home without blood loss and broken bones?'

He gave a mirthless laugh. 'I would love to say yes, but unfortunately there are times when things don't always go to plan.'

Jean nodded. 'Glad it's not just me then.'

Nathan chuckled. 'No, it's not just you. My point though, is that today, you have shown me how you use the skills you've been given. I've also seen that you and Daniel seem to have created a good working relationship.' He felt his throat tighten and tried to swallow while attempting to look and sound perfectly normal. By the look of concern on Jean's face he wasn't entirely sure he had succeeded. Taking in a long low breath he picked up his brandy glass and swallowed the rest of the contents in one before continuing. Jean just watched and said nothing. 'Daniel is particularly good at observation and is very fast on his feet. I think with your empathic skills, you could both work well together.' He knew that his decision was right, but he hated to have to admit it to himself. 'You have a place within our little band Jean. A useful one, that I have no doubt will become invaluable.

120

What I do need though is for you to realise we have our strengths too, and that includes me.'

Jean raised an eyebrow. 'The man-in-charge?'

Nathan was silent for a moment then shook his head.

'No, not 'the man-in-charge'. I lead yes, but that is because my strengths lie in strategy. I have an aptitude for being able to see a problem, then work a way through it. Admittedly it's not always that clean cut, and often it's pretty much a spur of the moment thing. But it is what I do, and as such, I make decisions to ensure the best possible way of achieving a desirable outcome. And so far we have all managed to stay alive. Just.

'My problem Jean, is that you do things without discussing them first. It's very difficult to make a plan when someone completely ignores it and starts doing their own thing.'

Jean bit her lip and sighed. 'I understand what you are saying. I don't deliberately try to be awkward, and I'm not saying I will be able to change overnight. But I will try.'

She looked down at her hands and the glass still full of brandy. Nathan sat in silence, waiting. She didn't look up when she spoke.

'Do you really think I have place here?'

Nathan smiled at her. This time it was he who reached out and held her hand.

'Yes, I do, and we welcome it. The Retreat will always be your home, no matter where you are in the universe, it will always be where you can return. I also stand by my words that things are about to get interesting for all of us.' He paused and took another long deep breath. 'But I also want you to know, that you will always have a place to stay here, in Denfield. You have spent too long on your own, and as we, and I mean Damien, Daniel and the others, have a lot of business here on Earth we spend most of our time here now. It is also your home world, and no doubt you will want to spend some time getting to know it again. So, I offer you my home as a place to stay, if you want to of course. If you choose to make somewhere else your home, by all means do so. But I have to admit I would appreciate the company.'

Jean sat in stunned silence.

'However, for now, we both need to sleep. It's very late, so I'll show you to your room and we can catch up with everyone else tomorrow.' He looked down at her barely touched brandy. 'Are you going to finish that?'

Jean looked at him guiltily and shook her head. Without a second glance he picked up the glass and finished off the contents. Standing up, she winced again as her battered body objected to the movement. She retrieved her pack and Nathan led her through the kitchen door and back into the hall. They made their up the grand wooden staircase and around the balcony. As they passed one of the rooms he pointed to it saying.

'This is my room. If you need anything just knock, though you should have everything you need in your own room.'

He then moved on past and they came to another door that he opened, beckoning her to enter. He stood at the door and watched as she walked around the room. Reaching the huge bed she laid down her pack and turned to him.

122

'Thank you Nathan, you have no idea how much I appreciate this.'

He returned her smile and wished her goodnight before closing the door quietly behind him.

Jean turned on one of the lamps beside the bed and went to close the curtains. Before she pulled them to, she took in the vast, moonlit grounds; it really was a beautiful home. After exploring the bathroom, she couldn't resist the urge to stand under the shower and its hot deluge of water. When she finally made it into her big comfortable bed, it was barely moments before she succumbed to her exhaustion and fell into a deep dreamless sleep.

8

Ħell's Angel

The warm and inviting sheets enveloped his naked body, feeling the softness of the fine cotton beneath his fingers, sinking deeper into the inviting comfort of the bed.

Shit, not another bloody dream.

Bales shot open his eyes, then immediately shut them again, as blinding light hit the back of his eyeballs; and for the second time in as many days, he tried to open his eyes to daylight with a raging hangover. He covered his face with his hands and groaned, was it really only two days since he woke to that bloody policeman banging on his door with the awful news. He ground his teeth in disgust at the memory. More thoughts flitted into his mind; someone pissing on him, embarrassment of being caught with his dick out, and the smell of blood as he vented his anger on the drunk.

He froze as he felt movement beside him. Slowly bringing his hands down from his face he squinted to try and focus.

'Who's there?'

'Hello Victor.'

His stomach lurched. Whoever this was, their voice made his skin crawl.

He tried to sit up, but a firm hand from someone else pushed him back hard against the pillows.

'Now, now Victor, you just lie still for a moment.'

Bales tried to ease down the panic that was rising within him. If this was a dream he wanted his dusky nubile woman back. He still couldn't see very well with the glare of light in his eyes, and he tried to shield them with his hand. Someone was moving again and the room slowly came into a dim focus as blinds were lowered against the glare. When he finally focused on his visitors, he was in two minds to ask them to have the blinds raised again.

It must have been the man who pushed him down that had closed the blinds as he was now standing behind his companion. Both of them watched Bales closely, he felt like a fly being studied by toads before being consumed as a passing snack. But it was their dead eyes that scared him most. He'd heard it said that a man's eyes were the window to their soul. If that was the case then Bales had never been more sure that these two were devoid of anything resembling a soul or any other form of spirit.

His skin crawled, and he felt sweat form on his brow, slowly dripping down his face and into his pillow. It took a while before he realised he was holding his breath. Afraid of breaking the silence he let out a long sigh, closing his eyes as the gentle hiss seemed to reverberate around the walls.

The man standing closest to him smiled. It wasn't a pleasant one and Bales wasn't reassured.

Had the toad decided it was time for his snack?

Bales fought to keep his panic in check and decided to fall back on his old favourite, bombastic bravado. He may not feel very brave but he was damned if he was going to let them know that.

He forced himself to sit up and noticed with some satisfaction that the silent man scowled. Bales took that as a small victory on his part. Bolstered further, he forced his voice to be as authoritative as he could, though even he had to admit that it sounded thinner than he would have liked.

'Where am I? And who are you?' He stuck his meagre chin out to make his point. The silent man continued to scowl but the other one just gave a mirthless grin, his lifeless eyes unwavering in their gaze upon him. Bales gulped.

'Later Victor. For now, eat your breakfast and then get dressed before joining us. We will speak later.'

Then before he could argue any further, they left the room and closed the door quietly behind them.

Alone, Bales looked around the room. It was small, with only the single bed, a table was pushed against one wall with a covered food platter waiting for him. Alongside was a hard chair that contained his neatly folded clothes. In one corner there was a sink and a mirror, with his personal shaving kit and toiletries on a small shelf above the sink.

Someone had been down his pack.

126

He didn't like this one bit. He shuddered at the thought of someone rummaging through his most personal possessions. He got out of bed and went to the sink, picking up the items he checked them carefully; yes they were definitely his. The reflection of his own movement made him look up, and he caught the image of himself in the mirror. He winced when he saw the man looking back at him. Unshaven with an unhealthy pallor about his cheeks, he wasn't looking his best no matter how much he tried to kid himself.

Picking up his shaving kit he began the familiar process of removing the stubble that had formed on his chin. Following the same routine he had done all his life as a man, noticing with despair, grey hairs amongst the scrapings. He automatically looked at his hairline and saw the tell-tale signs of grey forming there too. He was rewarded for his momentary distraction with a nick to his chin. Swearing, he looked around and grabbed a towel to mop up the blood flowing freely. It took a while for the wound to dry sufficiently so that he could carry on with his ablutions. By the time he had finished and had pulled on his clothes, which he noticed had been laundered and were now free of all embarrassing bodily fluids, the food that lay under the cover had gone cold. But cold soup was better than no soup, and his stomach appreciated it, as well as the large chunks of bread and cheese all the same.

Bales had checked his pack to make sure everything was still there, noticing with despair that his knife was missing. Adding his toilet bag to the pack he gave one final glance around the small room, then opened the door and looked out.

The door opened onto a long corridor that ran into the distance in both directions. There was no visible source of light but it was brightly lit all the same. Bales drew his eyebrows together in thought and looked back into his room. When he had woken he was sure it was hard sunlight that had flooded the space and his aching head, but looking back to the corridor he couldn't see anything so bright to cause that much dazzling light.

While he tried to consider this anomaly he felt the door behind him begin to close, as if there were a force behind it pushing hard. Bales instinctively resisted, but the door just pushed back harder, and with one final shove he found himself hurled into the corridor. He spun round, sure there were several hidden eyes watching him, but if they were, he had no idea where from. In apprehension his eyes darted up and down the corridor, warily taking in his surroundings. The walls were whitewashed and the floor was flagged with a marble like stone. He couldn't see a solid ceiling, only the glow of a light that blurred the edges around the tops of the walls, while all along the corridor lining each side, were innumerable doors.

His training had already kicked in. Cautious, he listened out for anything anomalous, but the whole situation was one big anomaly. He couldn't stand still, he had to move. So choosing a direction, he made his way down his elected path.

His boots rang out on the stone floor, reverberating off the walls and closed doors. Despite his footfalls, he could still hear faint whisperings of people on the other side of the

128

doors; occasionally he would stop and try one, but always, they were locked. The voices were muffled and no matter how hard he tried, he couldn't make out any words, either familiar or foreign.

He carried on walking along the corridor, unaware of time, it could have been ten or twenty minutes, he had no idea. The length of the passageway seemed to go on forever. Eventually he stopped and looked behind him, it felt as if the doors he had passed were disappearing into the distance. Pausing a moment, he became aware that something was different about the view behind him, something that wasn't there before. Concentrating his mind, he looked harder into the dim shadows, trying to figure out what was wrong.

He froze, it suddenly hit him that the corridor was no longer so bright behind, it was getting darker. As he watched, he saw in horror, that the darkness was following him. Fear shot up his spine and Bales forced his legs to move. Turning he began to walk quicker, his boots ringing out his steps. He looked behind him again, he was sure the darkness was nearer, it couldn't have been that close before.

Spinning back round he quickened his step and began to run, his breathing became laboured against the exertion. Legs pounded as he fought to leave the darkness behind him, soon he was sprinting. The lactic acid in his legs burned while sweat ran down his back in rivulets.

He dare not stop moving. The fingers of darkness were slowly catching up. He could feel it closing in, getting nearer, trying to trip him up.

His peripheral vision picked up shadows that seemed to reach out for his body as he frantically tried to get away.

Dear gods it was nearly upon him.

Screaming with the exertion, his body was pushed to its limits, but he couldn't let the nightmare of the unknown take him. His heart felt as if it would burst when suddenly, he hit something hard head on.

Reeling backwards from the impact he thought he heard a door in the distance slam, while he now found himself sprawled out on the ground, trying to suck in oxygen to his unexercised lungs.

Fuck

His brain began to slowly try and figure out what the hell had just happened. It took a few moments for him to realise that he wasn't lying on the stone floor of the corridor but on fresh, green grass. He could feel each blade against his fingers as he slowly moved his hands. He squinted against the bright light as he tried to open his eyes.

At this rate I'm going to go blind before the day is out.

Groaning again, he brought his hand up to eyes to shield his vision, before attempting to open them again. Squinting to ward off the brightness, Bales let his vision slowly clear, venturing to peer from beneath his fingers.

It was then he saw, with no small relief, that the bright light was in fact a sun. His senses gradually returning he could hear birdsong, feel the heat of the sun on his bare skin, the scent of flowers filling his nostrils.

His body objected as he tried to sit up, but he was determined, ignoring his aches and pains he forced himself to stand. Looking around he discovered he was in a beautiful garden, full of trees and flowers in blossom. Turning slowly, he eventually saw the object he had run so hard into. It was

130

the base of a large statue of a naked man and woman in a very suggestive embrace.

Bales looked behind him searching for the door that he must have come through, but he couldn't see it. He spun round again and looked in all directions, but still there was no evidence of an entrance.

'Glad you could join us Victor.'

He shot round at the sound of the voice. His spine tingled alarmingly. The two men he had met previously were now sitting at an iron garden table. He would have sworn on his life that they weren't there a moment ago, but here they were now, sitting having tea in the sunshine.

'Would you like some tea Victor? Please, sit down and join us.'

The man pulled out a chair and indicated that Bales should sit, then continued to pour out tea into three china cups. Bales reluctantly sat down, cautiously watching the two men. He didn't like the way they looked at a him, especially the silent one. The sweat on his back went cold under their scrutiny despite the heat of the sun.

'Were the hell am I? And you still haven't told me who you are.'

'Now Victor. Where are your manners? Drink your tea and we will talk. You will learn all you need to know… when we are ready to tell you.'

Bales felt himself bristle at the idea that these strangers should deem to tell him about manners.

Who the fuck do they think they are?

However, with reluctance, he sat down. Extending his hand to pick up the teacup, he noticed that beside the saucer, his knife sat, still in its sheath. He subconsciously reached out and briefly touched the soft familiar leather. But instinctively he didn't pick it up. Instead he moved his hands to his cup and picked it up, holding it in both hands as he always did, balanced between his fingertips.

Gellan watched, a small sneer flickered across his features. He had no love for this pathetic excuse of a man, but he was useful at the moment and so braced himself against the annoying habits displayed by the ridiculous human. Beside him Duran sat in his usual silence, merely resting impassive eyes on Bales like a hungry shark. Once he was satisfied that he finally had his full attention, Gellan began to speak, and Bales listened intently.

9

Christopher

Chris Jackson opened his eyes and rubbed at them, trying to focus on the time displayed on his phone.

0800

At least it was a Saturday, so his alarm wasn't set to go off at some ungodly hour. He turned over, trying not to wake the figure of the man beside him. Quietly watching the gentle, rhythmic rise and fall of his chest as he slept. The duvet had partly fallen away overnight, and John Corvier's long frame lay sprawled out, causing Chris to yet again catch his breath in awe of this man's body. He took his time, studying every inch of exposed skin covering the hard muscle and sinews of those solid, long bones. Hungry eyes finally settled onto John's face, beautiful and strong like the rest of his body, and

Chris couldn't help but feel his own body respond. He longed to reach out and touch the Knight, feel the warmth of his skin against his fingers, to explore and play.

But that wasn't what John desired now, he required sleep more than anything at the moment. Chris could barely contain his pleasure that he was the first person John had turned to when he came home; the first person he wanted to see of all the people in the whole universe.

Leaving him to sleep, Chris got up and made his way to the bathroom, hoping that by then he will be in a better state of mind to have the pee he desperately needed. However, looking down at his own nakedness, *it still might take a minute*, he thought wryly to himself. Once he finally managed to finish relieving himself he went to the kitchen to put the kettle on; coffee was his life source in the morning. While he waited for the water to boil, he thought about the previous evening and John's sudden arrival at his door.

It had been around midnight and he had been entertaining a few friends from his work. They had been playing computer games all evening whilst consuming several bottles of beer, interspersed with a considerable amount of vodka. He winced when he remembered the discarded bottles lying on the floor next to the empty pizza boxes in his living room.

It had all the usual signs of the beginning of a good all night session, when there had been a knock on the door to Chris' first floor flat. However, it was late, and he was cautious about anyone calling at that time of night. He was thankful that his front door didn't lead straight into his living room, but when he checked the monitor and saw the figure of John standing there he practically threw the door open. When he came face to face with him though, he had to check it was definitely the same man he knew and was beginning to care very much for; he looked exhausted and dead on his feet. His features were drawn in the bright light of the hallway, and it was difficult for Chris to make out the striking eyes that had often had his heart skipping a beat. Even his voice was exhausted.

'Christopher, thank the gods you are still awake. I know it's late, but do you mind if I come in?'

The only other person to call him by his full name was his mother, and that was usually if she was chewing his ear about something. If anyone else called him Christopher he usually set them straight in no uncertain terms, but somehow he couldn't imagine John calling him Chris.

'Shit John, where the hell have you been? You look awful.'

He caught his hand and pulled him into the flat, John ducking his head just in time before braining himself on the top of the door jamb.

'Thanks, and I was hoping to make this my new look.'

There was a sudden sound of laughter coming from behind the closed living room door and John looked sharply at Chris.

'Shit. I'm sorry, it didn't occur to me you'd have guests. I'll leave you to it.'

John turned to leave and duck under the front door again but Chris stopped him.

'Not a chance, you're not going anywhere. Come in and I'll soon get everyone out. Do you want anything to eat? There's no pizza left, but you can have a rummage around

135

the fridge, I'm sure there's the basis for a sandwich in there somewhere.'

John gave him an exhausted, grateful smile, allowing himself to be lead into the kitchen where he didn't need to be encouraged any further in investigating the prospect of food. Chris left him to it and went back into the living room, letting his friends know the night's entertainment was now at an end. There was a considerable amount of protesting and one or two threatening a sit in, but eventually Chris managed to get the last of them out, with several extra bottles of beer as bribery. By the time he returned to the kitchen, John was tucking into a sandwich that Chris was pretty sure contained most of the contents of his fridge, whilst washing it down with a large glass of milk.

'Are you going to tell me what you've been up to, or am I going to be left in the dark? Again.'

John swallowed the mouthful of sandwich he had been chewing and held Chris's gaze. This time the ring of gold around the speckled brown of John's eyes was bright and hard; Chris found himself the first to look away, biting his lip in frustration. John had been upfront and frank about who he was and what he did, pretty early on in their relationship. Though it may have taken a while for the enormity of it all to sink in, he was grateful nonetheless for the Knight's honesty. But so many times he had been left, not knowing when, and if, he was going to see John again. It was quite frankly doing his head in.

'Tomorrow.'

Chris looked up and saw that the hardness in the eyes looking at him had softened. Leaning forward, John took one of Chris' hands in his.

'We'll talk tomorrow, and I promise I will tell you everything you want to know. But be warned, it may take some time and I'm not even sure I've got all the details right yet.'

Chris squeezed his hand and smiled. It was more than he had expected, he wasn't going to push it. 'Ok. Tomorrow.'

John said nothing more until he had finished off the rest of his sandwich with two more mouthfuls, then washed it down with the remaining milk.

'Right, now I need a shower and to sleep.' He smiled, though Chris was pretty sure it took him some effort. 'Please.' He sounded more exhausted than ever.

Gathering up the empty plate and glass, Chris put them in the sink, before leading John towards the bedroom and the ensuite bathroom. Once inside, John practically fell out of his clothes, and Chris watched as he stood under the hot water of the shower. His heart sank at the sight of the bruises that covered the big man's body, he was black and blue.

When John finally re-emerged from the bathroom he saw Chris watching him.

'You had better tell me everything tomorrow, including how the fuck you got all those bruises.'

John sighed and made his way to the bed. 'I promise. But now I just need to sleep.'

Chris said nothing, which was probably wise, because within moments of John's head hitting the pillow he was sound asleep. With nothing more to be said that evening,

Chris just stripped himself and climbed into bed beside him. His heart ached as he gazed at the now familiar scars that criss-crossed the Knight's body; not even the bruises that were spreading and turning a sickly yellow could hide the wreckage that scoured his back.

Sighing, Chris turned off the bedside light. Then reaching out, he gently touched John's battered body, pulling back suddenly as John turned to face him.

'I'm sorry, I didn't mean to wake you.'

John didn't say anything, as he pulled Chris towards him, holding him close, running fingers though his hair before finding his mouth with his own. Too tired to contemplate anything more vigorous, John finished the kiss with a weary smile, Chris returning it in understanding. As they both lay in each others arms Chris was wakeful a while longer as John slept peacefully beside him.

'Good morning.'

Chris nearly dropped the cup of coffee he was holding.

Shit

He was abruptly brought out of his reverie, turning to see the naked form of John in the kitchen doorway. As Chris hadn't bothered to dress when he left the bedroom, he found himself unable to hide his, very obvious, sudden arousal. John grinned.

'What are you laughing at?'

'Me? Would I dare laugh?'

Then reaching for Chris' hand, John pulled him out of the kitchen and back towards the bedroom, all thoughts of coffee forgotten.

10

A Familiar
Scowl

J ean lifted her head and felt the warmth of the
morning sun on her face, breathing in the sweet
smell of the flowers that grew in tubs and planters
all around the patio, once again admiring the view
that had taken her breath away. Paths of grass and stone,
woven through the areas of flowers, trees and pergolas,
disappeared into hidden tree dappled glades. She allowed
her senses to soak up the joyous nature of early summer, as
all around was the constant sound of birdsong. The natural
cycle of life played itself out, even the role of death; young

were being born, their doting parents needed to feed their offspring.

Briefly closing her eyes, Jean revelled in the mid-morning sunshine. Having slept soundly the night before, she felt more calm and relaxed than she could ever remember being, even tempted to think she could possibly be safe; but it would take more than a couple of days in this little corner of Devonshire paradise to accept that idea. Yes, the Knights were more than capable of looking after themselves, but would that extend to her wellbeing too? She wasn't so sure. But for now, she basked in a rare moment she didn't want to end.

She looked over to the man sitting across the table. He was also looking out over the gardens, his legs stretched out in front of him, with hands relaxed in his lap, elbows resting on the armrests of his chair. The remains of their breakfast still on the table, plates containing several rounds of toast, a cafetière and two mugs of half drunk coffee. They were already onto their second refills.

Nathan was aware that Jean was watching him and it was a few moments before he looked up and met her gaze. He smiled.

'I'm afraid that the fare here at Denfield has been pretty lacking, I really do need to sort out some decent food for the fridge and larder. I'll speak to Janet later and she will take great delight in filling my shelves, no doubt declaring how hopeless I am at looking after myself.'

Jean furrowed her brows.

'Janet?'

'My housekeeper. Well I use the term loosely. She comes in once a week to make sure I'm still alive, but she has been visiting her family in New Zealand for the past three weeks. I told her I could fend for myself in the meantime, but I'm not entirely sure she was convinced.'

Jean was inclined to agree with Janet on this one, but didn't think it was wise to say so. Besides, she was just pleased that the animal, that had been resting somewhere near her heart, was getting itself comfortable again after the initial mention of this other woman called Janet.

Everyone started to arrive around ten o'clock; with Stephen first, soon followed by Daniel, each greeting Jean warmly, as if meeting an old friend. Nathan had apparently given prior warning about the current state of his bare larder and everyone ensured they brought ample food supplies with them.

When Damien and Ty arrived, Jean was pleased to see Ty looking in one piece still, though his arm was now strapped up. When he saw Jean he gave her a big one armed hug, that was returned warmly but carefully. He grinned despite the wince he gave when his damaged ribs objected. She looked at him apologetically, remembering how he had received his injuries, believing he'd been crushed under tree logs and the relentless butchering of the Kaimiren. Then the overwhelming relief which followed when she realised that he had survived. He smiled back and kissed her forehead. She was moved at how much she cared for this man she had only known for a few days.

Damien joined them and also gave Jean a smile and a hug, whispering in her ear so only she could hear.

141

'The incident with the chair and the airlock, we don't need to worry Ty with that do we?'

Jean pulled back slightly and looked up into his face, she got the sense he was more embarrassed than concerned, and gave him a wry grin.

'My lips are sealed.'

'What are you two conspiring about?' Ty was looking at them both suspiciously.

Jean and Damien tried very hard to look innocent, but failed miserably.

'Nothing.' They said in unison.

'Hmmmmm.' He was gearing up to push it further when John and Chris arrived.

As it was a glorious day, and everyone was still out on the terrace, all eyes turned curiously on the new arrivals; on Chris in particular, who reddened at the attention. John, however, was perfectly at ease and seemed unaware of his companion's discomfort, giving everyone a big grin.

'Good morning.'

There was a general round of good mornings from everyone, before another episode of silence as they all, once more, trained their gaze onto Chris. Jean wasn't sure if she should search out a bucket for him, she didn't think Nathan would be overly pleased if the poor lad threw up in one of his flower pots. At last John seemed to be aware that Chris wasn't looking quite right.

'Are you alright?'

Chris looked at him and then behind him, Jean thought he was going to make a run for it.

'That, was not good. I don't like it.'

142

Before John could answer, Nathan stepped forward with his hand extended.

'You must be Christopher, I'm Nathan and welcome to Denfield. I take it that is the first time you've translocated?' He didn't wait for an answer. 'It will get better, it's probably because you weren't ready for it. Next time will be easier.'

Chris blinked and then seemed to snap back, holding out his hand to receive Nathan's.

'Pleasure to meet you, and er… thank you for having me. I'm not sure I will ever get used to that though.'

John shared a glance with Nathan in thanks, then made the rest of the introductions himself, indicating everyone in turn and then with a grin he looked at Chris.

'Everyone, this is Christopher Marchent, he's a Teacher at the Glasgow School of Art.'

'You're an artist?' Nathan looked intrigued.

Chris seemed a lot more comfortable talking about something he knew and smilled. 'Sort of, my interest lies mainly with the history of art.'

'Really? A subject close to my own heart.'

Chris grinned back.

Jean thought it might be an idea to give the poor guy a break, she glanced at Nathan who nodded as she held her hand out to Chris, indicating he follow her.

'Christopher, lovely to meet you, I think a cup of tea is definitely in order now, do you want to come and help?'

Jean thought that he would consider creating a three course dinner if it meant that everyone would stop staring at him. He followed her into the kitchen and they left the Knights to continue talking on the terrace.

'Thanks for that.'

'Not a problem. It must be very intimidating to meet everyone like that if you are not used to it, I thought you were going to be sick at one point.'

Just then more people arrived. Simon, carrying a large box of food which he brought into the kitchen, followed by John. Behind them, Paul and Anna were holding their own offerings.

Simon gave Chris a collaborative wink as John made the introductions before they both returned outside. Paul and Anna stayed with Jean and Chris, while Paul made an inventory of the food on display. Jean looked at the pile and wondered how they were going to eat it all, before glancing outside and berating herself for asking such a bloody stupid question.

Glancing at Chris, who seemed to be getting a more healthy colour back into his face, Jean thought he still looked bewildered.

'Are you ok?'

He laughed, 'Yes I'm fine, but I've just realised that I've never felt so bloody short, and I'm six foot tall.'

Jean and Anna glanced at one another and chuckled. Anna put an hand on his shoulder. 'Well, you can imagine how I feel then.'

He looked down at her and laughed back.

Moving to Jean's side, Anna watched her for a moment. 'And how are you? It's good to see you all made it back in one piece then?'

'Yep, despite several efforts to the contrary. But first of all, I need to thank you for what you did in Parva. You saved my life.'

'Your actions saved everyone else, in comparison I didn't do anything.'

Jean shook her head. 'We must agree to differ on that one, but it is good to see you again.'

They shared a brief hug, then Anna looked at her wryly. 'There is one major advantage of you being here of course.'

Jean raised an eyebrow questioningly.

'At least now I'm not the only woman around. It's about time I had some backup.'

Paul drew his brows together. 'And what do you need back up for?'

Anna and Jean looked at each other but said nothing, smiling as if they shared a great secret.

'What?' Paul looked at Chris for support.

'I can't help you, I don't know anyone here, except for the information John has told me. I'm still trying to get over the fact that one second I'm in Glasgow city, then the next I'm in the middle of the Devonshire countryside.'

Anna sympathised. 'Don't worry, you'll soon get used to it, as if you are stepping off of a bus.'

Chris didn't look convinced but appreciated the words.

'I wouldn't worry about not knowing anybody else, John hasn't told us a thing about you either, you probably know more about us than we do about you.' Paul was talking as he investigated the piles of food before him.

'He didn't tell you about me?'

'Not a thing. First we heard about you was yesterday in the middle of outer space somewhere.' He wiggled his fingers towards the sky as if to emphasise a strange other place. 'Then he left almost immediately, saying he was on his way to see you.'

Jean sensed the danger and scowled at Paul as she put her hand on Chris' arm.

'Christopher, John has told you what has been happening in Kelan and the rest of the Empire?'

Chris sighed. 'Yes, he told me about everyone, and about Ephea and her sisters.'

She nodded. 'Then you must also know that anyone associated with John and the rest of the Knights were potentially in danger. Anna and Ty have had limited contact with Paul and Damien since it all started. I'm pretty sure that John's only reason for not mentioning you was to keep you safe. The fact that you're here now shows how much he wants you to meet everyone, and them you.'

Chris sighed. 'Yes, you're right, I'm sorry, it's just a lot to take in.'

'Of course it is, and no-one expects it to be easy straight away.' She handed him a tray of mugs. 'Here, take these outside.'

Chris did as he was told and Jean watched him leave before turning and letting her gaze rest on Paul.

You knew exactly what you were doing there.

He held her gaze, the silence hanging between them. Anna picked up the second tray, with teapots and milk and thrust them at her husband, who reluctantly dropped his eyes. He shot a look of annoyance at his wife, but she ignored him.

'Jean there seems to be a fair bit of food piling up in this kitchen. Help me put some of it away so we know what we are dealing with will you? Paul, that tea will not pour itself.'

Anna then picked up a pile of foodstuff and headed for the larder, indicating to her husband that he had been well and truly dismissed. Paul scowled again, which Jean was beginning to consider was his default setting, and took the tray outside.

Picking up a pile of food herself, Jean followed Anna into the larder, considering the irony that this woman, who was not only married to one of the most powerful men in the Empire, but was herself a high ranking knight in the Order, was now rummaging through Nathan's pantry on her hands and knees. From somewhere within the depths of the cupboard, Anna's voice echoed.

'That man has to seriously sort his life out.'

Jean was about to suggest that, as his wife, perhaps she had some say in that, when Anna turned around with a box of what seemed to be sage and onion stuffing mix. The packaging looked old and battered.

'Look at this. He's a health hazard to himself.'

'Nathan?'

'Yes, of course Nathan, who else?'

Jean thought it better to keep quiet. She liked Anna, and she understood her loyalties to her husband, but she also got the feeling that love may have blinded her to some of his less pleasant qualities. Glancing at the crumpled box currently being waved under her nose, she nodded.

147

'Nathan has asked me to stay here in Denfield for a while, and with nothing better to do I may as well put my domestic head on. I need to feel as if I'm doing something useful, and to be fair I don't think either of us can live on toast and scrambled eggs for long.'

'You will have the women of Earth reaching for their banners, declaring the oppression of women in the kitchen.'

Jean rolled her eyes. 'I'm hardly oppressed, and to be honest I would quite like the challenge. Nothing wrong with wanting a good kitchen and home to run smoothly. Besides, it's a hell of a lot better than dodging punches and sword thrusts.'

Anna began to laugh.

'What's so funny.'

'You called Denfield home.'

'I didn't mean anything, it's Nathan's home I'm just happy to help while I'm here.'

Anna had her back to Jean now, so failed to see the strangely familiar scowl that crossed her face.

Saying nothing more, she dropped the offending stuffing mix into an empty box lying on the floor. It had been commandeered as a make shift bin and was rapidly being filled with out-of-date boxes, many of which were items, Jean realised, were bought when she was still alive — the first time.

11

The Dumire

Once everyone had arrived and settled down with refreshments at hand, Nathan began the meeting as they all sat enjoying the sun while relaxing on the terrace. As far as Chris could ascertain, it was an informal affair, discussing issues raised by the High Council on the mysterious world of Kelan. There were also mentions of other people too. Apparently a General, who had managed to upset a lot of people by the sound of it, had absconded from the city of Parva before the Midsummer celebrations. He was currently AWOL, wanted for questioning by the Order, the police and any other person who could get their hands on him. Chris thought it probably wise if the elusive Bales kept his *rat faced, slime ball head* down for a bit. Jean's words, not his.

He didn't truly appreciate what was going on during the meeting. Anna and Ty, like him were pretty quiet throughout the proceedings, though they did seem to have more understanding of the topics discussed. Jean stayed out of the High Council business, only remarking on the progress of rounding up small pockets of Patrol members and the issue of Bales.

However, one subject did grab his attention; the discussion regarding a group of people she and the Knights had encountered called Vaupír. He was only half listening until the word vampire was brought up. Ears pricked, he listened in curiously, he was also gratified to see that he wasn't the only one fascinated by what Jean had to say.

The business of the Empire and the aftermath of their battle with the Kaimiren was settled and put to the side. Chris watched as Nathan sat back in his seat and considered Jean for a moment. When she became aware of his interest she held his gaze until he started speaking.

'So, now we come to the part of 'any other business'. I doubt if I am the only one curious regarding the unexpected arrival of a …a…' he looked enquiringly at Jean. 'What is the collective term for vampires?'

She shrugged. 'No idea, you can ask them next time you meet one.'

'Hmmm, well maybe we'll let that one hang. Anyway, having met my first vampire…'

'Vaupír.'

Nathan paused and spread his hands in acknowledgement. 'My apologies, Vaupír. Perhaps you can clarify the difference when you explain who they are and what this *Kyawann* is.'

Jean gave him a resigned smile as if she had been expecting this question, but was not overly keen on answering it. All around, Chris noticed he wasn't the only one listening intently to her answer.

'Fair enough, I suppose I should start at the beginning. Bearing in mind, that I was completely unaware of the other six Sectors before I arrived on Kelan, I have understood the design and creation of Kyawann to a greater extent myself now.

'Anyway, as we know, when the universe was still in its infancy, the Seventh Sector suffered under the influence of the Ti'akai, causing enough concern that it was eventually severed from the other six Sectors. While this had its own catastrophic influences on many parts of the Seventh Sector, it did however save it from utter destruction. It would appear that this process also caused the creation of Kyawann. A place that envelops the whole of the Seventh Sector, almost like a shell I suppose.'

Nathan held up his hand. 'I'm sorry, I have a problem with that, I have never been aware of any barriers that have existed between any Sectors other than the ones that I have created myself.'

Jean shook her head. 'Kyawann is not a barrier, it is a place that exists outside the confines of time and space as we see it. A separate dimension I suppose you could call it. Unless you were specifically looking for it, I doubt you would even know it is there.'

151

Nathan looked at her dubiously, but said nothing more other than to indicate she should carry on.

'So, if we consider those early days of the universe, life barely even a flicker in the quagmires that swirled around the newly formed worlds. The borders between the universe and the Kyawann were still flexible. Life within the other six Sectors, I would assume, had evolved pretty much consistently, the Ti'akai controlling the emergence of life quite rigorously. However, as the Ti'akai is no longer present in the Seventh Sector, such controls didn't exist. In part, life co-existed, regenerating within the Seventh Sector until the Kyawann was fully formed and cut off from the universe forever, taking with it life that can only exist freely along that plane.

'Ancestors of the creatures that lived within that turbulent time evolved in the Seventh Sector, genetics being the only curb to their ability to flourish extensively. Pockets of hybrid creatures have survived, the Vaupír being one of them; sharing characteristics of their cousins, but at the same time, not being quite the same.'

'So, what is the difference between a Vaupír and a vampire?' Paul asked.

'Quite simply, Vaupír are real, living beings who have a penchant for the fresher aspects of their menu, they are highly intelligent and don't take kindly to outsiders. But they are extremely loyal and good to have on your side in a fight; just don't piss them off.

'Vampires, however, are figments of people's imaginations. Probably born out of genetic memory from all those eons ago. Your good old common or garden variety of

152

werewolves, demons and evil spirits have no doubt sprung from the same historic memories of our ancestors through our genes.'

Nathan looked up sharply. 'Wait a minute, are you saying there are werewolves and demons within Kyawann too?'

Jean sighed heavily. 'No, I'm saying the inhabitants of Kyawann have marked resemblances to our own nightmares. They are real, but our nightmares are merely an unconscious delve into our genetic memories. Taking the most frightening horrors of the unknown and creating monsters to fit those characteristics. Vaupír, Teiver, spujki and Alyca are only a few of the people of Kyawann that we have villainised into the monsters we terrify each other with.'

Paul still looked dubious. 'Well, misplaced concern or not, those Vaupír on Franco's ship were not up for any opportunities to open, friendly discussion.'

'Ah yes, this is true. But Vaupír, just as humans, have their good guys and bad guys. It seems that Gellan and Duran have a nose for sniffing our the less amicable sort.'

Chris, like everyone else, listened intently to Jean throughout her whole description of the place she called Kyawann, along with its terrifying inhabitants. He was relieved to see he wasn't the only one who looked uncomfortable with this new knowledge. It took a fair bit of self control to not suddenly get up and make a run for it in the opposite direction, he wasn't even sure why he was here at this meeting. When it was finished and talk was made of lunch, he had to smile when John and Simon were the most eager to get underway. Paul disappeared into the kitchen with Nathan and everyone else began to talk amongst themselves. However, before John could engage anyone else in conversation, Chris caught his elbow and pulled him aside.

'John, can we talk?'

John looked surprised at the urgency of his voice. 'Of course.' He indicated one of two stone staircases, that ran down to the walled garden from either end of the terrace. The two began to descend, making their way around the walled garden. John looked across to Chris with concern. 'Is everything alright Christopher?'

Chris was silent for a moment, not sure what to say now he actually had John's attention. In the end he just dived straight in.

'What *am I* doing here John? Surely you don't need me while you all sort out your politics.'

John looked at his sharply. 'You don't think any of this has anything to do with you?'

Chris stopped walking. They had taken a path that ran within the perimeter of the garden wall and were now walking amongst the shade of trees. The heavy aroma of jasmine and honeysuckle hung in the air around them. Chris thought it would have been romantic if he didn't feel so confused and irritated.

'What on Earth would be said, that you think I would have anything to do with?'

A flicker of annoyance crossed John's face and Chris felt a brief flutter of doubt tingle in his spine, taking no mean effort to force himself not to step back, steadfastly holding John's gaze.

'I am not suggesting you had any part to play in the discussions.' John's voice was quiet but controlled, Chris was under no illusion that he was making an effort to keep his temper under control. 'At least not for the moment.' He closed his eyes and took a long slow breath. 'What do you think of the people who were there today?

Chris was slightly taken aback by the change in direction of the conversation, and took a few seconds to contemplate the question.

Was this some kind of test? Did he have to pass to stay with John?

John seemed to read his mind.

'That was not a trick question Christopher. I would like to know your opinion.'

Chris stopped again. Seeing John turn and wait patiently as if indulging a child, he felt his colour rise with his annoyance. However, if John noticed anything he chose to ignore it. Closing his eyes, he tried to concentrate on John's question.

Chris wasn't an aggressive man, often walking away from trouble rather than have to deal with it. In fact, he would be the first to admit he avoided any form of confrontation if he could. But on the odd occasion, his Celtic roots raised its head above the parapet. He gritted his teeth, determined not to let his anger show. Apparently he failed.

John put his head to one side and Chris felt his eyes boring into his own.

'What *is* the matter Christopher?'

'Why do you do that?'

John blinked, confused.

'Do what?'

155

'That whole, waiting patiently, quietly understated sensitivity thing? I'm not a child that needs to be understood.'

John stood back, and for a while just stared hard at Chris. When he spoke it was with the same quiet tone, but this time with a harder edge.

'For a start, perhaps you should stop acting like a child.'

Chris made to argue, his face belying the anger beneath; if John wanted a good old fashioned slanging match he would be happy to give him one. But John got in first.

'No. Whatever grievance you have, it is not with me, and I will not be party to your need to resolve past resentments. I asked you a perfectly good question, with no hidden agendas. As for the sensitivity of my tone…'

He took a long deep breath. Chris now felt his anger, not just ebbing away, but practically running in the opposite direction.

Continuing in the same quiet tone John broke the uncomfortable silence. 'Twenty-four hours ago, I stood with most of the men back up there at the house, along with Jean, and we faced an enemy that was hell bent on destroying us. I have spent most my life facing enemies with that same agenda. To do this job, I have to turn to a part of me that is capable of literally tearing a man apart. It's not anger that drives me, but the knowledge of what could happen if I don't succeed. I truly hope you never have to be in the position of taking the life of another being, witness the moment they breathe their last. It is a responsibility that we share as Guardians, and one that should never be taken lightly. I deal with that by the only way I know, and that is to

156

keep it buried inside, hidden under a veneer of what you call *quiet understated sensitivity.'*

John stopped and looked away. He seemed to catch himself, closing his eyes while he tried to calm his breathing. Chris got the impression he was working hard to keep his emotions down and in check.

'I'm sorry.'

John spun round and snapped open his eyes.

'What?'

This time Chris couldn't control the urge to step back. Suddenly John seemed twice his, already considerable, size and Chris got an uncomfortable insight of what it would be like for someone on the wrong end of a very sharp and pointy sword. He held his hands up, palms outward, his voice a little stronger, though he noted not by much.

'I'm sorry, I was out of order. I understand and I shouldn't have said those things. I'm just so bloody confused with everything and everyone.'

He looked away, biting his lip to control the emotions that threatened to spill out. He heard John force out his breath and felt him move forward and wrap his arms around him. Chris was shocked to feel the big man shake as he held him and for a while, the two stood together in a silent embrace.

Feeling calmer as the moments passed, Chris spoke first. 'As a group I like them.'

John pulled back to look at Chris. 'But?'

'But, throughout the meeting there was a tension. I don't know what it was, but there was something there, I could feel it.'

He looked up at John from his own six foot height; he still felt short.

'What exactly is Paul's problem?'

John winced. 'Ah, Paul.'

'Yeah, what is it with him?'

He looked at him sharply. 'Has he said something to you?'

Chris shrugged. 'Not so much, but in the kitchen earlier, he did imply that there was a problem with you not telling the others about me. As if you didn't want them to know.'

John's face clouded. 'That is not the case at all.'

Chris squeezed his arm. 'I know. Jean was there and explained that it was because you wanted to keep me safe.' He smiled as he felt John relax.

'Yes, our Miss Carter has shown her perception of a situation is as accurate as always.'

'I assume that is also the reason you haven't told me about Ty and Anna, for their safety.'

'Yes, exactly.'

John smiled and Chris could feel himself harden as a completely different emotion started to take over. He also realised he was not alone in his predicament and a whole new tension sparked between them. Chris was now thankful for the very mature gardens and their excessive cover.

When they finally resumed their walk around the path, John held Chris' hand and grinned.

'You see, you have learnt something about us while you've been here.'

He chuckled. 'Only bits, and I would hardly call it learning.'

'Christopher, that little group of people up there are without doubt, the most important people in my life.' He looked over at Chris. 'And that includes you. The politics you heard are nothing more than what we have done hundreds if not thousands of times before. It is a part of our lives we can literally do in our sleep, but it is outwith the dealings of the Empire that is our real work. As I've said before, what we do is extremely dangerous and not without its consequences. Yes, there is tension, and with the arrival of Jean there has been, and still will be, a certain amount of tension for some time to come. However, I actually think that is mostly going to be a good thing. We're a bunch of very old men who have allowed ourselves to be set in our ways for far too long. Jean is going to disrupt that way of life, and if I'm honest, I'm quite looking forward to it.'

Chris smiled but said nothing, just wanting John to keep talking while they strolled amongst the trees, enjoying the sun on their skin.

'So, despite the issues any of us have with each other. When we are working, all that is put to one side. I trust every one of those people up there with my life, and that includes Ty and Anna. I also want them to consider you in the same way. Trust is something we are extremely careful about. The amount of civilians, I suppose you could call them, that have been let into our little band has been very small.'

Chris was curious. 'How many?'

'Three, including you.'

Chris stopped again and John sighed.

'You know, if you keep stopping like this we are going to miss lunch.'

Chris felt his own stomach grumble at the thought of food and so started walking again. This time picking up the pace.

'Why haven't you been close to anyone else before? After all these years?'

'Ah well, that's a different subject altogether, one that has taken a slightly complicated turn recently.'

'Are you going to tell me?'

John looked ahead and indicated a garden bench nestled alongside several rosebushes that were already coming out in bloom. They were nearly two-thirds of the way around the walled garden by now. Chris allowed himself to be led to the bench. There was a loud buzzing amongst the flowers and he looked around apprehensively for little bees and those vicious beasts of Satan himself, wasps.

'What about lunch?'

John shrugged. 'We're fine. They'll shout when it's ready.'

Taking Chris' reluctance as concern over missing lunch he tried to reassure him.

'It's alright, honestly. I was only joking earlier, we won't miss any food.'

Chris wasn't happy about the continuing buzzing and he sat down gingerly at first. John seemed unaware of his discomfort and once he was satisfied that they were both comfortable he began.

'Do you remember when I said earlier about being able to 'literally run the Empire in our sleep'?'

Chris nodded, aware there was a flash of black and yellow flying around them, far too close for comfort.

'Well, in a way, that is exactly what we do, or did, much of the time.'

Chris scoffed. 'You're asleep when you should be running the Empire? I bet that wouldn't go down well amongst your people.'

John rolled his eyes. 'We're not actually asleep as in going to bed. It's called the Dumire.' He sighed. 'Maybe it's better if I start at the beginning. Imagine living for ten thousand years. Don't think of it as just a number, but how long that is in time, that is ten whole millennia. In Earth's history, that would be approximately when the last ice age began to retreat within the northern hemisphere.' He watched as Chris began to consider the enormity of the length of time he was talking about. 'Now you understand what I mean, imagine having lived every single one of those days.'

Chris stared ahead of him. The buzzing around him forgotten and the beautiful sight and smells of the garden around them went out of focus. He tried as hard as he could, but he was still unable to get his head around living for ten thousand years.

'It would send me mad. How is it possible to do that?'

'The best way to explain is probably the scenario of driving a familiar journey. How many times have you arrived at your destination and not been able to remember exactly how you arrived there? You must have negotiated all of the twists and turns in the road, even accommodated for other road users. But you can't actually recall any of it.'

Chris nodded. 'Are you saying that you do the same when governing the Empire?'

161

'Yes, sort of. Bear in mind there is the High Council that actually oversees the everyday Imperial business. So, between disappearing to other worlds for some impending disaster in the universe, and occasionally sorting out odd issues that arise that the Council needs help with, we basically switch off. We go through the motions, keeping out of the way of the general hubbub of life.'

'So that's why you've not been close to anyone before, because you haven't been aware of those around you?'

'Pretty much, yes.'

'That seems very sad. I understand the mechanics and why it happens, but still…'

Chris looked up and flinched as a wasp flew between them. John ignored it.

'So what has changed? What about Anna and Ty? What about me?'

'Ah well, that's the thing. I'm tempted to say that the whole nightmare of Ephea and her sisters have kept us on our toes, and subsequently more aware, but to be fair it's been happening since before then. Probably since we started spending time here on Earth. There has been a lot of work and preparation for our own various projects here. But I also think it's because coming here is the first place we've been to where no-one knows who we are. We haven't been in the middle of solving someones else's battles either, so we've been able to socialise, make friends with those who don't have to prove anything. Or even those who are looking to climb the greasy pole of politics.'

'And of course you met me.'

John smiled. 'And I met you.'

'So why am I actually here John?'

'Because I want you to meet my family and see what we do. Not just to socialise, but to work, which does mean a certain amount of wining and dining. You'd be surprised just how much work is done over a glass of wine and a room full of revellers. I want you to be part of that with me, but to do so you need to appreciate who we really are. Do you understand what I am saying?

Chris felt himself gulp.

'You want me to stand with you at your functions, dinners and parties?'

'Well, I would like to think there is a lot of personal time too, but yes, your social life would become considerably busier.'

'But how the hell am I supposed to know what to do?'

John leaned forward and grasped Chris' hand.

'You just need to be you.'

'You really think I can do this?'

'No doubt at all.'

Chris looked into John's golden eyes. He knew he couldn't have refused him this even if he tried. His face broke into a big grin.

'Do I get a tiara?'

John laughed. 'No, you don't get a bloody tiara.'

'Damn, I suppose I will have to learn to slum it then.'

John leaned in and kissed him before standing up, pulling Chris with him.

'Well, now we've got that settled let's get some lunch. I'm starving.'

163

Chris laughed with him, just glad to get away from the buzzing rose bushes.

Nathan stood and watched the two men make their way back to the house, they looked happy and at ease in each other's company. How strange it seemed to see his friend enjoying the intimacy that had been denied all of them for so long, but now seemed so natural as to not be strange at all. He smiled as he considered John's happiness, whilst also considering his own emptiness that welled up and held his heart in its cold embrace. Closing his eyes to steady his thoughts and emotions, he breathed deeply, becoming aware of another dark emotion threatening the empty void — jealousy. Not because he would wish to take the happiness that John and Christopher deserved, but because he already knew what his heart yearned for. An intimate touch, a private moment shared, an understanding between two people; with the only one his heart desired.

But she wasn't his, and it seemed another had already claimed her for his own.

As if on cue, the laughter of two people sharing a joke forced their way into his thoughts. Determined not to react, he kept his gaze on John and Christopher as they climbed the steps to the terrace.

'It's good to see them so happy.'

Nathan froze, Damien's words slammed around his head like a hammer determined to destroy the outward calm he was fighting to maintain. He looked at his cousin as he stood beside him. In doing so, out of the corner of his eye he saw Jean and Daniel seated at the table, comfortable and relaxed

164

as two people enjoying each other's company. Not engaging in an orgy of wanton sex as his imagination was resolved to believe. Confusion must have crossed his face because Damien pointed towards the two men approaching from the garden. Nathan turned his head and followed his gaze, gripping the balustrade while he attempted to settle his thoughts as they veered off wildly in different directions. He could feel Damien watching him, and when he faced him again he made sure his face was back to as it should be, even if his insides were churning like a raging tempest.

Smiling he nodded his agreement.

'It certainly is, and you and Ty too. Of course, even Paul has found a niche of happiness.' He inclined his head towards Paul and Anna as they called everyone to lunch.

But Nathan could never deny any of those around him their joy of finally finding the possibility of love, especially his best friend and cousin, whom he considered closer than a brother. He looked again for Jean and Daniel and saw, with some satisfaction, that Daniel was now talking with Stephen. But Jean was nowhere to be seen…

'Are you two coming to join us for lunch or are you going to stand and watch?'

Gulping, Nathan's mouth went dry as Jean was now so very close, standing next to him, grinning at the pair of them. How long had she been standing there? He could normally feel if someone was approaching, but it seemed his thoughts and emotions had clouded his senses. For the first time he was beginning to feel vulnerable, and considering how many times he had had his life threatened, that was some feat. While he floundered, Damien answered. 'We're on our way.'

Jean smiled and looked back at Nathan as if to check that he was coming too. Suddenly the cold dark emptiness and jealousy flew away, and he revelled in the warmth of her smile. His face felt strange as he returned her expression, while he indicated that he would follow her. For some reason he was still unable to release his throat to talk properly.

As Nathan followed Jean to the table, Damien looked over to Daniel, who had also been watching closely. Raising an eyebrow he cocked his head slightly to one side, the other man simply gave a small nod in agreement to the silent communication.

12

Disorderly Conduct

It was just over a week later and Jean stretched out under the covers of her bed. Not having closed the curtains the previous evening, Jean opened her eyes to brilliant sunshine pouring through the windows. When she had the opportunity to sleep with the promise of a rising sun in the morning she preferred not to obscure the view. Too many nights on a spaceship with artificial night and day lighting made sure she appreciated the glory of a morning sun. Checking the clock that ticked quietly on her bedside table she saw it was nearly six o'clock. Sighing to herself she knew she couldn't lay there all day, so rolling onto her back she rubbed her eyes and stared up at the ceiling, making the most of the warm, cosy bed coverings.

Convincing herself that she was about to throw back the duvet at any moment, there was a sudden knock at the door and Nathan stuck his head into the room. Jean couldn't help but try and run her fingers through her bed tousled hair. She dreaded to think what she looked like, but it annoyed her that she should even be worried about it.

'Good morning.'

'Good morning, is everyone alright?'

After her initial concern about the state of her own bedhead, Jean realised that Nathan wasn't only bidding her a good day. He himself was wearing what Jean assumed was his version of comfy casual wear, loose fitting sweatshirt and trousers.

'Can I come in?'

It still amused Jean that Nathan and the Knights were always so polite, even when they were in less than congenial moods. Most of the people she knew would have charged in and demanded her attention whether she was up or not.

'Of course.' Not sure if she should actually make an effort to get out of bed, or try to act as if it was perfectly normal for men to walk in and hold a conversation with her while she huddled under the covers. She sat up and tried to at least look as if she was going to be shifting her backside out of bed soon. Nathan came into the room and she noted, with some satisfaction, that he looked as uncomfortable as she did.

168

'Jean, I'm sorry to disturb you, but I've just had the watch leader on the gates banging on the front door stating there was an urgent message for you.'

Jean was caught between shock and confusion. 'Me? But who knows I'm here?'

'Well, the watch does obviously, and as such so does some of the Order in Parva. If anyone is trying to get a message to you it will come here eventually.' He paused and folded his arms, attempting another scowl which eventually turned into a lopsided grin. 'I don't think however, that whoever sent the message realised it would be me stomping down the stairs to answer the door to a very apologetic Lieutenant on my doorstep.'

Jean smiled despite herself. 'So who is the one responsible for dragging you out of your bed so early?'

'A Captain Niall Rivers, a farmer of your acquaintance I believe, and one time Captain of the Order.'

Without any more worries about the state she was in, Jean was immediately out of bed and stood in front of Nathan, concern etched across her face.'

'Niall? What's happened? Is he alright? Is it the twins? Layne? George? Please tell me Dana is alright.'

Nathan stepped back despite himself and held his hands up.

'Hold on, I don't know the details, but from what I can gather, he is worried about someone named George.'

Jean had already told the Knights about the Patrol Captain, Karen Johnson, and her intimidation of Niall and his family, but she had deliberately kept information limited. The mention of George sent a chill down her spine, he had already almost died at the hands of Johnson. While Jean took Niall and his family to Aria in a desperate attempt to save his life, Johnson had disappeared. A fact that still rankled Jean when she realised that in her haste to help the lad, she had not made sure the Patrol Captain was sufficiently dispatched. Had she returned and finished the job with George? Spinning round Jean made her way to the bathroom, already stripping off her bedclothes and making for the shower.

'I have to go immediately.' She stopped suddenly turning around to face Nathan who was looking at her with an odd look on his face. 'I am so sorry, you must think I'm very rude. Thank you for letting me know so quickly.' Then she headed back towards the shower, unaware that Nathan had let himself out of her room with a grin fixed firmly in place.

It was still early by the time Jean made it down to the kitchen. She had expected to just leave immediately, but Nathan was there, cups of tea in hand and taking charge of the toaster.

'I would give it some time before you set off to see Captain Rivers and his wayward farmhand, they are a few hours behind us so you can at least enjoy a breakfast before you leave.'

Jean looked at him suspiciously. 'How far behind? He does live on a farm.'

Nathan put the tea on the table and gathered the toast, indicating that Jean sit; butter and jam already sat waiting.

'British Summer Time is around one hour behind Parva, which is in turn is two hours ahead of Rassen. So at the moment, the time at Niall's farm is about five thirty. I'd give them an hour before you land on their doorstep.'

Jean sighed, picking up some toast and lathering it in butter and jam. Nathan raised an eyebrow at the artery busting amount but said nothing.

'So what time did Niall send the message?'

Nathan shrugged. 'From what I can gather, your friend George was found brawling in the street not long after being turfed out of a tavern by a very disgruntled innkeeper. Taking into consideration the fact that Captain Rivers had to be brought to the local police station, before then relaying his message to you, I would say it was about four hours since he contacted Parva.' Nathan helped himself to toast and snaffled the rest of the butter and jam before Jean got any ideas of acquiring more. 'That is of course assuming I got the message as soon as it arrived at the gatehouse here, they may have been waiting until a more acceptable time to wake the house. I admit, I would not have been pleased at being woken any earlier than I had.'

Jean winced, she tried to imagine Nathan being woken in the middle of the night and dismissed the thought immediately. She didn't think he would have been quite so accommodating.

'I've also taken the liberty of contacting Stephen, I believe he was responsible for tending the injuries incurred by Captain Rivers. He has said he would like to accompany you to the farm and assess how his patient is getting on.'

Jean looked at him suspiciously, did he not trust her? Nathan shook his head and chuckled, he seemed to read her mind.

'We all remember the time when Captain Rivers and Sergeant Chorey were attacked by the local drug dealers. It was a sad time for us all and Stephen was particularly upset that he couldn't save the Captain's leg as well as mend his back. Fortunately, Sergeant Chorey didn't have any family, but his death hit those that knew him hard. Earth didn't make any friends that day.'

Jean didn't know what to say, the fact that Nathan even knew who Niall was, let alone remembered him, was impressive. To have an emotional connection to the incident that injured him was staggering. Certainly not something she had encountered from senior officers elsewhere, let alone members of the ruling faction.

Nathan checked his watch. 'Stephen should be here within the hour, plenty of time for another cup of tea I think.'

Jean took the hint and stood up and made her way to the kettle. There was always time for another cup of tea in her book.

Stephen and Jean stood outside the gates to Niall's farm and looked out towards the surrounding countryside, enjoying the sun on their faces. Stephen had turned up at Denfield shortly before seven thirty, and only after a cup of coffee was he ready to leave with Jean to discover what George had done that warranted Niall to be so concerned. Now, as they had approached the farm, it seemed inconceivable that a beautiful day in such a picturesque location could possibly be marred by the worries of mere people. But worried Niall was, and so they turned and made their way through the gate that led into the yard.

Jean smiled to herself as the scene brought happy memories flooding back; from the chaos when the bull had managed to get loose when she first arrived, to when she, Layne and George had eaten their lunch by the barn in the mid-day sun. Allowing a frown to cross her face, only when the memory of seeing Naill and his family, intimidated by Captain Johnson and her thugs, forcing George to show her where the family enjoyed a rare chance of a picnic.

There was no-one in the yard at the moment and Stephen looked around, his brow furrowed. 'It's rather quiet for a working farm surely.'

Jean smiled and shook her head. 'Not at this time, they would have finished their early chores and are probably in the house settling down to a well earned breakfast.'

Stephen nodded and grinned. 'I wonder if we have timed it just right.'

Jean looked at him sharply. 'Timed it for what?'

'Breakfast of course, I'm starving.'

'You're always starving.'

Chuckling, Stephen nodded and started towards the house. 'Never turn down a meal when it's offered, you never know when the next one will be.'

Jean just shook her head. While she agreed with the sentiments she somehow couldn't see the doctor wasting away with hunger anytime soon. Hurrying to catch up she followed the Knight to the cottage door. Stephen waited for her before knocking, indicating that she should go first.

'You know the family better than I do.'

It seemed that Dana remembered her only too well. As Jean opened the door and entered, she was stunned by Dana's angry tones as they rang out across the kitchen.

'You. This is all your fault. You have some nerve coming back here. Get out of my house before I have Niall...'

The rest of Dana's tirade was lost in a strangled gargle as she finally saw the figure of the man following Jean through the door. It was at this point the rest of the room had noticed Stephen too and were quickly coming to their feet. Dana just stood in stunned silence by the range while Niall came forward to greet Jean and her unexpected companion.

'My Lord, please come in. We weren't expecting one of the Knights themselves to join us. Please sit down.' He nudged Layne, who was standing with his mouth wide open, to move over allowing Stephen and Jean to sit at the table. Niall then smiled at Jean, and before she could say anything he had caught her in a big bear hug. 'By the gods Jean it is good to see you. Come sit down, we have just started breakfast.'

As he led her over to sit between him and Stephen, Jean finally got a clear view of the of the young man she knew as a kind and gentle farmhand; the sight of him shocked her. George sat across the table and looked far from having led a calm simple life. His face was black and blue, his left eye swollen, and there was some evidence of an attempt to stem the bleeding from a cut above his eyebrow. He held his left arm across his chest as if protecting it, and winced with every breath he took. Stephen took one look at him and moved around the table to assess the state of his injuries. George attempted to push him away, but one look from the

174

Knight and he relented, allowing himself to be examined. He winced again but didn't argue as Stephen laid a hand on his shoulder.

Jean looked over to Niall who was by now explaining quietly to Dana that Jean was here by his request. She didn't seem too happy about it but didn't argue either. Instead her glance travelled towards the Knight and George before she busied herself with making breakfast, deciding that ignoring her husband and Jean was the best way to deal with the situation.

'Niall, what has happened?'

The farmer glanced to George and shook his head. When the lad looked at him with accusing eyes, Jean realised he obviously had no idea that she had been summoned either and was taking it as a personal slight. However, he didn't say anything as Stephen was in the process of using the force of his energy to ease his injuries and Jean got the impression it wasn't the most comfortable experience in the world. But George grit his teeth and refused to look at her, bearing the pain in silence.

Niall sighed and sat down beside Jean, rubbing his eyes, he didn't look as if he'd had any sleep. Finally he dropped his hands to the table and slumped his shoulders before explaining the reason he had asked Jean back to their farm.

'Life has been a bit different since you left us all those months ago Jean.'

Stephen looked up and glanced at the two of them, but said nothing before continuing his healing administrations.

Niall went on. 'George here was in Aria for a couple of weeks before coming home, but he's not been the same since.'

The farm hand looked up scowling, there was a fierceness in his eyes.

'It's no good looking like that lad, you can't argue with the truth.'

Dana, humphed in agreement as she laid the breakfast out. Stephen couldn't resist a smile when he saw the huge plates of bacon and eggs. Satisfied he had finished with George he settled himself down at the table and grinned up at Dana who blushed at the attention.

'Mrs Rivers this looks delicious. It is quite unexpected but appreciated all the same.'

Jean nearly choked on the hot tea and shot him a look of incredulity. He ignored her and proceeded to load his plate before indicating to Niall that he should continue with his story.

'So what do you think was responsible for this change in temperament of this young man Captain?'

George and Layne looked up puzzled, wondering who Lord Stephen could possibly be addressing. Jean caught their glances and answered for Niall, who was looking a bit nonplussed. He probably hadn't been addressed by his rank since he left the Order, but according to Nathan, everyone kept their rank even after retirement and she informed them so. Niall went red under the scrutiny of the young men who had only ever known him as a farmer, even if they did know his history.

Niall gave an embarrassed cough before answering.

176

'You have to understand that life around here was very different after you left Jean.' He met her sharp gaze, but it was brief; looking back at the table top and fiddling with his thumbnail as he continued. 'A lot of people suffered at the hands of Johnson and her thugs in their pursuit of you. When you left so suddenly there was a certain amount of tension, people felt abandoned. There were also those who voiced their displeasure.' Niall glanced quickly at Dana, who raised an eyebrow and sniffed. Jean wasn't surprised but she noticed that Stephen hadn't missed the gesture either. 'Of course there were those who stood up for you, and as such the inevitable arguments, that often ensued into an all out brawl.

'After a while things calmed down, and most people moved on. But George here decided on his own one man campaign to uphold your honour. Even when news arrived of the battle at Parva and your involvement, there were those who George felt were not shamed into admitting they were wrong. Unfortunately last night was one fight that got the better of him.'

Watching George as he sat in silence throughout Niall's account, she was appalled at how much the once quiet, peaceful young man now looked mutinous behind his bruises. It was then, as she considered how much his actions must have affected the family, that Jean realised the twins were nowhere to be seen. Normally they would be tucking into breakfast with the rest of the family.

'Niall, where are the twins?'

George suddenly put his head in his hands, wincing as his fingers touched the sore parts of his face, which was pretty

177

much all of it. Dana, looked ready to start another tirade but Niall managed to preempt her, gaining another scowl from his wife in the process.

'They are staying with friends, we didn't want them seeing George like this. It's upset them enough seeing him get so angry, to see his face bruised and battered would be too much. They will be back when George leaves.'

Jean sat up straight. 'Leaving? Where is he going?'

'Well, that all depends on him. The only reason he is here is so that he can make his decision with his family. Otherwise he would still be locked up in the local police station.'

'What decision do you have to make George?' Jean asked quietly

Stephen nodded his head as if understanding. 'The Militia.'

She looked at him questioningly. 'You spoke about this Militia before.'

Finishing a mouthful of breakfast, Stephen put his knife and fork down and clasped his hands together over his plate. 'While the Order is, by any army's measure, huge, it can't possibly fulfil all of its obligations on its own. Also, while it takes approximately two to four years for someone to fully train as a knight, depending on what they want to specialise in, not everyone is prepared to, or has the inclination, to go through that kind of training. But people do still want to have a career, or at least have some involvement within the military. Of course there is the fact that during times of peace there isn't the need to keep a fully armed garrison. So the Militia, predominantly made up of volunteers who train with the knights at local garrisons, are ready to be called upon at time of need. Amongst this Militia though is a smaller contingency of permanent soldiers, regiments that work alongside the knights within their garrisons. For most, this is good honest work that they enjoy. For a few, some go on to join the ranks of the Order by training at Pernia.' He looked down at his cooling breakfast and picked up his knife and fork again. George stirred beside him but said nothing.

'But what does this mean for George? You're practically pressing him into the army.'

Stephen looked at her steadily and there was an uncomfortable silence in the room. Jean didn't care, this was George they were talking about. Quiet, kind George. In the army of all things!

The Knight sighed and put his cutlery down again and looked sadly at the unfinished remains.

'I can assure you, the Empire is not in the habit of conscripting, or press-ganging even, anyone who does not want to join the ranks of the Militia. However, you have to remember that for whatever the reasons, however passionate or honourable he may feel his actions have been, George has consistently breached the peace over a very short period of time.'

He sat back and looked at George who did his best to keep his eyes down and averted. Listening to Stephen, it now occurred to Jean that he knew a lot more about George and his plight than she had been led to believe. He had obviously been privy to far more information than she had. She felt herself bristling at the thought, but before she could say anything, Stephen was speaking again.

'The future for George at the moment is to face a judge in court, with the very real possibility of a custodial sentence.' Jean looked shocked and made to speak but Stephen put his hand up to stay her. 'It is not often that someone has the choice that George has been given, unruly soldiers who have no wish to fight are of no use to the army at all. The Militia is not a punishment, but an opportunity for him to move on with his life, rather than the likelihood of a path that he may very likely regret.'

There was the sound of someone sniffing and Jean looked up to see Dana turned away, her head bowed. George had been a part of their little family for so long, the idea of him having to leave, especially under such circumstances would be difficult to deal with. Jean was under no illusion who Dana held responsible for this turn of events however, and Jean didn't blame her. She felt responsible enough already.

It was George himself who broke the awkward silence first. Sitting up straight he looked at Niall first and then at Dana and Layne, who seemed forlorn and lost at his best friend's plight; a man he had come to consider as a brother. Then George settled his gaze on Stephen and slowly breathed in as if to steady himself; if not to protect his sore ribcage.

'I want to join the Militia.' Stephen nodded but was surprised when George continued. 'But I don't want to just be a soldier, I want to eventually have the chance to go to Pernia. I want to become a knight.'

Behind him Dana gasped, but George ignored her. Niall and Jean exchanged a glance but Stephen held his gaze.

'Young man, if you truly aspire to the Order and show the aptitude required, then there is no reason why you shouldn't succeed. But be warned, hot headed young men need to learn to cool their anger and focus their emotions if they intend to travel that path. It is not something that can, or should, be approached halfheartedly, or without forethought.' He looked to Niall across the table. 'Captain Rivers here is a fine man who has many friends who remember him in the Order, as well as the sacrifice he and Sergeant Chorey made. He is a good knight, and in the short time you have before joining your garrison I suggest you speak with him and listen to what he has to say.'

George peered over at Niall. The two men said nothing, but an understanding seemed to have been reached, and for the first time Jean sensed an easing in the atmosphere in the room. Not however, from the area that encompassed Dana, she now looked at Jean with open hostility and it took everything Jean had to hold her gaze. Eventually Dana looked away, covering her anger with the banging of pots and plates as she cleared the breakfast things. Including, much to Stephen's dismay, the Knight's half eaten breakfast. Seeing that any further offers of food or drink would not be forthcoming, the Knight suggested that he check over Niall and see how his injuries had healed since he last saw him. Pleased to have the focus taken away from him, Jean saw George relax and so took the opportunity to take him outside into the yard.

When they both stood in the sunshine, the chickens scratched at the ground while the geese settled on the grass to take in the heat of the day. Jean looked at George and his bruised and battered face.

'Oh George, what have we come to now? What on earth possessed you to start brawling in bars and the street?'

She was relieved to see the young man lose some of the air of arrogance that had hung around him, and was surprised at the level of emotion that emanated from him, determination and love. Jean looked away, a lump forming in her throat.

'I'm sorry Jean, you're the last person I want to hurt, but I couldn't just let those people tell lies about you. They said you were a bad influence, an unwelcome foreigner that had no right to be here and put everyone in danger.' As George spoke, Jean had a good idea who had been spreading a lot of these views around and she bit her lip. Niall had his hands full there, and Dana's grievance won't stop once George is finally on his way to his new life.

'But why George, why worry what other people think about me? I've lived with pissing people off for a very long time, these people are pretty benign compared to the level of hate I'm used to.'

George shook his head. 'It's not about what people think of you as such, it's about me. It's not even about what others think, it's what I think.'

He had begun to garble as he rushed to get the thoughts and emotions out that he bottled up for so long. Jean had to listen carefully to understand what he was saying.

'That bitch Johnson, I felt so helpless. Niall and Dana are like parents to me, and I led her straight to them. If you hadn't been there she would have killed them and no-one

182

would have known. I swore as I lay in my bed at Aria that I would never let down the people I care for again. I want to be able to fight, to protect them, not let them come to harm. And being a labourer on a farm is not going to help. Lord Stephen is right, the Militia is where I ought to start. And Jean, I swear, one day I will go to Pernia and I will leave there a knight. No one I love will have to get hurt again, because I will be ready for them. I'll be able to fight, and be strong enough to protect them, like you do.'

By now tears were streaming down George's face, the passion in his voice nearly broke Jean's heart, but she had to be his voice of reason. While passion and determination were excellent qualities, they were not all he was going to need if he was determined in his goal. She took his hand and squeezed, trying to keep his attention and listen to her words.

'George, listen to me. Pretty soon you are going to be off to join a garrison where you will learn to become a member of a regiment that will become part of the Militia. Eventually you will serve alongside the knights of the Order, but you have to understand, that for all the reasons you feel now, once you start training you are going to need a lot more than passion to get you through. Yes, you are strong, you've worked most of your life on a farm, and yes I have no doubt you can hold your own in a fight. But that is not what makes a good soldier. You have to learn discipline, and I don't just mean being told what to do. It's about disciplining yourself, knowing your limits and knowing when to push them. But also know when to stop, to stand back and know when to walk away, and that will be one of the hardest things you will learn. I believe in you George, I know you can do this, but be prepared that there will be times when you will doubt yourself, and when you will get it wrong; what matters is that you learn from your mistakes and try again. I'm telling you this because I want you to succeed in your dream, but you will only do that if you truly understand what your dream will cost you.'

The young man looked hard into Jean's eyes and after a while he smiled. It was an awkward one because his face was obviously still sore, but Jean felt the honesty behind it.

'Are you going to leave us Jean?'

'Well, I can't stay here, Stephen and I have to get back.'

'No, I mean, will you be leaving the Empire, going back to where you came from?'

It was at that point that Jean knew the answer to that very same question that had haunted her for so long now. A lump formed in her throat as she realised how much it actually meant to her.

'No George, I'm not going anywhere.'

Behind them, they heard Niall and Stephen leaving the house and glancing back, Jean got the impression that they had been there for some time. They both brushed at their faces before Jean joined Stephen and they took their leave and said their farewells to Niall and George. Niall hugged Jean until she thought her ribs would crack, promising she would visit soon and vowed to keep up to date with George's progress.

Once they were outside the farm gates, and before they made to travel back to Denfield, Stephen turned to Jean with a wry grin and asked if she was ready to go home. Returning his smile she nodded and then looked away, there must be

184

dust in the air as her eyes, once again, seemed to be watering for some reason.

'Yes, let's go home.'

Part 2:

A State of

Misgivings

13

Suspicions

I t had been several weeks since the Knights had first met Jean, though Nathan hadn't seen much of her in that time. After her visit to Captain River's farm she had made a point of visiting others whom she had met since arriving on Kelan; including Mrs Moore, who Nathan discovered, made particularly delicious cakes after Jean's first visit. She had also spent a fair amount of time with Sergeant Croft and Inspector Graves of the Parva City Constabulary.

Between them they had taken it upon themselves to devise a means of re-establishing local police forces within small towns and villages. Encouraging some semblance of normality in Parva, before the pair had then proceeded to ensure the same work was carried out elsewhere within the

Empire. Nathan had been impressed at how the two women had taken up the challenge, ferociously dealing with the issues of unrest that had upset so much of the Imperial populous. They had put up with so much over the previous five years, and with the opportunity for many to voice their dissatisfaction it had not been a simple case of everything back to normal. There, understandably, a lot of questions that needed to be answered, by those who had pledged loyalty to the Duchess Ephea and her Patrols, but predominantly by Nathan himself.

Nathan agreed to endorse the suggestions made by Jean and the two police officers, implementing them via the High Council. He had hoped a written statement distributed throughout the Empire would be enough, but Jean wasn't convinced. She deliberately wanted him to avoid the cities, saying that, while the cities had been affected, it was the people within the countryside that had seen their livelihoods crumble under Ephea's regime. Not just because of the affect on the markets, but because the Order had been forced to remain within their barracks, the economies that would normally rely on the social aspect of the military presence suffered.

He still wasn't sure how it had happened, but a conversation during a rare opportunity to enjoy each others company over dinner at Denfield, had him practically eating out of her hand.

'Nathan. Do you remember after the battle with the Kaimiren you gave that speech to the people of the city?'

188

Having just popped a rather hot potato into his mouth, Nathan had no choice other than to nod his head to say he remembered.

'Why did you feel it was necessary to say something then? Wouldn't it have been better to put out a well worded letter that could be sent out via the press? More people would have seen it.'

Managing to swallow the still rather warm potato, he watched Jean for a moment before answering.

'I agree, a carefully worded letter would have given me an opportunity to assess every sentence, word and comma. I could have made sure that there were no political time-bombs waiting for me; it would have been clear, concise and to the point, as well as clinical, uninspiring tosh.'

Jean raised an eyebrow at the vehemence with which he spoke.

Putting his knife and fork down, Nathan spread his hands. 'When I stood in front of those people in Parva, it was immediately after a highly emotional and terrifying time for the city. Many had witnessed the battle itself, and those who didn't were no doubt given the full gory details after; very likely with many impressive embellishments. But that's the point, people were confused and frightened, they needed reassurance then and there, not later in some article in the media. Whether I like it or not, I am the Emperor and there are millions of people who, in time of crisis, need to know that I can lead them out of danger. For too long they have had to deal with the knowledge that I might not be able to do that anymore. By standing up in front of that crowd I not only gave them reassurance that the danger was passed, but that there was still hope for the future; a future that they all had a vital part to play in. They will then do a much better job of relaying the positive news to anyone who will listen. Far better than the Press any day.'

He paused and picked up his fork, eyeing his dinner plate before looking back at Jean.

'Do you understand what I mean?'

Jean nodded her head slowly, seeming to think about his words carefully.

'So what you are saying is, people are more likely to recover from the difficulties they have had to deal with in recent years, if they could physically see a positive response from the people they have come to trust the most?'

'Pretty much yes.'

'Hmmm. Like the police returning back to their posts in towns and villages?'

'Yes, absolutely, they have a huge part to play in reassuring people that things are returning to normal.'

'It must be a bit unnerving though.'

Nathan paused, another forkful of food was placed back onto his plate.

'What must be unnerving?'

'Well, those police officers had a pretty tough time of it before they were finally relieved of their posts. There were many injuries, one poor soul even lost his life.'

Looking back, Nathan realised he should have seen the warning signs long before this, but at the time he carried on, completely oblivious.

'Believe me, no-one regrets that more than I.'

Jean gave him a sympathetic look. 'I can imagine you do.' She moved her food absently around her plate. 'And of course, as well as returning to their local beat, our brave constabulary have to instil confidence in their ranks from the people they serve.'

'Yes, it's not going to be easy.'

'So, what they really need is a good injection of confidence from someone they know they can trust.'

It was at this point Nathan finally began to twig that something wasn't quite all it seemed.

'I'm sure a member of their local Council could make a rousing speech.'

'A member of their local Council?' Jean looked incredulous. 'So, it's true what they say, the people of Parva are more important than the rest of the Empire.'

Nathan nearly choked on the last morsel he had finally managed to eat. 'That is utter rubbish and you know it.'

'Well, that's what it may look like from outside the city.' Jean spread her hands and shrugged her shoulders. Nathan felt himself being backed into a corner.

'Now hold on. What exactly are you suggesting?'

'I'm not sure I'm suggesting anything; I'm only making conversation. It was just a thought I had while I was pottering around the other day.'

'Hmmm.' Picking up his wine glass, he believed he had managed to dodge that particular missile.

'But it's obviously not something you feel is necessary then?'

His eyes watered as he felt the liquid catch in his throat and threaten to go down the wrong way.

191

'What do you mean?'

'Well, if you were as worried about the thoughts and feelings of the rest of the Empire as you do those of Parva, you would jump at the chance to reassure them, surely?'

Nathan put his glass down carefully. 'You think I should visit every town and village in the Empire, making a speech to reassure the populous that all will be well from now on?'

Jean laughed and shook her head. 'No, of course not. That would be ridiculous.' She picked up her own glass and took as sip. 'Not every town and village, just the main ones on days when there will be plenty of visitors from the surrounding areas. Like market day. Also, with plenty of notice, people will travel to hear you if they know that you will be there. How often do they get to see their Emperor in the flesh so to speak? It will also be a huge boost to the local economies, just when they need it. And think of all the good press you'll get?'

Nathan was speechless.

Needless to say, Jean's general table talk had suddenly culminated into a discussion over a full report that outlined his part in the re-establishment of the local police force, and their part in boosting the local economy, while also reinforcing his own public image. He wasn't sure if he should be impressed or manipulated.

But Jean was right. By making a personal effort to speak to the people of the Empire, they had been far more encouraged to see the benefits of not causing anymore chaos. It didn't take long for them to realise how better off they were, and word soon spread to keep the peace and get on with rebuilding their lives. A working model was adopted by the High Council in Parva, which was then implemented throughout the Empire through local sub-committees.

Now, he was sitting in his own office, having completed a particularly whirlwind three weeks travelling the Empire with Jean, Sergeant Croft and Inspector Graves. His return was greeted with much relief from Damien and Daniel, who had been left to hold the reins while he was away. He found he didn't feel in the slightest bit guilty, and considered the whole experience a huge success. His presence in the towns of the Empire had been received with much enthusiasm, and he had rather enjoyed the experience, more than he had expected to.

However, on returning to Parva, the old worries started to make their presence known again. While he had allowed himself a brief respite from the burdens of his Office, he couldn't ignore them anymore. And memories that he had hoped to bury were now making their unwelcome way into his thoughts again.

Nathan contemplated the screen of the phone nestling in his hand. Unlike the basic mobile phones that Sergeant Croft and her fellow police officers were allowed to use, Nathan and the Knights had the most up to date smart phones. To be fair, they hadn't evolved much beyond the initial boom of media technology that excelled at the beginning of the twenty-first century, but with Simon's expertise and John's understanding of the materials used, this device had pretty much all the bells and whistles available.

He had to admit that the use of mobile phones had proven to be more beneficial than he had expected. He was also still being pressurised from ministers within the High

Council to make them more available to the wider community. It was something he still vehemently fought against; yes its value as a means of communication was undoubtedly useful, but to open the Empire to the threats associated with the internet and the ease with which it could subvert wasn't something he was willing to accept, no matter what the Council thought.

A pressing issue he also had to consider was regarding the crystals that Jean had been collecting over the centuries. They were his crystals, no-one else had created them, he had made them, and he had to sort out the problem. There were still members of the Order that relied on them spread throughout the universe; many on covert operations. The crystals were their only means of returning back to the safety of the Empire, without any communication that could exist outwith the Empire, they had no other way of getting home. Even Jean's computer NiCI was unable to use communications that traversed those distances. Though he had included the asteroid that was NiCI's base within the boundaries of the energy that united the Primary worlds. That way Jean was able to maintain contact with her ship and any communications it may receive, but if the spaceship moved away from its base, Jean lost contact with it.

Simon was already working on a solution along with Jean, but they had nothing to report and Nathan was aware that he had to do something soon; people were dying and disappearing, he couldn't ignore it. There were of course those few who had been born with the ability to translocate themselves. But while Nathan may have the capability to move entire armies across the void of space, those who had this ability could only translocate themselves, no-one else. There were even fewer of these people who could translocate outside of the Empire, and of those, there were a mere handful he would trust with the covert operations of the universe.

Running his fingers through his thick mop of hair, he was unaware, or even cared, that it stood up on end, giving him a wild, slightly manic, look. He was tired through lack of sleep as his mind constantly raced through the issues that plagued him. It wasn't as if he wasn't used to dealing with difficult problems, it was his day job after all. But this time his concerns were much closer to home.

The whole business with Gellan and Duran; the other Knights, Jean (he allowed himself a smile as he thought of her), and then of course, there was Ixeer raising its head again.

Ixeer, always somewhere in the darkest realms of his mind; a menace lurking, reminding him of his failure that almost proved deadly. The scars that refused to fully heal that scoured his back, had been feeling particularly sore of late, a constant reminder of his humiliation. Even when he did finally snatch a few hours sleep, the images of that one mission haunted him. Now he didn't know what was worse, no sleep at all or knowing what he will see when he closed his eyes.

Glancing at the paperwork spread out over his desk, he rubbed his eyes and decided that he was getting nowhere; he needed to get out of the office for a while. Thinking about the message he had received earlier from Jean saying that she was about to enjoy the afternoon sun along the Hoe in

Plymouth, he made a decision. He would go home, and take the car out to the south Devon coast to join her.

Recently, she had been taking tentative steps to relive the memories of her family. Nathan was convinced it wasn't a good idea, but she seemed resolute in her decision. He supported her, but was wary of a time when she would push it too far. He knew all about remembering family history, and it wasn't something he was too keen to relive himself.

Gathering up the files in front of him, he locked them in the drawers of his huge oak desk, before making his way to the door, pausing to look back at his large office; determined to commit the scene to memory as accurately as possible. Another issue that had concerned him lately, was that someone seemed to be rifling through his office. It was subtle, but he knew the signs. However, he also knew that no-one could just enter his office illicitly, as there were considerable security protections surrounding it as well as those rooms of Damien and Daniel. Even Val, his most trusted secretary, didn't enter unless he was there. Yet someone, somehow, had been in his office uninvited. But there was no-one, or anything, that existed within the universe that could penetrate his protections. Which of course leaves the only other possibility; whoever it was, wasn't part of the universe, they existed outside of it — amongst the gods.

The more he thought of it the more it made sense, but still Nathan didn't want to accept the notion completely. The thought of any of the gods actually entering the realm of the universe uninvited was shocking, even for him. But the simple fact of it was Gellan and Duran had already done just that; they had met with Franco and his fellow Kaimiren owners. What would stop them from going a step further and actually entering the Empire, his very office? There were lines that couldn't be crossed when it came to the laws of the gods and the existence of the universe. The whole point of the creation of the Guardians — the Knights and Jean — was to ensure any adverse issues that arose were dealt with by a force that existed within the fabric of the cosmos. The only concession to the gods' involvement being that they would control when and where the Guardians were needed. But Gellan and Duran had been removed from such auspicious positions a long time ago, by Anasara herself.

Anasara, the one they knew affectionately as the Mother of all creation, an enigma that even Nathan would never consider defying. But Gellan and that psychopath, Duran, driven by their hatred of the man who had seen to their downfall, had even been willing to incite her wrath and cause chaos.

Turning back to the door, he twisted the handle and left the office, closing it quietly behind him. Val looked up and he let her know he was leaving early, giving her instructions before he left. He paused as a sudden thought crossed his mind that had Val may have possibly let someone into his office? Dismissing the notion just as quickly, as both impossible and ridiculous, he gave her a smile that he hoped looked reassuring.

He felt uncomfortable as she looked at him oddly, suggesting concern. She had already asked him on several occasions if he was alright, and he had answered that everything was fine each time. However, she didn't seem convinced then and she didn't look too sure now. But he didn't have time to try and placate her concerns, so ensuring she had everything she needed he left her to it, then made his way through the main office to the stairs that would lead down to the atrium hall. He glanced at those working there and wondered if he wasn't being bit paranoid in speculating whether he could actually trust them all. Were some still loyal to Ephea's memory? Did some follow the literature that had been distributed during the riots in Parva and other cities of the Empire?

Descending the stairs and entering the atrium, he crossed the ornately decorated floor of the huge, sunlit hall. It had been busy today, with members of the Council meeting in the Chambers for one of the six-weekly sessions. It had been Daniel and Stephen who had chaired the gathering, apparently it had been quite a lively affair. Nathan had felt guilty when he suggested to Daniel that he would wait until he read his report rather than listen to a blow by blow account of the goings on personally; pleading too much work. Daniel wasn't fooled however, but he knew Nathan and, while showing concern for the tiredness of his friend, left the subject alone. He assured him he would have the paperwork sorted and on his desk by the next morning.

Those who worked in the Palace saw their Emperor and the Knights regularly making their way around the complex buildings and gardens, even venturing out into the city again as they did before Ephea and her sisters changed everything. But today, for some reason he was gaining more curious glances than he would normally expect. He made a point of

198

ignoring them however, wanting to get back to Denfield as quickly as possible.

He made his way along the corridor that would lead him to the tunnel that passed through the thick solid granite of the caldera walls; linking the Palace to the home the Knights fondly called the Retreat. Giving a nod to acknowledge the two members of the Order on watch at the Palace end of the tunnel, he made his way down towards the Retreat and through the gardens to its big oak front door.

The watch that had always stood guard at the entrance to the Retreat had been placed there by the Council to great amusement of the Knights; how two members of the Order were expected to act as protection to seven Guardians who were bigger, stronger and considerably more experienced was ridiculous. But they had conceded that if it, like many of the routines they had to endure, made the people they served happy, they would put up with it. Besides, it was useful for picking up the mail and catching unwanted visitors.

Today, however, there was no mail and the Retreat would be empty at this hour. The housekeeper had already been and overseen the final flourishes to the redecorating that had brightened up their home. The gardeners were still hard at work in the gardens, making remarkable headway into the jungle that had sprouted over the previous five years. It was beginning to take shape, and the Knights knew better than to interfere with their head gardener when she was in full inspiration mode. Even Nathan left her too it, preferring to wait until the work was finally finished before undertaking any adjustments of his own; and even then he would make sure they were minimal.

He made his way inside via the large oak front door, wrinkling his nose at the strong smell of paint; but he wasn't going to be staying here for a few days yet — there was a formal dinner they all had to attend, so that would mark the first night they would return to the Retreat officially.

Crossing the hallway, towards the kitchen and to the back door which would take him into the gardens, he passed a large mirror that hung on the wall. He caught a brief image of himself and stopped short. His hair was still standing on end, and his face also looked drawn with dark circles under his eyes giving him a distinct haunted look; no wonder he was getting odd looks from everyone. Making an effort to try and tame his hair, he checked his reflection again; there was nothing he could do about the tiredness in his eyes, but at least he didn't look as if he'd been in a scuffle with someone.

Satisfied he had done all he could, he made his way out of the Retreat and down through the gardens to the gazebo. A roofed area that gave some weather protection over the one part of Parva that allowed for translocation. It was a very small area and highly protected, and like similar spots in all the homes on Earth occupied by the Knights, this one could only be accessed by those with express permission. Privacy and security still had to be maintained.

Acknowledging the gardeners at work as he passed, he finally made it to his destination. It had been one of the first parts of the garden to be cleared and repaired, with the plants and trees cut back to form a colourful backdrop. The mid-summer flowers were in bloom and filling the air with their perfume. Nathan smiled and enjoyed a brief respite from his worries. Then his thoughts turned to Denfield and he was gone.

Arriving home at Denfield he quickly made his way into the kitchen, thinking that maybe he could make reservations for dinner in Plymouth for him and Jean. He decided to search his phone for the number of the new Chinese restaurant that had recently opened in the Barbican. Taking out his phone to start messaging Jean to tell her of his plans, the device began to ring. He smiled to himself, it seemed he didn't need to message Jean after all, she was calling him instead. Pressing the icon that would open the call, he put the phone to his ear.

'Hello, I was just about to message you.'

Suddenly his innards turned to ice, he knew instantly something was wrong. The seconds it took Jean to speak seemed like hours of silence; her voice a whisper filled with pain and fear.

'Nathan…help me!'

14

The

Lighthouse

Victor Bales stood at the base of the red and white tower of Smeaton's lighthouse. It was mid-summer and the tourists were out in force along Plymouth's famous Hoe. Children ran around their parents as they enjoyed a stroll along the front, while couples sat upon the grass; the sun warming their skin while they languished in the holiday atmosphere. Out in the bay the sea sparkled in the sunlight, while the white stone of the Plymouth Naval Memorial gleamed on the rise. It was a hot summer's day in Devon and the beautiful weather didn't look as if it was going to leave anytime soon.

But Bales didn't care, his only interest was in the woman making her way across the lawn from the memorial to the promenade of the Hoe. Wearing a light summer dress, a wide brimmed hat and sun glasses, she could have been any lone tourist enjoying her ice cream in the sun; but Bales knew her.

She was the woman who destroyed everything he had; even that bastard Nathan was oblivious until she came along. Victor allowed himself a small smile, she wouldn't be so relaxed if she knew he was there, watching, just as he had been watching for weeks. Always in crowds of course, he wasn't stupid. He knew enough that it wouldn't take long for her to figure out she was being watched if he was alone. However, while he was here, standing in obscurity amongst the tourists enjoying the Hoe, she remained blissfully oblivious.

His mind wandered to when he first saw her here on Earth some weeks before. He had been surveying the antics of the Emperor when he spotted the two of them together, he was quite shocked when they were both walking along the village streets of Stanton, nestled next to Nathan's home of Denfield. Then he considered that this was exactly the sort of thing she would do, somehow she had always managed to inveigle her way into the lives of people with influence. The last time he saw her was with that idiot Coniston; Lord Damien's lap dog.

It had been too dangerous for him to return to Kelan, let alone Parva. After fleeing the city when the police discovered his wife's body, he was unaware of the events that had occurred since. But obviously that little bitch had managed to turn the Emperor's head somehow.

Seeing Jean so relaxed and alone, Bales contemplated how vulnerable she was. He had spoken to Gellan and Duran about his concerns over this woman, that she had far more connections than was normal for someone who was a stranger to the city of Parva. He had no idea who she was, but he knew she had influence amongst those who mattered. But despite Bales' concerns, Gellan and Duran were untroubled. He knew that as gods they would have had little, if any, input into the ways of the universe and its inhabitants. As far as he could remember from his classes at school, the gods were instrumental in the creation and care of the cosmos only in its infancy. Now, they could only rely on the Guardians to resolve issues that arose due to corruption in the fabric of the universe. And then the gods could control only where the Guardians were sent, not what they did when they got there.

Bales also knew from his history lessons that once upon a time, it was Gellan himself who instructed where the Guardians; Nathan and the other Knights, were sent. But something had happened in the long and distant past that had seen Gellan and his cohort, Duran, exiled from the high court of gods. Now they were virtually blind to the goings on in the universe; only able to affect small incidents within time so as to create their desired effects further down the line. While he still didn't know what had gone wrong, he was aware that Gellan was seething that the latest plan, which had taken so long for him to put in place, had been thwarted at the last moment.

But the exiled gods had spent no time in mulling over their failings. They were, even now, working hard to achieve their final goal; and he, Victor Bales, was in the thick of it. They didn't even have to work at persuading him, as soon as he heard what they wanted from him he jumped at the chance; especially when he discovered the prize he would earn for his efforts. But, for now he allowed himself time to indulge in watching the Carter woman, oblivious to her vulnerability.

He brought his mind back to Jean as she continued her slow amble over the lawn, working her way among the picnickers and kissing couples. It was then he realised that his musing had taken up more time than he thought; she was barely feet away from him now. Turning his head to the side and pulling the peak of his baseball cap down, his heart hammered as she walked passed. Allowing his breath to ease out slowly, he looked in her direction out of the corner of his eye.

Suddenly he froze, she had stopped just feet away. She was looking up at the lighthouse, one hand on the top of her hat as her head was raised, the other hand still lightly clutching the half-eaten ice-cream.

He had no idea when he made the decision to attack, but within moments he had covered that small space of open ground between them and his knife was in his hand.

The look of surprise in her eyes was worth it to Bales; shock and pain were etched into her face. Then at the moment she recognised him, he felt a thrill of pure satisfaction.

Yes bitch, it's me.

The only regret he had, was that as the knife plunged into her chest, Jean had instinctively reached up and grabbed the hilt; making the possibility of twisting and retrieving his favourite blade nigh on impossible without some form of fight. But too many people were looking in their direction now, their curiosity aroused.

Turning away, Bales was aware of voices shouting around him; but he didn't care. He had killed the bitch, and the feelings of triumph flowed throughout his body.

Someone reached out to apprehend him, but his newly acquired skill of translocation (a small gift from Gellan) meant whoever it was, had only fresh air in their hands. Quite inexplicably, the small man with the baseball cap, who had stabbed an unarmed woman, was suddenly nowhere to be seen.

15

A Place By The Sea

Nathan spun on his heel and rushed out of the French doors, barely even aware if he had closed them properly or not, his brain consumed with the need to get to Jean as fast as possible; the sound of terror in her voice ringing in his ears. A few strides across the terrace and he was at the spot where he could translocate away from Denfield, his mind set on her signature that had become ingrained into his consciousness. There had come a point, soon after Jean had settled into Denfield, when he could tell where she was, even if her presence was in a totally different part of the universe. Pinpointing her position on the Hoe in Plymouth was as easy as if he could see her on the other side of a window. Such was the accuracy of his knowledge of her signature, when he arrived on the Hoe it was within yards of Jean herself, amongst the confused and shocked crowds that milled around her.

He didn't bother about the baffled looks he gained from the crowds as he suddenly arrived in their midst. All he cared about was getting to Jean. Pushing people out of the way and ignoring the shouts of indignation, he knelt down beside her; the look of terror and pain in her eyes tearing at his heart. But it was the dagger protruding from her chest, with her hands grasped around the hilt that made his guts wrench in horror.

She was resting on her knees, he could see it took her a huge effort to remain upright, but to try and lie down on her own could prove fatal. He moved behind her quickly to gently hold her and help her stay upright. Someone kindly donated a jacket, and along with his own, Nathan tried to keep Jean warm, despite the heat of the Devonshire afternoon sun. From somewhere close by, the sound of sirens were heard as the emergency services approached, sending ripples of panic up his spine, he couldn't let them take her away.

Calling Stephen on his phone, the doctor was with them within seconds, laying his hands over Jean, assessing the extent of the injuries the dagger had caused. Meanwhile, Nathan had called Damien and he too, along with the other Knights appeared by their sides within moments.

By now, the oddity of these strange men and their sudden appearance, apparently from no-where, dressed in some kind of uniform they didn't recognise, was causing some concern amongst the crowd. They were treated with suspicion when five of the Knights began to push the crowd back; their annoyance becoming audible at being forced to take orders from men who had no authority to do so. There was much pushing and shoving, and the threat of more violent action was only abated when the local constabulary arrived.

It looked as if the police were going to take the side of the crowd until Damien approached the most senior officer there and had a quiet word. The police officer looked momentarily nonplussed, but after a quick exchange over their radio with an unknown person back in an unknown office, the officer barked commands that they were to help with dispersing the crowd. The constables complied, and despite the shouts of indignation, soon there was an area created around Jean, Nathan and Stephen.

The five Knights stood, spaced evenly about the three of them, facing outward. The police and the crowd outside looked on, their morbid curiosity even overriding the indignation of the strangers' behaviour. The paramedics had also arrived and pushed their way through to the cleared ground, insisting that Nathan and Stephen withdraw, until an irate Stephen produced a card that seemed to be some form of identification, and told them to stand back and not interfere. Like the senior police officer, they were reluctant at first, but eventually did as they were bid; cautiously watching, refusing to leave the clearing completely.

Pretty soon the police had taken control and were taking statements from the crowd, while they eyed the Knights suspiciously. They kept well away as directed, but the accusations of people appearing and disappearing into thin air did little to ease their minds. For now they would put the allegations down to too much sun and ice cream, followed by one too many in the local pubs; at least until they got back to the station. There was something strange about the men and the way they dressed and held themselves.

Despite all the confusion that went on around them, the three people within the clearing were oblivious. Nathan placed the side of his head against Jean's, letting her lean back against him while he supported her back. She was still awake and was looking at Stephen with horror and fear. It took no time at all for Stephen to make his assessment and he looked up at Nathan, concern etched across his face. He took a slow intake of breath and leaned down, close to Jean's ear, speaking quietly enough that only Jean and Nathan could hear.

'Jean, I need you to listen carefully. Ideally you should be in Aria, where I can operate in the best conditions.' He paused and glanced up at Nathan, who felt the stone, that had settled uncomfortably in his stomach, lurch violently. 'But the blade has caught so close to your heart, any movement could be catastrophic. I'm also reluctant to render you unconscious to do this procedure as you will no longer be able to keep yourself upright. I need to you be aware and react when necessary, but I am afraid the pain would be too much unless you are unconscious.'

Nathan reached out and caught Stephen's shoulder. 'What are you going to do?'

'I want to pull the blade out. But, it has damaged major blood vessels, and while it remains in place it is the only thing that is stopping them from rupturing completely. Fortunately, Jean had the sense to stop whoever did this from taking the knife out. It has saved her life.' He didn't say *so far*, but the thought hung in the air between them.

Nathan looked panic stricken, but Stephen held up his hand.

'But, if I can heal the wound from behind as I remove the blade slowly I can minimise any damage, at least until I can get her in a safe enough position for her to travel to Aria.'

Nathan sighed. 'Do what you have to do. I will take care of Jean, she won't feel a thing. If you want her to do anything just say, but she won't be able to verbally respond.'

Looking up and searching for Damien, Nathan called for his attention.

'Whatever happens here, make sure we are not disturbed. Under any circumstances.'

Damien nodded and Nathan knew the other Knights understood too. It took a lot of effort to force themselves to not draw their own swords to prove a point to the crowd; but they all knew that if a time came, they wouldn't hesitate to do so.

Satisfied, Nathan turned back to Stephen and said. 'When you have finished, just tap my shoulder.'

Stephen had no idea what Nathan was going to do, but he didn't argue. Then, placing his hands gently on either side of Jean's head, ensuring she was resting safely against his chest, Nathan closed his eyes.

Almost immediately, Stephen saw Nathan seemed to zone out, then feeling Jean relax under his own hands he was aware that time was not on his side, and he began his dangerous and potentially fatal procedure to save Jeans's life.

Placing his left arm around Jean, and putting his hand against her back, he set his mind so that he could navigate his senses towards the dagger and the deadly wound it had made within her body. Her now slowly beating heart resonated comfortingly around his own mind, he could feel the sensation of blood moving throughout her body. The warmth of bone and tissue surrounding the cold invasion of steel told him where he needed to start; then with his right hand grasping the hilt of the dagger he began to slowly draw it out.

While the natural suction of tissue would normally render removing a blade extremely difficult, he was able to relax the damaged muscles just enough to allow the knife to move. As the tip of the blade left an opening in the damaged soft tissue, Stephen used his skill to knit the wound together.

This alone would have been extremely painful, let alone withdrawing the blade. He didn't look at Nathan as he worked, but silently he hoped to the gods he knew what he was doing. It was going to be a long process, but despite the terrible wound, Stephen felt that they may actually have a chance of succeeding. So slowly and meticulously, he continued his work.

All around the cleared ground there was silence. The crowds that had long before been enjoying a summer's day on the Hoe, were now entranced by the strange men and, in particular, the man who appeared to be taking the dagger out of the woman who had been savagely attacked. Slowly the sun began to drop to the west as Stephen worked on.

Nathan opened his eyes, he already felt the sweat running down his back; his thick dark uniform was not the most appropriate clothing under the blazing heat of the sun. Squinting his eyes he raised his hand to adjust to the glare from the bright golden sands, that stretched for miles along the shoreline of an azure blue sea. He saw Jean standing a short way off, her feet hidden amongst the slowly crashing waves. She seemed momentarily confused; wearing her light summer dress and wide brimmed hat, while standing barefoot in the golden sands as the waves swirled around her ankles. Spreading her fingers in front of her, she studied them intently, before bending her knees and dropping her hand into the frothing foam. Standing up she allowed the wet sand she clutched within her fingers to fall in globules, disappearing amongst the rippling waves.

And all the while, Nathan stood in silence and watched.

Her gaze took in the view out to sea, to the unbroken horizon, before turning her head to see the rest of her surroundings. When she saw Nathan she smiled, and without further hesitation, Nathan went to her, suddenly desperate to let her know she was safe here. As he moved, he realised he was no longer wearing his uniform, but instead white cotton trousers and shirt, his feet were bare like Jean's.

213

She watched him approach, taking off her hat and letting it fall from her hand. As it landed in the sea it faded away, as if it was never there. The smell of the salty air and the warmth of the sun enveloped them as they drew together at the shore, standing close to each other, but not quite touching.

She put her head to one side, her smile still lighting up her features.

'So where are we exactly? How did you know to bring me here?'

Nathan returned her smile, the turmoil that had clattered round his brain was momentarily calmed.

'I didn't, you brought us here, I just opened the way for us. This is your safe place, somewhere you can feel at peace.'

Jean looked impressed. 'I had know idea you could do this.'

'Neither did I to be honest, it was something that I was aware of as a possibility, but never something I have done in practice. The souls of two people have to be particularly close for it to happen.'

He was suddenly aware that he had said much more than he had intended and looked at Jean nervously, afraid she may be annoyed at his presumption; or even worse, laugh!

But Jean just took his hands in her own and was quiet for a while before speaking.

'Is it looking really bad?'

Nathan sighed. 'Stephen is concerned. He couldn't completely put you to sleep; he needs you to be responsive during the procedure. Only when he indicates to me will we be both able to come round. At the moment we are relying on the others to keep us safe.'

He watched as a look of concern flitted across Jean's face, he squeezed her fingers gently while they still rested in his own.

'It will all be fine. I have every faith in Stephen. We can leave him to his work while you're here.' He paused, a burning question gnawing at his mind, wanting immediate answers. 'But there is one thing you can help with. Do you know who did this to you?'

With the change of subject and Nathan's quiet tone Jean relaxed again, slowly nodding her head.

'Yes, in fact I do. Strangely enough, it was a certain General of the Order, and father of a murdered rapist.'

Nathan found himself quite shocked at this revelation.

'Victor Bales?'

'The very one, though I note you didn't call him General.'

Nathan scowled.

'He is currently a fugitive of the Empire, having left Parva soon after his wife was found hanged in their garden. There are issues he still has yet to answer to any satisfaction of the police, or the Order. He is a wanted man that I have had many knights searching for over the past few weeks. The question is, how did he find you, and how did he manage to attack you so easily? And where the hell is he now?'

Nathan could feel the familiar dark panic begin to rise again. Jean placed her hand on his chest, she looked worried as her eyes locked onto his own. He could feel his heart thumping under her touch, sure she could feel it hammering against his chest. But if she did, she didn't show any signs.

'I think I can answer all of those questions, even if some guesswork is needed.

'First of all, I have been far too lax in my own security of late. Too wrapped up in my desire to remember the past, I left my myself open to the dangers of the present. But, I can assure you it won't happen again.' She raised a finger as if to make a point. 'And don't even think about suggesting a body guard.'

Nathan had the grace to look guilty, as that was exactly what he was thinking. Instead he just agreed.

'Fair enough, but I think all of us should be more vigilant from now on!'

Jean smiled again and continued. 'Secondly, regarding Bales, do you know if he had the ability to translocate?'

The air was suddenly filled with his laughter. 'Absolutely not.'

'You don't think it's a secret he might have kept to himself?'

'Definitely not. Victor Bales may not be a big man, but his ego is plenty large enough. If he had any skills to boast about, let alone translocation, he would have made sure everybody knew about it and at every opportunity possible.'

Jean nodded. 'Agreed. Then it is a skill he has picked up recently.'

Nathan drew his eyebrows together. He didn't want to ask the question but he did anyway.

'How?'

'I think we both know the possible answer to that one. I saw, and felt him disappear myself. And considering recent history, I would suggest that our two rogue gods have had something to do with it, don't you?'

Nathan felt the huge stone in his stomach plummet further. Gellan and Duran again. This time actually attacking Jean.

'Nathan, are you alright?'

Jean was now holding his hand tighter and the hand that had rested on his chest moved up to caress his cheek, she looked concerned. So many emotions swirled around him, his head swam in panic and fear. He wanted to just pull Jean to him and keep her close, promising never to let her come to harm again. But even he knew that was an impossible hope.

Seeming to sense the turmoil that raged within him, Jean tried to speak, but Nathan never heard what she wanted to say. Forced back to the reality of the scene still taking place on Plymouth Hoe, he found himself once more sitting within the circle of Knights. Despite the warm evening and once more dressed in his uniform, Nathan felt chilled. His eyes shot to the figure of Jean, her head still resting against his chest, the borrowed jacket around her shoulders. A blanket had been placed over her and Stephen leaned back and stretched out his cramping back and shoulder muscles. As he glanced at Nathan he creased his brows.

'Are you alright?'

Nathan was aware that his anguish was very much apparent on his face, he just mumbled that he was fine and looked for Damien amongst the other Knights in the evening

217

half light. He caught his eye as he turned at Stephen's concerned words. 'Is everything still well here?'

Damien nodded. 'We still have paramedics around, and the police are not entirely happy at the moment, but the crowd have thoroughly enjoyed themselves. Nothing like the prospect of a good tragedy to keep them occupied. There has been some outrage that something has caused everyone's phones to malfunction. The local press have turned up as well, they are probably regretting only having their digital cameras too. There were a lot of people annoyed at losing an opportunity for their moment of fame on social media.'

Nathan gave him a knowing grin, it took him barely a thought to knock out all electronic equipment when he had first arrived at the scene. A few hundred witnesses was one thing, having it all recorded for prosperity was entirely another. He looked back at Stephen.

'Is everything done, will Jean be alright now?'

Stephen smiled, he looked exhausted; the operation must have taken it out of him, both physically and mentally. Nathan looked down as Jean started to stir and he instinctively placed his hand on her shoulder. She looked up at his touch and he answered her unasked question.

'It's fine. Stephen says the operation went well.'

Jean glanced over at Stephen and gave him a tired but grateful smile which he returned. They both looked relieved and Stephen spoke to her quietly. 'I want to get you to Aria as soon as I can. The operation was a success, but the wounds are still vulnerable.'

Then turning to Nathan with a troubled look he said. 'How are we going to translocate from here?'

Nathan considered this before glancing at the blanket still draped over Jean.

'We let the paramedics take her to the hospital. You ride with them and Daniel will arrive with another ambulance and relevant documents. You sign her over, agreeing that she is to be transferred to a private hospital. Once you are out of sight of anyone, we all translocate to Aria.'

Stephen didn't look entirely convinced and Daniel had turned at the sound of his name. If Nathan had to be honest, which he would rather not have to, he was making it up as he was going along. He had no idea if it had any chance of working, but it was all they had to go with unless someone else came up with something better; and Nathan knew the chances of anyone even attempting that was highly unlikely. They were more than happy to let him do all the thinking, especially when the results could go so spectacularly wrong. He rubbed his eyes, he was exhausted.

Stephen stood and started giving orders to the paramedics, who didn't look pleased about it at all; but they begrudgingly complied. Soon, Jean and Stephen were whisked away with blues and twos playing. While Daniel was compiling documents, John was sent to find them transport that could be passed off as a private ambulance.

Despite the possibilities of so many things that could have gone wrong, the plan actually worked and ran pretty smoothly. A black van had been acquired to pass off as a private ambulance. Nathan didn't enquire as to how John had procured one so quickly, he just hoped he managed to return it to its rightful owners before they realised it was missing. Jean found herself lying on a bare metal floor surrounded by tired and hungry Knights for the two minutes it took for them to get away from the prying eyes at the hospital. It didn't take long before she was tucked up in a hospital bed in Aria under the watchful eye of Stephen and the Knights however; all thankful that she was at last home and safe.

By the time she had fallen asleep, the Knights had satisfied themselves that they could do no more for her at the moment, and so had left her in the capable hands of Stephen and his medical staff. Only Nathan remained, unwilling to leave Jean just yet.

He rubbed his exhausted eyes as he sat in a comfortable easy chair in a quiet waiting room. He had no idea when he finally drifted off to sleep, but at some point someone had come in to check on him, he thought it could only have been Stephen. Leaving him to sleep, he had covered him with the same blanket that had covered Jean. And so, at least for a while, Nathan finally slept.

16

Johnson

Floella Johnson looked at her watch, 3:45pm, she would have to get moving soon, Tommy would be bringing the kids over for their dinner tonight. She wanted to make something special for them; it had been so long since she last saw the twins. Her son and his ex-wife had finally agreed the divorce settlement just over a year ago, but she and Derek had only seen the grandkids four times since.

That cow, Floella still couldn't bring herself to say her ex-daughter-in-law's name, had made it as difficult as possible for Tommy to get custody. The last straw was when she moved up state with her new *boyfriend* — boy being the operative word — making it a four hour long trip just for Tommy to pick up the kids. But now *the cow* wanted to swan off on a fancy holiday with the *boyfriend;* she probably got his flights half price on a cheap 'bring your kids' deal. Floella grinned to herself. Despite the vitriol she felt behind the sentiments, she couldn't help but be thankful that at least Tommy got to keep the kids for two whole weeks.

She had spent all last night baking. The poor little darlings needed feeding up, having no doubt had enough of all that healthy crap their mother forced down their throats. A good dose of wholesome food is what they needed.

She looked at her watch again, 3:55pm. The machines around the bed beeped and flashed, just as they always beeped and flashed. Tubes running in and out of the pale body that lay upon the hospital bed; it was like something out of a science fiction movie. But this was no fiction, it was very real. Again, Floella felt the pangs of guilt run through her ample body.

For several months now she had travelled everyday to the Royal Melbourne Hospital; talking to her daughter as if she was listening to every word. All about Tommy and *the cow*, news about the grandkids and even what the weather was doing; anything at all the doctors had said. And so she talked, reading magazines and books until she hated the sound of her own voice. But she carried on, she had to do something to try and make up for the guilt she felt inside.

Even now she could see every moment of that awful night when her poor daughter came home. Tears welled in her eyes, and as she blinked they fell freely down her cheeks. She remembered the sound of the dogs barking themselves mental in the yard, which had interrupted their telly viewing, so she'd had to force Derek to get up and see what was going on out there.

'Why the fuck can't you go and look?'

Floella had given him a filthy look.

'Because if you were half the man you pretend to be down the pub, you would want to protect me. What if I went out and someone attacked me?'

Derek had given her a look that suggested that anyone who would consider attacking her would need his bumps felt, but he kept that one to himself. Instead he just grumbled something about it being ok if they attacked him instead then, before lifting his bulk off the sofa and heading for the back yard, yelling at the dogs to pipe down or he'll show them what for.

It was moments later he came crashing through the back door shouting for Floella to call the police and paramedics.

She had looked at her husband as if he had grown two heads.

'What the fuck are you on about? What's happened?'

Derek had grabbed the phone himself and was heading back to the yard, shouting loudly into the handset that someone had better get there quick.

Ice had gripped Floella's heart, what the hell had frightened Derek so much that he would act so frantic? Who was out there? Curiosity forced her to go and see, but fear made her think twice before following her husband out. As she stood just inside the door she could see him standing over a body; *was he crying?*

Still undecided as to what she should do, Derek suddenly turned to her, the phone hanging limply in his hands, tears now streaming down his face.

'It's Karen Flo, some bastard has attacked our Karen.'

Trying to snap out of her stupor, Floella looked again at the body.

What was he saying? Where was Karen? Who was that lying there?

In the distance there was the distinctive sound of sirens, their wail bringing back the reality of Derek's words. Now she ran, nearly falling down the steps from the veranda to the cold hard earth of the yard.

Then she was there, looking down on the still, silent body of her daughter, covered in blood and unconscious. Letting out an almighty wail of grief, Floella had fallen to her knees. She didn't remember much about the paramedics running through the house and into the yard; she had no idea which of the police gently took her arm and tried to make her stand so the medics could do their work. But it must have happened because the rest of night had been spent pacing the hospital corridors, drinking endless cups of God awful coffee, and praying to a god she didn't even believe in.

When Tommy had arrived he took over talking to the doctors and nurses, Derek and Floella weren't much use anyway. They kept repeating the same questions, then immediately forgetting the answers; their minds scattered by their shock and misery. The stupid thing was, they hadn't seen their daughter for many years, turning their back on her when she had been thrown out of the army for selling drugs, regretting their decision as soon as she had walked away.

They had no idea what had happened to her, where she had gone, or even if she was still alive. But there she lay on an operating table, fighting for her life, and it was as if she had never been away. Their little girl, who had climbed trees with her brother, learnt to drive the truck with her father, and laughed while baking with her mum, seriously ill; and all they wanted was the chance to say sorry.

The police had searched everywhere, looked at CCTV and talked to everyone and anyone that could be convinced to speak. But there was nothing. No-one knew anything. Even the yard had very little blood on the ground compared to that which the doctors said she had lost. It was as if she had just materialised from nowhere; but of course, that was impossible.

The doctors had warned them that when, and if, Karen ever woke up, she may have some form of brain damage, but they would only know that when she eventually regained consciousness. But what they were absolutely sure of, was that Karen would never walk again. Her spine had been severed completely, even her basic bodily functions were likely to be impeded. If she woke up, Karen would need round the clock care, and Floella knew that her daughter would hate it. Half of her wanted to see Karen open her eyes, give her an opportunity to tell her how much she was sorry, how much she missed her. But the other half prayed she never woke up, never had to endure the misery that she would undertake everyday.

A final check of her watch, 4:20pm, she had to get moving, the traffic would already be building up. Gathering her coat that rested in her lap, Floella stood and bent over

225

her daughter's resting body. Running her fingers lightly down the side of her right cheek, she leant forward and kissed her forehead, just as she used to do when she was a little girl. A final sigh and Floella turned away from her sleeping daughter and silently passed through the door into the corridor, hurrying to get to the car and home before the traffic became too busy.

So taken up with her need to leave the smell and depression of the hospital behind, she barely noticed the two figures in the corridor that stood looking out of the window, gazing at the late afternoon Melbourne skyline.

If she had taken more notice, she may have been more cautious. Each figure watched her reflection as she passed, turning only to see her walk through the double doors at the end of the corridor. Eventually, the two individuals checked they were completely alone, and no medical staff were around to interrupt them. Then they made their way to the room that Floella had just left.

No cameras saw their passing, they had inexplicably stopped working. Opening the door they stepped inside where Karen Johnson, one time Captain of the Emperor's wife Ephea's notorious Patrols, lay sleeping.

Then closing the door behind them, Gellan and Duran approached the bed in silence.

17

Contemplati

on

J ean was leaning against the window pane, letting her head rest against the cool glass. Outside, the rain that had fallen overnight, was slowly drying up in the warm, summer, morning sun. This was her second day staying at the Retreat in Parva, and she had to admit she was feeling far more settled into its surroundings than she thought she would be at first.

Having spent the best part of a week at the hospital in Aria, under the strict instructions of Stephen, she was glad to get out of the place. She couldn't complain about the treatment, or even the surroundings there, but at the end of the day it was still a hospital and Jean couldn't wait to get home. Stephen had refused point blank to let her leave until he was absolutely satisfied that she had completely healed. She had attempted to protest at the beginning, but soon learnt, particularly under the advice of Daniel, that it was better to do as Stephen instructed or she could end up stuck in there even longer. Apparently even Nathan doesn't argue anymore; they just all make an effort to not have to undergo his ministrations.

Home.

She had to smile to herself, it had been nearly three months since the battle with the Kaimiren at the Palace gates, and despite her reservations at first, she couldn't help but look forward to the prospect of going back to the comforting embrace of Denfield. Biting her lip, she tried not to focus on the fact that the owner of the house was a pretty big draw too; even if the place felt quite empty when he had to work elsewhere within the Empire on the odd evenings.

But instead, they had all travelled to the Retreat. There had been plenty of renovation work in both the gardens and the house. Fresh paint had been liberally applied to most of the walls, and the gardens had undertaken a particularly enthusiast prune by the gardeners. Jean had likened it to a hippy undergoing a ferocious number one hair cut; brutal, but interesting to see what was lying beneath the undergrowth.

It had been decided that Jean's release from Aria should coincide with the Knights returning to the Retreat. Apparently, they had a particularly important dinner they

228

were all to attend the following evening, so they had made a point of celebrating in private, making sure Jean was thoroughly spoilt and welcomed to the fold. She was also relieved to learn that she was not required to attend the dinner with the Knights. It hadn't occurred to her that they would expect her to attend any functions, though Nathan had been adamant that as a Guardian, she had a status that had gained a certain amount of public attention.

Besides, why should she get away with not having to attend the bloody things?

His words, not hers.

As she gazed out over the gardens, a movement to her left caught her attention. A figure was making his way across the lawns. During the first few days of living amongst the Knights, Jean had often mistaken the distant figure of Damien for his cousin Nathan, so extraordinarily similar were they. But pretty soon they were as easy to distinguish to her as night was to day. So it was with interest, she watched Nathan stride out across the grass. She assumed he was making his way to the rose beds, having learned of his love of roses in his garden at Denfield. Jean had to admit he had quite the knack for producing amazing blooms in abundance; plenty of vases around Denfield displayed the results of his green finger ministrations.

But still, she couldn't ignore the concern growing inside her. Aware that something had been affecting Nathan's mood for some time, she hoped that after their encounter in her safe space on the beach, he would be more forthcoming with his thoughts. She was convinced he was going to tell her something important before he was pulled away, back to the reality of Plymouth Hoe and Stephen's desperate attempt to save her life.

According to Stephen and Daniel, Nathan had remained at her side in the hospital the whole time she was unconscious. She recalled him being there briefly when she woke up, but after that, he had apparently left and she didn't see him again until they all turned up at the Retreat. She couldn't deny it, she wasn't so much concerned, as down right worried sick. But if she had learnt nothing else about the Emperor Nathan L'guire, it was that when he wanted to keep something to himself, there was very little chance of prying any more information out of him. So, she decided that the best course of action for now would be to keep an eye on him, and just be around in the unlikelihood that he would finally open up and tell her what the hell was on his mind.

As the day was promising to be another hot one, Jean decided a good walk through the newly landscaped gardens was in order, and a chance to possibly gain an insight into how to grow roses without the prospect of committing rosa genocide.

Leaving her room she walked out onto the balcony that ran around the first floor and down the big sweeping staircase to the hall below. There was no-one there at that time of day, only Nathan. Jean had the sneaking suspicion that Stephen had insisted that there was always someone around with her, and it seemed that Nathan was allocated this morning's slot. Jean would have dearly loved to get a bit pissed off with this constant mothering, but if she had to be brutally honest, it was a comfort to know that she actually felt safe knowing the Knights were there.

She quickly made two cups of tea, and headed towards the back door. While in the kitchen she reflected on the previous day's lunch at the big wooden table; everyone was present except for John. When she had asked where he was, and why wasn't he going to the auspicious dinner that was to take place this evening, she was met with indignation, particularly from Simon.

'If it was that easy to get out of having to parade around and make pleasant small talk as an entertainment for other people's pleasure, believe me, we would all be elsewhere right now. But no, John is currently visiting the Smithsonian in Washington. Something to do with a geological exhibit regarding new scientific research. Christopher is with him.'

Jean smiled. 'He does know that NiCI has an entire database that he can analyse to his heart's content.'

All the Knights gave her a sharp look, but Simon got in first.

'So you are quite happy for us to visit your ship in order to gain such information?'

Jean laughed. 'Of course, please feel free. I have already made sure that NiCI is aware of who you are, you all have complete security clearance.' Looking at the faces that stared back at her, Jean felt she should probably elaborate. 'I thought you realised this, if there is anything you want to find out, NiCI is completely at your disposal.'

There was moment's pause before Daniel broke the silence.

'Well that's Simon set up for the foreseeable future, and by the look of it Stephen and Paul too. You may not get your ship back now you have opened that can of worms.'

Everyone around the table laughed, Jean smiled and put her head to one side.

'But seriously, he should have said, I'm sure Christopher would have enjoyed the experience too.'

'Hardly romantic though is it?'

Jean smirked. 'I don't know. It could get quite interesting if you turn off the artificial gravity.'

There was the sound of choking as Paul had taken a gulp of tea at that same moment, and Jean didn't miss the glance between Damien and Ty.

But then, without any warning, she was hit by a huge wave of testosterone and she regretted her innuendo immediately. It would be one thing to be in a room full of randy male teenagers, but it was nothing compared to the levels of hormone spikes the Knights were capable of creating.

She gasped and brought her hand up as she tried to catch her breath.

'Guys, please try to the keep the testosterone levels to a minimum, empath in the room.'

There were several evil grins exchanged around the table, followed by a lot of sniggering. Jean could only roll her eyes in exasperation

Standing up, she opened the kitchen window and enjoyed the fresh air on her face as she tried to refocus her hormonally battered brain. She had made a conscious effort not to build so many emotional walls while she was around

232

the Knights. Knowing that she could normally sense an individual's emotional state without any problem. However, when around the Knights, whether on their own or in a group, it was more of an emotional soup; difficult to attribute particular feelings to any individual. So instead of building walls she had endeavoured to try and filter the levels rather than block them; all very well until they hit her with a collective blast of emotions.

She had to admit, their conversations became a lot easier and relaxed once they'd had the awkward discussion about the ownership and control of brattine, the metal mined solely on the Primary World of Lode. It had all started when Simon was sitting at Denfield's kitchen table immersed in a magazine dedicated to some seriously expensive cars on Earth. Apparently, Simon was rather taken with a particularly sporty model with a price tag that made Jean's eyes water. She decided that she had to say something when Nathan had joined in Simon's appraisal of the motor's mechanical engineering.

'So, who's going to pay for this little toy you have rather taken a shine too?'

Both men had looked at her a bit nonplussed and Simon shrugged his shoulders as if the answer was obvious.

'Well, I am, obviously.'

'Oh, really? So once the tax payers have handed over their hard earned cash, it becomes yours to do with what you like? Including buying expensive cars!'

The two men looked at each other, then back at Jean, before they both started laughing. A bit put out that they should think taking advantage of the Empire's citizens was a laughing matter, Jean was all set to tell them both exactly what she thought. Nathan, obviously seeing the danger quickly tried to head off the impending tirade.

'Hold on, it's not what you think. No one is taking advantage of anyone.'

Jean didn't look convinced. 'Really? So, what about the metal brattine, you don't think that holding complete monopoly of its mines is taking advantage?'

Again, the two men shared a look before Nathan suggested that Jean sit at the table with them and he would explain everything.

'To be honest, this is something we should have discussed with you a while ago, I know Damien and Daniel are sorting the paperwork out, but I really should have mentioned something.'

It was now Jean's turn to look confused. 'I have no idea what you're talking about.'

Nathan smiled and Jean looked away, feeling her colour rise, though he continued talking as if he hadn't noticed anything. Simon however, seemed to have gained a daft grin that Jean thought suggested he hadn't missed her discomfort. She tried to concentrate on Nathan's words to divert her mind.

'First of all, we don't take any revenue from taxes at all. All public money is spent solely on public funding; education, health and public services etc. We take nothing.'

'Then how can you afford all this?' Jean looked around Denfield, then back at Nathan.'

'Ah, now we get back to the subject of the mines. Yes, you are quite correct, we do hold sole monopoly on the control and distribution of brattine throughout the Empire. And yes, we do take any final profit from the mines and distribute it between the eight of us.'

'Eight?'

'Bear with me, I'll get to that. If you looked at the accounts regarding the mines, and Damien would be happy to show you, you will probably be quite surprised at how little profit is actually made. However, through our own investments we have managed to ensure we live a considerably comfortable lifestyle. Though, having the mind of a brilliant accountant around does help. And no, as the Empire itself is run by the High Council, there is no conflict of interest. Our involvement is purely to ensure the Council is above reproach and the security and well being of the Empire is adhered to.'

'So you keep the mines to yourself so you have enough ready cash available to invest and make more money?'

Nathan sighed. 'No, we keep control of the mines so that it is not abused. As I said before, the profits are not great with the mining on Lode, metals are only extracted at a level on a par with demand. Any other business would require a constant flow of ore out of the mines to justify its investment. Most of the main profit that we receive actually goes back into keeping the mining communities there. It's a small industry compared to the size of the total trade in the use of brattine. Most of the brattine currently in use has been recycled, or has had no need to be replaced.'

'So, everything you own is through your own business acumen?'

'Basically, yes.'

235

Jean sat in silence for a while, as Nathan and Simon watched her.

'You said you would explain why it's split eight ways.'

'Ah, yes. Well as you know, James was one of us until his death some several centuries ago.' He glanced at Simon who gave him a sad smile back. 'Now, even though we lost James, Damien has been looking after his financial interests since then. You see, we know we have always meant to be eight, and I think we will all agree that James was never really comfortable in his role as a Guardian. He always felt as if he was just filling in.'

Simon nodded his agreement. 'To be honest, we hardly ever saw him unless we were off on one of our escapades elsewhere in the universe, and that was because he had no choice.'

Nathan concurred. 'Exactly. And then you came along.' He paused. 'So technically, any profits made from James' share of the mines now belongs to you. And as Damien has been looking after the accounts pertaining to those profits, they all belong to you too. I think you will find you are quite a wealthy woman in your own right. But as I said earlier, Damien and Daniel are sorting out the relevant paperwork, but no doubt you will be hearing from them soon.'

Jean just stared at the both of them, unsure of what to say or do. But as Nathan had said, it wasn't long before Damien and Daniel had sat Jean down with all the relevant paperwork and accounts. Now, Jean wasn't without sufficient means herself, but even she was quite shocked at the numbers involved. It was something she was still coming to terms with.

Now, as she walked through the Retreat's gardens she was brought back to the figure of Nathan while he set himself to digging over a large area of loam. She again considered what he was really thinking. As an empath himself, even if it wasn't necessarily to the levels that Jean could sense, she knew he probably felt the similar soup like affect that she did. She would have loved to know what he was really feeling now, but was relieved that he was also unlikely to sense the feeling that still churned inside her. She'd given up trying to dampen down their effect, and just put up with the knowledge that she was going to feel like a lovesick teenager for some time yet.

Nevertheless, despite Stephen's instance that it was Jean who was to be kept under a careful eye, for now she was prompted to consider that Nathan was more likely to be the one in need of supervision.

He looked up and smiled as she came to a halt beside him, offering him a cup of hot steaming tea that he took gratefully. He studied her for a moment.

'How are you feeling today?'

'Good, I'm sure there is no more need for everyone to fuss around as if I'm made of glass.'

Nathan held her gaze before speaking.

'You frightened the hell out of us...out of me. We just want to make sure you are alright. Besides, Stephen is enjoying himself.'

Sighing, Jean nodded and smiled.

'I'm sure you could find many more interesting things to do than babysitting me.'

'Nope, I'm quite happy, it's not often I get the chance to work in this garden now, so I'll take the opportunity while I can. Anyway, I enjoy the company.'

Jean saw a look pass across his face but couldn't discern its meaning, Nathan had taken a gulp of his tea and quickly looked away; earning a coughing fit as the hot liquid hit the back of his throat.

'Are *you* alright?'

Nathan nodded frantically as he tried to catch his breath. Then, as he regained some form of self composure, he started to laugh.

'What's so funny now?'

'It just occurred to me that Gellan and Duran have taken so much trouble to try and kill me off, and I nearly do them a service and choke on a hot cup of tea.'

Jean shook her head, and also started to laugh. It was good to see him look happy for once, even if it was just for a brief moment amongst his precious roses.

18

The

Militiaman

George jumped.

'FEWSON. What the bloody hell are you doing with that broom? I'd have had more luck sweeping the yard with a piss-pot for all the use you are at the moment.'

Flinching at the sudden roar in his left ear from Sergeant Ehring, he bit back a scathing retort. He'd been sweeping the yard for nigh on an hour now, but the wind was a nightmare. It wasn't a particularly large yard, but the wind blowing through the arch from the main parade ground, caused

239

swirls of debris to lift and scatter across its cobbled surface. Overlooked by the single storey buildings housing the garrison admin offices, George was painfully aware of eyes watching his hopeless progress in his task and he could feel his anger rising. Every time he managed to clear the space, a gust of wind would whip up his pile of leaves and debris, scattering them everywhere. He was just about to let his Sergeant know exactly what he could do with his piss-pot, when Ehring turned away and disappeared into the tool shed at the side of the yard.

At first, George thought he was to be, once more, left alone to tackle the fickle elements. Then a nasty suspicion crossed his mind. If Ehring returned with a piss-pot in his hands, he would come dangerously close to throwing his broom to the ground and storming out of the yard, and to hell with the consequences. But as the Sergeant approached, it became apparent that he was actually carrying a dustpan with a hinged lid and a hand brush.

'Look here Fewson, this place is notorious as a wind tunnel. If you think you can sweep it all in one go you'll be here forever. Tackle it a bit at a time, clearing up when you have a pile big enough to pick up. It may seem like more work, but it will be quicker in the long run.'

George took the dust pan and brush feeling ridiculous. It was obvious when you thought about it.

'I thought you were brought up on a farm Fewson?'

'I was, but we didn't have to pick up every twig and leaf that blew out of the trees. We'd never have got any work done.'

George had lost his mutinous glare, but still looked unhappy about his situation. He'd barely been in his new garrison, at Comston, for a week. He was the only full-time resident member of the Militia stationed there, while the rest of the barracks was made up of members of the Order. Major Dillon was the garrison Commander, with Captain Lee and two Lieutenants, along with Sergeant Ehring, making up the military personnel. There were civilians also working at the post, but they stayed in the village that had grown outside its walls. One of these was a full time cook, who came in daily to feed those who lived within the stronghold. Though he would be joined by another cook when the cadets arrived the following week.

Comston was predominantly a training establishment for the instruction of Militia within the North West of Lorimar. While it had been quiet during the previous five years of Ephea's regime, there was a renewed effort to once more build up the Militia numbers within the Empire. Until the new cadets arrived, George had the feeling he was so low in the pecking order, he doubted he even registered as having a rank.

While he brooded over the unfortunate lot of his life, Ehring had been studying him. The knight was himself not long out of Pernia, having just passed his final training at the Citadel there. Comston was his first post and he was desperate to make a good first impression. Especially as Major Dillon was a veteran of more than one of the Emperor's campaigns outside of the Empire, and she didn't suffer fools gladly. George, however, wasn't happy that the

241

Sergeant's progress through the Order was going to be at his expense.

'Look Fewson, I know it seems bloody stupid sweeping a yard on a windy day. But if you think of it as less of a chore and more of a challenge, you'll find life a lot easier.'

Taken aback by the knight's sudden change in attitude, George was confused.

'What do you mean?'

Ehring looked down at the remains of the last pile George had endeavoured to sweep up.

'If you look at this as a chore, you'll eventually get so frustrated, you'll either break the broom handle over your knee and storm out of the garrison, which I wouldn't advise, as I would have to be the one to bring you back and I won't be happy. Or, you'll be sweeping by the light of a half dozen orbs at midnight.

'If however, you see it as a challenge, then you begin to look for ways to overcome the problem. 'The young knight sighed. 'No-one is out to get you. It's just about teaching your brain to think in a different way. Soon we will receive our next intake of trainee Militia. They'll be from all walks of life, and have varying degrees of experience. But they've all volunteered, and we will all have to muck in to make sure we get the best out of them.

'As you are our resident, full-time member of the Militia, they will probably spend a lot of time running to you with the most ridiculous of problems. You'll be their font of knowledge when they haven't a clue what they are doing. It's my job to make sure you are capable of handling that responsibility. Do you understand now?'

242

George nodded. 'Yes, I understand.'

'Good lad, now get this bloody yard swept.'

The young man watched the knight walk away before setting his mind back to his task thoughtfully. Ehring had told him he had a purpose after all in his new home. It may not be a huge responsibility, but he had a job to do, a place at the table next to the Order. He might not be there yet, but it was a start.

Resuming his sweeping with a renewed vigour, he thought back to when he was at Fallport, his first stop on his journey with his new career in the Militia. He had a fierce fire still burning in his chest, determined to overcome the frightened animal he had been when Johnston had humiliated him in front of Niall and Jean.

He had spent so long building up the frustration and fury within, that when someone gave him the opportunity to vent his anger, it had been with violent consequences. The chance to become someone more than just George Fewson had kept him focused on his travels to Comston, a garrison some eighty miles South East of Parva. It was a relatively small fortification, with a village springing up alongside as the knights within looked for a respite from the confines of the garrison when off duty.

During the five years the Order had been effectively confined to barracks, Comston had become a quiet, small community. Now that life was coming back to normality, and the Militia were requiring more troops for training, Comston was once more becoming a busy little community again.

Before his posting at Comston, George spent some time at Fallport, the nearest garrison, to Niall and his family on

243

their farm. It had been a tearful departure from a home he had come to love and until recently, expected to spend the rest of his life. But all of that had changed and he was looking forward to his new life in the army. At Fallport, he had joined with other men and women wishing to make up the local branch of their Militia, and where his initial training had taken place. The Militia was predominantly made up of members who already had full time work in civilian life, and their role was to make up military numbers if and when required.

No-one expected to have to actually go into battle, that's what the knights were for, surely!

However, George was there on a full time capacity. He spent much of his time at Fallport, when he wasn't training with the others, helping out at the garrison. He had already proved his worth with the horses, and he was even spared the more menial work in the kitchens in order to help out in the stables. He had spent his entire life working with animals, but it was working with Jean that had given him the confidence to demonstrate how much they trusted him.

But it hadn't come easy, the first few weeks had seen him given the most unpleasant duties as punishments for causing arguments and fights with the rest of the cadets. Though his undoing, and main reason for reassessing his situation, was when he decided to piss off an old knight called Raynard, without doubt, the biggest knight George had ever seen. Raynard had arrived at Fallport after travelling on the road for over a week. No-one knew what he was actually there for, except that he had gone directly to the garrison commander on his arrival. He was exhausted, hungry and desperate to quench his thirst with a decent pint in the adjacent Town of Fallport. George didn't go out of his way to annoy the knight, but when he started a scuffle with Carrie — a butcher's boy from Rassen — and Raynard's pint went flying, it was the last straw. Raynard had bodily picked George up, which was no mean feat considering George was not a small man, and taken him outside the inn. Then pinning him again the wall had placed his angry face so close to George's, their noses nearly touched.

'What the hell is wrong with you boy?'

George shook his head desperately.

'Nothing Sir. I'm so sorry!'

'Then why can't an honest man sit at his table, eat a meal and enjoy a drink, without idiots like you causing fights?'

'It was just a misunderstanding Sir. A difference of opinion that got out of hand.'

Raynard, still holding the front of George's shirt, stood back and looked at him.

'Have I seen you up at the garrison?'

'Yes Sir, I took your horse when you arrived, I'm training with the Militia. I'm a permanent member of staff there.'

'What did you do?'

George blinked. 'Pardon?'

'What did you do that gave you a choice between the Militia or prison?'

George felt himself flush, he was thankful the light was poor so the old knight didn't see his embarrassment.

'I was in a fight and someone accidentally got hurt.'

Raynard shook his head and let go of the younger man.

'So they palmed a no good, useless, hothead onto the Order instead of filling up their own cells.'

George bristled. 'I am not useless. I'm here because one day I am going to join the Order myself.'

The knight just stood and looked at him for a moment in stunned silence, then threw back his head and let out an almighty roar of laughter. George was mortified and leapt at the knight, intending to hit out with all the force of his anger that he could. But, instead, the knight swerved to the side and shoved the lad onto the dusty cobbles of the road. George was already making his way to his feet when he turned and came face to face with the wrong end of a very sharp sword blade.

'Stay down lad, it would be wise for you to not act rashly right now.'

George couldn't take is eyes off the blade, and settled himself down on the ground, not daring to move. Satisfied, that George was calm once more and that he had his full attention, Raynard sheathed his sword.

'I think you've had enough for one night lad, get off back to your barracks and get an early night.' He started to make his way back into the inn when he turned back and grinned. 'You're going to need it.'

George frowned at the knight's back, but did as he was told. He had got away with it once with the old knight, but he doubted he would do so again.

The next morning, George was woken early by the night watch. He was told he was to be accompanying Raynard when he travelled today, so to be up and ready to leave by daybreak. George couldn't believe his luck, he was actually going out on Order business. He washed and got dressed in his Militia uniform as fast has he could. It didn't take long for him to saddle a horse and be mounted, ready for the knight when he left.

Raynard eventually came out of the barracks and crossed towards the stables where a groom was standing waiting with his horse. While donning his riding gloves he spied George watching him, waiting. He indicated to the groom to wait and approached George with a frown etched upon his forehead.

'And what exactly do you think you are doing?'

George looked confused.

'Sir, I was told to be ready to leave with you this morning while you ride out.'

Raynard nodded his head.

'That is quite right, I did. But I didn't say anything about you riding a horse, and I suggest you take that uniform off too.' He ignored George's look of shock and indignation. 'When you can control your temper and can enter an establishment without brawling, you may earn the right to polish the buttons on that uniform young man. Until then you can wear the clothes of the common man, and you can walk until I'm satisfied you are worthy of more than cleaning the shit off that beast's backside. Now get down and go and change. I'll give you five minutes before I leave, after that you can run and catch up.'

With that, Raynard turned on his heel and made his way to his own horse. George was mortified, by now the rest of the garrison was waking up to the new day and people were already moving around. Many of which were looking curiously at Raynard and George.

'Four minutes lad.' Raynard bellowed.

One of the grooms rushed out and took hold of George's reins. 'Don't keep him waiting Fewson, get moving.'

George dismounted and rushed to his barracks. Pulling off his uniform he climbed into his own clothes, wiping angrily at the tears of shame that fell down his face. By the time he had reached the main gates, Raynard was walking his horse through them. Without even looking his way he shouted down to the stricken young man.

'Well done lad, well done.'

George said nothing, he kept his head down as he passed the knights on the gates and walked beside Raynard's horse in mortified silence.

The rest of the day had George running errands for the knight. He carried notes to various people around the countryside, they would then read the note, write something in reply and then seal the note before handing it back to George. For two days George said nothing, but continued on with his tasks, assuming that the knight had important work that required much secrecy. If nothing else, he would prove that he could be trusted and not let the knight down, even if he didn't like him, he was a member of the Order; and George desperately wanted to get his uniform back.

On the third day, George had been delivering his third note of the morning to a shop in a quiet little village, he gave a note to the woman to whom it was addressed and waited, as usual, for her to open it, write her reply and seal it. The woman wasn't alone however, her daughter was also there.

248

She was about the same age as George, and she was intrigued by all the cloak and dagger of the situation. Looking over the woman's shoulder she started to giggle, George frowned.

'You shouldn't be looking at that, what do you think you are doing?'

The girl looked up and bit her lip.

'I'm sorry, but it is funny.'

George was furious.

'How dare you, this is Order business, you shouldn't even be here. I will report your actions to Captain Raynard.'

The girl put her hand to her face and started to laugh again.

'Mother, please tell him, you can't let him leave without knowing.'

'It says I shouldn't say anything.'

The girl frowned, and took the note from her mother.

'I don't care what the note says, here you should read this. I don't know why he has done this, but it doesn't seem right to me. I'm sorry.'

George was totally confused, he was torn between proving his trust to the Order, and wanting to know what the girl was talking about. In the end, the girl sighed and read the details out to him.

'*Please read this note in silence, the lad has no idea what this errand is for so please do not tell him, just acknowledge receipt and return it, sealed.* It then goes on to confirm an order for cheese for the garrison at Fallport. That's what my mother does, she makes cheese.'

He felt sick and a hot redness began to rise up his cheeks to the roots of his hair. The girl and her mother watched him with a mixture of amusement and pity; he turned and ran out of the house. He saw the knight sitting on his horse waiting for him to return, his forearms resting easy on the saddle. George wanted to drag him down to the ground and hit him until his smug face was a bloody mess; but then the girl came out behind him.

'Well Sir, I am sure you have quite enjoyed your joke, but this house does not take kindly to ridiculing others for your own amusement. Here is your reply from my mother, I hope you are pleased with yourself.'

She threw the note on the ground in front of the horse and stalked back towards the house, glancing at George as she passed, her anger reflecting George's own. A few passing people looked around at the disturbance, some even openly stood and stared, hoping for more of a spectacle. But George had had enough of being the centre of other people's jokes and now he just glared, daring the knight to laugh. But Raynard didn't laugh, instead he got down from his horse and picked up the note still lying on the ground. Then taking up the reins he started to lead his horse back up the road that led out the village. Looking over to George, he inclined his head and just said. 'Come on lad. Let's find somewhere to talk.'

They walked for a while, Raynard leading his horse, with George a short way behind, scowling at the knight's back. Eventually they stopped under the shade of some trees and Raynard opened one of his packs, handing out some bread and cheese along with a canteen of water.

'Here, take this.'

George just looked at him and did nothing.

'Starving yourself is not going to help you.'

The young man took the food begrudgingly, but only because he was particularly hungry, though he would be damned if he would admit it. They both ate in silence for a while before Raynard spoke.

'I suppose you want to know what this has all been about?'

'I doubt if wanting to humiliate someone and then go back and laugh about it with everyone back at the garrison, requires much explanation.'

'Is that what you think this was about? Wanting to humiliate you?'

'What else has it gained?'

'Well, for a start, I've managed to ensure the garrison's stores will be well stocked for winter.' George gave him a black look. 'But that isn't what you want to know is it?'

George just looked away.

'I know who you are. I know that you have spent the years since the death of your father working for Niall and Dana on their farm.' That caught the young man's attention. 'Oh yes, I know Niall very well, he was my Lieutenant before he earned his promotion. A good man, such a shame what happened.'

They both sat in silence for a moment, considering the horror that had befallen Niall, forcing his early retirement from a career he loved. Then Raynard spoke again.

'I also know that you have quite the friendship with this mysterious Jean Carter who has recently gained the favour

251

of the Emperor and the Knights. Even to the point where Lord Stephen himself has put a recommendation forward for you.' He gave a small laugh. 'I see by the look on your face you didn't know that. But it's true, somewhere, and somehow, you have managed to convince one of the most powerful men in the Empire that you are good enough, to not only wear the uniform of the Militia, but to possibly reach the heights of the Order. It's just a shame that you don't have the same faith as they do.'

George sat up straight. 'What does that mean? You are the one who made me take my uniform off, made be walk beside you as you rode along like a prince with a pole shoved up his arse.'

Raynard blinked, then let out a bellowing laugh.

'A prince with a pole shoved up his arse. That's a new one on me I have to admit.'

As he laughed, George tried to stay angry, but the knight's humour was too infectious, soon he was chuckling too, and eventually he had to succumb and join in.

'Now that is better. A man that is willing to laugh at himself can laugh at the world without guilt.'

'What does that mean?'

'It means young man, that you are so full of anger for yourself, how can you possibly be anything but angry with the world.'

'What makes you think I'm angry with me?'

'Aren't you?'

George made to reply, then thought about it, before nodding his head.'

'I suppose I am.'

'Talk about it, come on. We have plenty of time, that was the last supplier I needed to see, so we have all afternoon.' George frowned and Raynard sighed. 'It took you this long to find out what this charade was all about, I was concerned I would have to start making errands up.'

'But it was a secret, all the subterfuge.'

'I never once told you that what we were doing was secret, all you had to do was ask. But you were so full of anger, you let the obvious pass you by. Don't let your emotions cloud your judgement, one day it may get you killed. Now, tell me what is eating you up inside.'

And so George told him all about Jean coming to the farm, and Johnson and her thugs, about Niall and Layne and the picnic up by the falls. He found that once he started to speak he couldn't stop, and everything came out. His humiliation at the hands of Johnson, and how useless and guilty he had felt when he was forced to lead them to the family he loved so dearly. Raynard listened and said nothing until George had finally finished.

'Aye, that would account for the anger, and even why you would want join the Militia, to make sure that next time you would be in a position to help your family. But why the Order? Why go that far? Has it always been something you wanted to do?'

George sighed and shook his head. 'If I'm honest, no. I was brought up a farmhand, and the only aspirations I really had was to maybe own a smallholding myself one day. But now? Now I want to be more than just someone who has achieved what he expected. Yes, I want to be able to protect my family, but I want more than that now. I want to make a difference so that I don't have to react to the next bully who comes along, I want to make sure that bully doesn't want to come along in the first place.' George looked up and caught Raynard's eye. 'Does that sound ridiculous?'

'No lad, that's not ridiculous at all, I understand exactly what you mean. The question is, how much do you want to achieve that?'

'More than anything, I really do believe I can do this.'

'Aye, and I believe you. But unless you learn to keep that anger of yours in check, it will never happen.'

George looked down at his hands. 'I understand.'

'Do you?'

'Yes.' He sat up straight. 'Yes, I do understand. I also realise how much of an idiot I've been.'

'Ah well, we all feel like at times. Some of us more than others, but it's how you react and deal with it that counts.'

Raynard looked at his watch. 'We had better get moving if we are going to get back to Fallport in time for dinner.' He stood, and taking his horse's reins he mounted up. 'Here give me your hand, we'll be a lot faster if we don't have to wait for you to trip over every other stone on the road.'

George grinned and taking the knight's hand pulled himself up behind.

'Besides, we need to get moving, you've got a lot of buttons to polish on that uniform or yours.'

Both men laughed amiably this time as Raynald urged his horse forward, back to the garrison of Fallport.

Bringing his mind back to his sweeping task at Comston, George smiled at the memory whilst he dumped the last of the cleared yard in the bin. Ehring stuck his head out of a door and shouted to him to hurry up, and that dinner was ready. Still grinning, George made his way inside as his stomach reminded him it was indeed time for dinner.

19

An Unlikely Encounter

Andy Lawrence savoured his pint of London Pride as the golden, amber liquid passed smoothly down his throat. Licking his lips he placed the glass down on the dark, well worn, wooden table in front of him. He could hear the voice of the man sitting opposite droning on, but chose to ignore him. It had been a long time since he had sat in The George Inn, a listed pub in London made famous by Charles Dickens, and frequented by tourists and workers of the city alike. It was noisy, with business in full swing; they had been lucky to get a table in the corner. It was only due to Fred's insistence that the two lads, in their cheap Marks and Spencer's suits, no longer wanted to utilise the space, that they had managed to acquire it at all.

Now, six men huddled around the wooden table, heads close so they could all hear what was being said. All except Andy, he had no idea what made him come to this meeting, Fred had said it was an opportunity to get back at the Empire for the shit they had had to put up with over the last few months. Andy, didn't really care, he was glad to be back on Earth, and would rather put the whole awful experience behind him.

It was only because a few years ago, his Mrs had called the cops on him that he decided to make himself scarce. She had never bothered about the odd bruise before; silly cow should have been thankful he kept her safe. But apparently she had met some women who had formed a group. Next thing he knows, she's got a pepper spray and running up the stairs to the bathroom screaming that the police are on their way.

Fuck, this was all her fault.

He gripped the glass again and took another mouthful of beer. Glances from Fred reminded him he needed to keep his temper under control. Good old Fred, he was always there when he needed him. Not willing to wait around to have to explain to the police that the silly bitch was just overreacting and always was a drama queen, he had landed on Fred's doorstep when his friend had other visitors. Turned out they were recruiting for some bird called Ephea who was having a bit of husband trouble, and 'did we want to earn a bit of easy cash?'

It seemed like a good idea at the time. That was until some seriously voodoo shit started going down. It was nearly a week before he and Fred had finally accepted they hadn't been drugged and were actually on another planet, on the other side of the universe. However, once reality had set in, they were disappointed that apparently aliens were just like them — and not even an electric socket to charge his phone either. But it was easy money as they had said, and for most of the time they were just throwing their weight around, keeping the locals in check.

They had been sent to the city of Lorimar on the East Coast of the land also called Lorimar. He and Fred had soon made sure everyone knew he was in charge, seeing as he was the biggest after all. Despite the prominence of Lorimar as the principle city of the area, it was quite small in relation to the Imperial city of Parva. The people here were tougher however, working most of their lives on the fertile land that Lorimar was famous for. At first there was a fair bit of resistance when the Patrols had arrived, and they thought they were in trouble when Lord Damien, the Duke of Lorimar himself had turned up. He had listened to his people's pleas for help, but instead of eradicating the Patrols from the city, he had turned away and left its people to their fate. The will of the people had crumbled not long after that, feeling abandoned and cheated. When news of cities within the rest of the Empire had also suffered the same treatment, Andy could almost watch the fire die in the peoples' eyes. After that it had been easy.

Until that day. The Midsummer Festival the locals called it. It had been late in the afternoon in Lorimar when news arrived that a battle had taken place in Parva. And whatever shackles Ephea had wrapped round the Emperor, had finally been stripped away. The Knights were once more in charge and they let the knights of the Order out of their cages. If nothing else, Andy had been impressed with the speed at which the Patrols had been hunted down by the Order and the police. Only because Andy and Fred had been lucky enough to be near one of the public portals, had they managed to overpower the public officials who regulated the gates. They were never sure what the fate of those two men was, but one had at least a broken arm and possibly a broken jaw; the other one however, was losing a lot of blood from the stab wound that Fred had expertly applied. But they didn't care, they had managed to finally get off the world of Kelan and back to Earth. Even if it was only with the clothes they had on their backs, at least they were alive, and they didn't have to face the prospect of time in the prison at Belan.

Of course, now the problem was, those members of the Patrols that had managed to escape, also knew that there were active members of the Order working on Earth. Many a time Andy and Fred had talked about telling the world about their exploits on Kelan, all about life on other worlds. But who was going to believe them? And of course, as soon as they opened their mouths they would probably have half a dozen knights knocking on their doors. No, it wasn't worth the hassle.

So, here they were, sitting in a pub in Southwark along with three other ex-patrol members, listening to some ex-

Order member droning on about how hard done by he'd been.

Tosser.

Andy didn't like him as soon as the little creep entered the bar. He'd worked his way across the floor between groups of people drinking, and still managed to look like an oily slime ball without having to say a word. Once Bales had told them who he was — it was less of an introduction and more of a proclamation — he had well and truly ensured that no-one was going to trust him; he was lucky it was chucking it down outside and they still had their pints to finish, or they would have all told him to piss off right there and then.

He had whined on about how the Emperor and some bird called Jean had managed to ruin a nice cushy number he'd been enjoying under the patronage of Ephea — whatever that meant. Gathered around him, the Patrol members had watched with distaste as he picked up his half pint of lager with both hands and proceeded to sip his drink as if it would choke him if he took a decent gulp. He gave them all the creeps.

At last Bales had stopped speaking and sat in silence at the table. His fingers perched on the wooden surface as if he would fall off his stool if he let go. Andy shook his head to himself. He would be the first to admit that there was very little love lost between himself and the Order, but even he knew that they were men and women you would think twice about pissing off. They were well trained, highly disciplined and ferociously loyal to the Knights and the Emperor.

So how the fuck did you become a General?

260

Becoming aware that Bales was now staring straight at him, Andy had a horrible cold chill run down his back. While the others followed Bales' gaze, Andy tried to think of ways to get the focus off himself.

'Oi, Vic. How come all you lot have the same names as us then? Like your boss Nathan and all that? Are you all closet Englishmen at heart?'

The other men around the table sniggered into their own beers; peering over their glasses, waiting for Bales' response. They were surprised when it came.

'I beg your pardon?'

Andy was warming to his theme now and grinned. 'Well, look at you, *Vic*, I had a cousin called Vic. Right tosser he was too.'

Andy glanced at the others, who were beginning to enjoy the game.

Bales took another agonisingly long time to pick up his glass and sip at the contents, before placing it slowly down onto the beer mat in front of him. It was a few minutes before he raised his eyes to meet Andy's.

'The name Victor, is a very old and traditional name on the world of Candor. It became popular on Earth when it was adopted as a name by the Romans when a Candorian by that name helped them conquer the savages that plagued the area at that time. Let's face it, if it wasn't for the input from the Empire over the centuries, the people of Earth would still be living in the slime and filth of the swamps. Nathan may be a fool to allow the people of the Empire to gain so many privileges, but even he had to appreciate that, without not a considerable amount of help, Earth needed quite a large *leg*

261

up on the road to civilisation. In my view, you've still a long way to go.'

Ignoring the dark looks of the men around him, Bales picked up his drink again, then seeming to think better he put his glass back down.

'So what are you saying? Nathan, Damien and all the other Knights have influenced Earth's history so much that their names were adopted? Even I know they are names in the bible.'

Bales didn't even bother to hide his contempt. 'Yes, you idiot. Nathan and the Knights are ten thousand years old; you were still trapped in the last ice age when they were born. Though in your case your mother was probably still swinging through the trees.'

Andy's anger rose, and despite Fred's urgings to sit down, he had leaned across the table and grabbed the front of Bales' shirt. He was pleased to see the little git flinch, fear emanating from every pore. Other people in the bar began to look around and, feeling Fred's hand on his arm, forced himself to let go of Bales and sit back down. It didn't stop him from speaking his mind though.

'Look here you little shit. I have better things to do than listen to your winging on about how the Empire has done you wrong. I'm here for the money, so let's get to the point, then we can all fuck off home and never have to see your ugly mug again.' He sat and stared belligerently at Bales. 'Besides if it wasn't for that bloody Carter woman, your precious Knights would all be dead now.'

Andy smirked at the look of confusion on Bales' face.

262

'Carter woman? You mean Jean Carter? What does she have to do with anything?'

Andy and Fred shared looks with the other Patrol members.

'You don't know?'

Bales shook his head slowly, he didn't look so comfortable now. Andy crossed his arms across his chest; feeling smug that he had finally got one up on the pompous prat.

'It was the morning of the Midsummer Festival, load of armed soldiers attacked the city of Parva, a few of your comrades copped it on the way. They were all set to see off old Nathan and his boys, when Carter dropped by and the whole plan went tits up. Quite an impressive massacre from what we heard. Then the Emperor did a resounding speech and now everyone's licking his arse again. So him and the Knights and that Carter bird went off to fight another day.'

Bales slumped down in his seat. This was obviously news to him.

'What happened afterwards?'

Andy shrugged his shoulders.

'No idea, don't give a shit. That's all we heard before we did a runner on account of a few pissed off members of the Order with one or two scores to settle.'

It took a few moments, but eventually Bales looked up, his face once more an impassive mask.

'This is all very well, but Jean Carter won't be interfering in any of our plans from now on?'

'Oh, yeah? And how would you know that?'

'Because I know that *Miss Carter* has fallen foul of a vicious knife attack recently. She won't be bothering anyone else, anymore.'

Fred then sat up. 'You talking about the knife attack in Plymouth a few weeks ago?'

It was Bales turn to smirk this time. 'Indeed, I believe it was.'

'Well maybe you should be more thorough from now on mate. It says here that the woman who was attacked was operated on by some guy at the scene. Apparently she's alive and expected to make a full recovery.'

The colour drained from Bales' face. Fred and Andy grinned at each other and the sound of chuckling could be heard coming from the rest of the table. But slowly the mirth began to ebb away, even the people standing around, drinking amongst their own friends, seemed to sense a change in the atmosphere.

Bales stared at Fred and then at Andy. Blinking slowly he sat himself up as straight as his stature would allow. Once more Andy felt the feeling of cold dread start to climb up his spine, he felt he could never be warm again. The life in the ex-knight's eyes seemed to drain away, leaving the feeling of death and emptiness in their gaze.

Bales spoke quietly, his voice held no emotion at all.

'A week today, meet at this address, 10 o'clock. Don't be late.'

Bales stood up, leaving a scrap of paper on the beer stained table, an address was scrawled across its rumpled surface. Then, turning on his heel, he left the pub without another word. People standing in his way moved aside, unsure why they didn't want the creepy little guy to touch them.

Around the table, the five remaining men stared at the paper that rested on the table. Picking up Bales' forgotten half pint, Andy drained the glass and placed it back on the table with a dull thud, before making a declaration to the rest of the group.

'Twat.'

There was agreement all around the table, followed by sniggering and finishing of drinks, but there was the unmistakable air of fear that rested among them now. Andy stood up and made his way to the bar.

'So, who's up for another round?'

Fred watched his friend cross the room and then glanced at the other men at the table. He got the distinct impression he wasn't the only one who had an uneasy feeling in the pit of his stomach.

20

Family Ties

n athan glanced at his watch again.

Where the hell is Jean? She should have been home an hour ago.

He started to pace around the room, head down, in deep thought. Sensing Stephen watching from his seat at the kitchen table made him even more on edge. Nathan stopped and glared out of the windows, over the landscape beyond the walled garden, before closing his eyes and letting his breath out slowly; trying to settle his thoughts. He would rather have kept Jean at the Retreat after leaving the hospital at Aria, but she had insisted that she wanted to get back to doing some useful work. Even to the point of making some barely veiled threats if she wasn't allowed to leave soon.

However, despite Nathan's protests, Stephen was determined to give Jean a clean bill of health.

And so it was, they had finally returned to Denfield, and if he had to be honest with himself, he had to admit that he was glad to be back home; he just wished that Jean wasn't so damn independent and oblivious to the danger she was in.

Since their return to Denfield, Jean had been determined to pass her driving test, whilst taking up the reins of the running of the house with his housekeeper Janet. Who was apparently pleased that she could spend more time with her grandchildren now they were growing up, both here in England and abroad in New Zealand. Nathan had initially been quite put out that Janet hadn't talked to him about her desire to spend more time with her family. When he had asked why she hadn't said anything before, she replied that she simply didn't want to let him down. This of course made him feel even more guilty for a number of days afterwards, and he had taken to making himself scarce when Janet came on the one day that she had agreed with Jean to help out.

Eventually, Jean had decided that running a house with just the two of them rattling around in it wasn't going to tax her very much, setting her sights on Tom Fairbanks, Nathan's estate manager. He was sceptical at first, but soon he was happy enough for Jean to take on much of the responsibility once Nathan had given his blessing. As such, she was often seen working with the estate's tenant farmers and overseeing the general upkeep of estate properties rented out.

Nathan wondered at times whether he should be put out with how much Jean had taken an interest in his affairs; but she insisted that she had to do something to pay back his generosity, and besides, she hadn't enjoyed her work so much in years. Of course he hadn't argued, it was good to spend evenings discussing the day's business of the house and its estate. With all the extra work that had built up over the past five years, it was one thing less to worry about, and he had to admit, Jean was very good at it.

But he couldn't get the simple worry, worming away around his brain, that Bales had tried to kill Jean once, and it was more than likely that the horrible little bastard was now working very closely with Gellan and Duran.

And now Jean was late!

Stephen was still watching him from across the room. It was the doctor who had called the meeting, and Jean knew that he was adamant that she should be there. Nathan smiled, despite himself, when he considered that, although the issues with Ephea had passed, meetings still often took place at Denfield rather than at the Palace or the Retreat.

He checked his watch again, just as Damien and Daniel arrived. Stephen had asked that only the eight of them be present, which was intriguing in itself. Nathan usually tried to include partners in most of their meetings. As it was ironically still a whole new experience for any of them to have the opportunity to conduct their own private relationships, he wanted to make sure everyone partook in most informal discussions where possible. Daniel had even gone so far to call them *family meetings,* and despite Nathan's efforts, the name had stuck. So, for this *family meeting* to take place with just the Knights and Jean was unusual. Stephen was being deliberately mysterious about the point of their gathering, however. This was yet another reason why he wanted Jean to get there quickly; he wanted to know what was going on, he didn't like surprises.

There was a sudden loud noise coming from the hall, followed by Jean's voice apologising.

'Sorry. Only me. Dropped the bloody box.'

Feeling relief wash over him, Nathan hurried to the hall with the others to see Jean shaking her coat off and hanging it up on the hooks by the door. Before hefting a large cardboard box, that had obviously seen better days, across the hall to the kitchen. As she passed the Knights, she saw the looks of confusion on their faces and grinned.

'Toys from the Banks family for the 'bring and buy sale' in the church hall this weekend. Asked if I could drop them off at the vicarage.'

Then, without another word she took the box through to the boot room situated beside the kitchen, and came back to wash her hands in the sink.

Nathan hadn't said anything since she arrived, but when Jean took one look at his face, he knew she had figured out what he was thinking.

'Nathan, I am so sorry I'm late. It seems everyone has something to gripe about at the moment, so of course everything took longer. No excuses though, I simply didn't notice how late it was.' Nathan still wasn't happy and Jean came up to him, placing her hand on his arm, her voice lowered as she spoke. 'I really am sorry, I promise to be more careful next time.'

He felt the eyes of the others watching him again, he had to fight the urge to take hold of Jean and tell her how afraid he had been, how close he had been to translocating to wherever she was, and to hell with what anyone thought. But instead, he just inclined his head and mumbled something about not letting it happen again. The way Jean looked at him suggested she understood exactly how he felt. He also thought he saw concern cross her face too.

At that moment Paul, Simon and John arrived and were making their way through the French windows. But Nathan didn't miss Daniel and Damien's troubled glances in his direction when they thought he wasn't looking. However, for now, all concerns were put aside, as greetings were made and the important details of making teas and coffees for everyone was sorted. Paul had brought a particularly delicious looking cake that Daniel decided needed protecting from John and Simon's hungry eyes.

'Hands off you two, everyone else gets a bit first.'

Simon looked hurt. 'What exactly does that mean?'

'It means your portions always seem considerably larger than anyone else's, so you'll have to wait.'

Daniel then compounded his point by taking the cake away, finding the biggest carving knife he could, before proceeding to slice the cake up into equal portions.

Simon was indignant. 'That's just bloody rude.'

John agreed and without another word both seemed to feel it was necessary that this process required adjudication. The irony that Daniel, as the highest ranking Judge in the Empire, was to be scrutinised in cutting up a cake fairly, didn't go un-noticed by the rest of the room. By the time the cake was placed on the table by Daniel, Simon and John had also sat themselves heavily on the seat either side of him; a little too close for comfort judging by the look on Daniel's face.

They were all seated on the sofas around the wood burning stove situated at one end of the large kitchen. Though it was unlit due to the unseasonally warm weather at the end of September.

By the time the refreshments and cake had deemed to be equally shared out amongst the eight of them, Stephen was practically dancing in his seat in anticipation for them to get the meeting started. His interest, further aroused by the doctor's agitation, encouraged Nathan to get the proceedings started. Smiling at the man now glaring at him, he suggested that he finally take the floor and let them know what was so important.

As the doctor stood and faced everyone, the room became silent and all eyes were on him as he began.

'Well, as we have all stuffed ourselves on cake, I'll try to get to the point before you start to fall asleep. As you know, a few weeks ago, Jean was unfortunate enough to be attacked in Plymouth and suffered an almost fatal stabbing. While she was in Aria I took the opportunity to take a blood sample for analysis, and before anyone says anything, yes I did get permission!'

He rolled his eyes at Jean who grinned back.

'As you also know, there is a databank containing all the DNA taken as standard now of members of the Order; included in this is our own. However, these samples have alway remained completely separate from analysis, for obvious reasons. Until now that is.

271

No doubt, you all know that I am not the most computer literate man around. My job is to put people back together, I have no idea about all this technical stuff.

However, over the past few years, there has been a continuing effort to add all DNA samples to a computer database. I'm not going to say whether I'm for or against the idea, but I'm keeping an eye on progress. Anyway, as mentioned before, all details of our own DNA samples have been deliberately kept separate from this database. That is until one of my more exuberant lab technicians had entered Jean's DNA into his computer and decided to, *have a look around,* his words, not mine.'

Stephen glanced around at the faces watching him and smiled.

'It seems there are quite a few surprises hidden amongst the depths of our collective family history.'

Nathan narrowed his eyes, he wasn't sure if he was ready for any nasty surprises, but Stephen now had the bit between his teeth and he was going to tell all, whether Nathan liked it or not.

'First of all, our young laboratory technician decided to do a full comparison of all our DNA, including Jean's, and see what came up. Before you say anything, when I first heard what he had to say, I had his findings checked independently, and then did a separate check myself. Each time, the results came back the same.'

Everyone looked at each other and then back at Stephen, it wasn't often he was this animated about his work outside of a medical lecture. They were all thoroughly intrigued

272

now, especially when he turned specifically to Daniel and grinned.

'Daniel, as you, and everyone else here knows, it's been some years since you found out that James, who we all thought was your step-brother from Malin's previous marriage, was in fact, your real father.'

Stephen's face softened as he watched his friend deal with several emotions at once. Daniel didn't speak at first, he just nodded before eventually replying.

'Well, James always was a secretive bastard, it would have been better to know beforehand that he was my father, rather than living for all that time thinking that bastard my mother was married to, was anything to do with me. But that was James for you, never did like doing anything the easy way.'

His fellow Knights nodded and smiled, while Jean looked on, bemused and curious; it seemed that James' reputation for being a charming rogue had continued long after his death. But they didn't have to wait to contemplate the further vagaries of James, as Stephen had started to talk again.

'But it has now come to our attention, that James may not have only consoled Daniel's mother, Perrin, throughout her miserable marriage.'

Daniel sat up, Simon and John had to physically move away as he brought himself to attention at the edge of his seat.

'What are you saying?'

For the first time, Stephen paused, whatever he had to say was going cause a reaction, and he wasn't sure which way it would go. He took a moment before delivering the next bit of information.

'You have a brother amongst us. One of us was also fathered by our rather promiscuous James.'

The Knights all stared at Daniel, then back at Stephen, who was obviously now thoroughly enjoying himself.

'Stephen.' Nathan's voice was dangerously low. 'If you have something to say, then do so, or you will very likely be strung up until you do. If they don't, I will.'

Stephen eyed the others and took his point, his gaze then rested deliberately on one Knight in particular and sighed.

'It's you Paul, you are Daniel's half brother.'

There was total silence in the room as everyone now stared at Paul, who just slowly shook his head in disbelief.

Then all of a sudden he jumped out of his seat and made his way to the other end of the kitchen, pacing and running his hands through his hair as if the action would somehow make this news easier to understand.

Nathan stood and took Stephen's arm, his face deadly serious.

'Are you absolutely sure about this?'

'Yes, I told you, I have checked the results myself. There is no doubt, James is the father of both Daniel and Paul.'

Nodding, he then looked over to Paul who was now standing by the French windows with his hands on his hips, he looked distraught. Nathan didn't blame him, he could only imagine how he felt at that moment; anger, confusion, relief?

Paul turned away and rubbed at his eyes, no-one in the room said anything, but Daniel went to him.

'Paul, I know this is a shock, especially after all this time, but at least you know now.'

'But why didn't he say anything? After everything that happened, why couldn't he just let us know?'

'I wish I could answer that, I really do. I always put it down to the fact he never wanted responsibility, hated being in one place for too long. Children didn't really fit into to the lifestyle he had created for himself.'

'But him, that bastard Josh.' Paul began to raise his voice as emotion began to well up inside him. 'I thought he was part of me. I've spent all this time terrified I was going to become like him, and it turns out we're not even related!'

Paul's anger burst out, but Daniel didn't flinch, he didn't even move. Balling his fists, Paul looked as if he was going to hit something, or someone. He became agitated as he moved about the kitchen space. When he spoke, they weren't sure if he was speaking to anyone in particular or the room as a whole.

'It's over? I don't have to second guess everything anymore? Everything he did, to my mother, to me and my brothers, it's nothing to do with me?'

Daniel smiled. 'Paul, we never thought you would be like him, irrespective of who your real father was. The only one who doubted yourself was you.'

Paul seemed to slump, as if finally giving up a futile fight, leaning against a kitchen worktop. Daniel moved to his side and put his arm around his shoulders. Paul lifted his face to the man he had known all his life, but was now his new brother and hugged him.

It took a while until Nathan felt the waves of emotions, that had started to spin around the room, begin to settle. He looked at Jean, who sat quietly on the sofa beside him. When she returned his gaze he saw the effort it took for her to keep the commotion at bay. Only when Damien had taken the initiative to refill the tea and coffee, and had placed everything on the coffee table, did Nathan realise he had been holding Jean's hand. Guiltily, if reluctantly, he let go. A look from Damien told him he had seen it too but he said nothing, while Nathan tried to brush over the moment by talking to Stephen, he laughed as he stood.

'Well, if you wanted to create an impact Stephen, you definitely succeeded.'

Stephen shook his head.

'That was only part of what I've found out.' He eyed the replenished cups on the table. 'By the time I've finished you may want to bring out something a bit stronger.'

'There's more?'

'Oh yes, there's more. You might want to sit back down.'

By now everyone was back in their own seats on the sofa, they had all heard what Stephen had said, and like Nathan, looked as if they were bracing themselves. Stephen took up his position in front of the group again and began.

'I wish I could tell you Paul, that the emotional journey was finished, but I'm afraid there is still more to come.'

Paul looked shocked. 'What? Surely there can't be anything else?'

Stephen smiled. 'Bear with me. I said at the beginning that this all came about because Jean's DNA was added to our particular part of the databank. What the subsequent analysis brought up was quite surprising.'

Stephen turned to Jean, who didn't look too pleased about the prospect.

'It seems that Jean's selection as a fellow Guardian hasn't been a random act after all. The analysis has also shown that Jean, is in fact related to at least two members of this group.' He paused as he let this new bit of information settle in, but then continued when he saw the black look Nathan was giving him. 'Jean, your DNA shows that Paul, is in fact, your grandfather, or great-grandfather, certainly no further back than that.'

'That's impossible! How!'

Paul was out of his seat again, though this time he didn't move from the seating area, he was glowering at Stephen, who just shook his head.

'I don't think diagrams are necessary are they? All I can say is, at some point during the early part of the twentieth century, you conceived a child that would eventually lead to the birth of Jean.'

Paul looked as if he was going to argue, but then his face changed and he looked over at Jean; he looked stricken.

'I didn't know she was pregnant. I would never have left her alone if I'd known. I swear, I'm so sorry!'

Jean shook her head.

'I don't understand. Who are you talking about?'

'Ellie, Ellie Miles.'

Jean put her hand to her face and shook her head.

'She was my great-grandmother, her son William was my grandfather.'

'William? She had a son called William?'

'Yes, but she was married, my granddad had older, and younger, siblings.'

An uncomfortable silence now settled on the room. Paul sat down and looked away, putting his head in his hands.

'I know, but it wasn't what it looks like.'

'Really? Because it seems to only look one way to me.'

Paul frowned as Jean stared at him, daring him to say otherwise.

'At that time, the First World War was raging, Ellie and I met when we were all dealing with some pretty horrendous shit that was happening in Europe. The world had turned upside down and her husband had been away at the front for months. I'm not going to pretend. We were two people who sought comfort in each other, and neither of us had regrets about it. Had we, as Guardians, not been called away on a mission elsewhere in the universe, things may have been different. But by the time we finished and returned home, the war had become something we couldn't control. Earth at that time was a boiling pot of political turmoil, it was decades before it was deemed possible to do anything there that would have any positive impact. We withdrew and let the world get on with it.

'But if I knew Ellie was pregnant I would never have left her. Do you really think I would do that?'

Jean looked hard at him for a long while. Then she shook her head. 'No, I don't think you would have abandoned her if you knew. But that doesn't change the fact that she was married.'

Nathan agreed. 'No, it doesn't. But it happened nonetheless, and you are here today as a result of it.'

Jean spun round and glared at him.

'What if her husband had found out and threw her out?'

'Did he?'

'Well, no. Actually my grandfather always said he had a wonderful childhood.'

'Then that is all that matters.'

'The end justified the means?'

'No, of course it doesn't, but what is done is done. No-one can change that, so we carry on, knowing that Paul is your great-grandfather.' He thought for a moment then carried on. 'Of course, that also makes Daniel here, your great-uncle.'

Everyone looked at Daniel, who was now choking on the coffee he was drinking when Nathan hit him with this startling bit of information. When he finally caught his breath, he grinned. 'Well, this is turning into a productive day, I've gained a brother and a niece, all in the space of half an hour. Not bad going, even if I do say so myself.'

Jean shook her head and looked back at Paul, who by now looked distraught. She threw up her hands and sighed.

'Oh what the hell, I'm not angry with you Paul. It was just a bit of a shock that's all. I'm not going to judge anyone who had to live through those times. My grandfather was a lovely man, along with my grandmother; I wish you had had the opportunity to meet him.'

Paul gave her an emotional smile.

Nathan caught Stephen's eye. 'Have you finally finished with all of the surprises now? Shall I just fetch the brandy?'

But Stephen shook his head and Nathan's heart sank. 'Now what?'

Stephen shrugged. 'I'll wait for you to get the brandy.'

So, without another word, Nathan made his way to his cellar, he had a feeling this was going require at least two bottles. Using the time to think about everything he had heard so far from Stephen's revelations, he had to admit that despite the surprising content of his news, it was all positive on the whole. Paul had spent his entire life terrified he would end up like the man he thought was his father, and now he knows it was pointless.

He frowned, it didn't change the fact that if James had been honest from the start, both Paul and Daniel would have been spared a lot of unnecessary pain. But that was James for you. He had lived by his own rules and to hell with everyone else.

And then there was Jean, it made a lot more sense now that they knew her connection to the family, but again, the news came with a sting in the tail. Nathan thought back to the time when Paul must have met this elusive Ellie. It was true, times were very different for Earth back then, who was he to judge what happened between two people seeking solace in a world turned upside down?

But there was one bit of information that he couldn't deny had raised his spirits, if only for a short while. Jean was Daniel's great-niece, they were related closely by blood. He knew he should feel guilty for being glad over the news, but he didn't.

By the time he returned to the kitchen, everyone was talking amongst themselves. Paul and Jean were sitting next to each other in quiet conversation, and from his own seat, Daniel was watching them in silence.

Once the brandy had been passed around, Jean had chosen to have more tea, everyone again sat back in their chairs, bracing themselves in anticipation for Stephen's next revelation.

Nathan stretched out his legs and crossed his arms.

'Well, come on then Stephen, let's have it.'

Stephen grinned and looked out at the wary faces watching him.

'First of all, unlike the last two discoveries, this next bit of information is based more on theory and less on actual proof.'

'But you are certain of your theory?'

Stephen glanced at Nathan. 'Yes, I'm pretty certain.'

Nathan didn't say anything, but his face must have told Stephen he had better be a darn sight more than *pretty certain*. Stephen took a deep breath and held up a diagram he had drawn on a large piece of paper pinned to a board. Leaning it on a dining chair he had grabbed earlier, he referred to its contents.

'As you can see, this is a diagram of our family tree, I've even added James and his contribution to the gene pool.' All but Jean nodded and returned their attention back to Stephen. Jean took a few more moments to assess the names that had been written there.

'Now, since Jean's blood was analysed, some awkward questions have been raised regarding what we know of our families, As they stand, a lot doesn't add up.' He glanced over to Nathan again, who was now looking very suspicious,

281

before carrying on quickly. 'If we follow Jean's DNA through the female mitochondrial line — in other words, directly through mother to daughter — we find a match to Adriana, Gerhalt's wife and Nathan, Damien and Daniel's grandmother.'

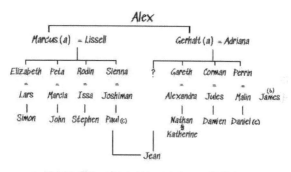

a = Adopted, b = Malin's son from a previous marriage, c = James' illegitimate sons

'But if Paul is her grandfather, how can that be?' Nathan was now sitting forward in his chair, arms on his knees, looking intently at Stephen.

'To put it simply, Jean is the link between both sides of the family. She is related to both Marcus and Gerhalt.'

Jean sat forward. 'I don't understand, Marcus and Gerhalt are brothers, the family is already linked. You're all cousins right?'

Nathan shook his head. 'Yes, we are cousins, but we're are not all related to each other.'

'You are going to have to explain that one.'

Nathan pointed to Stephen's diagram.

'I'll start at the beginning. Ten thousand years ago, there was no Empire, the primary worlds had nothing to do with each other, still separated by the vastness of space. The people of Kelan, were made of up of several clans that worked together, most of the time that is. Now the clans themselves consisted of many different families, but they all had one Chief that represented that clan, and of those Chiefs, one was the principle Chief, an Overlord if you like. Alex was that Overlord at the time.

'Unfortunately, while he and his forefathers were chosen for this role because of their expertise, they had one devastating problem. For several generations, they were plagued by a terrible disease. It left their minds clear but from early adulthood they became physically crippled. It was a long and slow debilitating process, until they eventually died, still relatively young men.

'Alex decided that he wasn't going to let this happen anymore, that the disease would stop with him. He never married, and he died, like his own father, in his forties. But before his illness took hold, Alex decided he wanted to travel. So he gained permission from his father and he set off on his adventures. He wrote several books about his escapades, they are worth a read, even now. But there came a time when he began to see, and feel, the early signs that the disease had finally caught up with him.

One night, while he was in a small town, he fell and hurt himself quite badly. Two boys found him, alone and vulnerable and he believed at that point he was going to die at the hands of some thieves. But, instead the boys took him to a place of safety, and helped him to regain his strength.

He learned during that time that they were orphans, living on the streets. They had met in the gutters, and over the years, had kept each other safe. Alex was so grateful for their help, he offered them a reward if they helped him get back home to Parva.

During their time together he learned all about them and they about him. A bond soon grew between the three of them, so that when Alex finally arrived home, he told his father of his plans to never marry and have children of his own, instead adopting the two boys, Marcus and Gerhalt.

And so it is they who inherited the responsibility of the Clans when Alex died. Gerhalt was considered the Overlord, but Marcus had skills in creativity and invention. Together, the two young men built up the clans into a more cohesive community. My father, Gareth, took up the role of Overlord after his father's death. But that is a whole different story.'

Jean had been listening intently. 'Wow, now I understand. So you, Damien and Daniel are cousins; and Paul, Stephen, John and Simon are another set of cousins?'

Nathan smiled and nodded. 'Exactly.'

'And that's where it gets interesting.' Everyone turned back to Stephen.

Nathan held up his hand in surrender. 'Well, you had better get on with it then.'

'Yes, well, as you can see, Marcus and Lissell had four children, and it was always assumed that Gerhalt and Adriana had only three. But, I believe that wasn't actually the case. As I said, if we follow Jean's DNA we can trace it back to Adriana. We know this through the DNA of Nathan, Damien, Daniel and Katherine; we still have Nathan's sister's

DNA on record. But that is where the problem lies. We know Katherine couldn't have children from an accident she had when she was a young girl, and the only other female we know of is Perrin, Daniel's mother, but we also know she didn't have any more children other than Daniel. So there has to be another issue from Gerhalt and Adriana.'

Stephen held out his hands, as if he had just produced a magic trick and was waiting for an applause. He looked disappointed when he was met with a resounding silence.

'Do you understand what I've said? Do you want me to explain it again?'

'No, we get the drift.' Nathan's voice was quiet, dangerously so.

Jean looked around. 'So you are saying, ten thousand years ago, an aunt of Nathan, Damien and Daniel, was my grandmother?'

'Yes, that is exactly what I'm saying.'

'Bloody hell. So what happened to her? She obviously had at least one daughter, hence me, but why don't any of you seem to know anything about her?'

All eyes were now turned on Nathan.

'What the hell are you all looking at me for? I'm as surprised as you are.'

John crossed his arms. 'But are you really? Is this just another little secret we don't know about?'

Nathan felt his anger rise; *always the same arguments*.

'How many times do I have to tell you, I am not keeping secrets from you.' The edge in his voice put paid to any further comment, but he didn't miss the looks that passed

285

between some of the others. He balled his fists and had to force himself not to react; *always the same damn story.*

'Is there any way of finding out who this other sister is?' Jean was now looking at Nathan with concern, but he was relieved to see, not suspicion. He shrugged.

'There may be something in the vaults, it's the only place that would allow documents to remain preserved for that long. Otherwise I have no idea.'

'Well, that's a good place to start, Daniel, do you fancy helping me do some digging?'

Her newly found uncle grinned. 'I think I can do that, it will be interesting to see what is down there, you never know what we may find.'

'Good, and hopefully we'll solve this mystery, and find out why no-one has heard of this strange, elusive member of the family.'

She then picked up an empty glass from the table. 'I think I'm about ready for one of those brandies now.'

Part Three:

To Hell &

Back

21

The Rift

Bales wrinkled his nose as he stood outside the sprawling mass of redbrick Victorian architecture, he wasn't a fan. Dark clouds had been steadily gathering since early that morning, and the first vestiges of precipitation were beginning to fall in big wet globules. Hunching his shoulders against the impending deluge, and shielding his face as the wind whipped the rain into his eyes. He made his way quickly to the open door that led into the derelict warehouse.

Dear gods, he hated London and its weather, he hated the country; in fact, he hated the whole stinking Planet. The sooner he was away from Earth, the sooner he would be happy. He hadn't realised just how much he would miss

Kelan and its people. Even memories of Parva were beginning to tug at his heart. But that would have to wait, for now, he had to keep to the plan and do as he was told. He could revel in the joys of going home when his work was done.

His hand reached up to the sore bruise that was blooming nicely on his right cheek, his guts and ribs were also hurting like hell. Gellan and Duran hadn't taken his impromptu attempt, and subsequent failure, to dispose of Jean Carter well. In fact, had Duran been allowed to continue his onslaught on his defenceless body, Bales was pretty sure he would have carried on well after his life had left it. But Gellan had the sense to know that Bales was still worth more to them alive, for the moment anyway, so he was spared any further reminders to keep his nose clean and out of trouble.

There was a short narrow corridor leading from the entrance to the warehouse proper itself. It smelled of piss and pigeon shit, but Bales didn't care, today they would take a big step closer to destroying Nathan and his Knights; and with any luck, that Carter bitch too. Though what part she had to play in helping the Knights after he left Parva and Kelan, he had no idea, even Gellan and Duran were none the wiser. But Lawrence and his fellow Patrolmen seemed convinced that she had something to do with ruining the gods' carefully laid plans. It riled him that, yet again, she had got in the way of his plans, she was beginning to become an itch that was too annoying to ignore.

He paused momentarily in the doorway that led into the vast empty space of the warehouse. The roof was leaking, and already puddles were beginning to form in the cracked concrete floor. Several cars were parked in the centre of the space, while five men were milling around, their furtive manner suggesting they didn't trust anyone, especially Bales. They looked around nervously at each other, peering into the shadows for the possibility of ambush. Bales grinned to himself, their time on Kelan hadn't been a total waste of time then. He was also pleased to see that everyone had turned up, even that mouthy bastard Andy Lawrence.

Gellan had stipulated that at least four men were needed for their plan to work, so a spare would no doubt be a bonus. His sore stomach and ribs let him know it would appreciate the reprieve.

Considering, not for the first time, the outline of the plan that Gellan had sketched for him, the little details he knew were enough to both terrify and excite him. He had no idea how their scheme would work, but as far as he was concerned he wasn't going to argue. Once more he brushed his fingers across his cheek, before entering the vast warehouse space.

The Patrolmen turned at his approach and he checked himself, suddenly aware of the impending danger he was in. The warehouse was conveniently out of the way of prying eyes, but it also meant there was no way of seeking help if the Patrolmen decided to attack. Of course he could translocate away, but he didn't think Gellan would be impressed by cowardice, and his ribs twinged at the thought. He could feel the sweat bead on his forehead and run down his back despite the rain outside having cooled the air within the warehouse considerably. He was beginning to think it wiser to start backing away, it was only the thought of Gellan

290

letting Duran finish the previous evening's beating that forced him to stay. If he could have translocated the Patrolmen himself to wherever Gellan wanted them he would have done so right there and then. But unfortunately, he had no idea where that was, and he was also only able to translocate himself; he didn't have the power to take anyone else with him.

As the Patrolmen started to approach, they all had looks that suggested they hadn't forgotten he had also been a member of the Order, they still had a score to settle and this seemed an ideal time for retribution. On the point of almost trying his luck with the wrath of Gellan and his pet insane sidekick, a voice rang out around the thick brick walls surrounding them.

'Good morning gentlemen.'

The Patrolmen spun round, searching for the origin of the voice. Two figures had appeared from nowhere and now stood beside the parked cars. The sight of them was strange, Bales had not actually seen the two gods appearing on Earth before; they seemed very slightly blurred around the edges, as if what was inside was too much for their bodily forms to cope with. Their presence made him feel ill-at-ease to look at, and Bales was aware that he wasn't the only one to feel uncomfortable. The Patrolmen took an involuntary step back, they glanced at one another, each looking as if he were about to bolt for the doors, and to hell with their cars.

Gellan passed a brief eye over the men before settling his gaze on Bales. He nodded his satisfaction.

'Well done Victor, shall we go?'

Bales didn't even have time to respond, within a moment the warehouse was far behind, and the gates of hell beckoned.

It took a moment for Bales to realise that they had actually arrived anywhere at all. He couldn't see anything, he couldn't feel anything, in fact, he wasn't sure if he was even standing on anything. While he didn't appear to be floating, he was aware of feeling very heavy indeed. He sensed, rather than felt, a weight envelop him, his energy seemed to be draining away. He was so tired his thoughts had become random nonsense.

Maybe if I just closed my eyes for a moment.

As he let his eyes droop and his body slackened there was an almighty crash from somewhere, and a brilliant light rudely invaded his senses. His eyes shot open, his head was suddenly throbbing, while his confused brain tried to figure out what the hell was going on. The lights and noises weren't outside his body, but within it, filling him with a vibrating sound and light that coursed through every cell and nerve.

Just when he thought he couldn't bear it anymore, he smashed hard into a solid floor, landing on his back, his body sprawled against the impact.

Was it a floor?

Could it be the ceiling?

He began to panic while his mind reeled.

I'm lying on the ceiling?

It took all the will he could muster to open his eyes, but when he did, all he wanted to do was close them again.

He tried to focus his brain and gain some kind of persecutive of his surroundings, but nothing would stay sharp, nothing would stay still long enough to allow him to focus. Holding his hand to his forehead, he could only imagine he must have hit his head as he landed.

A sudden movement to his left caught his attention as someone was trying to sit up, he was sure he should recognise him somehow, but the memory kept disappearing from his grasp like smoke. Trying to move himself, he winced, his body ached everywhere. It was as if he was carrying a huge weight, pushing him down further into the floor.

Finally, his training began to kick in. He attempted to sit up, he needed to get off of the floor, he was vulnerable lying here. He had to move and find somewhere safe. Forcing his hands against the surface of the floor, he pushed his body up, making himself kneel. Suddenly the invisible weight that had seemed so heavy was lightened, he felt as light as a feather. Making a final determined push he was on his feet, his heaviness gone. But the change in sensations in his confused brain recoiled at all the dizzying contradictions; he threw up.

As his empty stomach lurched, he slowly looked around him. The familiar man was there again, along with others.

Had he seen them before too?

They all looked confused and terrified; huddled together, staring at a point somewhere over his shoulder.

Bales followed their gaze, turning carefully. Three figures stood before them. Two were so bright they appeared blurred, but their eyes were as dead as corpses. The third figure stood between them, smaller and horribly deformed *its* eyes full of desperate hunger, while its tongue licked at a lipless maw filled with sharp vicious teeth.

A voice, barely a whisper but full of contempt, spoke behind him.

'What the fuck have you got us into Bales?'

Turning his head slightly, Bales tried to think who's voice that was. He furrowed his brows, his thoughts seemed to be wading through thick mud.

Lawrence, of course.

'Is he your choice?'

Bales' head snapped round, Gellan was now apparently reading his mind. Without a word he hardly inclined his head in acknowledgement.

Then the screams began.

Lawrence tried desperately to rip the chains that crawled up his body, they seemed alive, like iron snakes tightening their grip around his arms and legs, squeezing his body as he writhed, moving up towards his panic stricken face. He pleaded for help, but his fellows just stared in horror, terrified they would be next to feel the links slither around their bodies.

Without warning, Lawrence's legs were yanked from underneath him by an unseen force. Slowly he was dragged along the cold, hard ground, while he kicked and screamed, desperate to get away. About ten feet away, the floor seemed to blur and liquify, raising up to become a protruding rock, solidifying into a misshapen platform.

The chained man fought harder, eyes bulging with panic; screaming his agony and terror. Eventually, the chains and unknown force dragged him onto the uneven surface of the altar like structure. His arms and legs stretched wide, while a final chain wrapped over his screaming mouth, pulling tight to yank his head back, exposing his throat and dulling his screams to a desperate whimper.

The chains about his torso loosened so he was stretched backwards over the stone. He couldn't move, his bowels opened, the final defilement of his body surrendering to its horrific, unknown fate. But he didn't care, his eyes were fixed on the hideous creature that now stood beside him, its maddened eyes searching his for the fear it so desperately hungered.

Its fingers, like stiletto blades, tore through his clothing, ripping the cloth, exposing his bare flesh. It couldn't get to his arms and legs, they were too tightly bound by chains; but the man's fleshy belly, groin and throat were enough for the creature to feed, it could smell his terror and taste the tang of fear in the air. Slowly and deliberately it began its feast with relish.

Lawrence tried to scream, the chains across his mouth muffled the sound, but there was no mistaking his cries of agony; but still the creature worked, slicing and peeling skin and viscera. His audience of Patrolmen looked for somewhere to run and hide, but there was nowhere to go, all they could do was cover their ears and squeeze their eyes shut, desperate not to witness the horror that took place. Finally, the creature had its fill, crouching atop the helpless remains of the man forced to live through his torment, it executed the killing blow that would free him from his relentless torture.

Bales had watched the scene with nothing more than mere curiosity, he was sure he should probably feel something; horror? Revulsion? But no, quiet indifference had enshrouded his thoughts. Only when Gellan came to stand at his side, did he become aware that others existed outside the macabre tableau that had taken place merely feet away.

'So Victor, are you now ready for your prize?'

Again, Bales said no words, but Gellan knew his simple response.

Yes.

Seemingly satisfied, Gellan lifted his shoulders and stretched out his neck, as if a working out a tension that had set in, though his face remained expressionless. Ensuring he had Bales' full attention he spoke again, his voice echoing around unseen walls.

'Kneel before me and accept what is rightfully yours.'

Bales complied. He could do nothing else. Gellan placed both his hands upon the kneeling man's head and closed his own eyes in concentration.

Bales felt a heat so strong emanate from Gellan's hands, travelling down his spine like hot liquid metal, along his arms and down his legs. It was like a furnace beginning to rage within his body, he tried to flinch away but he couldn't move. Then he became aware of someone behind him, Duran placed his hands on Bales' shoulders and the fire at once exploded within him. At the point where he didn't think he could possibly bear it any longer, something changed, shifted; the fire was less raging pain, and more an inferno of desire. Then he slowly felt it, the something else, someone else. It was the strangest feeling, it was as if he had entered a room with other people, they meant nothing to him, but to them he was everything. Wherever he went, they would be there, he would never be alone again.

A voice interrupted his thoughts, he didn't want to leave the room, but he couldn't disobey the commands.

'Victor Bales, rise.'

Bales stood, the pain of the heat now abated to a beautiful smouldering fire. Tears fell down his cheeks, and Gellan smiled.

'Welcome Keeper of Souls, your time has come at last.'

Gellan and Duran both stepped away from him and Bales flexed his shoulders, he was strong and full of energy, at last he felt he was ready for the task he knew he was born for. Glancing behind him he looked at the men standing there; confused and terrified, their own cheeks streaked with tears.

Bales grinned, satisfied.

Now you are mine.

Gorging on the dead remains of Lawrence, the creature never saw the attack when it came. It was too late to react as its own misshapen body, drenched in blood and viscera, was snatched away as Gellan swooped down and caught it by the back of the neck.

Without a second's pause, Gellan opened its throat, its own life blood spraying across the dead man's remains and the black stone on which he was still sprawled and chained.

The creature's blood burned into flesh and rock, the body fizzing as if consumed by acid. With only a few fragments of bone and flesh clinging to the chains still wrapped around the raised altar like stone. Gellan held the lifeless body of the creature over the rock surface, allowing the body to exsanguinate, while the rock surface boiled before slowly beginning to liquify. Bales sensed the first vestiges of power within him begin to rise up through his body.

Satisfied that a point had been reached, Gellan thrust the creature's body into the fluid over the blistering rock, a crack appeared and heat began to spew out. Duran joined Gellan and added his own immense power, pushing the pathetic body further into the rift.

Bales felt the new power within him flow, adding to the force of the two gods. He felt invincible.

An almighty crack recoiled around the space, the body of the creature finally disappearing into the rock surface, where a sickly green fire now erupted. The flames leapt and engulfed the gods as they endeavoured to keep the fissure open, and Bales could feel the heat of the tongues of fire lick at his own bare skin, searing where they touched.

Now, new screams could be heard, evil, self-pitying agony mixed with angry determination. It took a moment for Bales to realise it was Gellan and Duran themselves, howling in terror and agony.

There was another huge crack, and this time the rock that had stood as sacrificial alter to both Lawrence and his tormentor, exploded. Bales was thrown back, landing hard on the stone floor, his body limp from the energy drained from him by Gellan and Duran.

He blinked, his eyes felt raw and dry from the heat of the green fire, his body numb from the violent force of his landing. He tentatively rolled onto his back. To his left, the Patrolmen now lay in an unmoving heap. He instinctively knew they were alive, he just didn't know why he should be so sure. To his right, Gellan and Duran were slowly coming to their knees having also been thrown by the force of the explosion. Both stared at their hands in horror, turning them over as if in disbelief that they should be there. Duran opened his mouth in a silent scream, while Gellan howled in despair; an animal like guttural sound. Both gods looked to each other and Bales could see them shaking violently as if from shock.

But they were soon forgotten when he perceived, rather than saw, movement from within the rift where the altar had been. Bales, still lying on the floor, kicked out with his legs and forced his arms to drag him backwards, instinct roaring through his brain to get the hell out of there.

But it was too late.

Something, both dark and terrible was coming through the rift.

22

The Silent Enemy

Standing under the hot shower, Nathan let the heat surround his body like a scalding wave of reality. Grounding his mind to the present, forcing his thoughts to stay within the boundary of his bathroom walls.

All too often recently, he had found himself looking over his shoulder, convinced he was being followed. Even when he doubled back to seek out his stalker, he could find no trace of his shadow. But he knew they were there, he could feel their presence lurking at the edge of his thoughts.

Always before though, whoever it was following him never pursued him to his home at Denfield or the Retreat.

That was until last night.

It had been a dinner like any of the countless functions he had attended before over the years. He and Damien had returned to the Retreat after the other Knights, having spoken to the head of the High Council, Field Marshal Inchgower, privately after the proceedings had finished.

Once they returned, it was such a pleasant late summer evening, that they had taken a late night-cap on the patio before Daimien retired, leaving Nathan to the peace of the evening air.

But that was when he sensed someone out amongst the bushes, watching from across the manicured lawn. Nathan sat alone before the silent house, while the other Knights slept, completely unaware of the prowler in the shadows. He was reluctant to wake any of them until he had established exactly who was out there. Whoever it was, they had no-one else with them, he was more than capable of dealing with them himself.

Pulling out his dagger that, like his sword remained unseen until drawn, he scanned his immediate surroundings. He may not have the acute senses of Jean's empathic skills, but he caught the tell-tale presence of someone near; though as he approached, they seemed to melt away.

He found himself at a loss, and he was caught on the back foot. Apart from the gazebo as a means of entering and exiting the Retreat, there was a gate that led directly to the stable yard. This was locked and protected as a rule. Only Paul used this gate usually, as a quicker and more convenient means of getting to his own work domain amongst the livery. No-one else would have need to use it and, like the gazebo, was restricted in its use to the Knights and Jean.

A thorough search of the area found nothing however, the gate remained locked, and Nathan could find no evidence of anyone having recently used it. Again, that same dread began to seep up his spine. Who could be out there that would have the kind of power needed to penetrate his own security?

His mind immediately went to Jean back in Denfield, and once more the panic gripped him. He wasn't even aware at first that he was running through the gardens towards the gazebo in a desperate need to get to Denfield.

He had to know she was safe, his mind refusing to allowing him peace until he saw her himself.

Even as he entered his own kitchen and rushed through the hall to scale the great wooden staircase, his senses were already seeking out her familiar signature, looking for evidence that she was still here. But, by the time he reached her bedroom door he knew she was there, her mind quiet and at peace.

He closed his eyes and rested his head against the warmth of the wooden door to her room. Grasping the handle he turned it gently, terrified of the possibility that he should wake her. He would have no excuses should she find him watching her, but he had to see with his own eyes, the possibility of losing her again was too great to not be sure.

Relief washed over him as he saw her quietly sleeping, oblivious to the turmoil that coursed through his mind.

Backing out quietly, he closed the door behind him. Leaving her to sleep, he returned to the Retreat, still completely at a loss as to who his shadow was. But by the time he had made his way to his own bed in the house at Parva, he no longer felt the menacing presence.

Sleep eluded him though. No matter what he did, he could not shut his brain down to the possibility of danger to Jean or the Knights who depended on him. When he finally gave up and made his way to the shower, the sun was still yet to rise over Parva.

He made to turn off the hot deluge of water before he left the shower, intending to dress and find something to eat in the kitchen.

Then it hit him.

There was an overwhelming feeling of knowing he wasn't alone, but by then it was too late. Before he had time to react, the stranger struck.

23

The Fallen

Gellan gazed sullenly out of the window onto a rain soaked landscape, such as it was. It had been raining for hours, and the dark clouds overhead didn't offer much hope of it ending anytime soon. He frowned at the foul weather, it mirrored his mood perfectly.

The house in which they were staying was warm and dry enough, set back far from the road and no-one seemed bothered about its occupants. He glanced at the corner of the room and wrinkled his nose, he was going to have to do something about them too, as they provided another insult to their current predicament; awareness of decomposing bodies. The smell was quite revolting, he would get Duran to take them out of the house and dispose of them somewhere, preferably down wind. The couple hadn't really put up a fight, the woman stopped screaming quite quickly once Duran had broken her neck, the old man had given up the struggle soon after that, his own grief and fear making it easy to despatch him as quickly as his wife.

So now they were encamped in this house far out in the middle of nowhere, trying to come to terms with their situation, and more importantly, how to deal with the whole horrendous predicament they found themselves in. He heard Duran enter the room and felt the heaviness of his heart, its weight seemed to cling to his own.

His heart! How ridiculous!

Feeling Duran's eyes boring into his exposed and unprotected back, he bit his lip as a trickle of fear slid down his spine.

'Well, my friend, we have some thinking to do.'

He turned away from the dreary scene outside and looked at the sad face of the man before him. Because, no matter how much they tried to ignore it, the facts were simple, Duran, his one faithful friend amongst the throng of deities that existed to serve the Lady Mother, had been sunk, like Gellan, to exist amongst the pestilence of the human race. Reduced to mere men, the rats of the universe, no longer one of the exalted. His stomach churned at the thought, a feeling he hated. All the emotions that ran around his body, thoughts that exploded into his head, unfamiliar and detested, threatened to send him insane.

Even here, in some backwater of Kelan, he considered the irony. As gods they were forbidden to walk among the worlds of the Empire, only on Earth were they allowed to

305

visit briefly due to the lack of T'akai. Nathan's protections had ensured their presence was impossible, hence their need to use the weak will of humans to do their bidding. Even their meeting years ago with Royston Morecross had to be manipulated so that he and his daughter, Ephea, had to travel to Earth.

He looked up sharply, in the silence, Duran's thoughts ran through his own mind, demanding answers, the underlying threat more evident as his anger flared.

He snorted in disgust.

'I don't know, I have been trying to think of a way out of this since we arrived on this stinking world. Have you got any better ideas?'

Duran furrowed his brows. Gellan couldn't read his thoughts, but the palpable sense of betrayal and disappointment emanated from him. Again that unmistakable hint of menace.

'So, this is my fault now is it? You seemed to think it was a wonderful idea, in fact you couldn't imagine a better way of dealing with the matter. But now, you think it might have been a mistake?'

Duran looked away and spied the bodies. Without looking at Gellan he went over to the woman first and picked her up, slinging her across his shoulder and made for the door.

Gellan spat out his frustration, his anger exploding, daring his friend to turn and do something, anything to break the interminable silence.

'THIS IS NOT MY FAULT.'

Duran stopped with his hand on the door handle but didn't turn around.

Gellan's voice reduced to a hiss.

'We did everything we had to. Only a Keeper of Souls can open the gates, Victor did all he had to do; the catalyst of the sacrifice and our combined effort should have been enough.'

The silent man eventually turned, the woman's head hitting the wall as he did so. They ignored the sickening thud. Gellan held out his hands in supplication.

'I know this is hard, it sickens me too. We should have been able to complete the rite and step back unscathed, but something went wrong.'

He looked down at his own hands, his eyes blurred, reaching up he felt wetness on his cheeks. He brushed away at them and anger flared through him again.

'This is his fault, Nathan L'guire, Emperor and Duke of Pernia, Guardian of the universe, Saviour of the *weak and tormented*. Human creatures that would do better if they died, other than continue to be a miserable blight on the glory of the universe.'

Taking a step towards Duran he grabbed his unladen shoulder.

'He will pay for this. Once he and his sycophantic Knights are dead, the power generated will be enough to give us back our true forms.' He plucked at the stolen clothes he wore. 'We can leave these repulsive bodies behind and take back everything we have lost due to *that man*.'

Duran studied him for a while, again Gellan could hardly discern any communication; *was he losing what was left of his power too?* Turning back to the door Duran opened it, just before he passed through he stopped, inclining his head, and Gellan felt relief flood over him.

'Yes my friend, we will get the bastard.'

The silent man closed the door behind him and once again Gellan was alone, mumbling to himself. Crossing back to the window he placed his head onto the cold glass.

We have to beat him, we have to win.

'Victor Bales cannot, must not, fail!'

24

A Tragic

Encounter

George Fewson stood amongst the tall woodland trees and breathed in the cool early autumn air. The sun had finally risen and they had been on the move since before dawn. All around him, his fellow Militia were also enjoying a brief break from their current task of tracking. The training troop comprised of fifteen cadets, half of the total number currently attached to Comston, the second group were due to take over in three days.

There were three knights in charge, including Sergeant Ehring along with two members of the Order who had travelled with the cadets. On this day, they had left their base camp having been split into three companies, and were heading off into the forest in different directions. Each group under the guidance of a knight.

However, George had been tracking with his father since he could walk, and later with Niall and Layne, but he had not pushed himself to the front as he may have done previously. He watched the others work and if they seemed to have problems he was ready to help out, otherwise he remained quietly observant. Sergeant Ehring knew of his past, but he seemed to approve of George's decision as went through the motions, listening to instructions and following orders.

It hadn't always been so easy, it had taken a while for him to come to terms with the discipline required of the Militia, especially under the watchful eye of the Order, now however, he was content to spend less time fighting the system, and concentrate more on finding his own role within the machine he wanted so much to be a part of.

Sitting amongst the trees with the rest of his group, he remembered Raynard's words from so many weeks ago and smiled to himself. He wondered what the old knight would think if he saw him now.

Suddenly, he become aware that something was wrong, very wrong. He sat up and listened, his ears straining, but there was nothing, absolutely nothing, no birds, no rustling of twigs and leaves as animals moved around the undergrowth, nothing. It was as if the world had suddenly stood still. Catching Ehring's eye, he could see by the knight's face he was also concerned. By now the other four members of the group had seen their sergeant tense and realised something was wrong. They all stood still, listening, holding their breath.

The sound, when it came, was like a shockwave blasting through the trees; the clamour of many people crashing through dense undergrowth. Then the screams, awful howls of pain and terror filled the air, George felt his blood run cold. The five Militia cadets looked to their knight in panic; what was going on? What should they do?

Sergeant Ehring called them together, ordering them to stay put while he went to find out what was happening. Just before he left he pulled George aside.

'If I don't return, get as many people back to Comston as you can.'

George tried not to show the panic in his voice. 'What do you think is out there?'

'I have no idea, but it doesn't sound good does it? George, I'm relying on you to keep people safe, don't let me down.'

And with that the knight was away. George joined the others again, urging them to make sure they were ready to move immediately.

'Aren't we going to wait for the knight to come back?' A young woman with an unfortunate overbite looked wildly at George.

'It's just a precaution in case we have to be prepared to move when he gets back, he won't be impressed if he has to wait for us all to gather ourselves together.'

311

There was more screaming and crashing coming from a different direction now, it seemed closer. George had a nasty feeling it was somewhere near their basecamp.

After what seemed forever, but could only have been minutes, the screaming and crashing stopped. The silence was ominous.

The tension in the air was so thick he was almost hoping the screaming would start again to drown out the thumping of his heart against his chest. But still Ehring failed to return. George knew he had to get the rest of his group moving. Looking at Carrie, a fellow he knew from his time at Fallport, he saw his own fear reflected in his eyes, but he couldn't let that cloud his judgement now, urging the others on, he finally persuaded them to follow him back to the basecamp. Once there he hoped to find someone who could give them the answers to the questions running through his brain at that moment.

Somewhere in the distance were the sounds of something moving around, they were no longer running, but moving slowly through the forest. Instinctively, George and his small group hunkered down, moving silently, their eyes and ears alert. When they finally arrived at the basecamp, the sight froze them all to the spot. Every member of one of the other groups lay dead, their bodies scattered around the clearing, some looked as if they had been hacked at viciously, while others looked horribly deformed, as if they had been pulled apart. The area was awash with the remains of blood and viscera.

Making a concerted effort to keep the contents of his breakfast down, George forced himself to move.

Encouraging the others to follow, they skirted around the horror until they saw two bodies at the entrance to a path that led back into the trees. They thought they might have been part of the other group, it was difficult to say with all the blood and gore. The dead remains of a knight lay further up the path and George felt himself relieved it wasn't Sergeant Ehring. Then, felt guilty when he considered the poor man had died trying to save a band of virtually unarmed Militia.

The ferrous smell of blood and worse hung heavy in the air, mingling with fear and anticipation. George knew they couldn't stay here, whoever had committed this atrocious act was probably very close, maybe even watching them.

A sound behind them made them freeze with fear, turning slowly they looked into the darkness of the trees, edging backwards, ready to flee at the slightest moment. But what came staggering into sight made them all cry in anguish; Ehring covered in blood, lurched towards them. His right arm was a bloody mangled mess, blood from a head wound poured down his face so he could barely see, while his left arm was clenched against a gaping wound in his side.

George rushed to him, calling for the others to help, but the knight would have none of it.

'No, I'm already dead, but you must leave here now, go back to the garrison as fast as you can and warn them.'

'But what of the others? We have to find them.'

The knight grabbed at George's jacket, blood flowed from the wound as he let it go.

'They are all dead, you are the only ones left. Go now while you can. Tell them hell is here, demons are amongst us.'

Then, before George could quiz him any further, the knight gave his last gurgling breath and died in his arms, his sightless eyes reflecting the terror he had witnessed.

'What do we do now?' The girl with the overbite was looking frantically around.

Somewhere within the trees there was a sound of someone moving. Ehring had said that everyone was dead, and the looks on the others' faces echoed what George was thinking.

He took a deep breath. 'Run.'

They didn't need telling twice. Every one of them turned on their heels and ran, hell bent on getting the sound of whoever, whatever, was behind them as far away as possible, none of them daring to look back, terrified of what they might see.

As they pushed through the trees they finally came out onto a clear area that bounded the River Elvian, still running high after a week of constant summer rains. Only last spring, the bridge, that had normally spanned its waters, was washed away by a terrible storm. The bridge that stood in its place now was a structure of wood and rope that the Comston garrison had erected as a temporary measure while the permanent one was being built.

When they reached the bridge, somewhere behind them they heard the sound of undergrowth being crushed. George stopped and turned, urging the others to cross the river.

314

When he looked back, he saw the most terrifying creature he had ever seen.

It had to be nine feet tall, its skin an oily blue. All around the sides and back of its head, a bone like crest protruded upwards, like a half crown moulded to its skull. It wore a short kilt and armour on its torso, otherwise its arms and legs were bare, as were its huge feet.

But George couldn't take his gaze away from the grisly sight of his friend, Carrie, hanging limply in its massive hand. His head at an unnatural angle, the silent scream etched in his young dead face. In the beast's other hand, a knife rested, drying blood covering its blade.

On the bridge, the other three remaining members of their group stood transfixed in horror. George jumped onto the bridge and screamed at them to run, he followed behind, unsheathing his own long, sharp hunting knife. Leaping the final steps to the opposite shore he brought his blade down onto the ropes that lashed the wooden beams together. It took barely a moment for the others to see what he was doing and they too were now hacking furiously at the ropes.

Across the river, the beast had been joined by three more demon-like creatures. One had already stepped onto the bridge when the final ropes were released, and George and the other Militia cadets heaved with all their might against the structure. George found himself cursing the efficiency of the Order's engineers. But, with the ropes cut, part of the bridge had already sunk into the river, and the surging current helped their desperate efforts. There was a huge crack as the construction finally gave way and tumbled into the boiling river below. The demon already making the

315

crossing also fell, as the waters tossed the loosened beams like matchwood. For a moment, George thought the beast may have been pulled beneath its surface, but its accomplices had managed to grab it and pull it free of the water.

The beasts' howls of rage could be heard across the sound of the roaring river, even as they ran hell bent towards the garrison some two miles away. They could still hear their howling as they ran, or maybe it was the echo of their own terror ringing in their ears.

They never stopped once, adrenaline forcing them on, not daring to pause until they reached the garrison gates. The watch on duty, looked in stunned surprise as four Militia cadets slammed the open gates shut and barred them against whatever was outside. Once they heard the shocking tale that George told, he and the others were taken to the garrison commander, Major Dillon. They retold their story, of the terrible demon beasts and their dead friends that now lay across the river. George was thankful that she didn't question his account, and only interrupted when he told of the deaths of the other cadets and knights. He understood the look of pain that crossed her face, but he saw with relief, that she put her own emotions aside and set about dealing with the horrors that lurked outside the garrison's walls. Within the hour, the fortification was on high alert and the adjacent village was evacuated to within its walls. Already word was being sent to Parva, via the garrison portal, of an unknown force that lay somewhere within the forests north of Comston.

25

The

Nightmare

L urking somewhere in the shadows, Jean could sense the figure moving in for the kill, its slavering jaws hungered for her blood as it stalked its prey. Her body calm, her mind clear of everything but for the impending assault, she planted her feet and took long, slow breaths. Her hands clasped the handles of knives and she drew them from their place, nestled across the small of her back; already primed and ready to be loosed.

The attack, when it came, was swift, hard and brutal. She spun on her heels and braced for the impact of the huge,

317

blue, armoured body as it launched itself. She made to step back, but her foot was caught in something, as she tried to pull her knives from their sheath but her arms seemed to be pinned to her side. Unseen bindings tightened around her body, when suddenly she was falling, an endless descent into an abyss. Without warning the ground came up and she slammed into the hard surface, fighting to free herself from the ties that bound her.

She writhed in frustration, as invisible arms grabbed at her, wrapping around her body, the beast was upon her.

She screamed in fear and panic.

'Jean, Jean, wake up.'

The terrifying images exploded into oblivion, she opened her eyes to watery daylight and a familiar man's face looking down at her in confusion and worry. The light behind cast him in shadow, but she felt relief as she recognised his features.

'Nathan, thank the gods.'

She tried to move her arms but she was stuck fast in her sheets. The figure shook his head.

'It's not Nathan, Jean, it's me, Damien.'

Helping her to untangle herself from the sheets, Damien sat back on his heels and she realised her mistake. An easy one to make, the cousins were so alike, except for those damn eyes of course. Looking around she realised she must have thrown herself off the bed as she grappled within the bedsheets when the beast in her nightmare attacked. A sudden pang of familiarity passed over her and she took a moment to try and think what it was, but it disappeared just as quickly.

Damien helped her out of the sheets and she stood up and looked around.

'What are you doing here Damien? Where's Nathan?'

Damien's face looked stricken.

Fear gripped her heart. 'What's wrong? Where's Nathan? I thought he was with you at the Retreat last night.' She couldn't keep the sound of panic out of her own voice now.

'I don't know, he's disappeared, and I mean literally disappeared.'

Jean looked at him incredulously, while at the same time sending her senses outwards, looking for a sign of Nathan. She, like Nathan, was now so close to the Knights, she could seek out their signatures anywhere. Nathan, in particular, was easy to pin point with considerable accuracy. But no matter how she tried, she could sense the other Knights, but Nathan was nowhere to be found.

She began to grab at clothes and started to dress.

'What happened? When did it happen?'

Relief passed across Damien's face in the hope that Jean could possibly find a way to locate Nathan.

'This morning, about an hour ago, there was an horrendous noise coming from Nathan's room. It sounded like a battle going on, things were being smashed and there was shouting and crashing as something hit the floor. The door to his room was locked and it wasn't until the room went silent Simon and John were able to kick the door down.'

Jean headed for the bedroom door and Damien followed.

'Does Nathan usually lock his door at night?'

He shook his head. 'I've never known him to, especially at the Retreat, why should he?'

'You think someone else locked it?'

'They must have done. Whoever it was, the last thing they wanted was us to come running in, we'd have ripped them apart.'

She nodded thoughtfully. They made their way down the staircase into the hall and through to the kitchen. She had spent the night on her own and had only eaten a small dinner, she had thought then how big Denfield was without its master there; now it also felt cold, and empty as if it knew something sinister about his disappearance. She shook herself, this was fanciful thought that did nothing to help the situation.

'What was he like last night at this dinner you were all attending?'

Damien frowned and shrugged his shoulders. 'If I'm honest, I'd have to say distracted. Don't get me wrong, he was perfectly amiable with all the other guests, even gave his usual rousing after dinner speech. But he could do all of those things in his sleep.' He chewed his thumbnail, as he paused to think. 'He was there in body, but his mind seemed to be elsewhere. Just like he's been for quite a while.'

Jean sighed, it would appear she wasn't the only one who had been concerned about Nathan recently. She felt guilt drop in her stomach like a stone. Perhaps if she had been more forthcoming with her worries and talked to Nathan, he might not have been so distracted that someone could blindside him and do the unthinkable. But even as she and Damien closed the French doors and made their way to the only area of the garden where they could translocate from, she knew that *what ifs* and maybes were not going to help them now.

When they arrived under the gazebo in the garden at the Retreat, Jean and Damien didn't hang about walking to the house. Together they ran along the path and almost crashed through the back door into the boot room that lead into the kitchen and hallway. On hearing their arrival, Daniel and Paul were already heading down the stairs to greet them. Jean was on the bottom step as they met.

'Has there been any news?'

The two Knights shook their heads. Daniel urged her to follow them upstairs.

'Come and see for yourself, maybe you can get an idea of what happened.'

She followed, so many questions were shooting through her brain, but she wanted to see the scene for herself before she started interrogating the Knights. She reached the landing where Stephen, John and Simon were waiting outside Nathan's room. After the initial shock of finding him missing, they seemed reluctant to stay in the area, it was still his private space and it felt wrong to intrude.

Entering, she couldn't help but be shocked at the state of the room. Nathan's room was a large corner suite, overlooking the gardens. It was decorated in warm tones, its furnishings were comfortable and attractive; a room to relax in at the end of the day. It reflected the private Nathan that few people were privileged to meet. Masculine, warm, friendly and inviting. But not at the moment, now it looked as if a stampede of wild animals had passed through it.

321

Substantial looking furniture appeared to have been tossed aside, and broken. Bed linen was strewn across the floor, and personal items had been smashed against the walls.

But it was the blood that splattered the walls, floor and debris that was the most alarming.

Nevertheless, it was the underlying pulse that reverberated throughout the atmosphere that caught her attention. It was very faint, but Jean could feel it, like a rhythmic sound wave, constantly moving through the air. She recognised the faint, but consistent, essence of Nathan's energy, and she clutched at the palpable force, afraid of losing it.

Walking across the floor, she carefully avoided the broken glass and debris. She looked back towards the door and caught Stephen's eye.

'All the blood, is it Nathan's?

He nodded, but looked sick to admit it.

'Is there enough here for you to be worried?'

John looked incredulous. 'What kind stupid question is that?'

Stephen held up his hand. 'It's alright, it's a valid question, and no, if this is the extent of his blood loss then no, he isn't bleeding to death if that's what you mean. None of this is arterial, more likely cast off from an open wound.'

Jean closed her eyes in relief, that was something anyway.

He continued. 'There's more in the shower. That seems to be where the fight started, probably where he picked up the injury.'

Following Stephen's direction she made her way to the en-suite. Suppressing the desire to openly whistle, she walked into the room. It was enormous.

Wow, I've seen smaller apartments, I'll give you your due Nathan, you may not be an extravagant man, but boy do you know how to do class and style.

The floor was still wet and she had to hold onto a towel rail when she nearly slipped on the tiles. Blood still clung to the parts of the room that hadn't been drenched in water; the corner of one of the sinks, the side of the bath and the side of the door jam. The glass wall of the large walk-in shower had been smashed, and small grains of safety glass sparkled amongst the wet floor tiles.

'That must have taken some force to break, have you seen what was used to smash it?'

Damien had walked in beside her, also taking care on the wet surface.

'Nothing that we can see, whoever did it must have taken any weapons with them.'

'What about the shower, was it on or off when you got here?'

'On, Daniel nearly broke his neck trying to get across to turn it off.'

Jean turned carefully and went back into the bedroom, Damien followed. By now the others had entered the room too, though still reluctant to come any further than the vicinity of the doorway. She turned back to Damien.

'How did whoever was responsible for this get in? I thought the protections around Parva and the Retreat were impenetrable.'

323

'As far as we know, they are. Nothing is supposed to be able to get through. Even the gods would have to enter via the gates to the city, and they would need permission to even be within the Empire. Only those who Nathan allows into the Retreat can translocate to the gazebo. Daniel has spoken to the watch and they are adamant no-one passed them. The doors are locked at night, so whoever did this, has a power I've never seen; and to get past Nathan, I would have said it was impossible. But someone obviously did.'

'What have you done about searching beyond the Retreat?'

'Nothing.'

'Nothing?!'

'Nathan disappeared from this room, he didn't go of out the window, or through a door, whoever took him had means to get him far away from Parva, even the Empire. Sending out search parties without any idea of where to look will only cause panic. Whatever has happened to him, Nathan's fate lies with us.'

She looked around her again and spied the Knights, they were looking at her expectantly and she suddenly felt quite alone. As far as the Knights were concerned, the impossible had happened, the man who they expected to have all the answers was suddenly taken away. She felt angry, Nathan needed them all now and the Knights seemed lost, unwilling even to accept what had occurred.

Looking around the room again, thoughts began to form images in her mind, but they were a jumble of disconnected and distorted pictures. She bit her lip and decided to keep her own council, at least until she was more sure of the facts.

'Well, at least we know he's still alive, that's a blessing.'

Damien nodded. 'I agree, Nathan may play down his role within the Empire, but he is a lynch pin that holds much of it together. The fact that the force that links the primary worlds is still intact demonstrates he is still alive. Also, having seen the damage after the explosion of power when we lost James, I hate to think what the devastation of losing Nathan would be.'

Jean was relieved, at least they were positive still, there was hope yet. But standing around was not going to get Nathan back.

And while he may still be alive, they had no idea how much longer he had. She put her hand on Damien's arm and gave him the most encouraging smile she could muster.

'I'm going to try and connect with Nathan, even though I can't find his signature within the universe, I may still be able to join with his mind.'

He looked relieved. 'Like he did with you when Bales decided to use you as a pin cushion?'

'Exactly.'

The other Knights looked at each other, they had no idea what else to do, Damien returned Jean's smile. Then he did something totally unexpected. Drawing Jean towards him, he held her so her head rested against his shoulder. 'We're here when you need us, just tell us what to do.'

Despite her initial surprise, Jean felt comforted by Damien's emotional demonstration and she gratefully returned his embrace. She knew she shouldn't be angry with him, the Knights were as worried as she was and would do anything to get Nathan back. If she was their only hope, they would scour the universe to help.

She lifted her head and smiled. 'I know.'

Looking around the room again she decided the bed was probably the best place to start. It was the most intact piece of furniture in the room and it was where he had spent the most time over the last few hours. This should be where his presence would be strongest. She grasped the end bedstead and the energy that had been pulsing around the room flared up within her. Closing her eyes, she tried to concentrate on the focus of that energy, pushing through all the irrelevant substances that only served to confuse.

Jean was shocked at just how much power remained and now surged through her body. She felt her knees buckle as the weight of the force dragged her down. Her head reeled trying to push forward, looking for the slightest glimmer of Nathan's mind.

Dear gods Nathan, how do you cope with this?

The energy continued to well within her, and when she thought she would be completely overwhelmed, an image appeared in her own mind, a shadowed space; an area of darkness within the darkness. It confused her at first, was this Nathan's safe space? More shadows formed within the darkness, black on black, sinister shapes confounding her perception.

A dull light glimmered briefly and she tried to focus on the area where she had seen it. Nothing happened and she began to think she was making images up in her mind, a desperate attempt to find something in the endless expanse of nothingness.

There it was again, slightly brighter this time, and it lingered longer. Homing in on the vision she was sure wasn't a figment of her imagination, she moved her mind forward again. And then the light grew, from a pin prick of brightness, eventually growing to form a shape, a human shape. When she realised what she was actually looking at, Jean couldn't help but let out a cry of anguish.

Lying naked on his side, he was facing her, his legs drawn up to his chest, with his arms wrapped tightly around his knees, his head resting within his hands. Blood was smeared across his skin, mixed with a sickly sheen of sweat glistening in the dull light.

Though the atmosphere was hot, he was shivering, and all around him Jean sensed an overwhelming air of fear and despair. She tried to reach out to him, but a substance she didn't recognise surrounded him, like a gelatinous bubble. The air around him blurred and momentarily his image went out of focus. Then she felt, rather than heard, him moan in anguish and she moved back quickly, afraid of causing him anymore pain. Feeling frustration and anger well within her, she found it was difficult to speak in the thick, hot air, but she forced out the words, she had to know where he was.

'Nathan, can you hear me? It's me, Jean. I'm here for you!'

Jean felt a bubble of relief begin to glow within her when his head moved, as if listening for a noise in the distance.

'Nathan, it's me, Jean, can you hear me? Please Nathan.' Her voice begging him to hear her.

Lifting his head, his tired eyes looked out from a drawn and exhausted face. Jean's heart ached to see him like this, confused and afraid. Then she heard his voice; quiet and rasping, as if he hadn't spoken for a long time. Jean frowned, he looked as if he had been like this for some time, but it had been less than two hours since his disappearance.

'Jean? Is that you?'

The bubble of relief grew.

'Yes, Nathan, it's me. Tell me where you are, and we will come and get you.'

He shook his head, looking confused, he didn't seem to be able to see her.

'Out of time.'

Jean looked blank. 'What do you mean out of time? Please Nathan, don't give up hope, we will get there, just tell me where to go.'

He furrowed his brows, he seemed frustrated that she didn't understand.

'Out of time! I am, out of time!'

She finally understood what he meant, he wasn't making a statement of despair, he was telling her he was at a place that existed outside the boundaries of existence. She felt the air around him shift again, pain etched into his face and his body seemed to shiver with the vibrations of the thick atmosphere he lay within.

She had to hurry.

'How do I get there Nathan? You have to tell me. I know it hurts, but please try.'

Again he raised his head and tried to concentrate.

'Tell them, they will know.'

328

'You mean Damien and the others?'

He relaxed slightly, at last she understood something.

'I'll tell them and we will come and get you. Just hang in there Nathan, please.'

She couldn't keep the sound of fear and panic out of her voice and she hated herself for it, he needed to know she was there for him; strong and able, not weak and helpless, she must stay calm.

'I will be there soon, I promise, I won't leave you.'

For a moment she thought she saw a glimmer of a smile. But then she began to feel the pull as she returned back to reality, she had to leave and it was the hardest thing she was ever going to have to do. Just as the image of Nathan began to blur he once more looked out for her, and briefly she saw recognition on his face. Determination seemed to seize him, and in his familiar, strong, forceful voice that she hadn't heard since she had found him, here in this God awful place, he called out to her.

'Don't trust anyone.'

And then he was gone.

When Jean opened her eyes, she was lying on the floor, Stephen and Damien looking anxiously over her. Trying to sit up, her head swimming with the effort, she thought she was going to throw up. Stephen put a hand to her elbow.

'Steady Jean, take it easy.'

She shook her head. 'No, we don't have time, we have to go now.'

Damien and Stephen looked at each other, then as they helped her to sit up she saw the look of concern on the faces of the rest of the Knights. They had come further into the room now, probably when she fell to the floor.

Damien took her hand. 'You've seen him? He's alright?'

The look Jean gave him didn't give him the answer he wanted to hear, what she said made it sound even worse.

'He's in a bad way, he's in pain and he's cold and afraid. We need to hurry.'

'Do you know where he is?'

She nodded, which offered at least some hope. 'He said he was out of time, when I questioned it, he said you would know.'

'Out of time?'

The Knights seemed as confused as Jean had been, until Daniel answered.

'Pernia. We have to go to Pernia.'

Recognition passed between the men, and Damien nodded. 'Of course. Where else?'

Jean felt herself getting annoyed. 'Pernia? The island where the Order do all their training? Why there?'

'Pernia is Nathan's ancestral home; it is also where the Council Chamber is.'

'I take it you are not referring to the Imperial High Council?'

'No, this is something completely different.'

'Okay, so you are saying someone has taken him to Pernia? Because that did not look as if Nathan was lying on a big island off the east coast of the mainland.'

'No, the Council Chamber isn't technically on Pernia, but it can only be accessed from there.'

330

'Of course, nothing could be that simple could it?' Jean threw her hands up in the air in exasperation. 'Well, come on then, let's get down to the gazebo, the sooner we bring him home the better.' She grabbed hold of the side of the bed, which still pulsed slightly, and with Stephen's help, stood up.

The doctor was shaking this head and Jean sighed with exasperation.

'What now?'

'Nathan placed protections over the whole of Pernia. It is completely inaccessible other than by boat, and only by a few places along the coast, so the Order can train without any fear of attack. It doesn't even have an area set aside for us to translocate, we have to find our way there by sea.'

'You have got to be kidding me? Isn't anything ever easy?'

'I'm sorry, for us to get to the island we have to wait for the next tide.'

Daniel made his way to the door. 'I'll get someone to charter a boat for us.'

'No!'

Daniel spun round, confused. 'I have to organise a ship to get us there, we have no other choice.'

'No, I mean you can't tell anyone. Nathan said we can't trust anybody. When we do this, we have to do it ourselves, and certainly not from the harbour here in Parva.'

The Knight's looked stunned, but said nothing. It seemed as if by now they had resigned themselves to the fact that nothing was going to be easy about rescuing Nathan, so this additional bit of information was hardly a great surprise.

It was John who broke the silence.

'We should make our way to the fishing village of Bernick, we can find a boat there and then put in at one of the small coves on the south of the Island. There is an emergency route from the Citadel to the beach. It is a fair climb from there, but it is secluded and no-one should see us.'

'Aren't you afraid that anyone can access the Island from there if it's so easy to get to.'

John shook his head. 'No, the whole area is surrounded by solid defences, only those with keys can get through the locked gates, and I'm not talking normal keys.' He waved his fingers to prove the point. 'Only one of us can get through there from the beach, and only in an emergency will the gates open from the Citadel side.'

Jean didn't ask how the gates would know this but took his word for it.

'I see.' She smiled. 'So we translocate to Bernick'

'If we arrive at the cliff top above the village, it's a short decent to the harbour below. If we hurry we can make the next tide.'

'Better get moving then.'

Jean felt the atmosphere lift as they all left Nathan's ransacked room. They had a plan. They had no idea what they were going to do when they got to Pernia and the Council Chamber there, but at least they were doing something. Making their way across the hall and through the gardens to the gazebo, she sent out a silent prayer to Nathan.

Hold on Nathan, we're coming to get you.

26

Kendon

Kendon, the leader of the Kyawann rebels, stared down at the little human filled with rage. Personally he wouldn't think anything of picking him up and ripping him in two, watching all the dangly bits inside squelch out. However, he would have to bide his time as the one they called Bales currently held the fate of Kendon's entire army in his hands. But he could wait.

'What the fuck do you think you are doing letting your men roam around the countryside killing people? That was a Militia training team, led by the Order. And to top it all, some of them were allowed to escape.'

Bales' voice gradually rose with his anger, by the time he had finished, he was several octaves higher and out of breath. Kendon didn't flinch at the tirade, which seemed to make Bales even more angry.

'Don't forget Kendon, I brought you here, and I can just as easily send you back to the hell you came from.'

The huge Tievera put his head to one side, as if listening to a child not getting his own way.

'Why are you so concerned? My men were out on patrol and happened upon some humans, they saw an opportunity for some sport and took it. Some of them put up a good fight, even managed to kill one of my men, so what if a few got away? The fear they spread will help our cause when we finally meet on the field at this place you call Parva.'

Bales threw his hands in the air. 'Fool, they were Militia, they may only have been training, but they would have gone straight back to the garrison at Comston. The fact that they had the foresight to destroy the bridge in their flight demonstrates that they are not fools. Once arrived at the garrison, there wouldn't have been any panic, there would be a strict course of action taken. And the first person told will be that bastard Nathan; the Order will be out in force, hunting us down.'

'Then we will meet them, we are not afraid.'

'Idiot, the Order is not just any army, Nathan has access to tens of thousands of men, he can raise hundreds of thousands if needs be. The only thing on our side is that it will take him time to bring that number together on the field. We cannot afford to wait any longer, bring your men into line and prepare to march on Parva. If we are lucky we will be within sight of the city before nightfall tomorrow.'

'And if we are not?'

'Then be prepared to face the might of the Imperial army, and a very pissed off Emperor.' He turned as if to dismiss Kendon, but then seemed to think of something else. 'And while you're at it, make sure your men know that when I give an order from now on, they make sure they obey it.'

Then turning on his heel he left Kendon standing alone, seething while he tried to keep his temper under control. Somewhere behind him he heard his second-in-command, Roan, walk up and join him.

Kendon bristled. 'The man is an idiot. Who does he think he is? The arrogance of humans is even worse than we were led to believe.'

'Indeed, his Captains have been moving among the army. The Vaupír are looking for an opportunity to acquire one for a snack.'

Both Tievera smiled, it was a tempting thought to allow one of the human men to suddenly disappear, but that would not help their cause. Roan looked at Kendon thoughtfully.

'May I speak freely my Lord?'

'Of course, what is on your mind?'

'Are we sure this Bales is who he says he is? I mean, he gave an order that no-one was to leave the camp, but four of our troops were able to go out into the countryside to hunt. Surely that would be impossible if...'

Roan left it hanging, but Kendon got his drift, and he couldn't argue his reasoning. He stared out over the fires of the huge army encamped before him; hidden within a valley from prying eyes. Only those humans who had been living there knew of their existence, but they were not a problem.

335

They and their livestock had proved an appetising prize. He sighed and inclined his head to the Tievera next to him.

'I agree, this Bales is unlikely to be who he says he is, however, our presence here is tied to his wishes. If he chose to send us back to Kyawann then we could do little, if anything, about it.' He gave Roan a vicious grin. 'For now, anyway.'

'What do you want to do?'

'At the moment? Nothing. It still suits our purpose to be here, whether we will need to rely on Bales much longer is yet to be confirmed. However, this Emperor he seems so afraid of intrigues me. We will meet him on the field at this city of Parva, and when we have him in chains at our feet, we can perhaps use him in our favour.'

'What about Bales' concern that he can call up so big an army?'

Kendon scoffed. 'A human army be a match for us? No, I am not worried about such things. As Bales said, we will be there by tomorrow and we will take the field. Give the orders to break camp, we march within the hour.'

'Yes, my Lord.' He turned to leave when Kendon called him back.

'And Roan, Bales did have one useful suggestion. Our rebellious soldiers that took an illicit hunting trip, take their leader and make an example of him. The Vaupír are no doubt still looking for snacks.'

27

An Errand of Mercy

Jean and the Knights left Parva while it was still early morning. They arrived, as Damien had predicted, in time to catch the high tide. Having chartered a fishing smack and its small crew, they left the mainland and headed for the island of Pernia mid morning. The crew had taken up the commission to sail eagerly, the opportunity to be paid to go to sea and not have to fish for it was not to be taken lightly. They of course, also realised who their passengers were, even if they weren't forthcoming with their identities.

Once on board, the Knights and Jean were keen to get underway. The crew were curious as to why they would choose to travel from Bernick when they could have sailed from Parva. But Damien informed them of the exact location of their destination only once they had set sail. The crew had obviously been puzzled by these arrangements, but again, didn't dare question them.

As fishing boats go, there was the usual intense smell of fish throughout the vessel, but the small company didn't care, they were moving forward, but to what end none of them knew. Of course, Jean had never been to the island, let alone have any idea about this Council Chamber they needed to find. It would be dawn the following day before they arrived and she found it difficult to control her frustration, though she knew the Knights were as anxious as she was to get to Pernia.

At first, it was difficult to gain everyone's attention; despite the small size of the boat, they had wandered around the deck, finding their own ways of keeping their minds busy. John and Simon had offered to help the crew with setting the sails, whilst Damien chatted to the Captain. Paul and Stephen had made their way aft and they both sat in silence, staring out to sea; the concerned looks on their faces mirroring their companions.

Daniel had joined Jean in the prow of the ship, moving stored fishing nets and pots in order to find a place to sit. It was a snug fit for the two of them, but Jean found she didn't mind, at that moment she realised how alone she felt and appreciated Daniel's company. They had formed a close relationship since the battle at Parva. A shared confidence

338

had sealed a trust that neither had cause to regret. He was easy to talk to and she enjoyed his, often skewed, view of those around them. When he visited Denfield, he spent as much of his time talking with Jean as he did with Nathan; he was more like a brother to her than the great uncle he really was. Now, as he sat down, his arm draped along the rail behind her. Looking up she noticed he was watching her with concern, she tried to give him a reassuring smile, but he didn't look convinced. It was a while before he spoke, and when he did, his voice was quiet but suggested this was not going to be a prelude to small talk.

'Are you alright?'

Jean smiled sadly. 'Bearing up considering the circumstances'

He returned her smile. 'Fair enough, I should have expected nothing less.'

'Are *you* alright?'

He didn't answer straight away, and when he did it was with another question.

'What is it you're not telling us Jean?'

Taken by surprise, she had to think carefully how she was going to answer, especially with Daniel. He had a knack of knowing how to wheedle answers out of people before they realised it. She decided to go for his own tactic and answer with her own question.

'What makes you think I'm hiding anything?'

He raised an eyebrow and put his head to one side. 'I think we both know each other well enough by now to know when the other is keeping things to themselves, and I don't just mean your empathic skills. Back in Parva, you never questioned whether coming to Pernia was the right thing to do or not. For all we know, Nathan could be held in some part of the universe that we could be tearing down now to get to him; but you're still sure this is the right course of action. Why?'

Jean held his gaze before turning her head to look out to sea, somewhere on the horizon was the island of Pernia, she wished it would come into view faster. Daniel said nothing, he just waited, because he knew Jean would answer, she had to. Still staring across the open expanse of water, she closed her eyes, only speaking when she opened them again.

'I believe the force that took Nathan from his room in the Retreat, a place heavily protected by Nathan himself, wanted him away from any association with the universe or the even the gods themselves. A place that would take him out of time and space, a place that shouldn't exist.'

She paused, before again, choosing her words carefully. She turned and looked into Daniel's open and concerned face.

'I have no idea how to even start looking for somewhere like that, let alone try and get there. So, if Nathan believes you know what he means when he says *out of time*, then I am going to hang onto that glimmer of hope and not let go.'

Daniel continued to study her, even after she had finished. She knew he wanted to know more, but she wasn't even sure herself. He looked as if he was gearing up to further questions she wasn't prepared to answer. Fortunately, Damien chose that moment to join them. Daniel didn't look pleased at the interruption, but seemed reluctant to push his questions further with Damien there.

'I've spoken to the skipper, he reckons by dawn tomorrow we should be within sight of the shore under the Citadel; it will be another couple of hours before we sail round to the inlet we want.'

Jean couldn't hide her frustration.

'It's all taking so long, why does Nathan have so many protections around this bloody island? We could be there by now, and Nathan could be home, safe.'

Damien and Daniel shared a look, Jean didn't miss it and she could feel her anger rising.

'What? Why does everything have to be shrouded in protection? We can't leave the city unless its through specific points, and an island in the middle of the sea can only be accessed by ship. And on top of that, I had to spend seven thousand sodding years desperately looking for my home, only to find out it too has been hidden under a cloak of concealment.'

As she got into her stride, Jean's voice had began to rise, the other Knights and even some of the crew were now looking her way. Realising she had become the unwanted centre of attention she turned away and was resolutely staring back out to sea again, hoping the Knights would get the hint and leave her alone.

Apparently though, they had other ideas.

'What's going on?' Simon joined them and Jean groaned inwardly, she was going to have to brazen this one out. She turned around and realised that all the Knights were now gathered about the small space in the ship's prow. It was getting a bit cramped and Jean thought that with one good wave they would all be soaked in sea water. But she had reached the point where she really didn't care, all she wanted was to get to Pernia and find a way to reach Nathan.

Irritation gnawed at her mind, images of him lying in the dark, naked, afraid and in pain, tore at her heart, and everything they needed to do to get to him was thwarted by the very protections that Nathan had himself created. Anger flared up inside her again.

Bloody man, why do you have to make everything so bloody difficult?

Fear soon replaced anger. The thought of him dying alone in that awful place sent shudders of despair through her body. She couldn't lose him now, not when she had only just found him, they had so much to talk about and do. She needed to talk to him now, tell him how bloody annoying he was, tell him that she loved him.

She closed her eyes and fought back the tears threatening to fall down her cheeks, there, she had admitted it to herself at last.

Yes, Nathan L'guire, I love you, and you're stuck in the middle of nowhere, literally, so I can't even tell you.

She rubbed her face with her hands and opened her eyes, the Knights were still watching her in silence. Most men would look for the nearest escape route when a woman even so much as hinted at an emotional outburst, but then again, most men weren't ten thousand years old and had probably seen it all so many times before. Instead, they barely looked uncomfortable, seeming more concerned. They really weren't going to let her get out of this easily.

'I'm sorry, this is not normal for me to be so bloody emotional, but it's frustrating having to take things slowly. I just don't understand what is so special about this island and why this Council Chamber can only be accessed from there.'

As it seemed that Jean had stopped venting her anger and frustration on anyone who would listen, the Knights made themselves more comfortable. Fishing nets, pots and boxes were moved around under the unimpressed eye of the ship's skipper, until they were all sitting more or less comfortably. Damien broke the silence when they were finally settled.

'I know you're frustrated Jean, we all are, but we also know that trying to fight it will get us nowhere. We have to work together. I don't believe any one of us can do this alone and getting angry over something you can't control is not helping.'

Jean bit her lip, she felt suitably chastised and knew she thoroughly deserved it. It didn't help her mood, but she knew she had to keep her anger in check. The Knights weren't fools, they had been around even longer than she had, of course they were worried sick about Nathan, she didn't have a monopoly on him.

Feeling ridiculous now, she looked around guiltily and tried to put a smile on her face, not believing for one moment that it was convincing, but they seemed to appreciate the effort anyway. She had existed for centuries, dealt with horrors and emotions that would send most people mad, but here she was, feeling as if she was losing it over a man she had known for a matter of months. Sharing her pain with men who, until recently, didn't even know she existed. But as Damien suggested, it is what it is, they can't control it, but they can deal with it, together.

'I'm sorry, this isn't your fault and as you say, childish outbursts aren't helping anyone. It's just…' She trailed off, not certain of what she could really say that wouldn't betray feelings she wasn't sure of herself. Damien reached out and held her hand, they were sitting so squashed up to each other, it was more a gesture of goodwill than of intimacy.

'I know,'

Jean looked at him sharply.

What did he know?

He said nothing, but the grin that spread across his face made her flush and she felt herself gulp before looking away. Sure the others also knew what he was talking about, she decided she needed to change the subject.

'So what about Pernia and the Council Chamber, then? Tell me what you know about that.'

Damien spread his hands and relaxed against the side of the ship; sea spray hung in the air around them, but no-one seemed to care anymore.

'Well, the Council Chamber isn't exactly *at* Pernia, it would be more accurate to suggest it is accessible from The Citadel. But before that, maybe I should explain what Pernia and the Citadel actually is. First of all, it is Nathan's ancestral home. Apart from being our Emperor, he is also known as the Duke of Pernia.'

Jean nodded. 'Of course, the only title Ephea could rightly claim through marriage.'

'Exactly. He inherited this title from his father, Gareth, who decided this was where he wanted to set his family seat. At first my father Corman, his younger brother, thought it odd that Gareth should claim such a small area of land as

344

his own, while he could consider himself the Duke of the whole of Lorimar. But of course, Gareth had his mind set on more than just land on Kelan, his vision had a more galactic outlook.

'We had all been taught the knowledge of the Primary Worlds in school, just as every other child, as well as their importance within the structure of the universe. But Gareth saw an opportunity to bring these worlds under the authority of one government; unifying them in a bid to gain a foothold in every sector of the universe.

'While it seemed at first that he may achieve his goal, it soon became apparent that he had 'bitten off more than he could chew' as I believe they say on Earth. Our grandfather — his father — Gerhalt was still very much alive when Gareth started on his quest.

Gerhalt had already unified the clans within Kelan. There had been a huge advance in the creating of portals back then; they were still pretty primitive by today's standards, but they were effective nonetheless in bringing cultures from across the globe literally within a step of each other. There was an established court dealing with law and order already existing at Parva, though the city we know now was more of a fortified village within the walls of the caldera surrounding a small harbour. But as a centralised banking system was also established, there came a need to create more portals in order for people to access, what they considered, their administrative centre. Hence the reason Parva became the strategic centre it is today.

Pernia, being just across the sea, was perfect for Gareth to demonstrate how he thought himself separate from the rest of the administration. There was a portal there then, and he could travel to Parva knowing he could retreat to his own private island whenever he wanted.

'But I digress. For Gareth to use this strategy of opening portals to unite the seven Primary Worlds would seem, in theory at least, not such a bad idea. Of course the difference was, the people of these other worlds had no idea who he was, and had no intention of just handing over the governance of their lives to him or anyone else. And so it was that he then spent the rest of his life convincing these worlds that he was their best option for a leader. Needless to say, he wasn't entirely successful. This may have been down to the huge armies that he sent to impress upon these people his good intentions.

But apart from opening up the gateways between these worlds, and allowing people to pass across freely, while also opening the opportunities for some to trade and create economic alliances, his great plan wasn't very successful. In fact, it was his final foray into the Primary World of the Seventh Sector, Earth, that did for him in the end. He was killed during a battle in a place that is now known as Australia. Nathan and Katherine were six at the time.'

Jean looked incredulous. 'Sorry, are you saying that there were sufficient armies ten thousand years ago, on Earth, that could stand up to a force from Kelan? Surely not.'

Damien and the other Knights laughed. 'Don't be fooled by what you read about Earth's history, just because there are no longer records of the lives of the people back then, doesn't mean they were primitive and uncivilised. There is

346

much about Earth's history that is unlikely to be uncovered today.'

Jean had a sudden feeling of déjà vu. Listening to Niall telling her of the Empire and its influence on Earth, nothing was ever as it at first seemed.

'So what happened after Gareth died?'

'To be honest, nothing happened really. Gerhalt had been dead for a number of years by then, and Gareth's wars outwith Kelan's borders had been costly, both financially and in men. While it was accepted that Nathan would inherit his father's position, as a very young six year old he wouldn't be taking up the reins of power for many years yet. Alexandra, Nathan's mother was had also died, so my father brought him and Katherine from Pernia, to our home in Lorimar where he and my mother looked after them. He dealt with the administrative responsibilities, until the twins had finished their education and were in a position to take over. Of course, by then the whole idea of the Guardians was instigated by the gods and we all had very different roles to play.'

'So that is where you and Nathan grew close? When he and Katherine came to live with you I mean.'

Damien surprised Jean by laughing and shaking his head.

'Hell no. I am ten years older than Nathan, I was a spotty hormonal teenager of sixteen when their father died. I had no compunction to entertain two little children I had probably only met once before in my life, and that was soon after they were born. No, Nathan and I became better acquainted when they both came to me to learn how to use a sword without slicing off bits of their own anatomy.'

347

'You taught Nathan to use a sword?'

Daniel grinned. 'Damien is our own Master Swordsman, he makes sure we are all up to par, even now.'

Damien gave Jean a hard look. 'Yes, and a subject I have been meaning to have a word with you about.'

'What do you mean?'

'I have noticed you have picked up a few bad habits when you use your sword, at some point we need to deal with them.'

Jean felt herself bristle and was about to say something but Daniel spoke first, clearly intending to head off any potential controversy.

'I wouldn't bother arguing, he won't take no for an answer, and if he's not happy with your technique then it would do you good to listen. He really does know what he is talking about, even if it can get a bit painful in his demonstrations.'

There was unanimous agreement from the other Knights, who all seemed to have the same grimace on their faces. Jean made a mental note to make sure she improved her sword craft before being dragged into any practical classrooms with Damien. In an attempt to steer away from the subject of her apparent need for improvement in sword craft technique, Jean returned to the topic of Nathan and Pernia.

'So did Nathan and Katherine return to Pernia as they were growing up?'

Damien shook his head. 'No, Nathan had no desire to return to the place after our inauguration there as Guardians. He hated it; his mother had died giving birth to the twins there, and they had been virtually imprisoned

348

within the Citadel while Gareth spent his time away fighting. It was only Katherine who eventually returned and extended the building that stands there today and made it her own. Nathan only returned to effectively put the whole area into a protective bubble when she disappeared. That was predominantly to keep people out, as well as to preserve the estate; something similar to what he did at the Retreat, but for seven thousand years instead. The people who lived and worked on the farms and villages stayed, but had to sail to the mainland when the portal was removed. The rest of the island became impenetrable by anyone else. Only the local wildlife were prevalent there. Well, that is until about four hundred years ago; but that is a different story altogether and for telling another day.'

Jean was intrigued but didn't push the subject. 'But what about the Council Chamber?'

'Hmmm, yes, the Council Chamber. Well, to be honest, that is the odd thing about it all. We know it didn't exist when Gareth was alive, but when we all gathered there for our inauguration ceremony, it appeared as if it had always been part of the original structure. Very strange, but with all that was going on at the time, and everything that we had dealt with just to get to that point, it wasn't something we really questioned; well, not until a long time later.'

'So how do you know it's still there?'

'Because it is, or it isn't unless we've needed it, if you know what I mean.'

Jean felt the first pangs of panic begin to rise. 'You mean it might not be there when we arrive?'

Damien tried not to look uneasy, but it was pointless to try and fool the empath in the group. 'This is where Nathan wants us to be, I have no doubt about that. It's what we have to do when we get there I have concerns over.'

It was Jean's turn to place her hand over his in reassurance.

'If this bloody Chamber is there, we will find a way to Nathan. I just wish it wasn't taking so long for us to get there.'

She looked back out to sea, towards the direction of Pernia. 'So if Gareth never actually united the Primary worlds, how does the Empire exist?'

'Ah, well that is entirely down to Nathan. Where his father felt that brute strength and dominance was the way to gain power and influence, his son just utilised the common trade lines that had been set up over the years. It was James and I who first helped to create the treaties between the Prime Worlds. Then, with Daniel's help, these understandings were strengthened and eventually a trust was formed, after which the Empire came into existence. Ironically, Nathan found himself with the title of Emperor, which he hates by the way, he's been trying to shake it off ever since. But it helped to instil a trust in an authority that has kept a social and economic security for thousands of years, so there's not much he can do about it.'

Jean had to chuckle to herself and said. 'An Empire built on trust; well there's something you don't hear everyday.'

'Indeed.'

Before the sun began to sink below the horizon, the Skipper had come to inform them there was a storm heading down from the North. They all studied the northern horizon and groaned at the thin dark line that forewarned of the impending tempest.

Damien grimaced and turned to the weather worn Skipper.

'How much is this going to set us back?'

The sailor shook his head. 'That depends entirely on that beast out there. We can try and make a run for it before she hits, then make our way back to Pernia when she's passed. But if she catches up with us, we'll have to heave-to and throw out the sea anchor, then batten down the hatches until it's buggered off south.'

There was nothing else they could do. Jean and the Knights joined the rest of the crew to set the sails, in order to try and make a run for it towards the west of Pernia. By the time the storm caught up with them, the Skipper of the fishing smack gave the order to heave-to, then everyone took cover below decks to wait for the howling wind and rain to pass. They ate a basic meal and settled themselves down for a thoroughly cold, wet and miserable night.

The sun was high in the sky by the time the storm had begun to move away. Jean and the Knights had managed little sleep, the extra seven people on board would normally mean ousting the most junior of the crew out of their pits. But on the small smack, apart from the Skipper and his mate, the crew used hammocks strung up across the small area in the lower deck. The Knights eyed the sleeping conditions warily, they were soldiers, not sailors and preferred to seek out dark corners to get their heads down. Jean tried to sleep but images and thoughts of Nathan ran

351

through her mind, and with the storm raging outside she could only succumb to the occasional exhausted doze as the hours crawled by.

The wind was still high but the storm had passed to the south when everyone had gratefully escaped to the upper deck, breathing in the fresh air. Jean was eyeing the Knights and crew with undisguised disgust and John looked at her enquiringly.

'What's upset you so early in the day?'

She shook her head. 'I know this is a fishing vessel, and it's impossible to avoid the smell of fish, but to have to share a confined space with a load of men adds a whole layer of revolting odours.'

John looked quite offended. 'What do you mean?'

'How do you all function producing that many smells and noises? It cannot be healthy!'

John began to laugh, and when he was joined by the other Knights he gladly regaled them of Jean's distaste to their 'manly odours'. Needless to say, they all thought it was hilarious. Jean just shook her head, rolled her eyes and stomped up the deck muttering to herself.

The smack had been blown someway to the west of Pernia during the storm, and the Skipper was now giving his crew orders to make for the shores of Pernia. It was a delay Jean and the Knights could have done without, but there was nothing they could do. She looked towards the island and leant against the wooden rail. Closing her exhausted eyes, she concentrated on the image of Nathan and sent out her thoughts.

Hang in there Nathan, we're on our way.

28

Hell

Pain convulsed through Nathan's body, every muscle and tissue fibre screamed with agony. It seemed an eternity until it finally ceased; his body covered in a film of sweat from the effort. Inside he felt cold and empty, despite there being no movement of air around him, no source of heat either, but still he felt chilled to the bone.

As the last of the spasms left him feeling exhausted and confused, he tried to concentrate his mind, figure out where he was and why he was here. Or had he already done this, didn't he know where he was? The question seemed familiar, but the answers always seemed to escape him. Forcing down the feelings of panic that threatened to rise, he tried to calm his thoughts, focusing his mind inwards. At first his thoughts

353

were like wisps of smoke, and trying to catch them was impossible. But slowly they became solid and his heart sank as the truth emerged from the darkness.

For as long as he could remember, he had always had a connection with the energy of the universe, manipulating it to help form the protections that surrounded the Empire, Pernia, Parva and Denfield, amongst other places. He could feel the vibrations of its resonance, understood its nuances. It never felt strange. It was part of him, as he was part of it; until now.

His heart ached at the loss of something that was so fundamentally part of who he was. Now he understood, where he had been taken, he was outside the very fabric of existence itself. But he already knew this, he had figured all of this out before; if space didn't exist here, then neither did time. He shook his head to try and clear his brain.

How long had he been here? Hours? Days? Years?

Around him, a force so thick, he could feel it entering his lungs as he tried to breathe.

Was he breathing?

How could he breathe if air didn't exist here? But of course, if time didn't exist, he was most likely still living with his last breath in his lungs.

Though how much longer did he have until that finally faded away?

Already he sensed the edges of his mind begin to succumb to the fog that was clouding his brain.

Did this happen before? Or is this something new? Was this finally the start of the end?

He shook his head again, trying to clear his thoughts. Images rose up before him, people from his past flitted like shadows through his consciousness; friends, family even enemies. At one point he imagined talking to Jean, she seemed so close and he tried desperately to reach out to her. But he couldn't move, the effort seemed to cause the force around him to push harder into his tormented body, causing it to writhe in agony.

Even in his dreams he couldn't escape it seemed. He tried to remember the image of Jean's face, and all he saw was fear and concern; she was afraid and it tore at his heart to think she was so worried. He wanted to reassure her, tell her he would be fine, he would be home soon. But that would have been a lie, he couldn't get home, he was lost here, nowhere.

Eventually he succumbed to all the pain and guilt, the feelings of inadequacy and fear.

He had failed again.

Inside, his heart was breaking, for all the dreams that may have come to pass had he been a stronger man. He forced his eyes shut tight in his efforts to keep Jean's image alive in his mind. The vision of the woman who had barely just walked into his life, and who never knew how much love he wanted to give her.

Somewhere he heard her voice, he wasn't sure if it was in his mind, or somewhere out in the depths of the place that didn't exist.

'Hang in there Nathan, we're on our way.'

He wished with all his might it was true and not his desperate attempt to believe there was hope. As he tried to keep hold of the thoughts, he sent a single word in reply.

'Jean.'

355

29

Inchgower

Field Marshal Harvey Inchgower was not in a good mood, it should have been his day off. His grandchildren were due to visit and he and his wife were looking forward to seeing the boys. Even though every visit usually left their house as if a hurricane had blasted through it, Inchgower and Rebbie loved the sound of laughter and mayhem running about every room.

Today was his daughter's birthday, and she and her husband wanted to make some much needed precious time for just the two of them. As such, both the boys and their grandparents had looked forward to the day as much as the exhausted parents. But circumstances had taken over, and Inchgower had been forced to leave his wife crashing around the kitchen, furious that she was now left to look after two very boisterous boys on her own. His daughter and son-in-law had said they would arrange for another day, but of course, Rebbie would have none of it; it's difficult to be a martyr if people are understanding and try to make things easier for you.

There was an awkward silence as he made his way along the half mile of the Avenue up to the Palace with General Morris. But there were too many questions flitting through his mind to worry about how his wife would make him pay for his negligence; he was sure she would do all that for him later.

Things hadn't gone well when General Morris had arrived, leaving an escort outside the front of the house, he discovered Inchgower and his wife had only just settled down for breakfast with the rest of the family due to arrive any minute. The General had sense enough to look sorry for the intrusion; the temper of the Field Marshall's wife was well known in the higher social circles of the city.

'Sir, I am here on behalf of the High Council. A matter that requires your immediate attention has arisen.'

Inchgower waited for further information, but was annoyed when no more was forthcoming. Rebbie was eyeing the General with unguarded hostility and the man was looking extremely uncomfortable. Aware his wife's annoyance could very easily be focused his way, Inchgower snapped at his unwelcome visitor.

'General, if you've come here on my day off and expected me to leave my family because the High Council is having difficulty with an *urgent matter,* I can assure you I am not impressed. So, you can go back and tell the High Council to hold it together until tomorrow, when I will be back in my office ready to receive any urgent matters still outstanding.'

General Morris however, had been in the Order far too long to be intimidated by anyone, even if they were a retired Field Marshall and the Leader of the Imperial Council; though it was getting close to it.

'Sir, I cannot give you any more information here, other than this is extremely urgent. I implore you to come with me now.'

Inchgower was about to let the General know exactly where he could stick his imploring, especially as he could feel his wife's eyes boring into his neck. But something about the General's voice made him check himself. Something was wrong and it was obvious that he wasn't going to get any more information standing here. Giving a brief nod to Morris, he took in a slow breath and braced himself for the inevitable onslaught. Turning to his wife, he opened his arms and gave her the biggest smile he could. She didn't look impressed.

'Rebbie, darling……..'

The rest of the conversation went down hill rapidly. In fact it was less a conversation and more a one-sided tirade, with only the arrival of his daughter and her family as a brief respite. And brief it certainly was. Giving his daughter the most apologetic look he could, he grabbed his jacket and followed the General out of his house.

At least now Morris looked suitably terrified.

The two men had walked all the way to the Palace in silence, both feeling as if they were back as newly knighted members of the Order, about to get it in the neck from their senior officer for a misdemeanour.

Field Marshal Harvey Inchgower was sixty-two years old and had enjoyed a full and remarkable career behind him. Both his parents had been in the Order, and while it had been expected that he would follow in their footsteps, if he was asked he would have to say he couldn't imagine himself in any other career. While he was still a cadet at Pernia he had shown his skills at leadership, not only capable of making difficult decisions that others would baulk from, but also as a man that others rallied to. As he rose through the ranks, those under his command followed without question, even into situations that would ultimately cost lives.

He never forgot those who had fallen under his command; they were soldiers who understood the risks, but it didn't make it any easier to live with and he carried the burden of their sacrifice with him everyday.

His superiors were quick to realise his potential too, especially it seemed, the Emperor himself. The two had become friends when Inchgower was still a Colonel and was stationed at Parva. It was from this friendship that he had eventually become the Leader of the ultimate power within the Empire next to the Knights themselves.

While the High Council was made up of elected members, the position of Leader was always the choice of Nathan. As the person expected to stand in for the Emperor when he was away, such as his unexpected disappearances with the Knights on one of their missions, Nathan needed to know he had someone he could trust implicitly to take responsibility. It was a prestigious position that had been held by a distinguished few over the centuries. They had come from all walks of life, and strangely enough, not many had come from the ranks of the Order.

Nathan was explicit in his desire to not turn the Empire into a military state. Apparently, he was more interested in Inchgower's ability to gain the trust and respect of those under him than his military prowess. All through the Ephea years, as they were now being unofficially referred to, he had quietly led the government of the Empire, while the Knights worked with him from behind the scenes. It had worked well, so that even Ephea was unable to interfere with the High Council's authority.

Inchgower and Morris, along with their escort, now made their way through the huge double doors that led into the Palace atrium. The General had still said nothing regarding this mysterious issue that was so important, particularly one that should require the leader of the High Council to be dragged away from his family on his day off. But Inchgower became even more curious when Morris led him to a private room, instead of the usual meeting chambers. He gave a puzzled look at the General, who remained steadfastly silent as he opened the door into a room filled with a dozen men and women; only two of which were actually members of the Council. The rest of those present were senior members of the Order, along with, he noted with interest, Colonel Anna Priestly and Captain Ty Coniston, neither of whom would normally be considered senior enough to join such a prestigious gathering.

He acknowledged their presence but said nothing. Introductions were not needed, so joining everyone at the large conference table, he glanced up at the map that had been pinned to the wall opposite. It was of the west coast of Lorimar, and he could just make out pins that had been placed in an area located east of Parva.

He made himself comfortable and placed his arms on the table in front of him, his hands clasped together, resting easily on the wooden surface.

'Good morning everyone, I am assuming that someone is going to tell me what the hell is going on. I was under the impression this was High Council business, not an issue for the Order.'

It was Anna who spoke first, much to the consternation of the others around the table.

'Sir, our apologies for the intrusion into your personal time and the mystery surrounding your summons.' She didn't have the opportunity to continue before the man sitting next to Inchgower raised his voice.

'That will do Colonel.'

The Field Marshal wasn't impressed at Brigadier Otto's interruption and gave him a look that reflected his annoyance.

The senior officer flushed at the unspoken rebuke. 'My apologies Sir, but I think the Colonel should be made aware of her place. I don't even know why she is here, this is a significant meeting that does not concern her or the Captain here. I believe they should be removed before any further discussions are made.'

Inchgower studied him for a moment before turning to Anna, the murderous look on her face didn't go unnoticed. He had a feeling her presence here was significantly more pertinent than the Brigadier suggested. Her reply confirmed his fears.

Maintaining a calmness to her voice, there was no mistaking the steel note behind it. 'Brigadier, I am not here in the capacity of a Colonel of the Order, but as the Duchess and wife of the Duke of Pylia. As such, I sit here as the most senior person available for this meeting in Parva. I have asked Ty here to join me as representative of Lord Damien.' Ty looked positively alarmed as all eyes suddenly turned in his direction, but Anna continued. 'It was also I who called this meeting, including who should attend. I am hoping that your presence will not be a mistake.'

Her eyes bore into those of the furious man across the table, but he had the good sense not to argue. Inchgower, filled the moments of awkward silence that followed.

'Of course you are quite right my Lady, to a point.' Anna shot a confused look in his direction. 'You are quite correct, that as the Duchess of Pylia, Brigadier Otto should recognise your seniority.' He paused for a moment, watching her face change as she realised her mistake. 'Yes, my Lady, while the Emperor is away from the Empire, I stand in his stead.'

Anna flushed, but held his gaze. 'Of course, my apologise, I did not mean to speak out of turn.'

He watched as the rest of the table shifted uncomfortably. He returned his attention back to Anna and his expression softened.

362

'Think nothing for of it, there are obviously far more pressing matters to be dealt with here than who is king of the heap. This also brings up the first most important question — why are your husband and the Emperor not available at this time? I take it they have been called away on one of their missions.'

Anna inclined her head. 'My apologies Sir, and please call me Anna. While I may presume my presence here as a Duchess, I by no means expect deference to my rank. Secondly, wherever my husband is at the moment, it would appear that it is not on a mission requiring the attention of the Guardians.'

He frowned. 'Wherever he is? You mean you don't know?'

Anna shook her head. 'Early this morning, Ty and I had calls from both Paul and Damien stating they had to leave on a matter that required their immediate attention.' She looked down at her hands, Inchgower saw a look of deep concern on her face. 'Paul wouldn't give any further information other than that. I, of course came to Parva immediately, where I met Ty who told the same story. We have since heard that there were six Knights, along with Jean Carter, seen at the fishing village of Bernick chartering a fishing boat.'

'You said there were six Knights with Jean, who was missing?'

Anna looked around the table, her face as worried as the rest. 'Nathan, he was missing from the group.'

Inchgower frowned. 'Is the Emperor still in the Palace?'

Otto shook his head. 'We've had the Palace searched, no-one has seen him since the dinner he attended last night with the other Knights.'

Resting his chin on his clasped hands, Inchgower looked around the table. 'While this may be disconcerting, this is not the reason why you have brought me here. Even the Knights are allowed a private life, they don't have to tell us everything they do.'

This time it was General Morris who took up the story. 'We are concerned over the disappearance of the Knights because of news we have received of an incident that has occurred near the Comston garrison.' He held his hands together in front of him, as if trying to hold himself together, and took a deep breath. Inchgower found himself intrigued by whatever could make such a normally calm man seem so uncomfortable.

Morris continued. 'An hour ago, Major Dillon of the Comston garrison, along with a Militia cadet, arrived in Parva via portal. They described large blue, demon like, aliens having invaded Kelan. It would have been laughable if it wasn't for the fact that in their report they mention that all but four members of their fifteen strong Militia training company, and their three knights were massacred by these invaders.'

The Field Marshal sat up straight. 'All of them? Have these claims been verified?'

'The garrison is currently investigating, but a bridge was destroyed in the survivor's efforts to flee, so they are having to travel further up stream to cross the river. They will send word once more information is forthcoming. However, the two messengers are still here if you wish to speak with them yourself.'

Inchgower nodded. 'Indeed, I will. You say there have been other incidents.'

'There was a message from the main gate that a farmhand was demanding admittance, gabbling that his family was murdered in their sleep, and that blue men had destroyed his farm. The man was a mess when he arrived and he is currently being looked after at the Palace guardroom. They have given him food and he is resting before they try and gain some more coherent information.

It has been established that his farm is just south of the forests to the north of the River Elvian. In his flight to escape these invaders he had stopped to change horses at a farm on the way here. But even so, the horse and its rider were exhausted after having travelled most of night to get here. There are scouts currently sitting in the stables, prepared to ride out and find out what is going on as soon as orders are given.'

'Yes, that is an excellent idea, have them sent out immediately. I want to know any information as soon as it arrives. Ty, please have Major Dillon and this Militia cadet from Comston called.'

Ty left the room and returned a few minutes later with Major Dillon, along with a young man eyeing those around the table warily. After making a brief introduction, the young man who was called George Fewson, relayed everything that had happened that morning up until the point when they had run through the gates at Comston, demanding they be shut and barred.

No matter how much he tried, Inchgower found it hard to see the man as a dissembler. The confirmation being that Major Dillon, who he knew to be a solid and reliable member of the Order, was not known for her overreacting to unusual circumstances. And that Fewson was a man who was becoming a respected member of the Militia who also had aspirations of joining the Order.

Brigadier Otto wasn't so convinced. 'I don't see how it is possible for anyone to invade the Empire. The defence barriers set in place around the six Prime Worlds by the Emperor would be impossible to enter, and have never been broken. While Earth is an obvious possible weakness, there are so many protections between them and us, only authorised personnel are allowed through.'

Inchgower didn't like the way Otto used the words *them and us,* but for now he let it pass; but he did have to remind Otto of recent events.

'But the invaders known as Kaimiren were able to get here from the Seventh Sector. Also, Ephea's Patrol members have moved to and from Earth for the past five years.'

Otto looked uncomfortable but had his own ideas about that one. 'That may be so, but while it is not common knowledge, we here know that there was significant celestial influence involved.'

There was a silence in the room as the leader of the Imperial High Council considered the information set before him, he looked up at the concerned faces around the table.

'Considering the possibility of an invasion on Kelan soil, no matter how unlikely that is, we still have to take it seriously. Issue orders to the other garrisons that Parva is calling for them to send reinforcements to the city and to be prepared to translocate when needed. Bearing in mind the Emperor is not available to move such huge numbers of troops at once, they will have to use the crystals to travel. This of course is an issue on its own, to use so many crystals in close proximity could possibly be catastrophic, so they will have to arrive at a safe distance and make their way towards Parva.'

'But what of the threat from the east?' All eyes moved to Anna. 'If there is an army of invaders heading this way, to translocate a small body of knights anywhere near them could be fatal.'

'Yes, I agree. At the moment confine all troop movements to the north and south of the river between the forest and the city until more information is available.' He held up his hands as Otto made to speak. 'I know this course of action will cost a lot of time, but at the moment we will proceed with caution.'

With that, the small meeting ended and everyone was despatched to their tasks.

After a long day dealing with the sporadic information available regarding the invading army, it was now past midnight and Inchgower took off his glasses, closing his eyes before pinching the top of his nose. There was a start of a headache building behind his eyes and he opened his desk drawer to look for something to ease the dull throb. Having found some painkillers, he stood and made his way to the window where he poured himself a glass of water from the pitcher there. Once he'd taken a long drink with his tablets, he looked out over the darkened rain soaked city that

367

sprawled across the river on the South Bank; a few lights remained within houses, but otherwise, only the street lighting gave any indication that there was life there at all. The trees that lined the Avenue bent against the wind of the storm that blasted up the thoroughfare, and the knights of the duty watch on the gate had the guardroom door firmly shut and the gates barred. Only the foolhardy would be abroad on a night like this.

He stood at the rain lashed windows, having finished reading the reports of the training company massacre at Comston confirmed, along with the stories told by refugees fleeing from the west; talking of huge, blue monsters devastating villages and farmsteads. Troops of knights and Militia on their way to Parva were of some comfort, but there were reports from scouts that the invading army were at least forty-thousand strong.

Even if luck was on their side, the slow progress of moving troops in small groups, along an ever decreasing window of opportunity, would barely cover a quarter of that number.

When it was discovered that the Knights had charted a boat heading in the direction of Pernia, orders were given to set sail for the remote island immediately. But no ships had been able to leave on the next available tide that evening due to the sudden storm that had built to the north, heading south down the Pernia Strait. The weather report suggested nothing was leaving harbour until at least the following morning.

Inchgower sighed and closed the curtains. His headache was already breaking through his painkillers and he didn't think it would be dissipating any time soon. He knew he should try and get some sleep, but his brain was working too hard trying to answer impossible questions. Field Marshal Harvey Inchgower had to admit, for the first time in his career he needed help; he needed his Emperor, he needed Nathan.

Dear gods, my Lords where the hell are you?

30

Ducking &
Diving

Exhausted and sore from their cramped night on the fishing smack, the Knights and Jean were a bit damp round the edges after their clamber ashore. Looking up at the cliff face, it appeared a lot higher from the beach than it did from out at sea. Behind them, the fishing smack was sailing away, Damien had released them from their obligations once they had landed, putting out their nets to fish in the now calmer seas around Pernia.

They had all agreed their aim was to find Nathan. If they didn't succeed, the Knights would forget all subterfuge and they would send out every available man and woman to search for him. However, for now, they would abide by his wishes and remain resolute in their task, attempting to be as covert as was possible.

It was past midday and Jean looked skeptically at the ominous climb ahead of them. She glanced sideways at Damien.

'You expect us to climb that?'

He shook his head. 'Not climb exactly, if you look closely, there are steps carved into the cliff face.'

Jean eyed the surface and could just make out flights of steps, zigzagging their way up to the top. From this angle it was difficult to make them out, but once seen, it was obvious that they were there. Each step was only about one and a half metres wide, which seemed precariously narrow the further you went up the bluff.

'You have got to be kidding me!'

'No, this is it, our way into the Citadel.'

Damien appeared to be far too cheerful about the prospect as far as Jean was concerned. She looked up again and closed her eyes, she had no issue with heights, any nerves in that department had disappeared centuries ago. But with height came the wind blowing in from the sea, buffeting anyone daft enough to try and scale the rock face.

'Is this a route you've used often to access the Citadel?'

Damien shook his head. 'No, this is an exit for emergency use only, not as an easy means of access.'

He looked out to sea towards the west and gauged the sun as it made its way toward the horizon.

'We had better get moving, this is going to take a while and I don't fancy still clambering up there when it's dark.'

There was a lot of muttering in agreement from everyone, who were also painfully aware of the time, as they made their way to the bottom of the steps, Damien leading the way.

Jean fell in behind Daniel with Paul behind. An ominous growl pulled her up short and she turned to her newly acquainted grandfather.

'Was that your stomach?'

He grimaced. 'Yes, and I admit that I am in total agreement with its sentiments.'

They had managed to procure some food as they waited for the tide at Bernick; a hunt predominantly led by Simon and John, who refused point blank to sail on an empty stomach, a cause swiftly taken up by the rest of the Knights. Since then they had only eaten the meagre rations served on their sea voyage. Now, as they made their way up the cliff face, grumblings of hunger were mumbled amongst the Knights and Jean had to admit to herself that she was also feeling a tad peckish. She was well aware by now that her companions' capacity for food was pretty impressive, and she hoped they would find sustenance at some point in the Citadel before all their hunger fuelled grumpiness took hold.

As they climbed, Jean felt as if the steps were getting narrower. It was a long, steady, often precarious, slog to the top. At one point, as they flattened themselves, yet again, against the cliff face after another particularly strong gust of wind blasted them, Paul shared a startled look with Jean.

'All I can say is, it would have to be a pretty desperate life or death situation to want to climb down these bloody steps in an emergency.'

But as Daniel also pointed out, this was an emergency, only they needed to go up, instead of down to the beach. By the time they finally neared the cliff top, the sky was blood red and the last few flights had been daunting with darkness rapidly falling. They were all very happy when they made their way back from the edge of the precipice, taking a breather at a safe distance. Not that they could move inland very far, as about twenty yards from the edge, a fifteen foot solid stone wall impeded their way. Only a single door broke the monotony of the barrier as it disappeared into the distance either side of them.

Jean walked quickly over towards the entryway, intent on getting into the Citadel and finding Nathan at last. But when she arrived she found there was no door handle or lock, in fact it looked as if the door itself was melded into the stone of the wall.

She turned to the Knights and asked if anyone had an orb in order to see better; she still hadn't replaced the disintegrated torch she arrived on Kelan with. John dipped into an inside pocket of his coat and pulled out a small wooden box. When he opened it, an orb, no bigger than an inch across, was nestled inside. But despite its size, it still radiated a light that was bright enough to illuminate the whole door surface and the surrounding wall. Jean studied the door again, this time realising her first assumptions had been correct, there was no lock or handle, or any other means of opening it. If it wasn't for the fact that it was clearly made of wood, Jean would have said it was nothing more than a recess in the stone wall itself. She turned to Damien in exasperation.

'How the hell are we supposed to open the bloody thing? Or are we expected to climb over the wall?'

He folded his arms and leaned against the stonework.

Dear gods, does the man have no sense of urgency?

Jean bit back her impatience, glaring at him as if this would make him talk faster. When he did, he spoke with his usual calm laid back manner; Jean wanted to shake him.

'No, firstly, as soon as your head breaches the top of the wall, the protections that surround the Citadel will set off an alarm. This place would soon be swarming with members of the Order, and as we are trying to remain out of sight, that may not be a good idea.

'Secondly, we *can* use this door, but only because we are Guardians. Unless there is an emergency inside of course, which would allow it to be opened from that side.'

Jean stared at him, there was still a gaping hole in his information and she was now too tired and hungry to play at being polite for much longer.

'But how?! There's no handle.'

'Just try it and see.'

He put his head to one side, and gave her a smile that suggested he was enjoying her confusion. She scowled and had to push down the urge to throttle him, but at the moment they didn't have time; she did, however, consider saving the prospect until later.

Biting her lip in frustration, Jean closed her eyes and tried to control her impatience. Then taking another moment to look at the bleak wooden obstruction before her, she lifted her hand and let it hover over its surface. It was at that moment she felt it, the gentle vibration that emanated from the surface as if it was alive, along with a subtle hint of recognition.

Through her fingers she could feel the unmistakable energy of Nathan. She felt the essence of his energy from the protections that surrounded, not just the Citadel, but the island itself; warm and safe. For a brief second she contemplated just remaining there, soaking up his essence. But shaking herself off, she took control and pushed both her hands against the surface of the door. She gave a slight intake of breath as she felt a gentle click from within, before it pushed against her hand as it opened outward.

Jean glanced at Damien, who still had the annoyingly daft look on his face, and gave a brief nod. She reached out and grasped the now exposed door edge and pulled it open wide. Taking a step forward to enter the Citadel compound, she suddenly stopped, while the Knights, who had immediately tried to follow, almost catapulted Jean through the door, only Damien catching her stopped her falling.

He whispered in her ear. 'What's wrong?'

Barely making a sound, she whispered back. 'Three people coming.'

They all froze. The perimeter wall at this point, bordered an open green within a large garden. On either side of the door, high, overgrown bushes partially covered the entrance; Jean considered that obviously there had been little need for emergency exits recently. Tensing as she sensed the three figures stopping nearby, she and the Knights daren't move,

375

not even to step back and close the door, it would have made too much noise. Instead they stood in silence, barely breathing, hoping whoever it was would move on and enjoy their evening stroll elsewhere.

There was a sound of laughter and they saw, with relief, three figures come into view, but fortunately they were walking away from them across the lawn, to finally disappear within a copse of trees.

Damien whispered into Jean's ear again. 'Is it clear now?'

She nodded, and there was a collective sigh of relief.

Making their way through the entrance, they pulled the door closed. While keeping to the shadows of the undergrowth, they gathered together to assess the situation. During their journey on the boat to Pernia, they had discussed what they would have to do once they were inside the Citadel. Despite the precautions that Nathan had placed on the compound, there were constant patrols around the perimeter and the Citadel itself. Mainly to give the cadet knights plenty of practice at watch duties, but also to make sure there were no unwanted visitors. Apparently, no-one had yet to succeeded in penetrating the compound, which didn't bode well for their own enterprise. If it wasn't for Nathan's warning, they could walk up to the door and they would be gladly welcomed, given everything they needed for their stay. But Nathan did warn them, and even if this was considered one of the safest, and most protected, places in the universe, they would still honour his wishes.

So here they were, anticipating breaking into their own Citadel, trying to evade trainee knights, who followed the same rules of defence and duty the Knights had laid down

376

centuries ago. In the end, it was decided that Jean was probably their best bet to go first and sense for anyone within the vicinity. While there was always the possibility of confrontation, the preferred alternative was to make sure they didn't meet anyone at all.

And so it began, an elaborate game of cat and mouse; only there were a considerable number of cats roaming around, and the mice were much larger than your average rodent. By the time they had reached the main building, they had evaded several encounters with members of the watch, as well as those choosing to take advantage of the clement weather and enjoying an evening stroll. There were many occasions that involved ducking behind walls, undergrowth and even an elaborate statue of rollicking nymphs. Jean had raised an eyebrow at such an object in a military training establishment, but Daniel shook his head and muttered something about being a throwback from Katherine's time; he looked quite disgusted.

John was still picking several thistles out of his hair and clothing, his face suggested that any laughing at his decision to hide in a large prickly bush as two female cadets jogged past, apparently enjoying an evening run, was unwise.

But it was the sight of Paul, who now squelched his way along the path to join them, his face like thunder, that had everyone struggling to not laugh out loud. It didn't help his mood at all. Apparently, someone had recently decided to create an ornamental pond in the exact place that he had thrown himself into, whilst trying to dodge a pair of newly enrolled cadets, who where out patrolling the grounds. The ensuing tumult of thrashing water as a very surprised Paul

377

attempted not to drown in its the shallow depths had obviously caught the young cadets' attention.

'What the hell was that? Who's there?'

Both cadets came to an abrupt halt, unsure what they should do next; it was unprecedented that someone was actually prowling the grounds. This was their first duty, having arrived at Pernia barely a week ago. They were told it was just a routine walk around the grounds.

When no-one answered their call they looked at each other for help.

'What do we do now?'

'Haven't a bloody clue.'

One appeared to come up with a plan. 'I know, you stay here and I'll get help.'

'Why do I have to stay here?'

'Because I thought of it first.'

'Now hang on a minute…wait what's that?'

Just ahead there was a rustling of bushes and both cadets stood stock still, eyes bulging with fear and confusion. Then, as they both were about to turn tail and make a run for it, a raft of ducks broke through the bushes, quacking indignantly. The cadets' knees nearly gave way as both shock and relief took over. They also realised that they had both clutched at each other's uniforms. Separating pretty sharpish they brushed themselves down, looking around, hoping no-one had seen.

'Fucking ducks, next time they're going in the oven.'

His fellow agreed with his sentiments and they both made their way down the path quickly, vowing not to let anyone know of the humiliating incident.

Now Paul stood glowering in a rapidly spreading puddle of water. Assuring him that she wasn't finding the situation at all funny, a grinning Jean accompanied him as they followed Damien around the side of the building where there was a low door leading to a cellar. Simon had to wrench the door open when the lock refused to budge and they all piled quickly inside. John took out his pocket orb and rummaged around for more lighting, and by the time he rejoined them there was sufficient light to see their surroundings.

They had stumbled into a utility area, which included a small laundry. According to Stephen, most of the laundry was done in a separate building, but this was a small addition attached to the kitchen area for its staffs' own needs. Jean had a forage for dry clothing for Paul. She found several cooks whites, finally settling on a large jacket that was wide enough across the shoulders and long enough in the arms, but it was also obviously made for someone with a much wider girth. The only trousers they found that would fit were several inches too short, and Jean was taken back to when Ty and his neighbour, Captain Kate Bridger, put together a version of the Order's uniform for her. She sympathised with her grandfather. Once he put his own, still soggy, boots on, it wouldn't matter, but the overall image was of a chef who had recently lost a lot of weight through illness. His surly look didn't help the image.

Daniel slapped his brother on the shoulder. 'Cheer up Paul, when this is over you can whip up a few eggs and roast a few of those ducks, you certainly look the part.' Receiving a growl for his efforts, Daniel just grinned back.

In an effort to ward off the possible altercation that promised, Jean stepped in-between the two. She was thoroughly fed up now, this was taking far too long and it was getting late.

'So where is the best place to look for this Council Chamber we're here for?'

With relief, she noted Daniel took a step back and sat himself down on a cabinet full of tea towels.

'To be honest, it's not that often we have needed to find it, but when we have, it's usually been on the first floor, somewhere towards the west wing. But not always.'

'Well, that's all we've got for now, so it's a start. Let's go.'

She made to move but Paul put his hand on her shoulder.

'Hang on Jean, you can't just go wandering around here. You thought it was busy outside in the gardens, this building will have people roaming the corridors for most of the evening. The best thing for us to do is to wait here until it quietens down for the night.'

Jean felt her heart sink, more waiting around. She just wanted to find Nathan and take him home and to hell with whoever saw them. Paul must have seen the frustration on her face and he raised his hand to brush away a stray hair that had fallen across her cheek.

'I know, I want to get out there and find him too, but crashing around the Citadel and getting caught isn't going to help anyone.'

Biting her lip and looking away, she nodded. It wasn't just the thought of Nathan alone and in danger that tugged at her emotions this time, the look of concern on Paul's face had raised memories that had been buried long ago. A time

380

spent with her grandparents, following her grandfather around the garden as he worked. At that moment, it was like looking at the man who she had grown up with, standing in front of her once more.

Despite knowing the truth about her relationship with Paul and Daniel, it was only now she realised its significance. Her beloved grandfather was Paul's son, and thinking back, his mannerisms, even the way he spoke, were as familiar to her as if her grandfather was still here. Emotions welled up inside and she hadn't even realised she was hugging Paul until he wrapped his own arms around her and he spoke quietly in her ear.

'Are you alright Jean?'

She nodded into his shoulder and remained there for a few moments longer before leaning back and giving him a soggy smile.

'Yes, I'm fine, frustrated, but fine. So what do you suggest we do for the next few hours then?'

'Well, seeing as I am dressed for the part, I suppose we can have a hunt around for some food, I'm sure I can cobble something together.' He glanced over at Simon and John, who still resembled a slightly dishevelled thorn bush. 'Either that or we are going to have a riot on our hands.'

Jean followed his gaze and grinned. 'Good idea. Let's get moving.'

Everyone agreed and started to quietly make their way around the cellars in the hunt for anything to eat.

Paul was still holding Jean as he looked at her, his face full of concern.

'We will find him and bring him home.'

381

'I hope you're right Paul.'

Her voice almost cracked with the emotion she was feeling, he touched her chin and looked into her eyes and smiled.

'Of course I'm right, and when he's home, perhaps you two can finally sit down and have that talk you should both have had a long time ago.'

She was about to protest her innocence, but his look told her it would be a pointless exercise. She looked away.

'I don't think he's ready for me to make that much of an idiot of myself yet, do you?'

Paul shook his head and chuckled.

'You have no idea do you?'

'What do you mean?'

Paul didn't have the opportunity to answer as an excited Simon came over and shoved a cooked ham under their noses, soon followed by John with a box of vegetables.

Jean was impressed. 'I'm sure you two could find food in a barren cupboard.'

They both grinned as Paul let go of Jean and smiled back.

'Well, find me an empty kitchen and we'll see what we can do.'

Quietly making their way out of the cellars and moving around the underground corridors, they found their way into the main kitchen areas. All of which were thankfully empty now, though prepped and ready for the morning shift at breakfast. Daniel found a smaller kitchen area in a room off to the side and they all squeezed inside. They made themselves comfortable while Paul busied himself with providing food. Jean watched him work while the other Knights sat back and rested; one of the main rules of any mission, eat when you can and rest when you can, you never know when the opportunity will arise again.

Having eaten their meal of ham and vegetables with gusto, they waited a few more hours before Damien made his way to the door and beckoned Jean and Daniel to follow him.

'You two head out and have a look around, see if the place has quietened down.'

They both agreed and slipped out of the door, leaving the others to clear away their mess. Daniel led the way, and they eventually found themselves at a closed door, he turned to Jean and, pointlessly in her view, put his finger to his lips in a silent hush. She gave him an exasperated look, which he evidently chose to ignore. He was about to open the door when Jean placed her hand over his and pushed it closed, which earned her a sharp look. She couldn't help but imitate his actions by placing her finger to her lips, before silently indicating there were two people just on the other side of the entrance. Daniel grinned and had the grace to look sheepish.

Finally, Jean signalled that the way was clear and they opened the door. The contrast of the hall that they entered, to the maze of corridors they left behind, was stark. Even though it was dark outside, lit only by the full moon now rising in the sky, there were a few orb lamps left glowing on surfaces around the space. Full height windows that rose on either side of two huge wooden double doors, cast a silvery light into the room.

While details were hard to make out, Jean couldn't fail to see the quality of furniture that lined the walls; huge, solid tables and chairs, along with glass cabinets filled with glittering silverware. Paintings lined the walls, partially hidden in shadows, she was sure many of them were of the Knights themselves and various high ranking members of the Order down through the ages.

Dominating the hall was a double staircase that rose from the centre of the room and split in two at a mezzanine level, leading left and right to the upper first floor hidden from view.

The area was empty, but Jean could sense many others within the building. However, unlike before, people were now settling down, and there was a sense of peace resting over the Citadel; with just a hint of excitement underneath. She told Daniel of her feelings for the place and he nodded his understanding.

'This is a military training establishment, there will surely always be a certain amount of emotion around.'

She said nothing and he told her to stay there and he would get the others.

A few minutes later she was joined by the rest of the Knights, and they began make their way, cautiously, up the stairs to the first floor. Damien led them off to the lefthand side of the staircase, this apparently was where most of the administration offices were, as opposed to the accommodations that resided to the right of the building. Only once did they encounter anyone; two unfortunate young cadets who had been out patrolling along the corridors. The Knights pounced before they had a chance to

384

even realise anyone was there. Stephen had stepped up and sent them into a dreamless sleep, before Daniel and Paul placed them in an empty room to sleep off the rest of their watch.

'What happens when someone comes looking for them?' Jean asked.

'We'll worry about that when it happens.' Damien shrugged. 'Let's hope we find the Council Chamber before then.'

In the end, it wasn't so difficult to discover what they were looking for. Jean had found it strange how a room could just appear anywhere within a building, but not actually exist most of the time. However, when they finally found the door, or more likely, it found them as Jean later considered, she couldn't imagine anything more normal, in a very odd sort of way.

They travelled down a corridor that had a full length window at the end letting in the brilliant moonlight, passing several doors which seemed perfectly normal. But as they approached one, she felt an unmistakable pull, almost to the point where she couldn't bring herself to carry on up the corridor any further. Turning towards the entrance she saw that the other Knights had had the same feeling too.

'Our Council Chamber I take it?' she whispered.

The others nodded, but she noticed they didn't seem overly happy about it. Confused at their reticence, especially considering the importance of their quest, she wasn't sure what the problem was.

'Well, shall we go in then?'

They looked at her but didn't move. She bit back her impatience and pushed to the front of the group to open the door. It was then she realised that, like the door in the Citadel's perimeter wall, this one had no visible means of opening either. This time however, Jean didn't hesitate and she placed her hand on the wood.

The sensation that shot through her body shocked her.

Unlike before, when she could sense Nathan's energy running through the surface, this time it was a much harsher sensation. It was cold and hard, like frozen iron, and Jean had to force her hand away before she was physically sick.

Holding her hand as if it had been burned, she turned to Damien who looked at her with concern. But before he could ask if she was alright, the door clicked inwardly open. Appreciating the Knights' previous reluctance, Jean now stood back and waited until someone else made a move. There seemed to be a joint consensus that Damien had been nominated for the task and he didn't look too happy at the prospect, but he reached out and pushed open the door anyway. Leading the way forward, he entered while the others followed cautiously.

31

The Forest Awakens

ajor Torvil looked out over the parapet of Parva's caldera walls, watching the frightened, confused and desperate huddles of people making their way to the safety of the city.

Groups of refugees had been arriving at the gate since sunrise that morning, and as the sun began to dip towards the western horizon, it looked as if there were still plenty more people fleeing before the Demon army.

Their stories were fantastical and horrifying when first told to the duty watch. Tales of communities ripped apart by

387

monsters destroying everything in their path. Slowly, as more people told the same desperate tales, a picture emerged of a huge army heading towards the Northern forest. A horde of demons coming from the River Elvian and making their way, at great speed, up the valleys towards the North and the River Par.

From the Northern forest, the enemy could turn east or west. To the North, was the Ketler Mountain Range, that marked the boundary to frozen lands of Northern Lorimar. While it was possible the army could turn east to the farmlands of Rassen and beyond, it was more likely the horde would turn to the west, and make for Parva.

The stories talked of huge blue demon like men with strange crowns around their heads and monstrous fangs and claws. They set about their heinous destruction with enormous dog-like creatures, that were at least as big as horses, who walked on two legs as well as all fours. Other, smaller creatures, described as having evil eyes and deadly knives, caused havoc as they ran alongside their larger comrades. While wraithlike beings were seen to tear at the raw flesh of their victims, irrespective of whether they were alive or dead. A whole army of tens of thousands, moving at a rapid pace that overran the weak and slow. Everything in their path was destroyed or devoured.

It seemed the hordes of hell were heading Parva's way.

Aware of the terrain the enemy had to traverse to get to Parva, Major Torvil also anticipated the ferocious speed at which they had travelled over open farm land. However, this would be markedly reduced once they entered the Northern forest. There were a number roads that passed through the trees. But the forest itself was a dense growth of old and young, deciduous and evergreen trees, the varieties changing the further north the great woodland spread. There were many woodsmen who lived and worked amongst the timber giants of the forest. Their families grew up learning the lore of the forests, and of course there were members of these families that had joined the Order.

Major Torvill was one of those who had grown up beneath these ancient emerald canopies. His father was a woodsman, who had tended the forest and knew the secrets of the trees. He was also, like his fellow forest-men, an excellent hunter and tracker; melting into the undergrowth, as he pursued his quarry as wraiths amongst the silent trees. He had passed down this knowledge to his own children, and Torvil's sister took over from their father when he retired.

The army that headed towards the forest may be fast moving now, but once they entered the trees they would find a whole new, more deadly world. Small companies of the Order had already left the city to join with the woodsmen there. Many of whom were like Torvil and knew the lie of the forest like the back of their hands. And now it was Torvil's turn to wreak havoc upon the demons that threatened his home. He turned and made his way down the long staircase to meet with the rest of his small company. Captain Forrest waited with the others at the North Gate from the city leading from the Palace stables. They were to cross the bridges up river and, as with other members of the Order, enter and wait for the horde to come.

As they started out, Torvil shared a grim look of determination with Captain Forrest. Soon hell would feel the first bite from the teeth of the Imperial Army, as the great war machine began to stir.

32

The Sapphire Tree

J ean stood back from the doorway and let the Knights go first. She couldn't say why if asked, but she had a weird reluctance to enter the room. Even when everyone had made their way into the chamber, with Daniel holding the door open waiting for her, she still hesitated before finally crossing the threshold.

Taking a long slow breath, she stepped from the darkened corridor and raised her hand to shield her eyes from the glare of apparent daylight within the Chamber.

Blinking to try and focus, she was eventually able to take in her surroundings. They were within a circular room, it wasn't large, but spacious enough to accommodate three tiers of wooden benches curving with the contours of the walls. Two sets of benches, facing each other on either side of a raised dais with eight solid looking wooden chairs in a line upon it.

All around the walls were stained glass windows; three tall panes arranged behind the curved benches. Above the dais, a large single expanse of glass dominated the space with a scene depicting a tree in full leaf. However, it appeared to be of a night-time tableau with a full moon shining down on the abundance of leaves, turning them a vibrant blue. A sword was superimposed down the length of the tree, standing on its point with a simple gold coronet crowning the scene.

The colours of the stained glass were as vibrant as if they had just been painted, with the light from an unknown source streaming through, drenching the floor and walls with beautiful colours and abstract shapes.

It was easy enough to view the patterns set within the floor, as the Knights were making a concerted effort to not walk across its centre. Preferring to remain outside its perimeter, they avoided the six pointed star etched in gold, approximately twenty feet in diameter within the smooth stone flags.

The middle of the star held a circle with a strange pattern that didn't seem to depict anything other than random curves and lines. Jean puzzled over the markings for a short while, as something tugged at the back of her mind. She tried to catch it, but the click of the door closing gently

392

behind her blew the strands of memory away and it was gone. A slight shudder flitted down her spine, and she was relieved to see that she wasn't the only one in the room feeling uncomfortable.

Jean soon realised it was obvious this room was wasn't actually part of the Citadel in Pernia; for a start, it was definitely sunlight flooding through the coloured glass rather than moonlight. Also, the high wooden vaulted ceiling that rose above them, was unlikely to be rising through two further floors above, and there were far too many windows surrounding the room considering the central location of the corridor outside.

Time moved on as they all stood in silence, with no-one willing to be the first to speak. Jean began to feel the panic rising within her again, they had to find Nathan, and standing around kicking their heels, whilst achieving nothing was not going to bring him any nearer home.

Pushing aside her concerns, Jean breathed out and tentatively eased her senses forward, testing the area for anomalies beyond the expected; though as this whole environment shouldn't really exist she kept an open mind. Sensing a very faint, but still tangible presence of Nathan's signature, it took all her will to keep the tears of relief from escaping down her cheeks. At last she felt that their course of action was the right one and that there was every chance they were going to bring Nathan home. The only question now of course, was how?

Making her way around the room, she, like the others, steered clear of the star etched into the floor. Spending some time looking at the stained glass windows, she concentrated

393

on the main window behind the dais, taking a particular interest in the sword overlaying the tree. To most people it would be just another sword, it looked quite an ordinary weapon, except for the blood red stone that sat as its pommel, nothing about it was remarkable. But to Jean it was all too familiar to be coincidence, particularly in this strange place.

Shuddering, she looked away, trying to concentrate on the other six windows set into the curve of the walls. At first they seemed just random artwork, images depicting the whim of the artist that had created them. But they were odd, if that was the case, they were hardly scenes to invoke emotions of serenity or even any other feelings come to that. Jean got the impression they were like images you would find in a reference book, she couldn't make head nor tail of them.

Simon had joined her, and seeing the look of confusion on her face, explained their meaning.

'They are supposed to depict various aspects of each of our professions or expertise.'

The frown on Jean's forehead made him smile, and he pointed to one of the windows behind the benches in front of them.

'For example, that window there, what do you see?'

Jean glanced up at him, and then back at the window. It was a six sided shape where each opposite angle was attached by a line to create a six sided star within its centre; within the hexagon were lines crisscrossing to form many triangles. She had to blink several times as her brain switched from viewing a flat hexagon shape to a visual representation of a cube. She said as much to Simon who nodded at her response.

'Exactly, this is a visual representation of the equation for the theory of relativity.'

'E=mc^2, Einstein.'

'Ah yes, Einstein.' Simon grinned and glanced over at John who grinned back.

'What's that look for? He was the one who discovered about relativity and all that wasn't he?'

John gave her a look that suggested he was having to show patience with a difficult student. 'Yes, on Earth he was.'

Jean humphed. 'This is where you tell me that he nicked his idea from you I suppose?'

'I would never presume.' He shrugged. 'But he got there, eventually.'

Not quite sure what else to say to that, Jean deliberately clamped her jaw shut; sometimes it was just not worth the argument. Besides, they had much to do. She was about to look away when Simon, who was quite expressive when he demonstrated something he considered too technical for the listener, continued talking. Jean's jaw was beginning to ache.

'E=mc^2, is the correct formula but it is written slightly differently outside the Seventh Sector.'

As he spoke he drew shapes within the air haphazardly to emphasise his point. To her surprise glimmers of small sparks seemed to glow in front of him, but he was so immersed in his explanation he hadn't noticed.

Jean placed her hand on his arm. 'Simon, do that again.'

He stopped and looked at her questioningly, his hands still in front of him while halfway through a particular movement.

'Do what again?'

'That equation for relativity, make the symbols in the air again.'

Simon shrugged but obliged, this time concentrating on his actions. His eyes opened wide in astonishment as his hands moved in front of him. There, as clear as day, was the equation for relativity glowing red in mid-air before merging and becoming a simple glowing image of three intersecting lines.

He turned his head slowly and stared at Jean. 'Did you do that?'

'Me? No. This was you.'

They both turned round and shared astonished looks with the other Knights who were now watching with avid interest. When they glanced back, the glowing lines were slowly beginning to fade.

An idea began to tentatively form in Jean's mind, but she was almost too afraid to believe it could be that easy. Looking at the windows again, she asked the Knights a question which she prayed would give them a glimmer of hope.

'These windows, do they all depict a formula of some kind? And if they do, can you do the same as Simon?'

The Knights looked at each other and then at the windows. When no-one else moved Damien sighed and stepped forward, then looked behind him at a window showing an abstract drawing of lines overlapping each other. Jean eyed it dubiously and then raised an eyebrow at

Damien. As a mathematician, he had a fierce passion for numbers, even to the point of performing apparent impossibly complicated mathematical problems in his head. Jean considered this ability both fascinating and quite freaky.

'This should be interesting, what weird and wonderful equations are you going to come up with?'

Damien put his head to one side and raised an eyebrow.

'There is nothing *weird* about this equation, it's perfectly simple.' And he, like Simon, raised his hand and drew shapes in the air.

$Y = Mx + c$

'A straight line? That's it?'

He shrugged. 'These equations are not about being complicated, but about the basic forms of the subject they represent. A straight line is about as basic as it gets.'

Jean said nothing, instead, her gaze had fallen on the glowing figures that had now merged into a single line suspended in the air before Damien. Curiously, this time, unlike with Simon's equation, it didn't start to fade, but hung as bright as ever.

'Daniel, can you do your's, but next to Damien's one?'

In answer to the curious glances from everyone, she pointed to the floor below Damien's image; it was directly over the abstract markings etched into the centre of the six pointed star. Daniel immediately stepped forward and started drawing in the air.

If P then Q

Q

Then P

'Logic?'

Daniel nodded. 'The basis of any argument.'

Before Jean could say any more, Stephen had stepped forward and added his own set of figures. This time there were considerably more letters and Jean hadn't a clue what they were. As he finished, he looked up and announced his own addition as the equation for the first sequence of the chemical formula of DNA. Jean just took his word for it.

Then Paul stepped up drew a diagram of a rectangle with a series of squares inside. Jean grinned, she knew this one.

'The Fibonacci sequence.'

Paul nodded and smiled.

Then it was John's turn, Jean didn't recognise his equation either, and he looked up at her confused face. 'Ever heard of Friedmann? Einstien's field equations of gravitation?' He was surprised when Jean nodded.

'I have, but it doesn't look like that.'

'No, his theory is based on the composition and density of the universe in the Seventh Sector, which includes, what they call Dark Matter, the space between atoms. But, Dark Matter is only the result of the removal of the T'iakai, which has a completely different affect to its density. As such, the subsequent version of Friedmann's equation is actually much simpler.' He stood back from his own glowing figures, looking thoroughly satisfied with his explanation as they too merged into a simple image of a few lines. Apart from John, Jean noticed that the other Knights looked as dubious as she did.

Finally, Simon stepped up and added his own formula of relativity and stood back, spending as little time within the star shape as the others had done.

Damien looked at Jean. 'So what now?'

She shook her head, she had no idea. As the Knights still seemed reluctant to move into the centre of the room again, Jean decided to take the first step. Walking around the separate line images that still hung glowing above the floor, she studied the shapes as she went. Around the outside, the Knights were migrating to various points of the six pointed star on the floor, it seemed they had their own specific positions that they always went to.

'Should Jean have a formula to add maybe?' Daniel asked no-one in particular, and received a lot of shrugs and shaking of heads in ignorance as an answer. Jean put her hands on her hips and considered his question for a moment before shaking her head.

'I don't think so.' Indicating the windows on the wall she added. 'There are only six windows suggesting there are only six formula needed. Besides, I haven't got a clue what I would add.' While she spoke she continued to study the figures, avidly ignoring the red pommeled sword depicted in glass above her. She was onto her second lap around the glowing figures, when she suddenly stopped. Looking at the central abstract markings in the floor and back up to the glowing formula, checking several times before she asked Damien to confirm what she saw.

'If you stand here and look through the figures what do you see?'

Damien left his place on the outside of the star and joined her, looking through the formula as she had indicated. Then looked at the floor before answering her.

'It's not exactly the same, but pretty near.'

Jean checked again, then moving to the side she headed for the formula that Stephen had produced. Placing her hand against the glowing markings she found they moved freely at her touch. Giving a slight adjustment to its position, she turned back to Damien.

'Hows that now?'

'Amazing. It's an exact copy.' Damien looked shocked as he confirmed Jean's theory.

'Right gentlemen, you're going to have to bear with me here. Damien, if you could go back to your position, I don't know if it will make a difference, but let's not take any chances.'

Then, Jean spread out her arms so that she could hold the expanse of the markings within her hands, before she slowly brought the glowing forms together. Unsure of the effect of her actions, she had to fight the urge to close her eyes and wince at the possibility of something going bang. But instead, as the figures finally touched in front of her, she saw that not only did they keep their original forms, but seamlessly melded together. By the time she finished, there was a glowing disc within her hands that mirrored the abstract pattern on the floor. She gave the Knights around her a final glance, but they were all transfixed on the glowing disc.

Not having any other idea of what to do next ,she simply turned the disc over so that it now lay perpendicular to the

400

floor. A final check to ensure all of the shapes lined up, she took a deep breath and pushed the disc downwards. As it descended, the disc began to glow brighter until it was virtually impossible to look directly at it, and Jean was forced to close her eyes. She only knew the disc had finally touched the floor below when a jolt of pulsating energy shot up her arms and through her body.

Around her, she felt, rather than saw, a blinding light pass along the arms of the six pointed star and towards the Knights. It seemed as if the entire room was filled with an impossible light that penetrated her tightly shut eyelids, pulsating as it travelled through the Chamber. When just as suddenly, the light disappeared and the pulsating vibrations stopped.

Jean felt exhausted, as if all her energy had been sucked out in an instant and she fell forward heavily onto her hands and knees. Opening her eyes, she blinked rapidly to try and disperse the ghost of the bright light from the back of her retina. Around her she noted that the Knights had also been affected, but unlike Jean, they were down on one knee as they dealt with the after effects.

Feeling ridiculous on her hands and knees, Jean scrambled to her feet, feeling a bit light headed as she rose. Swaying slightly as she felt someone steady her from behind, she turned to see Daniel standing there. He said nothing, but he did give her a concerned look before letting her go. She frowned and nodded once before moving slightly to the side; now was not the time to show weakness.

In the silence that followed, everyone looked at each other. Nothing had changed, the Chamber looked exactly as it did before. And the worst thing of all, there was still no Nathan.

Had they done something wrong? Was this all a waste of time after all?

Then, from somewhere below their feet, there was the sound of stone scraping over stone and the floor suddenly lurched upwards. Jean and Daniel jumped back, while below them, the centre of the star and the place where the glowing key had entered the floor, was starting to move. Dropping slightly, the circular area was beginning to shimmer and fade. Curiosity getting the better of them brought the rest of the Knights to the rim of the circle and they all stood around as the ground below them opened up.

Finally, only a black space existed where the floor had been, a darkness so intense it seemed almost solid.

'There.'

Everyone jumped as John pointed down into the void. They all held their breath as they desperately looked for a glimmer of hope within the darkness, but as they looked deeper into the hole they also saw something appearing from the abyss.

Jean was never able to say whether the shape was at a distance and travelling nearer, or already close and only just becoming visible. But by the time they finally realised what the thing could be, it was already within reach.

Nathan's naked form was shivering as he lay curled within the darkness, just below the rim of the chamber floor. Around him, a strange slimy substance covered his body, leaving a film that made his features seemed blurred and indistinct.

All at once there was activity as coats were removed, while John and Simon reached down and pulled Nathan free of the void. As they lifted him, the floor below began to reform, and within moments, the stone floor, with the now familiar markings, had returned.

Stephen was already checking Nathan over, concern on his face told them all he wasn't out of the woods yet.

'He needs heat and fluids, now.'

Without saying anything, Simon had gathered Nathan's body, now wrapped in warming woollen coats, and lifted him into his arms. As a six foot three soldier, strong and battle fit, Nathan was far from a small man, yet Simon held him as if he were a sleeping child. Jean was reminded why Simon and John were considered the juggernauts of the group.

Daniel opened the door, and quickly the Knights passed through, with Jean following behind. Looking back, she gave the chamber a final glance, before gladly leaving and entering the darkened corridor of the Citadel once more.

Part four:

A Case of

Trials and

Errors

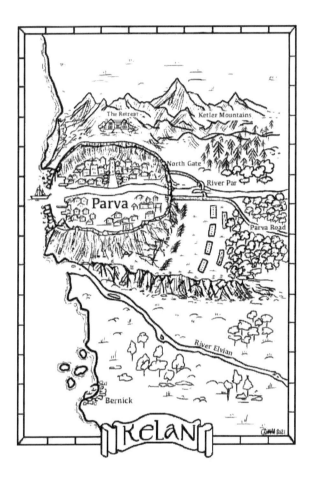

33

A Friend
Indeed

George watched the shapes cast by the shadows from the trees outside his window dance across the ceiling. With one hand relaxed behind his head and the other picking at a loose thread on his blanket, he lay in his bed, waiting for the sleep he knew would not come this evening. All around, the sounds and smells of others sleeping broke through the frustration that plagued his mind. It didn't help, that one of his fellow slumberers in their quarters had eaten something the previous evening that had affected their gastric system, the effects were now permeating offensively around the six man room he shared with three other men and women. He had been informed that two other knights were out on night duty.

George had been taken aback when he had been given a bed within the Order's barracks at the Palace; it seemed they were concerned with panicking the general public if his story of strange blue giants roaming the countryside and murdering people were to emerge. He was interested to hear that the only knights to actually stay in the barracks were lower ranking members of the Order, and those carrying out their scheduled duties. The rest lived in either rented accommodation, or in homes with their families, within the city.

The Order had treated him well, including the portion sizes of their food. He was now very much aware of the particularly large dinner he had worked his way through — apparently knights were expected to have a hearty appetite. But there was no getting away from the fact that he was considered with some curiosity, which grew as the day went on.

Having arrived in Parva the morning of two days ago with Major Dillon, travelling from the garrison at Comston via portal, he had been rigorously questioned about the events that had happened to his training group in the woods. While he understood that the knights needed as much information out of him as possible, he had ended the session feeling that it had been more of an interrogation rather than a matter of questions. At one point, he wondered what it would have been like to have actually done something wrong and required to undertake a rigorous cross-examination; but he quickly pushed that nasty thought firmly from his mind.

The most terrifying aspect of his time in Parva so far, had been when he was stood in front of a table surrounded by very senior members of the Order. He had no idea what their ranks were, but there was enough silver over their black uniforms that he thought it unlikely they would be doing night duties on the gate any time soon.

The only thing that forced him to keep his nerve were the images of his friends and colleagues; broken and torn, their bodies strewn around the woods. The thought of Ehring dying in his arms, and the sight of Carrie's body dangling from the monster's hand, his neck at an impossible angle, made his innards churn with horror and guilt. He knew those images would haunt him for the rest of his life.

George turned over onto his side, gazing at the wall opposite his bed. He closed his eyes shut against the images that refused to leave his mind. Tears of grief and frustration leaked out and ran down his nose and face. He brushed them away, angry at feeling sorry for himself, when there were people who would never see another day; people who had families who would grieve for their loved ones.

Despite the knights' precautions to keep the news of strange marauders in the countryside away from the general populous, the steady arrival of people escaping into the city, soon set the gossips' tongues wagging. There was talk of farms being overrun by monsters, animals being slaughtered and crops burning in their fields, mingled with terrifying stories of blue monsters with three heads and six legged horses as big as houses that breathed fire. So varied and obscure were the stories from the refugees, that in the end the High Council had issued a statement to clarify the events as they knew it; though that was sparse enough.

There was no denying that people were dying though, horrendous stories of families butchered in their homes as the invaders swept over villages and farms. Those who escaped were terrified, arriving at the city with nothing more than the clothes they stood up in and the families they clung to.

An evacuation was started of the city with the most vulnerable first. Time was not on their side and priorities had to be made, despite several of the city's wealthiest families fleeing to the portals demanding to leave first if they paid to jump the queue. The Order would have none of it, and pushed to the side, the rich and high ranking members of Parva society, forcing them to watch and wait as the elderly and young were escorted to the safety of elsewhere within the Empire. Only when the Order was satisfied the vulnerable were through, were the portals opened for free passage to anyone who wanted to evacuate the city.

Fortunately, reports from around the Empire confirmed that the only threat from these unknown invaders was upon Parva itself. Therefore, many people travelled to visit family and friends elsewhere in the Empire.

It was a quieter Parva that met the sunset that evening, but there were still those who chose to stay, or had nowhere else to run to. The whole year had been an ordeal that most would be glad to see the back of, and it seemed, for Parva at least, the nightmare hadn't ended yet.

One element of George's first visit to Parva had given him something to look forward to; Jean was here. Or she should have been. He was quite shocked at how much it upset him that she wasn't in Parva when he arrived. It soon turned to concern when he heard the mysterious circumstances of her disappearance from the city with the other Knights. He had outgrown his boyish crush for Jean long ago, he no longer day dreamed about fantasies that would have had Dana chasing him out of the house in disgust if she knew. But he still missed her, and he often thought about the times they spent at the farm together, a time when the world seemed a much smaller and peaceful place. He had wanted to meet her and tell of all that he had achieved, of his friends and of Raynard. He found himself grinning despite himself, he missed the old knight, he wished that he was there now, telling him not to be such a fool and to get on with his work.

George threw himself onto his back and studied the ceiling again. Where was Jean and the Emperor? Why hadn't the Emperor been with Jean and the Knights when they were seen in the fishing village of Bernick? These were questions that had been flying around the city amongst the tales of monsters and slaughter. There was little doubt now that the invaders were heading towards Parva. However, despite the Council and Order's attempts to form a defensive force large enough to defend the city, they needed the Emperor in order to move the numbers required, if they were to have any chance of beating back the demon hordes — as they were now being called.

It was no good, he was never going to sleep, and lying here would only increase his frustration. Flinging off his bedclothes, George got out of bed, washed, dressed in his pristine Militia uniform, and made his way out of the barracks. He left through the back entrance that led to the stables, he still found comfort among animals, and took time to speak to the long noses that looked out of their stalls as he passed. He was greeted politely, but curiously by members of the Order on duty at such an early hour, but otherwise he was left to his own devices. Making his way to the outer city caldera wall, he climbed the only tower that had access to the Palace compound. Catching his breath after the excursion to the parapet, he took a moment to enjoy the cooler air that circulated around the crenelated wall, and filled his lungs.

It was still dark as he looked out over the countryside to the east, but below the walls, were people who had arrived after the gates had been closed for the night. They had made sparse camps and their fires still burned where they huddled, waiting for the gates to open again. By the look of the makeshift shelters, it appeared that they had been provided with at least some means of keeping out the coldest of the elements. He considered the previous night's storm and was thankful for the poor souls below that weather had turned drier.

His eyes then scoured the forest in the distance. During the time he had spent here at the Palace barracks and stables, he knew that there were members of the Order and Militia out there, preparing to make the enemy's journey through the trees as difficult as possible.

He was a farmer, he had spent his life out in the open fields. While he could hunt and track as good as any man, he remembered his time in the forest further south and the

411

attack by the demons, he had been confused and afraid by the restrictions of the trees around him. Many of those out in the forest now though had spent their lives amongst the silent timber giants, they could attack stragglers and the unwary, before melting back into the trees; the enemy confused and powerless to do anything about it.

While they couldn't hope to reduce the numbers of the demon army significantly by any stretch of the imagination, they could instil the feelings of unease and panic amongst its ranks. The enemy would have to slow down and take precautions as they moved. By the time they reached the open fields before Parva, the enemy would have to navigate the Order's own version of hell.

He gazed out at the earthworks that had been constructed since dawn the previous day, and the last of the storm had blown itself out. The sappers were still working in shifts throughout the night, with gangs of volunteers reinforcing their ranks so as to be ready for when the hordes arrived. Long trenches were being dug across the fields before the Northern Forest, staggered rows of ditches with lethal stakes driven into their depths, forcing an advancing army to move around them, herding them towards the centre of the field. About a thousand metres from the city walls a line of palisades had been constructed. Tree trunks had been driven into the ground, sharpened into vicious stakes, alternatively standing upright then at a forty-five degree angle towards the enemy. Like the trenches, they were arranged to allow men to pass through, but not at once, herding them into smaller groups in order for archers to ply their deadly trade. The angel of the stakes meant that the

412

attacking army would struggle to push against the fortifications to bring them down, but the defending army would have no problem flattening them forward for ease of movement before a charge.

However, no matter how long it took, the hordes would still eventually arrive before Parva, looking to break down the gates and take the city. George's guts clenched, they were only a day away at the most. If they were forced, the enemy could be within the fields that surrounded Parva before mid afternoon. He turned and looked out over the city, across the sea to the direction of Pernia, the last place the Knights were thought to be heading, and he sent out a silent thought.

Please come back Jean, don't desert us now.

'Well lad, you're a long way from home.'

George spun round at the familiar voice and saw the figure of a man he knew well. Relief overwhelmed him, and he embraced the giant knight.

'Raynard.'

He almost wept at the sight of his friend, but then realised what he was doing and where he was and stepped back, apologising for his emotional outburst.

A huge grin split the bearded, Raynard's rugged features, and he slapped him heartily on the shoulders, keeping his hands in place as he spoke. George felt his knees buckle under the force.

'Dear gods lad, look at you, almost big enough to fill that uniform of yours.'

The fact that George was almost as tall as the knight, and had the strong hard body of a man used to working on a

413

farm all his life, seemed lost on Raynard. But he found himself grinning back, just pleased to see his friend again. A familiar face when he needed it.

'I've missed you Raynard you old bastard. It's good to see you again.'

Raynard looked indignant. 'Less of the old, still plenty left in this bag of bones, have you even started shaving yet?' He gave George a light tap on his chin. 'But aye, I've heard it was you who first brought word about our hellish invaders. I wasn't entirely surprised. If there's trouble about, I have a feeling you're going to find yourself in it somewhere.'

George bit his lip, he hadn't considered how much he had felt alone since the incident in the forest.

Was it really only yesterday?

Seeing Raynard's familiar face gave him a comfort he hadn't realised he needed. He shook his head sadly.

'Gods Raynard, I don't know if this is a battle that even the Order can fight, let alone win.'

Raynard looked at him for a while, saying nothing. Only the furrow between his brows showed his concern. Crossing his arms, he leaned against the parapet.

'Lad, it's not about whether we can win or not, it's about knowing that no matter what, we have to try.' He put his head to one side. 'Why do you think it takes so long to train a knight? It's not so they can have the shiniest buttons and look good on a horse. Though I do cut a pretty good figure mounted I must say.' He chuckled to himself for a moment before catching George's eye and straightening himself up. 'It is so that when the time comes, there is no question about whether we can or cannot. It's about using our resources to

414

make sure that whatever happens, we have done everything possible we could.'

George shook his head. 'But the Emperor is missing, along with Jean and the other Knights.' Thoughts and feelings of frustration had built up inside him so much, that to actually get them out and talk to someone he trusted was a relief.

Raynard shrugged, inclining his head as if in understanding.

'Aye, admittedly, that's bit of a bind, but the Order isn't about the Emperor, it's about the men and women who follow his example and live by his philosophies. Whatever happens tomorrow.' He lifted his arm to check his watch and shrugged when he couldn't make out the time in the darkness. 'Or today I should say, we will do what we have to and nothing less.'

George stood up straight, his eyes wide 'Will you be in the field to meet the enemy when they get here?'

Raynard nodded, eyeing George suspiciously. 'Aye lad, I've a command. Why?'

George stepped forward, his voice belaying his eagerness. 'Take me with you. Let me do something to fight these bastards.'

Shaking his head the knight pushed himself away from the wall.

'No, absolutely not.' Before George could argue, he held up his hand. 'I need to know that every person under my command knows exactly what they are doing. I won't have time to keep an eye out, making sure you're not getting

415

yourself killed. You'll stay here.' And to emphasise the matter he added. 'And that is an order.'

George bit his lip. He refused to be a coward again, letting others fight his battles for him; he still hadn't forgotten his humiliation at Niall's farm. But Raynard had been adamant and there was going to be no arguing with him. Instead he said nothing and just nodded his head, refusing to meet Raynard's eye.

The big knight's hands landed on his shoulders again, and despite himself George winced under the pressure. Still looking away he didn't see the look of suspicion and concern etched across the older man's face, as he studied him in the early morning gloom.

Dawn had at last broken in the east, and both men eventually stood gazing out towards the forest. Somewhere out there, was the enemy, plotting their assault on the city of Parva. And today the Empire would meet them on the fields outside the city walls, whether the Empire was ready or not.

34

Ħard Ꞡruths

Nathan L'guire, Emperor, Duke of Pernia and Guardian Knight twitched. It was barely noticeable, but he was sure he felt something. Concentrating hard, he tried to settle his foggy mind, while images flitted in and out of his view. The hallucinations had increased since…

Since when?

He felt himself frown, that was new, he couldn't remember the last time he was able to frown. Trying to focus on the wild images that haunted his thoughts, pictures of men and a woman swam around his head. Was he supposed to recognise these people? His heart ached when he saw them; on a small boat, climbing cliffs, huddled together in the dark. Everything felt as if it should be familiar, but he

417

couldn't remember why. When he saw them within a room filled with coloured light, he wanted to cry out in warning, but at the same time, reach out and beg for help. The effort to try and put the images together was exhausting, and the sweat on his body began to cool and he shivered.

He shivered!

The agony that had wracked his body was at last subsiding to a dull throbbing ache; as if he had tensed his muscles for too long. Yet despite the pain and exhaustion, he fought on, determined to push through the fog. He suddenly tensed, there was a voice, quietly spoken in hushed tones, but he was sure he heard it. Straining to hear anything else, there was another voice, still hushed, but the tone not so deep, a female voice?

Panic suddenly gripped him when unseen hands grabbed at his body, the sensation of touch burning at his skin. He wanted to cry out in agony, but his voice still failed him, his jaws locked firmly shut. The hands continued to pull at him and he felt himself lifted up, something wrapped his body and the pain of the hands touching him began to feel like a reassuring warmth.

Still unable to open his eyes, he felt nausea overcome him as he seemed to be moving through air, floating. Travelling through space, his awareness was slowly beginning to return, at first uncomfortable, a mix of sensations that were confusing, compounding his need to be sick. He fought back the bile that was threatening to rise in his throat, while his mind battled to come to terms with his situation.

Eventually, he became aware that he wasn't actually floating, but being carried by someone. He could feel their

418

body against his, whoever it was, their smell was also familiar and comforting. Trying again to open his eyes, he felt them slightly move apart. Buoyed by this progress, he worked at the process needed to do the simple task of opening his eyelids. Cold air brushed against his eyes making them water, and he reluctantly forced them shut again. But the next time he attempted to open them, he gingerly blinked, adjusting to the world around him. He was still confused and nothing would stay in focus. However, a light from an unseen source cast monstrous shadows on darkened walls, his heart pounded as he contemplated the fear that he was released from one hell only to be taken into another?

The figures still shifted around him, and whoever was carrying him moved at a quick, steady pace. Fear fuelled the need to survive, forcing its way through his confused thoughts and emotions, while he battled to move his aching body. Finally, he burst through the invisible constraints that bound him, his arms and legs convulsing against the sudden movement. While he struggled to free himself from the grasp of whoever held him, his abrupt actions had caused his captor to lose their hold on his body. He slammed into the hard surface of the floor, the impact sending a new wave of pain through his battered frame, and he moaned in pain.

He yelled out and felt relief at the sound of his own voice, despite feeling his throat and lungs object to the task. He tried to rise, kicking and punching, desperate to get away from the hands that wrestled with him. Crying out in frustration he suddenly felt panic as once more his desperate efforts to escape were hindered by hands forcing him back to the floor.

419

Then darkness began to overtake him, drifting off into a dreamless oblivion.

'Dear gods, what the hell was all that about?'

Damien was now sitting on Nathan's chest staring down at his cousin as if he were a mad man. He wasn't sure if he was breathing heavily from the exertion of pinning him to the floor or from the shock at how bloody strong Nathan was when he was pissed off.

Simon had hold of one of his arms while John had the other, Daniel and Paul had laid claim to a leg each.

'I don't know, but I couldn't hold him, and it didn't sound good when he landed on the floor.' Simon winced at the memory.

Stephen was still kneeling at the head of the now unconscious Nathan, he looked concerned.

'He's fine, it would take more than a fall like that to do any harm. I'm more concerned with his mental state than his physical one.' He looked up at Jean hovering over them all, with deep concern etched into her face, making it a question rather than a statement.

She shook her head, mirroring his concern. 'He has no idea what has happened to him, he probably woke up with the memory of yesterday still fresh in his mind. No wonder he panicked.'

Stephen seemed to agree. 'Well, he's asleep now, I'll wake him when he's lying down and not going to rouse the entire Citadel.'

Silently they agreed and tentatively began to move away from Nathan's unconscious body. Everyone had faith in

420

Stephen's ability to keep the man asleep, but this was Nathan after all, and you could never be too sure. Satisfied he wasn't going to suddenly wake up and cause a ruckus they all stood up, then Simon once more picked him up in his arms.

They moved quickly, climbing stairs and making their way along corridors until they were a further two floors up, somewhere on the other side of the building. Jean discovered they were now in an area reserved exclusively for the Knights when they visited Pernia. Fortunately, the area where the Council Chamber had manifested, and Nathan had noisily woken up, was away from the sleeping quarters. And so not for the first time, the Knights were thankful there were few watch patrols in the area. Though Damien had hinted that he may have to have a word with the Commanding Officer about the lack of security. But for now, they were glad they didn't have to explain to anyone else what they were doing carrying an unconscious, naked Emperor around the Citadel, after having arrived on the island secretly.

Their living quarters were, essentially, a series of bedrooms along the length of a long hallway, facing a large shared living space, a dining room and kitchen. Apparently the only room off limits was one used exclusively by Nathan as a study, but this was locked and no-one had any inclination to enter anyway.

Simon carried Nathan along the passage which ended with a full length window looking out towards the sea to the East. Stephen opened the door to the last room, and Simon entered with Jean following quickly behind. The rest of the Knights disappeared into separate rooms, agreeing to meet in the living room; once they had showered and changed

421

into clothes kept here for such situations. No-one suggested where Jean should go, but she was more interested in ensuring Nathan was safe and had no intention of leaving him.

She was aware that Stephen was considering her as she stood on the opposite side of the bed, Nathan now lying between them in a peaceful oblivion, with several blankets covering his body.

'He will sleep now until I wake him. I won't be long, I just need to shower and change, but I would rather he isn't left alone.'

Jean shook her head. 'I'm not going anywhere, if there is a bathroom here, I can sort myself out.'

Saying nothing, Stephen walked across the room to a door that opened onto Nathan's en-suite bathroom. When Jean joined him and looked in she wasn't surprised to see it was as large as the one in Nathan's room in the Retreat.

'Everything you need should be here. To be honest, Nathan rarely visits Pernia, but all of our quarters are always made ready should we turn up unexpectedly.' He walked back into the bedroom and indicated a large chest of drawers. 'Nathan usually keeps his shirts in here, they will probably be rather large for you, but I very much doubt if Nathan would mind if you wanted to change into something clean.'

Jean looked at him sharply. 'What does that mean?'

Stephen didn't answer, but grinned as he made his way to the door. 'I'll be back soon.'

He left, and Jean was sure she heard him chuckle. Frowning she made her way over to the man asleep on the bed, clasping his hand in hers as she sat down beside him. Concerned the effects of his experience could linger, she was pleased to feel that his chilled body was feeling warmer, sensing peace running though him now, his mind cleared of pain and confusion.

But he was exhausted.

She wished the Knights would let him sleep longer, but they needed to learn what had happened to bring him here and whether there was more danger lurking in the shadows. Jean had her own suspicions, but decided to keep quiet for now, she wanted to speak to Nathan first before she voiced her concerns.

Satisfied Nathan was safe for now, she retreated to the bathroom and took full advantage of the facilities on offer. Coming out refreshed and clean, she eyed up the dresser Stephen had indicated earlier and then had a sniff at her own shirt, After spending a night on a fishing boat and climbing cliff faces, she thought that perhaps Stephen had a point. Despite feeling awkward, she investigated the dresser drawers and found a crisp white cotton shirt. She had to roll the sleeves up and gave up trying to tuck its entire length into her trousers. Instead, she left it loose and buckled her belt around the waist, she felt slightly ridiculous but had to admit it was good to wear something clean. Returning to her seat beside the bed, by the time Stephen had come back into the room she was reading one of the books piled on the bedside table. She didn't notice the small smile that crossed the doctor's face when he saw that she had taken his advice, and acquired one of Nathan's shirts.

When Nathan opened his eyes, the first person he saw was a large blonde haired man eyeing him cautiously. He tried to sit up, but the doctor gently, but with some effort, pushed him back onto the bed.

'Just take it easy.'

Nathan blinked as he tried to figure out where the hell he was, and who this man was.

Recognition suddenly flooded into his mind.

'Stephen!'

'Ah, so now you know who I am, it wasn't so long ago I was evading some well aimed punches from you my friend.'

Nathan relaxed into the pillows and looked around the room, recognising the sparse furniture and the awful wood panelling around the walls.

'Pernia! How the hell did I get here?'

'How indeed? That is something we would all like to know.'

Nathan frowned, confusion etched across his face. A movement to his right made him turn his head, and he looked into the concerned features of a woman sitting beside him. He felt his heart lift and a flutter around his navel.

'Jean?'

'Hello Nathan, glad you could finally join us.'

She grinned at him and he smiled back, while she squeezed his hand. He gladly returned the gesture until Stephen broke through their little moment.

'Jean, if you want to join the others in the living room, I'll help Nathan get ready and we'll join you there.'

Nathan was about to protest that he was more than capable of sorting himself out, when Stephen's face suggested he wasn't open for negotiations. When Stephen took charge of a patient, he expected them to do as they were told, it didn't matter who they were. Jean nodded and stood up, giving his hand a final squeeze before she let it go and left the room quietly.

'Was that my shirt she was wearing?'

'Yes, I do believe it was. Now are you going to move or do you intend to lay around all day?'

Running his hand through his hair, which felt sticky at his touch, Nathan sat up slowly. He had to admit that it was probably a good idea that Stephen was still there, as walking to the bathroom his legs felt wobbly, and he was a bit lightheaded. Once the hot water from the shower hit his naked body, he had to steady himself against the wall, and while Stephen didn't say anything, Nathan knew he was there with a worried look on his face. He stood under the deluge for a while, appreciating the heat as it scoured away the stickiness that seemed to cover his body. Memories of his ordeal flitted through his mind and he bit back the urge to vent his emotions. He needed to be strong to face whoever, whatever, had done this to him.

Once he had dried himself, he viewed his image in the bathroom mirror and ran his hand through the stubble of his beard.

'Stephen, how long have I been away?'

'Almost forty-eight hours? Why?'

Nathan looked over sharply. 'Two days? Surely not.' Stephen said nothing but watched him carefully. 'It felt as if I was there forever, but you say it was only the day before yesterday?'

Stephen nodded. 'Admittedly it seems a lot longer, but yes, you disappeared only two days ago.'

Nathan looked back at his image, the frown apparent between his brows. Deciding that he didn't have the strength, or the inclination, to shave, he finished the rest of his ablutions and returned to the bedroom to dress.

Soon, he and Stephen were making their way to the living room and joined the rest of the Knights and Jean waiting for them. Passing the large window in the hallway facing east, a pink sky indicated the dawn of a new day, a small niggling sensation in the base of his spine suggested a feeling of unease despite the beauty of the vista. But he put this down to his recent circumstances and kept his own council before following Stephen down the hall.

As they entered the living room, everyone turned and stood, relief showed on all their faces. As one, they all made to come forward to greet him, stopping only when they saw the look on Stephen's face suggesting they should give him some space. Damien, however, walked straight up to Nathan and, despite warning looks from the doctor, embraced his cousin. His relief was obvious when it was returned, and when he looked into Nathan's blue eyes, he saw a calm clarity.

'It's good to have you back my friend.' Then, placing his hand on Nathan's shoulder. 'Who the hell did this to you?'

Nathan grasped his arms and shook his head, but said nothing.

There was a movement at the back of the room and Nathan looked up. Jean was standing there, watching him carefully. He gave, what he hoped, was a reassuring smile.

'You must know something.' Damien was reluctant to leave the subject and the sharpness of his question brought Nathan's focus back onto his cousin. For a moment he looked at him blankly before realising he was expected to answer. Trying to cover his confusion he stepped back and crossed his arms, he didn't like the vulnerability he was feeling and breathed in deeply to calm his nerves.

'What do you mean?'

Now it was Damien's turn to look confused, he turned back to the others in the room and they gave him a number of shrugs and shaking of heads. He studied Nathan before asking again.

'Nathan, two days ago, we were woken by a sound of all hell breaking loose in your bedroom. By the time we managed to get through the door, you were missing, the room was ransacked and your blood was spattered everywhere. What the hell happened?'

Confused, Nathan held his hand to his head, and felt a lump under his hairline, the jagged edges of dried blood under his fingers. Frowning, he tried to concentrate on the events of the previous morning, but he couldn't recall anything. His stomach churned and he began to feel sick again. Sitting heavily on the edge of a sofa he put his head in his hands, aware of others moving around the room, settling down too; all eager to hear what he had to say. Rubbing his face and allowing the roughness of his unshaved chin to course over the hard skin of his fingers, he finally placed his chin on his clasped hands while his elbows rested on his knees.

Around him, the room sat in silence. They wanted answers that he wasn't sure he was able to give, and whatever he said, they would probably think he was mad. But they had all travelled here, to Pernia, determined to bring him back from a living hell. He owed them something.

But first he had his own questions, and sitting up he looked around.

'How did you know to come here to find me?'

Damien, who was now sitting beside him, inclined his head to the back of the room.

'That was all down to Jean. I don't know how, but she was able to connect with you while she was in your room at the Retreat.'

Nathan turned around. Jean was leaning against the far wall, arms and legs crossed as if she was calm and relaxed, but he saw a glimpse of the apprehension within.

'You were there?'

Jean took a short while before answering, then nodding, she said. 'I pretty much did what you did to me in Plymouth after the Bales incident. You left a huge signature when you disappeared, and while I couldn't find you anywhere within the confines of the universe, I managed to latch on to a small remnant of where you were. It was difficult to hold onto, but it was enough to gain the information we needed to find you.'

When Jean made it obvious she wasn't saying anything more, Nathan asked. 'What information?'

Damien answered. 'You said you were nowhere. I admit it took a moment to figure out, but the Council Chamber is the only place I know that sounded like a possibility. It was a

428

nightmare though not telling anyone where we were going. Ty was not impressed when I called him, saying I was going to be away for a while and that I would speak to him soon. Anna and Christopher weren't too happy either.'

Nathan groaned and put his head in his hands again.

'I told you not to say anything?'

'You said not to trust anyone. We had to travel to Bernick to charter a boat that took us to the south of the island and the emergency exit via the cliff face there. That is a bloody long climb by the way. It didn't help that we had spent the night at sea in the middle of a storm either.'

'And the farce of trying to get through the gardens to the Citadel without being seen…' Paul's voice grumbled from the other side of the room. 'And, did you know they've built a bloody duck pond there now?'

Despite themselves, the Knights did have a chuckle at the thought of Paul's unfortunate swim the previous evening; even Paul had to grin eventually.

Damien enlightened Nathan's confusion. 'Paul had to dodge a couple of very green cadets. Unfortunately, the bush he jumped behind hid a new duck pond. It caused quite a stir.' He grinned. 'Anyway, we think we have managed to get here without being seen, but we still have no idea why.'

Nathan shook his head in bewilderment. 'I had no idea.' He spread his hands and gazed at his palms without really looking at them. 'I don't actually know what happened to bring me here to Pernia, but I suspect that Gellan and Duran had something to do with it. There have been too many strange things happening that can only be explained if those two were involved.'

429

There was a movement behind him, but everyone stayed silent as they listened.

'Someone has been in my office, moving things around. I don't know why, because it's very subtle, but if they were trying to unnerve me they were doing a damned good job. The attack on Jean pretty much sealed my suspicions, I've been trying to figure out how and why for weeks now, but I still haven't found any answers.'

He felt so tired, and to have to admit that he was unable to keep such a dangerous enemy away from their doors, leaving them vulnerable, was hard. But he had obviously failed them, they needed to know.

Damien shook his head. 'But how is that possible Nathan? I thought even the gods couldn't penetrate your protections, only when we are sent on a mission are they allowed to intervene, and that is under the supervision of Mother. And Gellan and Duran have been out of her favour for centuries.'

Nathan slammed his fisted hard onto his knees. 'I don't know. I wish I did, but I don't. Somehow they got through and there's nothing I can do about it.'

It wasn't often Nathan raised his voice, usually when he was angry he grew quieter, but this outburst surprised the Knights. Biting his bottom lip he made a concerted effort to calm himself again He closed his eyes and breathed deeply.

'The simple fact is, I don't know if I can protect anyone anymore. I've failed you all…again.'

Damien sat up. 'You haven't failed anyone. We can work this out. Gellan and Duran cannot get away with this. Once Mother finds out, she will have to act.'

Nathan shook his head and tried to protest, but there was movement from behind him and Jean's voice cut through the tense air in the room.

'Gellan and Duran didn't take you from your room in the Retreat, they haven't moved anything in your office, and to be honest, I very much doubt if they had anything to do with Bales' attack on me; he's fool enough to try that little stunt all on his own.'

Everyone turned in stunned silence and watched Jean approach Nathan.

Sitting down on the coffee table in front of him, checking first it wasn't going to collapse under her weight, she leaned forward with her arms on her knees, until his confused face was just inches away from hers.

'They didn't send you to that place Nathan. You did.'

Ignoring the sounds of outrage that continued around the room, Nathan studied Jean carefully. He couldn't understand why she would say something like that unless she meant it, but the whole idea was preposterous, and he told her so. She shook her head and held his hands in hers, he didn't object to the warmth of her palms as they rested in his, but his eyes never left her face, his voice was quiet.

'How could I possibly do that and not know?'

She sighed. 'The protections you have put in place still work, no-one, not even the gods can get through them, as Damien has already said.'

She paused for a moment, as if trying to choose her words carefully. He watched her closely, impatient to know what she knew.

431

'I have been worried about you for sometime, in particular since Bales' little stunt in Plymouth.

'You are exhausted Nathan. I've heard you walking about Denfield at all hours in the night, before then going to work early and not returning home 'til late. I can't imagine the last time you had a decent night's sleep.

'With regards to things moving around your office, I suspect that there are many aspects of your days at the moment that are difficult for you to recall at once; lunches, meetings? You may have acted normal in all of these cases, but I think you are compartmentalising each action in an attempt to maintain control. In the process, some things are easier to recall than others. For example, when you carry out some normal, everyday task without thinking about it, you may move familiar objects around. But if the next exercise you undertake requires more concentration, it is then that you notice things have moved on their own; when it was you who was responsible all along.'

Nathan shook his head in disbelief, but Jean continued.

'Concerning the events of two days ago, I think your exhaustion, confusion and anxiety over recent events, finally came to a head. Part of you has had enough, a desperate need to end the struggle that has plagued you these past months, the whole nightmare of Ephea and her family and the devastation that they have been responsible for over recent years, would have been hard enough to deal with. But I think that there is something else that is underlying, and recent events have only been the catalyst to, what I would consider, a catastrophic psychological event.

'While you have plunged further into your own personal darkness, your subconscious has finally stepped in and taken control. I don't know what you were doing exactly the other morning, but I believe that the state of your mind was such, that at a sub-cognitive level, you had become a threat to others. I've heard what happened to James and the subsequent destruction on his demise, I can only image what would occur if something similar happened to you. As such, I think you literally took yourself out of any possible scenario that could harm anyone, and the only place that could be is outside the known universe. You know about the Council Chamber and its unusual existence outside of space, I think you used that knowledge and energy to hide. Only when I was able to connect with you did your consciousness fight to be heard and call for help.'

She stopped and Nathan sat in stunned silence, his hands still resting in hers, but he felt as if he were somewhere else in the room. How could he be the one responsible for all of this? What kind of man had he become? No, this couldn't be right. He stood up with such a force that he almost pushed Jean to the floor. He made his way to the back of the room.

'No, that is a ridiculous notion, how can I do that? I have sworn to protect the universe and the people in it, not try and destroy it.'

'And that is what I am saying. You had no choice, your subconscious took over when it realised the threat that your actions would create. I'm not saying what you did was wrong, it's just the more likely explanation for the facts presented.'

He looked away and his mind raced. It couldn't be true, if he was going mad what use would he be to anyone? Damien brought him back to his senses by cutting through the uncomfortable silence in the room.

'So there is no conspiracy? No-one is out to kill Nathan? Is that what you are saying?'

'No, that is not what I am saying. What happened with Ephea and her sisters, along with the Kaimiren and Franco are all down to Gellan and Duran. And I don't for one moment believe they have given up on their pursuit to bring Nathan down. I just don't think we should let what has been happening here, be confused with the very real threat out there. My concern is what has set all of this off in the first place.'

She stood and joined Nathan, taking his hands in hers, while looking hard into his eyes.

'You've been around for ten-thousand years and seen and done things no human should have to deal with, yet you have coped just as the rest of us have over the centuries. But something has happened, and quite recently I suspect, that has made you doubt yourself.' She paused as his face betrayed the confirmation of what she said. 'Whatever it is, you need to talk about it, you can't let it fester like this.'

Nathan closed his eyes, how could he possibly admit out loud the horror of his worst failure to anyone, let alone Jean. When he opened them again, he let go of her hands and walked over to a window to tear himself away from her gaze, placing his hands on the sill. He looked out over the eastern sky, which was already lightening with the rising sun, his head resting against the coolness of the glass and he breathed slowly to steady his thoughts. He knew he had to tell her, she had a right to know what she was dealing with if they had any chance of working together in the future.

But could she forgive him?

'If what you are saying is true, does this mean I'm going mad?'

He felt her hand rest between his shoulder blades, a warm tingle ran through his body and all he wanted to do was take her in his arms and hold her until all the fear melted away. But she would never have that, not with the wreck of a man that he had become.

'Of course you're not going mad. You've had a terrible experience, and you are dealing with responsibilities that would overwhelm most people. You just need to learn to trust those around you, you need to talk Nathan.'

He turned back to the room, he could feel the pain emanating from the Knights, his friends, men he had spent his life with, men he had failed. Jean caught his eye, if he could feel such powerful emotions radiating around them, then she would feel it even more. He walked back into the centre of the room with Jean following. She looked to the other Knights as if hoping for some help from them.

It was Damien who spoke first, he shook his head slowly, his eyes belying the sadness he felt inside.

'I haven't told Ty the truth about what happened, I don't know if I could.'

'Anna doesn't knew either.' Paul hung his head as he too seemed to understand.

John also agreed. 'Christopher asks, but I have so far managed to evade the questions.'

Jean put her head to one side, curious, but said nothing. Nathan looked around the room and knew there was no going back now. His pain filled, exhausted eyes rested on Jean's.

'Ixeer, that is when it started.' He paused and looked back at his friends. 'I think it might be easier if we show her.'

There was a collective sigh, but without argument they all stood. Then as one, each Knight turned around, loosened their shirts and pulled them over their heads to reveal the scars that refused to fully heal, criss-crossing their backs. In some cases the wounds had been so deep they still looked angry and sore.

After a short while, they all turned and dressed, in silence, facing Jean with sad and pain filled faces. There was no mistaking the shock on her face, and who could blame her?

'Oh Gentlemen.' Her voice held no pity, but an acknowledgment that this was something that needed gentle handling. Taking Nathan's hand, she urged him to sit down again on the sofa next to Damien, while she pulled up a small armchair beside him. The other Knights followed, their faces masks of sadness and pain. Nathan wished he could spare them the need to remember the ominous details of that time, but he was resigned to his decision; Jean deserved to know. As he recalled those eventful days, his mind focused on the past and he spoke of the harrowing memories.

35

Ixeer

Nathan was exhausted, what he wouldn't give to curl up on the sofa and sleep the memories of Ixeer away. He worried an invisible mark on his thumb with his nail, oblivious to the red blotch appearing until Jean placed her hand over his. He looked up and closed his eyes. Focusing his mind he opened them again and began.

'You are right of course Jean, Ixeer didn't happen long ago, in fact it's been barely fifty years since...'

He didn't finish his sentence, but shook his head and sat up, breathing in deeply. He took one last look at the unhappy faces of those he held most dear, and gave Jean a sad smile.

'But to be fair, time is irrelevant in this case, it is the circumstances that have a bearing on this story.

'At the time, nothing in particular was happening within the Empire; Earth was still on the to do list, and the likes of Ephea hadn't even been born yet.

I say normal, that is until we received a message that there were raiders on the Aria and Lorima border. Intelligence was sparse, but if there were people plundering the Marchlands, it had to be sorted quickly. Needless to say, Stephen and Damien were keen to find out what was going on. They left, intending to make their way to the nearest garrison for more information, and investigate further. I have to add here that while on the whole, life within the Empire is pretty peaceful, it still has to deal with those little irritations, where chaos and mayhem run riot. So this news wasn't a total surprise.

'Daniel, Paul and I carried on back in Parva, while Simon and John continued at the university, expecting to hear soon that everything had been sorted and life would carry on as always once again. It wasn't until three days later and we hadn't heard anything from either Damien, or Stephen, that we considered that there may be more to these raiders than was first thought. It was decided that Paul, John and Simon would make their way to the area, and along with knights from the garrison at the city of Brooklake, they would endeavour to meet up with Damien and Stephen eventually.

'You have to remember, that as we still hadn't returned to Earth at this point, we were still to utilise their mobile phone technology, so most garrisons communicate directly via the portals they each have.

'However, when we lost contact with the others too, Daniel and I really began to be concerned. We translocated

438

to Brooklake and demanded to know what was going on with all these raiders and what had happened to the other Knights.

'I honestly expected to find that the raider problem had been settled days before, and everyone was now involved in some celebration party and had lost all concept of time. I'm sorry to say this was not an unusual occurrence, and so I still wasn't overly concerned. In fact, I had more to deal with Daniel's grumpiness because he believed he was missing out on the festivities.'

He glanced at Daniel, who raised an eyebrow. 'It was a valid point.'

Nathan gave him a smile while shaking his head, then continued.

'That is until we discovered that the garrison at Brooklake, and the subsequent garrisons we called on, had no idea about any raiders. They didn't even know that any of us were in the area, let alone aware of any Guardians visiting the garrison. As such, our concerns were raised by quite a few levels.

'Up until that point, I had no reason to track their whereabouts, but of course, by the time we realised they were actually missing I began to mentally search for their signatures. It was a shock at first to realise that they were no longer within the Empire. Anger had taken over at this point, and I was still foolish and arrogant enough to believe we could do something to bring them home.

'Dear gods, I couldn't have been more wrong.

'The moment I translocated us near to their position, we knew something was up. We had arrived within a wooded area where the trees looked sick, and the air was damp and fetid. Even as we drew our swords, a unit of five men appeared from behind the trees. They surrounded us while bearing crossbows; loaded and ready to loose. It seems they were waiting for us.

'I hate crossbows, nasty, vicious weapons.

'Of course, I could have translocated us straight out of there, but we still needed to find the others, and at least this way we had a chance of finding out where they were before making plans to get everyone home. It appears my arrogance knew no bounds.

'There was no way we could fend off five bows at once with just our swords, they had us surrounded and we had nowhere to run. Our only choice was to lay down our arms and let them take us. I should have realised something was amiss when they didn't even try to pick up our swords, they just left them on the ground. No-one would do that unless they knew who, or what, they were dealing with. If I hadn't considered that as odd, they then pulled out shackles made with lead with traces of lemium.'

Jean gave him a stunned look and he nodded. 'I know, we were shocked too, we couldn't figure out how these men were even able to lift the chains, let alone shackle us with them. We had no idea at the time how anyone could possibly get hold of such a metal; though I've got a good inkling now. The upshot of this however, is that we were well and truly trussed up and had no means of immediate escape.

Tied together we were surrounded by the bowmen, and trooped through the woodland until we came to a small fortress. Not a particularly big affair, it was poorly built and falling down in places, but they marched us through the gate and into the Bailey. Even here there was evidence of how run down the place was, the ground was nothing more than baked hard mud. Yet apparently they had access to knowledge and technology to create shackles to keep us chained.

'We were taken through a door in the Keep that led to steps going down, that's always an ominous sign, eventually coming out into a poorly lit corridor lined with solid looking doors. Foul water ran down the walls and the place stank of shit. Even now I can still recall that smell and feel my stomach churn at the thought.

'Before we were able to continue along the corridor though, Daniel was separated from my own chains. While he was still trussed up with the lemium shackles, they opened a cell and I had a brief view of what I thought, was Paul lying unconscious on the floor. The look on Daniel's face suggested he was as horrified as I was, before he was shoved inside and the door slammed shut.

'It was at that point I almost gave in to my vow not the use my energy to destroy the whole stinking shit-hole. However, I would have achieved nothing but anarchy, and I couldn't afford to succumb to that level; but dear gods I was close.

'By now they had dragged me into another room at the end of the corridor, it was so dark inside there was barely enough light to see a large solid wooden table lined with more shackles — it was of course too much to ask that they were the normal iron variety. I didn't have much time to consider what would happen next as they must have knocked

441

me out. The next thing I knew, I was waking up stripped naked, chained to the table and nursing a horrendous headache.'

He paused again, the memories of what had happened next flooding his mind, he felt sick. Taking a deep breath, he tried to fight down his nausea, the look on Jean's anxious face clenching at his heart. He wanted to get this over and done with quickly.

'I wasn't alone unfortunately, peering over the table was the face of the biggest, ugliest bastard you're ever likely to meet; I'm sure he dwarfed even Simon and John.

'I won't go into what he did next, but let's just say it involved several nasty looking metal instruments, a lot of pain and a hell of a lot of imagination on behalf of my ugly companion. I must have passed out at some point, because the next time I came round I had a visitor. He was, in comparison, the complete opposite to my ugly friend; he'd obviously spent a lot of time on his vanity and rarely ventured into his dungeons. He kept running his fingers through his hair which created a waft of magnolia scented perfume around him. I still can't stand the smell of magnolias to this day. He looked a bit green at the sight and aromas of his unwashed torture victim, I remember apologising and offered to freshen up next time he visited, but apparently he didn't have much of a sense of humour.

'Anyway, having dispatched with the small talk, I then found out the real reason for my current situation. I was expected to renounce the Imperial throne and to disband the Order, agreeing to leave the Empire altogether with the rest of the Guardians and never to return. If I hadn't been bleeding so heavily and in so much pain, I would have laughed.

'The fool had no idea.

'The irony was, I would have been more than happy to take him up on his offer. But of course, that would never be allowed to happen. Having had to decline his offer, he was obviously disappointed with my answer, and he made sure that the rest of my stay in that awful room would be used to ensure my ugly friend and I were to get more acquainted. Occasionally, the fop would return to see if I had changed my mind, and each time he left disappointed. Making sure of course, that I was aware of how unhappy he was through ugly's ministrations.'

Nathan knew making light of a part of his tortuous time was at odds with the horror he had endured. But it was the only way he could cope with recalling the harrowing images.

'I have no idea how long I was there for, but eventually they decided they needed a new tactic. Removing me from the now blood soaked table, while of course keeping the shackles in place on my wrists, I was then dragged out of my room of torture and up the stairs into the bright, watery light of the Bailey. By now I could barely stand, let alone fight, so tying me to a wooden A-frame, with my wrists above my head and both ankles bound to the base of each pole, wasn't going to be difficult.

'However, it was at that point I realised that what I had already endured at the hands of my captors, was nothing to what was coming. Arranged before me, lined in front of the Bailey wall, were my friends, all chained to their own wooden A frames, and all showing signs of having been

443

beaten, if not worse. Anger raged through me. If they had loosened my bonds at that point, I would have found the energy to fight the bastards for what they had done, maybe even pass over the line I had forbidden myself to cross.

'It wasn't long before I was joined by the little fat peacock. He told me that if I did as I was told, they would let my friends go free.'

Nathan shut his eyes to try and force back the tears that threatened. Jean ran her thumb over his hand, letting him know she was still there. He took comfort from her gesture and squeezed her hand back.

'It broke my heart to have no alternative but to refuse. I did take the opportunity to tell him that he would regret ever crossing me, and that one way or another he would pay. He didn't seem convinced however, and instead, instructed one of his men to set to my back with a metal tipped cat. I cannot describe the pain as my back was opened with each stroke, every bite of the lash made all my other tortures seem meaningless in comparison. When the peacock returned and made his demands again, I could hardly speak when I told him to fuck off.

'Then, without a second thought, he turned and motioned for my friends, those I consider closer than my brothers, to be subjected to the same brutal experience of the cat as I had. I cannot lie, at that point, it nearly broke me.

'Once they had finished inflicting their work, the fop's men left us exhausted, bleeding and barely conscious.

'Then our captors made their one fatal mistake.

'Believing we were too far gone to be of any further threat, they cut the bonds at our ankles and released our wrists from their shackles. Falling to the floor, I recall lying on the hard ground trying to focus on the others, seeing they too had been freed. This gave me the will to dig deep and find the strength I needed. Fuelled by revenge and anger, without the restraints of the lemium shackles, we could at last draw our own swords.

'We set upon our captors with such ferocity, not even I thought we were capable of. Soon our swords were biting through flesh and bone, relishing in the fear and shock of men falling to our blades. I admit, to see the horror on the peacock's face before I took his head off was good, but not as satisfying as disembowelling his ugly torturer had been.

'By the time our energy was finally spent and revenge had been sated, the Bailey was a blood bath. Anyone who had survived had done so only by fleeing for their lives, and by then we had no inclination to follow. Instead, in desperate need to get home, we returned to the safety of the Retreat, naked and covered in blood, both ours and that of our enemies.

Stephen had set about almost immediately trying to heal the wounds inflicted by the vicious cat, but for some reason they have never really healed properly; enough to not bleed anymore, but still raw, causing pain and discomfort if aggravated. As such, we have all carried these scars ever since.'

Having finished his tale, Nathan looked into Jean's eyes, desperate to see anything other than his own self loathing reflected there.

445

'Since that day, I have had to accept the knowledge that if I had taken more care, been more diligent, I could have made sure I was in a position to save everyone from the disaster of Ixeer. Instead, in my arrogance, I was responsible for the pain and torture inflicted on the people who I care for most.

'I swore from that day, that I would protect the ones I love and make sure I would never let them down again. But, as the last five years have demonstrated, I have failed them again. And only recently, I failed to keep you from harm in Plymouth.

'And all I can say to you all is that I am sorry, though I know it will never be enough. I must always live with the possibility that my failures will incur a cost that someone else will have to pay for with their life.

36

Dissension
In The Ranks

Bales watched his army march before him, sitting atop his spujki; a wolf like creature as large as a horse. The beasts had been furious that they should be expected to stoop so low as to carry humans on their backs. But Bales had threatened to send them back to Kyawann, and only fear of what would happen if they returned to their homeland made them acquiesce and allow Bales and his four Captains to climb upon their backs.

He looked out over the heads of his warriors, smirking to himself as he considered the moment the proud face of that conceited bastard Nathan, as his precious Order ran at the sight of his monster army bearing down on them; slaughtering and devouring their arrogant flesh. The images brought a pleasure to him he hadn't realised he could ever feel, so long had he needed to keep his true thoughts and feelings to himself. Now he was able to express his innermost desires and the Empire would be the first to feel his true power; he felt unstoppable.

Bales' army had been marching since before dawn two days ago. They had entered the forest the previous afternoon and had encountered the guerrilla attacks from the moment they were engulfed in the shaded darkness of the trees.

Already restricted by the close undergrowth, Bales and his army were forced to spread out along its lines. Now already slowed down by the food and provisions they had plundered from the farms and villages. Groups of his army's stragglers were soon victims to the expertise of the forest inhabitants; including those of the Order and the Militia. It didn't take long for the stories to travel down the lines of ghost-like wraiths seen flitting amongst the trees, taking the unwary, only to deposit their remains further down the road for their comrades in arms to find as they approached.

Soon Bales' army was beginning to show signs of alarm and fear. Their Commander, Kendon, and his own Captains were forced to slow their advancing columns down to ensure the rear troops were no longer targets for these hidden phantoms.

Bales was furious, he was fully aware of who these so called wraiths were, and ordered Kendon to force his men to fight back. But it seemed his mighty force was a suspicious lot, and as far as they were concerned they couldn't fight ghosts. Therefore, he had to endure the frustration of a twitchy, unnerved army of forty-thousand strong, determined to move at a pace that ensured they were safe from the evil that lurked in the trees. The irony wasn't lost on him.

Kendon now made his way back to Bales' position within the procession, his broad face looked up into that of Bales who delighted in the opportunity to look down on the beast. He wasn't sure if the creature was angry or not, his features were set in a permanent sneer, so he could have been delighted with his lot for all Bales knew. However, his tone when he spoke soon put paid to that idea.

'My Lord, why do you continue to ride back here instead of travelling at the head of the army. You should lead from the front, be an example to the warriors who follow you.'

Bales scoffed.

'Don't dare to tell me how lead my own army Kendon, I'm not stupid, that is where the danger is. I will stay where I should be, here where it is safe, knowing that my army is in a position to place themselves in danger in order to protect their leader. In case you had forgotten, there is an enemy out amongst the trees, would you let me fall into their hands?'

Kendon gave him a look that suggested that if he had his way, he would have dragged Bales into the trees himself and left him to his fate. But instead he answered. 'No Sir, of course not.'

449

Beneath him, Bales felt his spujku growl, a sentiment echoed by its fellows. The commander glanced at the beast and said nothing, only giving a cursory nod before returning to his position at the front of the column; his face now dark with anger.

They eventually emerged from the Northern Forest with the walls of the Caldera rising before them in the distance. For a moment he felt a brief pang of regret, seeing the flags bearing the Imperial Tree flying above the parapets. He could have had the perfect life there, but *he* had to ruin it all.

He noted with some satisfaction that an army was forming below the walls, he would get some gratification after all. Today he would earn his battle honours.

Field Marshall Inchgower fiddled with the lenses on his binoculars, trying to focus as far as possible at the enemy emerging from the forest. By his reckoning, they would be on the field by mid-afternoon. Lowering the binoculars he closed his eyes and took a long slow breath inwards, his usual habit to calm his nerves and keep his mind focussed was becoming harder to be effective. At the moment, the incoming hordes were nothing but a blur against the tree line, but it didn't change the fact that they had to be at least forty-thousand in number, and that didn't include the wolf like beasts that moved amongst them. It was difficult to tell, because some of these creatures walked upon all fours, whereas others stood upright. But that could just be because of the distance he was looking from and lack of focus.

Reports had been coming in from scouts and patrols returning from their forays into the forest. Apparently the horde may be terrifying to see and were large in numbers, but they were as susceptible to the blade as any mortal man. Also, they lacked discipline, and already there were those who tried to desert into the darkness of the trees, only to be cut down by the Order and Militia waiting there.

Looking down from the parapet he observed their own army now amassing before the city walls. They had gathered around ten thousand so far, and more were due to join them, but looking at the number bearing down on Parva, Inchgower couldn't help but fear for the citizens still within the city walls.

The Imperial army was strong and highly disciplined, but realistically, did they really stand a chance against such odds? Not for the first time that day, he turned his gaze west, and the isle of Pernia, praying to the gods for his Emperor's return; despite knowing these same gods had no interest in his, or any other human's business. But he was at the stage now, even beseeching dispassionate deities had become a necessity for his own declining faith.

Footsteps approaching brought him out of his reverie, and he turned to see General Morris looking as exhausted and worried as he did. 'What have you got for me General? Please tell me it's good news.'

His heart sank when the look on his friend's face suggested he was going to be disappointed, bracing himself, he listened to the latest information, while silently praying again for Nathan's return.

'Fewson, what the fuck are you doing down there?'

451

George jumped, he hadn't realised how deep in thought he'd been until the medic bawled down to him from the field hospital, situated outside the walls south-east of the city. Nestling in the city's shadow, it occupied a small plateau at the base of the caldera, that fell away to a small but steep sided ravine below. It acted as a natural defence and lookout point with access to the impending battlefield, but far enough away to afford some protection. Unless of course, the enemy prevailed and then it wouldn't make any difference anyway.

Only the very worst cases admitted to the field hospital would be transferred immediately to Aria or other hospitals, as the use of crystals was to be minimised. However, if Lord Stephen had been there, there would not have been a problem with the transference of patients. But of course, he was with Jean and the other Knights.

Despite Raynard's misgivings, George had managed to assign himself to the hospital by annoying a young medic knight so much, that she finally gave into him just for some peace.

'If you are determined to stay, make yourself useful in here.'

She had indicated an area full of temporary beds within the complex, separated from the main hub of the facility by canvas walls.

'Is this to be used a ward?'

The medic waggled her left hand and grimaced.

'Sort of. If nothing can be done for the mortally wounded, they will be brought here for care.'

'You want me to watch over the dead?'

George was indignant, he wanted to help, not sit amongst the dying.

The medic was furious.

'Who the bloody hell do you think you are? There are men and women willing to die to save the city, at the very least they should know that they wouldn't be dying alone.'

George felt his face colouring with shame and mumbled his sincere apologies.

'I'm sorry, of course I'll do everything I can.'

He looked away, mortified.

Satisfied he'd been suitably chastised, the medic left George to his own devises; there was little he could do until the battle began. He had wandered down to sit overlooking the valley, an outcrop of rock separating the agricultural fields and the drop to the valley below. He could hear the Order and Militia gathering, preparing for the battle before the city walls, the sights and smells of soldiers and horses filled the air.

Making his way up the rise to re-join the medic, they both turned when they heard a call that someone had seen the enemy. Looking towards the Northern Forest in the east, George found he had suddenly lost his ability to speak; his mouth had gone dry and his stomach churned. He last saw these creatures only two days ago and he felt the fear tingle down his spine at the memory. A hand on his shoulder made him start.

'Come on Fewson, we've got work to do.'

From their view from the Ketler Mountains that looked out over the fields around Parva's walls, Gellan and Duran watched their army below. Led by Bales and his Patrolmen Captains, they moved out of the trees in earnest towards the city.

At the wall's base, members of the Order and Militia amassed to meet their enemy.

Pleased with what he saw, Gellan smiled to himself. Despite the cold wind that blew down from the mountains, along with the constant hunger that plagued them everyday, they were, at last, nearer to their final goal. But Duran, wasn't happy, Gellan ground his teeth as, yet again, he had to calm him down.

'Yes, I know this plan has to work this time, I hate this revolting human form as much as you do. But look…' He flung his arm out to the fields below in frustration. '…we have an army that can engulf the pathetic humans gathering that Nathan calls his Order. We have even made particular precautions regarding that annoying Carter woman. So when this is finished, we will have the Empire on its knees, begging us to save them, offering gifts to placate, showing the reverence we are entitled to. Then, Anasara, our Mother, will understand her misguided loyalty to the unnecessary lives of the universe. Gathering us back into her arms, once more we will be in our rightful place amongst our bothers and sisters.'

Gellan gave Duran a sharp look, who stared back as impassively as ever, but his thoughts drilled through Gellan's mind. His repost was almost spat out in anger.

'It cannot fail, it has to work, and we will win.'

His gaze returned to the far off walls of Parva and his voice became barely a whisper.

'But if all else fails, we still have Johnson.'

37

A Cause For Concern

J ean gazed out to sea and breathed in the briny air, allowing it to fill her mind with memories of voyages past. The Bonnie Maid lifted with the swell, her prow cutting through the white tufted waves as they made their way from the Citadel on the Isle of Pernia, to the harbour at Parva. The midmorning sun reflecting bright golden patterns on the water's surface.

She looked over to the man sitting next to her. He too was looking out to sea, but the green tinge of his complexion and the concentration on his face, suggested this was more than likely to try and keep the contents of his stomach down, rather than enjoying the exhilaration of the voyage. Nathan turned to face her and, despite his queasiness, managed a smile. He held out his hand to her along the ships rail and she grinned back, taking his hand and put her head on his shoulder.

'How are you feeling now?'

'Wishing the world would stop moving.'

Jean chuckled. 'Your home is an island, how can you be seasick?'

'It may be my family home, but I have never really lived here. My mother preferred to live in Parva when she was pregnant with Katherine and I. When my father died, we spent most of our time with Damien and his family in Lorimar. In fact, it has only been this last few hundred years and the formation of the Order that the Citadel has been used since the disappearance of Katherine.' He frowned at an unspoken memory. 'She seemed to enjoy the isolation out here.'

She gave him a sad smile. It was difficult sometimes to reconcile the Katherine she knew with the one Nathan and the Knights had known.

They both relaxed into a comfortable silence, at ease in each other's company. Jean took in a long slow breath and her mind drifted back to the events of earlier that morning.

When Nathan had finished telling his devastating tale about Ixeer, the room had remained silent. Jean was used to the fact that now the closer she had become to the Knights, the more confused her senses were to their emotions; and she had completely given up trying to read Nathan. But at that moment the emotional energy was stark and raw; pain, shame and fear, her heart almost broke with the intensity of it. She tried to shield herself from the effects, but then realised that Nathan had felt the subtle change, he looked even more distraught. She desperately wanted to reassure him, make him understand he wasn't alone.

'Nathan, have you spoken about any of this to anyone else?'

She looked around the room, the sad look on the faces told her the answer.

Damien sighed. 'He won't speak to anyone. We've tried, but he refuses to talk about it.'

Jean was concerned. 'Have any of *you* talked about it?

She felt Nathan's body sag as if he carried a huge weight. She reached out and grasped his hands within hers.

Damien nodded sadly. 'We have, we came to terms with the whole episode a long time ago. We just haven't talked about it with anyone else.'

She pursed her lips, it wasn't ideal, but it was a start. Returning her attention back to Nathan, she opened her senses again, slowly and carefully. This time she focused on the man sitting before her, he was broken and in pain, and when she touched his face with her hand, he seemed surprised by the contact and flinched. She refused to move her hand however, and when she caught his gaze, his sadness was like a great wave washing over her.

She looked at Damien again.

458

'And do you blame him for what happened?'

Anger shot around the room, the look of consternation reflecting on every face.

'Of course not. How could we possibly blame him for something he had no control over.' Then, snorting in disgust he continued. 'But trying to convince him of that is impossible.'

Jean inclined her head. She understood his anger, he had to watch his best friend condemn himself everyday, knowing the pain he suffered but could do nothing to alleviate it. Moving closer to Nathan, Jean was now barely inches away.

'Are you listening to what Damien has to say? These are men you trust with your life, hold most dear to your heart. Yet you choose to ignore them when they try to help you.'

His eyes pleaded with her to not go on, but she refused to let it go.

'Instead of talking to the very people you trust, you kept this terrible guilt locked up inside, pushing it down until you could almost pretend it wasn't there. Until one day, Belby happens, a horrible catastrophe that digs deep into your conscience and drives your shame before you. Then one day, you can't hide from it anymore.

'With Ephea thrown into the mix, I'm surprised you've lasted this long. But you can't do this to yourself Nathan. Look at what has happened because you haven't shared your thoughts.'

Taking his face in both hands she looked hard into his eyes, this time she didn't berate herself for wanting to fall deeper within his gaze. Instead, she allowed herself to admit the truth that was always there. She loved this man more than anything she had ever known. Her heart, body and soul was his, and there was nothing she wanted to, or could, do about it. She surrendered unconditionally and accepted that she needed him now as much as he needed her; she would never leave him.

'How can you believe you are a man capable of harming your friends, your brothers? The people you love? Yesterday, your very soul took you to a place that you believed would keep others safe. A place that was slowly killing you. That is not the mark of a monster, it is the nature of a remarkable, selfless man, that deserves the love and respect of those around him. Who also inspires others to follow him into the bowels of hell itself if needs be.

'A man that I would not only follow, but would gladly walk beside without a second thought, while demons taunted our souls.'

Jean touched his forehead with her own and closed her eyes. Breathing in his scent and praying to the gods he didn't push her away. But Nathan just closed his own eyes and let the tears run freely down his cheeks, he didn't try to wipe them away. Without moving his head away from Jean he slowly shook his head.

'You don't know that.'

Jean pulled away and couldn't suppress a small affectionate laugh.

'Of course I do you idiot. I know, because I love you. If it came down to it, I would die for you. Let's face it, walking into hell is just another day at the office for us.'

Nathan looked stunned for a moment. When he spoke it was barely a whisper.

'You realise that I love you too, don't you?'

She could only stare at him. Her voice had abandoned her, while she thought her heart would burst with relief and joy. Then, taking her completely by surprise, he suddenly wrapped his arms around her and pulled her to him. His kiss was hard and desperate and her own passion charged her response, flinging her arms around his neck in happiness. He then buried his head in her shoulder as she hugged him back, her own tears flowing down her face. For a short while at least, they felt peace around them.

As one, the rest of the Knights rose, everyone wiping their faces as the relief and emotion swept over them too. Nodding to Jean, they made their way from the room. The door was pulled to, eventually leaving the pair of them alone, while Nathan broke down completely and sobbed his heart out.

Once the gates to his guilt, anger and fear were opened, there was nothing he could do to close them. At last the pain and sorrow that had plagued him for so long was released. When he had finally spent his tears, he and Jean spent their time alone talking. It wasn't going to be easy, but both of them knew that things were going to be better from now on.

By the time the Knights returned, the two were sitting together and at ease. The Knights had talked to the Citadel's commander and had arranged for breakfast to be brought in. Silence quickly ensued as the eight hungry Guardians tucked in.

Once they had finished their meal, Damien told everyone the odd conversation he had had with the Citadel commander, apparently there hadn't been any ships arriving from Parva since the day before yesterday. It had also come to light that fishing vessels hadn't seen any ships from Parva either. The Knights were obviously concerned to hear such news and Nathan said he would have a word with the Commander himself. Jean noticed that the opportunity to concentrate on something other than his own guilt seemed to perk him up. It was decided, in the meantime, to charter a vessel, back to the mainland and Parva, on the next tide. They would investigate the strange absence of shipping when they got back to Parva.

Now Jean was sitting with Nathan on the Bonnie Maid, the ship taking them home, her hand resting in his, while he looked as if he was still trying to keep his breakfast down. The green tinge around his ears hadn't abated. The other Knights left them alone and they appreciated their thoughtfulness. Even though little had been said between the two while onboard, they were both comforted by each others' company.

At some point in the voyage, Jean became aware of her phone vibrating in her pocket. It seemed that while the forces Nathan had created around the island prevented the devices from working, once they crossed out of the zone, they picked up a signal immediately. Reluctant to allow the device to intrude, Jean thought she had better review her messages anyway. Apologising to Nathan, she checked the screen and frowned.

'Nathan, I have to go.'

He looked up sharply.

'Why, what's happened?'

462

'Well, you remember that you set up a link between NiCI and Earth, so that I can receive messages, even from that far out into space? Well, she's just relayed a distress call sent by a friend. I have to find out what's going on.'

Moving away from the rail, Nathan winced, his stomach didn't appreciate the sudden shift in position.

'I'll go with you if there's trouble.'

Jean smiled and squeezed his hand, shaking her head.

'It's alright, I just need to see what he's got up to now.' Seeing him about to protest, Jean stopped him. 'No, I promise, if I need help I will contact you. The sooner I'm gone, the sooner I can come home.'

She caught herself as she realised that she now considered Kelan as home, or was that just anywhere Nathan was? He gave her a small smile and she felt the butterflies inside again, along with concern at the odd colour of his cheeks; he really didn't look well.

Jean glanced at the other Knights who were also looking avidly at their phones, something had definitely caught their attention too. She needed to leave now though, before she was bogged down by more protests. Leaning forward and kissing Nathan, she smiled and promised him to be back soon, before standing up and translocating away.

Despite his seasickness, Nathan felt uneasy about Jean leaving so quickly; something inside told him it was wrong. But could he really trust his instincts anymore? His thoughts were interrupted by Damien hurrying to his side, his worried frown suggesting he wasn't about to enquire after his cousins health.

463

'Where has Jean gone?'

'She had a problem to see to, after receiving a message from NiCl.'

'Well, she's not the only one. We need to get back to Parva now!'

The look on Damien's face told Nathan not to question his judgement. His stomach lurched again and he winced briefly, but taking a long slow breath he made a point of trying to ignore his nausea.

'Tell me on the way.'

A single wave to the ship's Skipper, who looked on curiously, and Nathan took the Knights to the Retreat. He listened intently with growing concern and foreboding, as Damien told him all about what he had learned concerning the alien army marching on the city of Parva.

38

Valern

When Jean arrived on the bridge of NiCI, the familiar sounds of the main life support and light systems vibrated around her. There was always a breathable atmosphere on the bridge for when she returned, but the rest of the ship was powered down to conserve energy until required.

Wrinkling her nose, Jean, again, realised how much she had become used to breathing fresh air that hadn't been processed through a recycling machine. She could taste the ionised particles, and the atmosphere was dry compared to the Devonshire countryside and the salty brine of Parva.

She didn't, however, have time to mull over the conditions of the universe. A distress call had been received from Marne and she had to find out if he was safe. The daft fool was probably trying to talk himself out of a dodgy deal, and was no doubt hanging by his thumbs from an unhappy father's rafters. But he had been there for Jean too many times for her to leave him to his fate, even if he did probably deserve it.

Checking NiCI's systems, Jean frowned. The distress signal was definitely Marne's signature, but it had been received from an odd location, one that was familiar, but still highly unlikely for a scoundrel like Marne.

She knew speculation would get her nowhere, she had to find out what trouble her wayward friend had found himself in now. She also wanted to get things dealt with quickly, there was still a lot of conversation she needed to have with Nathan, and an evening with Marne didn't figure in her plans.

Looking up from the console, she caught her reflection in the glass of the viewing screen. Despite the wind and sea spray, she seemed to have survived and managed to still look half decent. Of course, this might also have something to do with the big grin that had spread across her face as she thought of Nathan, encouraging her desire to return to Kelan as soon as possible.

Tucking a loose piece of hair behind her right ear, she returned to the centre of the spacecraft's bridge.

'Power down NiCI, it will be a while before I'm back again.'

Even as she thought of her destination, NiCI's systems were darkening, and once more the lights dimmed. Soon, only the blinking lights of the terminals glowed within the silent ship.

The religious house at Valern was an ecclesiastical outpost, created to serve as a retreat for those requiring a place to find peace, solitude and reflection. Jean considered it nothing more than a hidey-hole for those wanting to keep out of the way of the law, or more often than not, an overbearing spouse. But this wasn't really Marne's way. Normally, if he found things a bit too much, he would go on a bender for a week and wait until whatever was troubling him, finally disappeared with the resulting hangover. Besides, the only spouses Marne ever encountered where the ones after his hide. But the simple fact was, the distress signal had come from this location, within the stone edifice of Valern. Nestled amongst the snow shrouded forests that covered the surrounding mountains.

She had arrived a short distance away from the granite fortress like structure, unsure what she would encounter when she got there. Remaining hidden amongst the pine trees, she listened, sensing. The air was still, not a breath of wind stirred the trees, the snow deadening any sound.

It was odd, she didn't feel any danger, not even the remains of the distress expected after a traumatic event. Pushing out her senses further, the only trace of life she could discern was from within Valern itself, and that remained a tranquil calm. Only the presence of a few animals moving amongst the trees and burrowing under the snow encroached her senses; but nothing insidious, no potential danger. Still, there was nothing wrong with being cautious. Jean moved out from the protection of the trees and drew her daggers.

She approached the sanctuary, eyeing the wide open front doors with caution, watching the porter sitting on his stool inside an alcove to the left of the entrance. He was one of the religious clerics of the house wrapped in a thick woollen cloak to ward off the cold. He looked up as she approached and smiled, standing ready to greet her, only retreating back when he saw the blades in her hands.

Jean registered his concern immediately, a stark contrast to the peace around them. Awkwardly, she sheathed the daggers and held her empty palms up to show she came peacefully.

'It's alright, I'm not going to hurt anyone.'

The cleric didn't look convinced, and he pulled his cloak over his coarse spun habit more closely around him, as if the material were a shield against potential danger.

'Why is the White Vixen here and carrying arms if she doesn't mean to harm anyone?'

Jean groaned to herself. She had earned a number of names over the years, some even respectable in polite company. White Vixen was an old nickname from centuries earlier during a particularly over exuberant blonde phase. It wasn't a shade she ever intended to favour again, though unfortunately the name had stuck.

'You obviously know who I am, but I swear I am not here on any other business than one of mercy.'

The cleric looked confused. 'Mercy? Are you expecting trouble?'

Jean frowned, this was getting odder by the moment. 'I received a distress call from a friend of mine, it was sent from this point. Has there been any trouble here recently?'

The cleric shook his head, he looked puzzled. 'There has been nothing of note here for weeks. Well, except for those two unusual gentlemen this morning.'

Jean looked at him sharply, regretting it immediately as the porter flinched at the sudden movement.

'What two men? What did they look like?'

He was silent for a moment as he took the time to think. He shook his head and looked unhappy. 'I didn't like them, and that is an awful thing to say. But they didn't seem to be here for reflection or solitude; especially the silent one, I didn't like his eyes.'

Jean felt her stomach clench in fear. 'What did they do when they were here?'

He shrugged. 'Well, nothing to be honest. They stayed where you are now and asked about the possibility of joining us in the spring. But I got the impression they had no intention of coming back. It was curious, as I said, who travels all the way up here to just enquire about coming another day?'

Jean had to agree, it was indeed strange; unless you had a pretty good idea who the strangers were.

But why?

She turned away from the sanctuary and stared down the tree lined path that led some miles away to the nearest village.

Behind her the cleric was watching curiously as she muttered to herself.

'They didn't trek up the mountain, they came straight here and then sent a message for NiCI to pick up.'

Fear suddenly clutched at her heart. They didn't draw her up here into a trap, they drew her away from Kelan. From Nathan.

She spun back to the cleric. 'I've got to go, I'm sorry about the confusion.'

Then as quick as you like, she was gone, leaving a very confused porter to make his way back to his seat in the alcove by the door. He added a few more coals to his brazier, determined to try and keep the chill away that was beginning to settle within his soul. A feeling he was sure had nothing to do with the weather outside.

39

A Deadly Skirmish

George watched in horror as the monstrous army emerged from the Northern Forest and made their way across the open fields towards the City of Parva. He couldn't even contemplate counting their numbers, definitely tens of thousands, but if he dared to think about how many, he knew he would lose his nerve completely.

On they came, shaggy beasts that walked both upright and on all fours, their thick coats covered in a leather like armour. Their heads lolled slowly from side to side with their long slow gait, maws hanging open bearing long sharp teeth. Other monsters were amongst the throng, tall beings clad in metal, they seemed thin and wiry, but George wasn't fooled, to wear that much steel armour required strength, and the freedom with which they moved their bodies suggested they were agile with it too. Darting amongst the legs of the army, smaller creatures ran. They seemed desperate to join the fight, only a sharp bark or the occasional kick from their taller counterparts encouraged them to return to their lines.

The most prominent creatures that moved amongst the hoard were taller than a normal man, their bodies had a strange blue hue about them, hard muscles covered their huge frames with only their torso, neck and head covered in a protective armour. Boney crowns encircled the sides and back of their heads, and if George hadn't seen these evil creatures himself only yesterday morning, he would have assumed they were just adornments on their armour. But he knew better, they were as real as the beasts who bore them. He clenched his fists in anger. Hate filled up his heart, and the desire to strike down every one of the hideous monsters threatened to overwhelm him; only then he remembered words from Raynard forcing him to stay his ground.

A stone began to form in the pit of his stomach, fear and rage boiling together to form a solid ache. Fuelling his desire to save the people of Kelan from the terror threatening to destroy their Capital City, Parva, the centre of Imperial security and might. It had already lived and survived under the threat of anarchy, now it seemed it would be destroyed by monsters from another world, a world that must be the embodiment of hell itself.

He looked on, transfixed by the strange creatures that bore down on them. They didn't seem to be in any particular formation, but moved in a huge mass of beings he had only ever encountered in his darkest nightmares. Bristling with arms of swords, pikes and axes; armour of metal plate, mail and boiled leather. Yet there was something about the enemy that appeared wrong. Apart from their lack of discipline, the armour they wore wasn't whole. For some, they wore only a mismatch of plate and mail, some adorned with ornate patterns, alongside plain battered pieces. It looked as if they had scavenged the dead of a battlefield to glean what protection they could.

George reckoned the open land between the city walls and the edge of the forest to be at least three miles in distance. The sappers had been busy however, the change in the landscape since he had arrived at the city, some forty-eight hours ago, was considerable. Earthworks had been dug, and palisades erected along the defensive lines. The huge stake filled trenches that hampered their movement forward, were successfully forcing the enemy to slow down considerably. As the numbers behind drove the front ranks forward, the army was forced to negotiate the ditches. Sounds of those falling victim to the vicious staves below, rang out across the fields. But the enemy showed no thought to their fallen, instead they followed the lines forcing them into smaller groups, breaking up company lines and exposing their flanks.

473

Archers lined the palisades ranged out before the city walls, regularly firing arrows into their ranks, until eventually the horde was forced to halt their pace, their commanders keeping their forces away from the lethal shafts.

And still, the city of Parva waited.

Beneath the city walls, the Imperial Army gathered, their numbers were many; George had heard someone mention at least ten thousand strong. But in comparison to the approaching army, it seemed woefully inadequate. George felt sick, the stone that had formed in his stomach now seemed to emanate a cold that was beginning to chill him to the bone.

There was a shout from one of the units that had taken position near their field hospital, he looked over and scanned the serious faces of the men and women preparing to meet the enemy. A familiar face stood out, and he watched as the old knight, Raynard, sat upon his horse in quiet determination.

George bit his lip, what he wouldn't give to be alongside his friend now, while at the same time, terror gripped him as he wondered at the horror awaiting them all. He balled his fists in frustration, he wanted to do something, anything to help, but he was useless to act while others faced the imminent danger. For everything he had done since that day at Niall's farm, nothing had changed, and he hated himself for his impotence even more.

A sudden roar and trumpet sound brought him out of his reverie, George turned his head and followed the gaze of Raynard and his fellow knights, to look towards the sound. Another roar went up, this time louder, as the Knights and

Militia that had stood below the city walls were now joined by at least another thirty-thousand knights at arms along with Militia infantry bearing pikes and halberds; short swords at their sides ready to be drawn when fighting the enemy at close quarters.

Armour and shields shone against the black and silver of their surcoats, their war horses armoured like their riders. Bristling with arms they took their places to make battle for the defence of Parva.

Ahead of them, the silver insignia of the Knights shone out as they rode along the lines, taking their places before their army. However, it was the man who rode before them all, his own gold insignia bright against the black of the Order. At last the Emperor had returned, ready to lead the Imperial Army against the hoards of hell.

George punched the air and roared out his elation with the rest of the army, their spirits lifted by his very presence.

So relieved was he, that it was almost too late before he realised a small group of the enemy was bearing down on the ledge the field hospital was erected on. Led by one of the huge blue monsters, one of hairy beasts running alongside him, some fifty of the hoard were now set on attacking the unprotected medical facility. A small enemy contingent had scaled along the cliff face of the ravine that fell away to the south of the city. An apparent suicide mission against the Order, but a potential disaster for the hospital.

George couldn't move, fear had seized his body. He looked on in horror as his fate seemed already sealed.

An almighty crash reverberated around the air, freeing him from his stupor. The world before him seemed to blur

475

into a display of twisted bodies and flashing steel, as Raynard, along with his unit of knights, tore into the advancing enemy faction.

The screams and roars of battle rang out, while George looked on in dismay. It seemed to take forever, but in truth it was barely moments from when the enemy first attacked and when the knights smashed their way through their lines.

Completely caught off guard, the charging monsters reeled against the Order's attack, and for a moment it looked as if they would be overwhelmed. But then they counterattacked, forcing back the knights' charge.

There was nothing organised about the clash, it was now an all out brawl, as Raynard rallied his own knights again to push back. The mounted soldiers forcing their way forward, while the enemy dug in their heels, refusing to give way. Even though the monsters of the enemy were large and their weapons vicious and deadly, they lacked the discipline and proficiency of the Order. While they used weight and strength to fight, the knights and their horses moved quickly and efficiently, finding weaknesses in their defences and ill fitting armour.

Despite George's original fear that the sheer size and mass of the enemy would decide the fate of Parva, he saw now that it was strategy and skill that could hold the end of the battle in the balance.

Then the unthinkable happened, a hairy beast stood on its hind legs and lunged at Raynard and his mount. The horse screamed in agony as it went down in a shower of blood, an artery ripped open by the monster's claws. Raynard tried to jump free of his horse as he fell, but he

476

appeared to be caught in his stirrup and his legs were crushed under the unfortunate animal, before he could be completely free. A final blow from the beast ended the flailing animal's suffering, before the monster now turned his attention onto the knight trapped beneath his mount's body.

Raynard reached out for his fallen sword, but his numb fingers found only bare earth. He looked on in resigned horror as the beast made to lunge forward, its eyes blazing with the assurance of victory.

A yowl of pain and anger roared from its open maw, its eyes blazed with confusion and pain as the blade ripped into exposed flesh due to its ill fitting leather armour. Caught off balance, it stumbled as it spun round to see what had hindered its impending kill. Howling with rage it briefly saw a human, unprotected by armour, smashing a further blow towards its neck.

George had found Raynard's sword as he rushed towards the beast. Heedless of what he was going to do, all he knew was that he couldn't let his friend and mentor die at the hands of this monster. Barely aware of what he was doing, his body took over as he delivered blow after blow to the shaggy coat of the brute. Hacking at armour and flesh alike, anything to stop the beast in its deadly pursuit.

He had no fear now, only rage fuelled his assault as he slashed and stabbed at anything he could. It was said afterwards, by a knight who had witnessed his attack on the beast, that it was no doubt the unpredictability and ferocity that probably saved him from the monster's counterattack. Even as he rained down each blow, George was unaware of one of the smaller creatures leaping upon his back, scratching and biting at the young man. But George fought on, the blood from his own injuries mingling with the gore and blood from the beast.

Another creature threw itself onto George's chest, digging claw-like toes into his sides as it tried to scratch at his face. Dropping Raynard's sword, George grabbed at his latest attacker and threw it from him, he screamed in pain as its claws raked at his flesh in a desperate attempt to continue the onslaught. The creature hit the ground, but was already scrabbling to its feet as it made to leap back onto George's body. Stepping back to get away from the renewed attack, George fell over the lifeless legs of Raynard's horse. But as he went sprawling, he threw his weight behind him, crushing the creature on his back against the ground, knocking the wind out of it as he fell.

The hairy beast took the opportunity now, forgetting the sprawled body of Raynard, and set its intentions on seeing off the irritation that had caused it so much pain. George shut his eyes as the beast made to throw itself upon the young man.

But the killing blow never came.

Once again the beast's advance was thwarted, and when George opened his eyes, the beast's body crashed into the ground beside him, its throat pierced by a long steel tipped pike.

The second small creature now took its opportunity to strike back at George while he lay on the ground. Again it was about to leap at him but a heavy iron shod hoof cleaved its exposed head before it could leave the ground. A knight of the Order spun his horse round, its hooves pounding the earth and the helpless body of the creature. Soon there was nothing left but a bloody mess within the mud.

Beneath him, George felt the creature begin to move. Leaping up from his prone position on the ground, he turned and seized Raynard's sword and plunged it into the little body. Evil eyes stared back at him in enraged shock before the light disappeared from them in its agonised death.

He heard a voice shouting at him, he whirled round to see the mounted knight that had killed the hairy beast and trampled the second creature.

'Get out of here lad, and take him with you.'

Then he was gone, into the melee that had moved back towards the enemy lines, the Order pushing the monsters back.

His body wracked with pain and exhaustion from the fight and blood loss, George staggered, rather than ran, towards the body of Raynard, searching for signs of life. Despite his own injuries, all he could think was to get his friend to safety. The knight had managed to haul himself free of his horse while George had fought the beast, but the effort had been so great, he barely had the energy to stay alive. His blood soaked into the churned, muddied ground around him, and George forced himself to drag his friend's armour laden body to safety, unaware if he was alive or dead.

His years working on Niall's farm had made George strong, yet his lungs screamed with the effort of sucking in sufficient air. But he didn't care. He hauled his friend as far as the base of the ridge that held the field hospital, but in the end, even George's own body struggled to keep his legs beneath him. Falling to the ground he clutched at Raynard, willing him to still live, not leave him alone to die out here on the battlefield.

Looking around him, it took some moments for him to realise that the two armies were still standing in their positions on open fields. Throughout the whole skirmish below the ridge, neither lines had moved to attack or save their own. Anger welled up within him, had the Emperor thrown his own knights to the fate of the enemy? Tears ran down his mud and blood spattered face, his energy too spent to comprehend the treachery he felt inside.

His eyes closed against the pain that overwhelmed him, while his exhausted brain tried to make sense of all the shapes and voices that now milled around. Visions of monsters pawing at his body flitted across his mind, he screamed out in terror at their touch before he slowly slipped into oblivion. The last thing he remembered was somewhere in the distance, a blast of a horn sounding the retreat.

40

An Unexpected Turn Of Events

Bales frowned as he screwed up his eyes, trying to focus on the Imperial Army spread out under the walls of Parva. He wished he had some binoculars, but apparently the Kyawann army didn't require such technology. They said their eyesight allowed them to see much farther than mere human eyes; Bales believed it was more likely because they were too primitive and afraid of technology. Either way, he was left frustrated at the lack of clarity as he scanned the enemy lines. He snorted with disgust.

'Where is he?'

'Who Sir?'

Bales glanced at the man speaking beside him. One of his Patrol Captains considered him questioningly. His eyes were as dead as a corpse, Bales looked away quickly. His insides churned as he felt a small tug, as if one of the souls that resided within him, had found recognition and great loss in the man that stood beside him.

Pushing the uncomfortable feeling down, he gazed back out over the field at the tens of thousands of soldiers waiting to do battle.

'Nathan, that idiot who proclaims himself as Emperor. He's not there. And where the fuck is the rest of the Imperial Army? This should be a battle worthy of a great General, this will barely tire our front ranks.'

The Kyawann army, had by now, drawn their lines still some distance from those of the Imperial Army. The Order may not look huge in number, but they still had archers placed upon the ramparts of the city walls and in particular, ranged along the palisades set out across the fields. Bales considered there was no point in losing soldiers needlessly, just so trigger happy Militia can find their range by shooting deadly bolts and arrows into his army's ranks.

Bales had to admit he wasn't overly impressed with the attitude of his own troops so far either. His forces had been compelled to travel at speed, in order to arrive at Parva's gates before the Emperor could rally his own army. He didn't want the Order to have the opportunity to dig in defences before the caldera walls.

But Gellan and Duran had insisted that they were unable to deliver Bales and his warriors any nearer, due to the protections Nathan had put in place. Bales had the impression there was more to it than that. He wasn't sure, but the two gods seemed different since they opened the gates to Kyawann. Nevertheless, he had a job to do, and was determined to see it through. As far as he was concerned, this wasn't about petty arguments between the gods, this was all about his vengeance on the man he despised above all others. The Emperor Nathan.

He hadn't cared about the few troops he had lost in the forest, even those who had succumbed to the stake filled trenches, his numbers were sufficient to cope with the losses. But the reduction in their speed once they entered the trees had annoyed him. His angry outbursts had done nothing to encourage Kendon and his Captains to urge his army to move faster. Even now, as they made their way out of the trees and onto the field of impending battle, they were forced to slow down and reform their lines further back from the city and its army.

All the while, the Order watched and waited as Bales seethed in frustration.

Trees from the forest behind them had been felled to create a makeshift platform, so that Bales and his Captains could watch the battle unfold. It may be some way off from the front of his army, but Bales was more than happy to stay back and watch everything at a safer distance. It was far too dangerous to be any closer to where the actual fighting was taking place.

But the question still stood, why wasn't Nathan there?

Suddenly, there was an almighty roar from the city and Bales rushed forward on his platform, barely able to stop himself from falling head long into his troops below.

Screwing up his eyes as tight as he could to focus and still be able to see, he saw what had caused such excitement from the Imperial Army.

Riding forth were seven men. The black and gold of the Emperor, a marked contrast to that of the silver and black of the other six Knights that rode out either side of him.

'Yes.' Bales balled his fists and grinned, only just stopping short of punching the air with glee. 'Now things will start to get interesting.'

There was another roar and before the city wall, tens of thousands of knights of the Imperial Order and Militia appeared.

Spinning round to face his Captains, Bales ignored the feeling of longing and pain that erupted inside him. His eyes wild with elation as he envisaged the tremendous victory he must now surely achieve. The might of the of his own superior army, finally crushing Nathan's Empire.

A shout ran through his troops and Bales turned back to the field. A small group of his army had broken away, they were now rushing towards an area that had been set aside on a ledge as a field hospital; its identifying marks clear for all to see. Anger flashed within him, shouting out to the Tieveran Commander, Kendon, who was forced to stand with him on the platform, he demanded an explantation.

'What the fuck are they doing?'

'They saw the unprotected lines, and so made their way along the cliffs of the ravine in order to gain a victory for you General.'

Bales caught the sneer in his Commander's voice, but was distracted by movement near the front of his ranks, suggesting they were desperate to join in the charge.

He bellowed until his voice hurt.

'Stand fast all of you. No-one move. I will tell you all when to start the charge. The next man to move will end up on a spit. Do you understand me?'

By now the small, weasel like man was shaking with rage. His voice had raised in both decibels and octaves during his tirade. Kendon grimaced with disgust, but acknowledged his orders. When Bales finally seemed to be satisfied that his army was once more maintaining their positions, he allowed himself to calm down. He had no idea how these monsters were able to communicate across the mass of troops so quickly, but he was relieved nonetheless.

His eyes were sore from squinting so hard, it also took a few moments to gain back his composure. As such, he didn't see the figure rushing in front of the enemy lines, stopping when they reached the stirrup of the Emperor. Only when the horns blasted the retreat did he look up, confusion flashing across his features.

'What is he doing? He can't surrender now. He has to give me my victory. This is…'

Bales didn't finish his next tirade, the words had caught in his throat. Eyes wide with horror, he stood on the platform, unable to move. Finally he let out a barely perceptible exclamation as his plans for an almighty conquest began to unravel.

'Fuck.'

41

A Dash Of

Mercy

J ean knew there was something wrong as soon as she
arrived under the Gazebo at the Retreat. The
overwhelming sense of fear, anticipation and
adrenaline hung heavily in the air, even in this
tranquil space hidden away from the outside world. She
knew the signs only too well, they couldn't mean anything
else other than impending battle, and most likely a big one at
that.

She hurtled down the paths between the beautifully manicured lawns and flowerbeds, still displaying their late summer blooms. Conscious that Nathan and the other Knights were unlikely to be at the house with an impending battle about to take place around the city, she nevertheless had to make sure.

Yanking open the door to the boot room that led into the kitchen, she continued to run into the large hall, calling out if anyone was still around. The pervading silence confirmed her initial thoughts and she made for the front door leading to the tunnel that would take her up to the palace without stopping.

Barely aware if the door was closed behind her properly or not, she dashed through the tunnel, her boots echoing off the walls. The guards at their watch station between the Retreat and the Palace proper, stood watching at the noise and commotion. She ignored their gestures to wait and waved them away, it was pointless stopping to ask them what was going on, she would find out soon enough.

Running on until she came to the atrium, she passed through the large double doors that took her onto the broad stone steps. Not slowing, she continued down to the large parade square and the iron gates overlooking the Avenue. She pause briefly, however, before making for the guard room. She recognised the knight on duty as the newly promoted, Captain Kate Bridger, standing at the door when she arrived. Jean remembered her as the tenant living above Ty's apartments.

'What's going on Kate?'

She looked tired as she shook her head, concern and fear etched across her face. To Jean, she seemed to have aged overnight.

The young knight shook her head. 'Hell has come to our gates and threatens the city, Jean.'

Jean frowned. 'What are you talking about, Hell?'

'Monsters and demons marching to take Parva to its doom.'

Jean's blood ran cold. 'Don't be ridiculous, pull yourself together, if the city is under attack you need to keep your head to help the people within it.'

The Captain blinked at her harsh words and thrust her chin out.

'Are you suggesting I'm a coward?'

'Of course not, but fanciful thoughts are not helping anyone.'

'Then you tell me that those creatures out there are not real, because there are plenty of tales being told by survivors of the kind of evil they have brought with them.'

Jean shook her head in bewilderment. 'It's not possible, surely.'

Without waiting to hear anymore from Kate, Jean turned on her heels and took off down the small hill of the tree lined Avenue, towards the River Par, as fast as her legs would carry her. Once over the bridge, she turned left and hurtled towards the main city gates. The streets were deserted, but terrified faces looked out of windows, watching as she ran past. Shops had been closed and many were boarded up, it seemed the people of Parva were expecting trouble to enter

488

the city. Glancing up, she saw the city walls lined with archers standing ready with strung bows.

The gates, when she arrived, were closed; even a barrier had been raised to close off the river, allowing only the current to pass through small gaps created in the blockade. When the guards saw her running towards them, they opened the wicket to let her through.

She noticed that all the knights were now heavily armed, with swords drawn and shields carried. Light armour covered the most vulnerable parts of their bodies, allowing for ease of movement but still affording some protection against attack. Their faces were grim and resolute.

Nodding her thanks she passed through the gate, which was firmly closed behind her. Her first thought, as she took in the view of the impending battle field, was a resounding, *Oh Shit,* and now she understood why Captain Bridger was so alarmed.

Some hundred yards in front of the city walls were the rear guard of the Imperial Army. Mounted knights stood in ranks spanning the space from the south of the river to the ridge-line that dropped down into a steep ravine. To the north of the river, around two thousand knights guarded the narrow strip between the river and the cliff-face that abutted the city's caldera walls; the other side of which were the gardens of The Retreat.

Making her way quickly through the corridors that separated the different mounted units, she estimated there must be nigh on thirty or forty thousand troops lined up to face the enemy. Light and heavy cavalry made ready to charge at the first signal from their commanders; archers stood ready with strung bows and pitched arrows ready to fly; infantry soldiers, made up primarily of the Militia waited with halberds, pikes and short swords.

Glancing back to the city walls, Jean could make out the archers aiming at the front ranks of the enemy lines should they be stupid enough to come too close.

As she emerged from the mounted ranks she was able to see the enemy lines properly. They fidgeted, straining to throw themselves against the might of the Empire. She recognised the make up of these so called monsters, that had put the fear of the gods into the people of Kelan. A platform, far behind the enemy lines held a number of people who seemed to be watching the field with interest.

He hand instinctively went to her chest, a moment's memory of a previous battle where she had allowed herself to become too involved. She threw the notion aside, this was nothing like before. This was her home, and she would protect it no matter what.

The air was alive with tension, and she knew it wouldn't take much to set off either side. She didn't have time to gawp, however, she needed to find Nathan. A commotion to her right drew her attention, a skirmish was taking place where a group of the enemy had made an assault towards the ridge-line, that Jean now saw to be a field hospital. A unit of knights had charged and diverted the attack, pushing the enemy back towards their own lines. Archers from the south of the city had found the enemy targets with deadly accuracy.

Jean was relieved to see that neither side had taken the bait and charged forward of their lines. Though the enemy looked as if it was a struggle to hold them back much longer.

Standing before the front of the Imperial lines, she observed the Order's Commanders waiting with their units. And then, in front of them all were the Knights themselves, spread out along the ranks, ready to lead the charge when it came. Armed and clad lightly in steel, she knew they were as nervous as those they led, but no-one else on the field would know that.

She looked down the lines and sought out the only man she needed to speak to right now. When she saw him sitting on his horse, the black and gold of his surcoat picked him out for who he unmistakably was.

Without a second thought, she once more ran straight for the man who stood in front and centre of the Imperial Army. She passed Simon, who called after her, but she ignored him and anyone else who shouted for her. Only one thing mattered now, for whatever happened here, on the fields before the city of Parva, this was not the Empire's battle.

Somehow, she had to find a way to convince Nathan of the fact.

By the time she reached him, sitting upon his black horse Bron, her lungs felt as if they were on fire. Gulping in air, she seized onto his stirrup and hushed him to hear her out. She felt movement, as several people tried to intercept her, but Nathan raised his hand and sent them away.

Watching her catch her breath he frowned, while Jean looked up into his concerned face, framed by the steel of his helmet that shone bright in the afternoon sunlight. Finally

491

catching her breath, she asked the one question she prayed she knew the answer to. Grasping his stirrup tighter she implored him.

'Nathan, do you trust me?'

42

Retreat

n athan took in a long low breath.

Keeping his mind focused on the battle ahead. He and the Knights had consulted their Generals, and orders had been issued out amongst the officers and ranks of the Imperial Army. Highly trained and well disciplined, the Order and members of the Militia that waited behind him, stood ready. Many of which were veterans of previous campaigns on worlds far away within the voids of the universe.

But today they were here, ready to fight for their city and the Empire.

Still, his thoughts lingered on the memory of Jean. The events of the previous forty-eight hours seemed to have been of a different time altogether. Even the last few hours, those

493

spent in the Citadel and aboard the ship sailing back to Parva; his stomach churned as he remembered the waves of seasickness that caught him every time he made that awful trip. She had gone so quickly, and they'd had such little time to talk, he barely even had a chance to say goodbye. Now he could only hope that he would have the opportunity to see her again.

From the moment he arrived with the other Knights under the Gazebo in the garden, he had virtually no time to consider the previous events that had led up to his absence from the Empire and the city of Parva. However, he threw himself into the urgency of the situation whilst still listening to the bare details, related by Damien, as they made their way quickly to the house.

Field Marshall Inchgower had been frantically calling and sending messages, and when he had finally managed to speak to Damien his comments were brief and to the point.

The city is under attack, we need the Emperor here now.

Details were garbled, referring to blue giants and shaggy beasts, marching with other monsters that had devastated villages and farms on their journey to Parva.

Stopping briefly at the stable yard they made their way to Paul's own office and area where his staff usually gathered for meeting and briefings. There, they met with grooms who helped them to change into gambeson and plated boots. Finally, they made their way quickly to the top of the caldera walls. By the time they had arrived, archers were ranged along the battlements, and Inchgower was already detailing all that had occurred since their disappearance.

494

Aware how precious time was, Nathan spent those moments studying the force settling far out on the fields to the south of the River Par. He estimated about forty-thousand, though it was difficult to be more accurate, and considering his extensive experience in facing opposing armies, this enemy force appeared to lack any disciplined form.

Aware, also, that small companies of the Order and Militia had joined with woodsmen of the forest, causing mayhem within the trees. He was pleased to note they had successfully slowed the oncoming force down. The spiked trenches were also causing some disruption amongst their ranks. But he was no fool, this was going to be a hard fought battle.

The progress of the approaching army also seemed uncoordinated, though there did appear to be some form of control from individuals that moved amongst the horde, albeit rather brutally; he mentioned his thoughts to the other Knights and they agreed.

But it wasn't until he scanned the enemy ranks with the aid of his binoculars, and viewed the makeshift platform to the rear of the formation, did his anger finally begin to rise.

'What the fuck is he doing?'

Damien raised an eyebrow and looked askance at the man glowering while still looking through his lenses.

'Who?'

Nathan snatched the binoculars away from his face, and glared at Damien.

'Bales.'

Suddenly there were several sets of lenses scouring the enemy lines, followed by various colourful expletives.

Damien shook his head. 'There is no way Bales has organised this assault, he could barely organise a tea party.'

The others nodded, while Nathan played with his bottom lip as he thought.

'I agree, he is not a natural leader, but he is a man who knows how to gain favour from influential people. I have a feeling this is the work of Gellan and Duran again, this time they have employed the unscrupulous aptitude for disorder of our ex-General.'

'Is it something we should be concerned about?'

Nathan thought for a moment before slowly shaking his head. 'No, we treat this as any other threat to the Empire. Whatever reason Gellan and Duran have felt the need to use Bales for, it is not to lead an army. Our concern should be with these invaders themselves, we can worry about Bales later.'

He gave a final look out over the field, and assessed the vastly undermanned ranks of the Order and Militia below the walls. To the north of the river, a unit of mounted knights made ready to protect the only gate that led directly into the area designated as stables and paddocks for the horses of the Order. He was pleased to learn that earlier that night, under the cover of darkness, a detachment of Militia sappers had destroyed the only bridges that spanned the Par between the city and the forest to the east. But still he wanted to make sure there were no surprises.

'Add extra artillery here to protect the unit below, and add a Militia infantry detachment while we're at it. I doubt if they will make it across the river, but we'll not take any chances.'

He inspected the palisades that had been driven into the ground some several-hundred yards in front of the city walls. Sharpened tree trunks alternately placed upright and angled towards the enemy to form a series of solid wooden blockades.

Heavily armoured archers remained ready behind the palisades, occasionally firing arrows to find their range, catching any stray members of the enemy foolish enough to come too far forward of their lines.

Eventually, orders appeared to be given for the hordes to move back out of range until they were ready to engage in the battle proper. But still, lookouts kept an eye on movements ready for any foolhardy souls pushing their luck. They weren't impenetrable, but it did give some control of the offensive to the defenders for a while.

Turning, he gestured that they all get ready, he needed to bring an army to Parva to see off these unwanted invaders. He didn't doubt the Imperial army could win the day, but he felt sick that it was going to cost them dearly in good men and women to do so.

When he thought of the little man standing on the platform so far behind his own lines, Nathan clenched his fists in anger. Bales had a lot to answer for, and this time the arrogant little prick wasn't going to walk away.

The Knight's had their light armour brought to the stables and while grooms helped to fit breast plates and vambraces, they held council with Inchgower and their Generals. Confirming strategies for the impending battle. It was clear to the Knights they were deeply concerned about the approaching enemy, but with their Emperor and the Knights here, they knew that there was hope at last.

By the time Nathan and the Knights had ridden out of the main gates to the city, word had already spread that they had finally made it back to Parva. A huge cheer rang out from the Imperial Army as their Emperor rode the length of their lines, the Knights ranging out either side of him.

Making his way back to the centre of the army lines, he indicated for the Knights to take their places. When he was satisfied they were all where they should be, he signalled for the existing lines behind him to stand fast and for the Knights to move forward at a canter.

Once they were at a sufficient distance he released the energy in his mind and called forth the extra thirty-thousand knights of the Order and Militia he had previously given orders to prepare for translocation. The roar that had rung out when he joined the field was increased several times over, as the desperately needed reinforcements joined their ranks.

Suddenly, somewhere to his right, there was a rush as the enemy made a quick assault towards the ridge where the field hospital had been constructed. Their small numbers had managed to sneak through the steep valley below and make it behind the Imperial lines. Archers fired volleys into their ranks, but pulled back as a single unit of knights smashed into the invaders before they could reach the ridge and the unprotected medical facility.

Nathan could feel the tension rise around him as his own lines wanted to help their fellow knights. But he knew they would not move until he gave the order. The small unit tasked with protecting the hospital was on its own, they didn't expect reinforcements and it didn't come.

The front ranks of the enemy moved in hungry anticipation for the battle to begin, but someone, at least, had the sense to keep them in check.

Maybe Bales had remembered something of his training at Pernia after all.

In the brief time before the inevitable battle, Nathan recalled again the face of Jean, tinged with the feeling of regret that he hadn't had a chance to say goodbye to her should the day not go well for him. He was torn between wishing she could be there beside him, and thankful that she didn't have to face this horror, when a shout went out somewhere to his left. He looked up towards the sound, and again a shout went up, this time he recognised the name clearly. People were calling out for Jean.

A figure was running full pelt in front of the lines and Knights, ignoring the shouts as she made straight for Nathan. As she finally arrived at his side, she caught his stirrup and placed her hand on the side of his black horse, Bron.

He frowned as she tried to catch her breath, alarm and anguish etched across her face. But before he could ask what the hell was going on she drew nearer and placed her hand upon his knee and implored him.

'Nathan, do you trust me?'

The question took him by surprise for a moment, and his answer was far more brusque and impatient than he intended.

'Of course I trust you, but this is neither the time nor the place to be discussing that now. Get out of here Jean and we'll talk later.'

He couldn't be absolutely positive, but he was sure he just heard her growl.

'No, I have to know now, this is not your battle Nathan, you have to call a retreat and pull back your army.'

It was difficult to keep his voice low and calm in his shock at her unexpected demand.

'Have you lost your mind? If I pull back now I open the entire city to these monsters.'

'They are not monsters, and the only way to ensure the safety of the city is if you trust me.'

All around him, Nathan could feel the tension rising yet another notch, as those watching his exchange with Jean began to wonder if there was an even bigger problem on the horizon. He had to keep control of the situation, aware his voice was probably a lot firmer than he wanted it to be.

'Jean, I can't do this now. Leave the field or I will have you removed.'

'Don't be ridiculous. I am going to do what I have to with or without you, but for the safety of your army I urge you to trust me.'

Nathan looked at her sharply. 'What are you going to do?'

'I don't have time to explain, that's why you need to trust me. Please Nathan, pull back your army, now.'

His instincts told him to do as Jean said, but after the previous months of self doubt, and the now ever-present fear

500

of causing more pain due to making the wrong decision, he faltered.

But this was Jean, the woman who had more than once saved his life, who had stood unflinching beside him when facing horrendous odds, and refused to judge him when he hated himself. Now, all she asked was for him to trust her and he knew, there was never any doubt.

He turned to Damien, who was watching intently to their exchange, unaware of the content.

'Call the retreat. Pull everyone back.'

The relief on Jean's face was obvious. 'Thank you.'

Bringing his attention back to her he said adamantly. 'Whatever you do Jean, this is still my city, my people, if I need to defend them, I will.'

Jean looked quickly towards the enemy lines, then back at Nathan.

'Understood, but do not come forward of the palisades, this is important. And you still didn't answer my question.'

Despite himself he smiled. 'Of course I trust you. Now go and do whatever you have to, we can continue this conversation later.'

She returned his smile, and as the retreat rang out around the field, she made to turn away, stopping briefly before speaking.

'I love you.'

And then she was walking away, straight towards enemy lines.

'I love you too, Jean Carter.'

The archers and soldiers that had stood behind the palisades, keeping the enemy at bay, now pulled back towards their own lines. A dangerous, and potentially fatal move, one that required archers from the ranks to move forward to cover them as they retreated. In reality it was a procedure that was fairly quick in practice, but with an enemy looking for any weakness to exploit, it seemed to take forever.

But for Nathan, he knew his own army was highly trained and more than capable, without having to check their every movement. Instead, he kept his gaze on the back of the woman who was now picking up her pace, and silently making her way towards the enemy lines, through the withdrawing units.

43

An

Unexpected

Battle

nathan watched as Jean made her way quickly towards the palisades. He felt, rather than heard, a strange incantation that he couldn't quite decipher. He did, however, see the essence of fear that emanated from the foremost ranks of the enemy.

Before she passed through the central gap between the palisades, Jean turned her palms outward, her arms still at her sides, but slightly away from her body. Then he felt, a strange awareness that instinct told him to fear. He had to fight down the urge to run forward and stop Jean from going further.

All around him were shouts, as commanders gave their orders to stay still. Horses snorted and stamped their iron shod feet, while there were murmurs as riders calmed their mounts. But Jean had asked him to trust her, and he had to let her do what she needed to do, though nervous sweat was beginning to run down his spine.

Suddenly, it was as if the area between the two armies had come alive, as if a great door was opening, and what came through made his blood run cold.

Before them, rank after rank of soldiers came through the unseen door; and dear gods, they were more of the monsters that Bales had brought down on the city of Parva.

What the hell are you doing Jean?

He turned to Damien some way down the line, he couldn't see his reaction, but he could imagine the horror he was feeling too. He returned his gaze, watching the new military force Jean had brought through to his world of Kelan. But now he noted there was something very different about these creatures. While there were huge blue, horned giants, tall waif like men and more of those horrendous hairy beasts, these were well armed and well protected, with good fitting clean armour. They moved in a disciplined and ordered manner, and of utmost importance, still faced the enemy of Bales' army.

504

Jean was now standing with two of the waif like figures on either side of her. While they stood together, it appeared to be they who took charge of the emerging army, but conferred with her as they gave out their own orders in a language he could barely grasp.

Movement towards the tree line, almost three miles away, caused Nathan to delve into the small pack tied to his saddle and he took out his binoculars. He began to scan the rear of the opposing ranks. Noting, with alarm, more of the monsters appearing through the trees.

Had Bales kept them in reserve and now brought them out to face this new threat?

But then there was a rumble of noise coming from the forest area. Bales' army was beginning to surge towards the centre of their ranks, pulling back away from the new arrivals as they emerged. Screams were heard as some of the enemy hordes were pushed too far by their comrades and fell into the lethally spiked trenches.

Nathan understood, this new company had nothing to do with Bales, whose army was now surrounded by this new threat to the front and behind. With a steep ravine to one side and the River Par on the other.

He frowned, he wished he had more troops on the North bank now. If Bales' army chose to make a break for it across the river, despite the losses, there would inevitably be enough who would make it. His thoughts then turned to the ravine to the South, while deadly to any who fell from this height, those desperate enough may still try to flee the field by attempting the climb to safety.

505

His concerns were interrupted by a loud bellow that seemed to reverberate from the skies and he looked up sharply. He had to shield his eyes against the glare of the sun, and he wasn't sure at first if it was a trick of his sun dazzled sight; but then he saw the truth of it. He was stunned, and he was pretty sure he wasn't the only one.

An almighty sigh of despair was heard from the enemy as, emerging from the blinding light of the sun, five winged shapes appeared. Tracking their way across the sky towards them, gradually getting bigger as they approached.

The closer they came, the faster they seemed to fly, until a mighty gust of wind followed their wake as they swooped over the forest, across the battlefield and up over the walls of the city towards the sea beyond.

Standing in his stirrups, Nathan turned and watched their path as they rose in the air above the city. The most terrifying, beautiful and impossible creatures he had ever seen; and he'd seen a lot over the centuries.

Their bodies seemed to shimmer in the sunlight, changing from black to iridescent colours as they moved. Great bony heads that held an abundance of teeth, along with large, hawk like eyes, sitting upon their long strong necks, which arched as they slowed their flight, swooping once more over the field. Their bodies were some five to eight metres in length, with a further two for their necks and head, with long sinuous tails of another two metres. All in, Nathan estimated around nine to twelve metres, nose to tail.

Then, swooping north, their forearms spread to hold mighty wings, their hind legs were extended out in preparation to settle on the ridge of cliffs that led up to the foothills and the Ketler mountains to the North. With a final roar and a blast of fire, the five great beasts settled to gaze on the theatre arranged before them. Whether creatures of heroic myths, or children's faery stories, today the Empire played host to *dragons*.

Another enormous roar from the field brought back his attention, and the world suddenly reverberated with an explosion of noise. There was a moment of suspension, when the universe seemed to hold its breath, before the battlefield erupted into chaos, as the two monstrous armies collided.

The ground seemed to heave as the battle unfolded, and the explosion of noise was almost deafening. Surging into Bales army, Jean's warriors hacked into the ill disciplined and poorly drawn up lines of the enemy, viscously tearing through their ranks, surging over the dead to claw their way forward.

Jean's army smashed into the invaders, their panic soon replaced by dogged resignation and a determination to survive. They knew they weren't going to be given any quarter from this new adversary, and the only way out was to destroy before being destroyed.

The discipline of Jean's army cut into Bales' columns with efficient ferocity. Again Nathan looked through his lenses to see the platform that the hapless ex-General and his Captains stood upon, watching as it swayed dangerously.

A call from one of the men at Jean's side and Nathan was immediately brought back to the predicament of his own units, as several of the hairy beasts left the battle and turned towards the Imperial army.

Horses, already straining after the appearance of the dragons, stamped and snorted, with many knights fighting to calm, not only their own nerves, but those of their mounts too.

However, the beasts halted before the line of the Order and Militia, turned and faced the enemy again. Crouching down as a sprinter would before a race, but relaxed before the final call for the off. There were maybe a dozen of those beasts, that he was later to learn were called spujkis, strung out along the Imperial lines that still amassed in front of the city walls. Nathan doubted they would last long if they had to deal with a breach in their own army's lines, but to know that they would be there to help his own soldiers should the need arise, was a comfort at least.

This time, when Nathan looked over to Damien, his gaze was returned, both men stared with both alarm and confusion, while at the same time reassured.

All at once, another roar went up. This time the air vibrated with a long primeval cry, and the pair of them raked the cliffs to the North to see what was happening.

The dragons again took flight, this time though, instead of aiming for the skies, they swooped over the battlefield, scouring the troops below with searing flames. While seconds before, Jean's army pulled shields above their heads to protect their bodies, the metal apparently impervious to the immense heat. The enemy, however, screamed in agony as they burned from the holocaust. The smell of burning flesh mingled with the spilled body fluids of blood and worse, permeating from the field.

508

Nathan's stomach was only just settling from its trials at sea, the barrage of noxious smells threatened to overwhelm him with nausea again.

A loud splintering noise had him peering through his binoculars again and he saw, with some satisfaction, that with all the chaos from the fighting, Bales' own terrified troops were in danger of smashing his platform to pieces. At one point, one of his Captains fell screaming into the mayhem below, his tortured yells soon cut off as he was trampled underfoot.

Bales, wide-eyed with fury and horror, could only look on as his army was annihilated. He clung onto the disintegrating structure of his platform, while he desperately sought to find a way off the field and to safety. He yelled out to Kendon, who looked as terrified as he did, demanding that he *get him out of here.*

However, in an instant, the Tievera had disappeared. Bales blinked in confusion, but had no time to wonder what had happened as he felt strong claws grab at his body and haul him from his feet.

Finding himself flying through the air, the vice-like grip of the dragon that held him, squeezing to the point where he felt at least one rib give into the onslaught. He tried to call out in agony, but the wind was pushed out of him, and he could only wheeze as he tried desperately to breathe.

Wind rushed past his face, while below, he could see the devastation of his army spread out before him. Almost passing out with the lack of air in his lungs and the pain coursing through his chest, he was unprepared for the sudden impact of his bruised body hitting the ground as the dragon dropped him.

Dazed and winded, he opened his eyes and shook his head to try and clear his vision. Rough hands were immediately upon him pulling him to his feet; ignoring his shouts of agony. His arms and body were quickly caught up in chains, and so too were Kendon and his Patrol Captains. He did however catch a glimpse of the furious and disgusted look from Nathan as he sat upon his horse. But as he attempted to vent his own fury, the Emperor looked away, dismissing him entirely, and the disgraced General was hauled away with the others from the battlefield.

A horn was blown to the North and Nathan now saw that some desperate enemy soldiers had managed to make it across the river. In an attempt to flee, they had turned east towards the Northern Forest, but one of the dragons had other ideas and blasted them with a blistering firestorm. Those that managed to flee the worst of the onslaught ran back towards the city walls and the Imperial army that waited for them.

The archers on the walls fired at the terrified monsters, who fell under the relentless rain of arrows and bolts. As the survivors clawed their way nearer to the walls the signal went up and the artillery ceased firing and the cavalry swooped out in a pincer movement, forcing the now, exhausted and petrified, enemy into the way of the Militia infantry who tore them to pieces.

Three survivors tried to escape by jumping into the river, but they had no more strength to fight the current that dragged them under to a watery grave.

To the south, screams were heard from those plunging to their deaths in the ravine below, in their desperate attempts to escape. Any who clung to the cliff face to make the treacherous climb down, were soon burnt to cinders as one of the dragons scoured the precipice with more charring flames.

Jean's army had now made their way so far into the ranks of the enemy, some of Bales' troops had managed to fight their way through, and were now heading towards the city. Buoyed by the possibility of advantage, they charged at the Imperial lines, flooding through the gaps between the palisades. The waiting spujki met their advance with rabid brutality, but were far too few to deal with them alone.

Bearing Jean's warning to not come forward of the palisades, Nathan called out for the signal to make ready. Once given, the Order, led by the Emperor and the Knights charged into the oncoming rabble.

The exhausted monsters tried to claw at the horses as they bore down upon them, but armour plate protected their flanks, and the mounts kicked and trampled; trained not to run from the fight, but to work with their riders. The cavalry of the Order, cut into the poorly armoured bodies of the enemy, steel tipped lances smashing into bodies, impaling them into the ground.

Turning before they reached the palisades, the Order ran back through the disorganised enemy troops again, but this time only to clear the way for the infantry as they made their charge. Again, no quarter was given and none expected. Using halberds the Militia cut and thrust with vicious efficiency, resulting to their short swords only when they joined close enough with the enemy.

The Imperial army saw off the last of the invaders that had made it through the palisades, while Jean's army were now pulling back from the field.

The dead from the invaders lying where they had fallen, piles of them in places; cut down as they had scrambled in their haste to get away.

Relief coursing through his body, with bloodied sword in hand, Nathan searched the field, turning his stamping horse as he tried to find Jean amongst her army.

And then he saw her. She was already watching him with her two commanders still standing beside her. For a brief moment, they shared a smile, the chaos around them forgotten.

Then the shouting of orders being given, and soldiers reorganising, came rushing back in. The battle ended, now there was much to do, and many questions to be answered.

44

Ḥ'ntei

A muted quiet permeated the fields outside the caldera walls of Parva that afternoon. People moved around amongst the dead. Seeing to the wounded, assessing damage and looking for friends and colleagues; finding relief in their safety and discussing the events of the day in hushed tones.

The sounds of harness leather and buckles creaking, while unsettled horses were calmed, the dulled sound of their hooves stamping on the ground as they moved. Familiar sounds that spread throughout the afternoon air. But with the explosion of the battle that had echoed around the fields surrounding Parva, the atmosphere was more like a whisper on the wind.

Ensuring Damien and the other Knights were dealing with their Generals and Inchgower, Nathan urged Bron, towards Jean and her two companions that never left her side. They also made their way to meet him, and as they came nearer, Nathan strapped his helmet to his saddle and dismounted. Immediately, a knight was beside him, taking Bron's reins. Inclining his head to the young knight, Nathan continued on foot.

While he made progress across the ground, Nathan considered the force that Jean had brought to fight the invading hordes of Bales' army. They had fought with brutal efficiency, and now, as he watched them in the aftermath he saw the same mindset in their dealing with those that had fallen. The bodies of those that had died after breaching the palisades had been dragged back to be thrown with the dead now piling up in the fields where the main battle had taken place. So fast had they been, a company of knights had been posted to watch and ensure that members of the Imperial army were not carted off too. Nathan also observed that Jean's army were not distinguishing their own dead from those of the enemy, choosing to leave them piled together in bloodied tangled heaps.

When the enemy eventually engaged with the Order and Militia during the main battle, the only casualties were now nursing several injuries; ranging from serious to the odd cuts and bruises. Stephen had immediately taken charge of the assessment of the injured, making sure those who needed to translocate to Aria were despatched as soon as possible, while the less serious were seen to in the field medical facilities.

However, the casualties from the earlier skirmish that had taken place by the field hospital hadn't been so lucky. Several knights had died in their efforts to save the unprotected facility, though the numbers were still to be confirmed.

Paul was also busy organising care for the horses that had suffered injury or had fallen during the battle; his face suggested his patients hadn't faired as well as their human counterparts.

Approaching Jean, Nathan had an opportunity to assess her two companions. They seemed familiar, but it took a moment to figure out from where he had seen them before. They were tall and wiry, their armour was light and covered only the vital parts of their bodies. Their angular faces were distinctly human in character, yet their movements were almost catlike as they made their way across the ground.

Removing their half helmets, Nathan was able to see their features far more clearly. Then it struck him, the last time he had seen anyone like them was on Franco's spaceship. They were Vaupír, vampires from Kyawann, the separate dimension of the universe where new forms of life had been created when the Ti'akai had been removed from the Seventh Sector. Though those on Franco's ship had been cross-bred with humans, they had seemed larger in build, and while they were still big, were not so tall as these Vaupír. Also, now realising exactly who they were, he recounted how they had fought in this battle, quick and athletic, moving amongst the enemy as if in a strange deadly dance. The Vaupír on Franco's ship seemed clumsier by comparison.

Then, at last, he and Jean met again, they stole another smile before Jean introduced the Vaupír beside her.

515

'Nathan, this is Daci Alucard, Y'lin Yar of Kyawann.'

Nathan furrowed his brows and must have looked confused.

Jean grinned. 'He's effectively your counterpart in Kyawann.' Indicating the Vaupír on her other side. 'This is Mandril Le, his Second in Command.'

By now the other Knights had joined Nathan and they stood silently curious.

Around them, the clearing of the dead progressed.

Jean continued. 'Daci, this is Nathan L'guire, Emperor and, like me a Guardian.'

Daci didn't look surprised by this information and stepped forward to shake Nathan's outstretched hand, Mandril followed suit.

Jean introduced the rest of the Knights before Nathan spoke.

'We owe you a debt of gratitude today Daci.'

The Vaupír inclined his head, then shook it slowly. 'On the contrary, today has been an opportunity to rid Kyawann of a scourge that has played havoc among our people. My only regret is that we have involved humans in our affairs.'

Nathan raised another eyebrow. 'And what affairs would that be?'

Daci glanced at Jean before answering. The Tievera, known as Kendon, has been active in rousing the less contented members of our society, shall we say? There have always been those who prefer to seek a more unlawful means of profit. But Kendon has been particularly adept at rallying the most discontented to his cause. The rabble amassed here today is the largest contingency of his followers. There are

516

still a few groups in Kyawann that exist of course, but now this faction has been put down, they will be unlikely to cause any more trouble.'

Daci looked around.

'Where are the rebels that were taken from the field during the battle? I prefer not to stay any longer within the human realm than I have to. Kendon and his human cohorts have to answer for their crimes.'

Nathan nodded to John and Simon, who then left in search of their chained prisoners. He then turned back to Daci.

'Of course you will deal with Kendon as you see fit, but Bales and the other humans will be dealt with by me.'

Daci straightened and Mandril openly snarled; Nathan ignored him. The Vaupír's haughty attitude was beginning to annoy him, and he was as keen that their army was gone as they were. And he certainly wasn't going to hand over Bales to anyone.

Daci glanced at Jean again, a habit that wasn't lost on Nathan. Placing his hand on his own sword that hung at his side, the Vaupír drew himself up and glared at him.

'The humans violated the laws that govern the very existence of Kyawann, they must answer for their crimes.'

Before Nathan could answer however, there was a scuffle behind them. John and Simon came into view, along with half a dozen members of the order, dragging Kendon, Bales and three other men to stand before Nathan and Daci.

A group of Tievera and Vaupír soldiers stepped forward to grab at the prisoners, but the Knights put themselves in the way, hands twitching to draw unseen swords.

517

Daci was furious.

'What is this? I demand that you release these contemptible criminals into my hands.'

It was Nathan who glanced at Jean now; she was watching him carefully but remained silent.

'The humans stay here. The laws of the universe are my responsibility, and while Kendon has also violated these same laws, I will allow you to take him to do with as you please. But Bales and the others stay here to answer to me.'

Daci snarled and stepped forward, followed by Mandril. But this time, Jean moved and placed her hand on Daci's arm. He looked at her sharply then checked himself as she continued to move until she now stood beside Nathan.

'No Daci, you do not have authority here. Take Kendon and return home. Your presence here today has been invaluable as an opportunity to deal with the rebels. But you do not take the humans with you. Nathan will deal with them as he sees fit.'

'And how effective will that be? How can we know that the humans won't try and open the gates to Kyawann again?'

He thrust out his jaw and scowled down at Jean. The look she returned was cold and hard.

'Be careful Daci, you forget yourself.'

The Vaupír, realising he had pushed his limits, stepped back and inclined his head.

'My apologies, to you both.'

Nathan saw the look in the Vaupír's eyes, he may be sorry for overstepping the mark, but he still resented his authority being overridden.

By now they had gathered quite an audience, with the Imperial army standing in formation, sensing their Emperor may have need of them yet. The Kyawann army stood back, but watched cautiously.

Intent on taking the conversation away from less confrontational subjects, Nathan approached the sullen figure of Bales that stood in chains before him. He seemed even more insignificant than the last time he saw him, defeat seemed to have drained him of any resolve he may have had left. But he had answers that Nathan intended to obtain, and he wasn't concerned about the lengths required to do so. Bales refused to look at him as he came nearer.

'Where's all that arrogance now Bales? Without an army at your back, your insignificance speaks volumes.'

Bales snapped his head up and thrust out his chin in a defiant gesture.

'How significant would you be without the snivelling and fawning of the Order behind you? Especially with *them* licking your arse at the snap of your fingers.'

He cocked his head at the Knights standing behind Nathan. They did nothing but look on in distaste. Seeing the figure of Jean standing with them seemed to spark a burning rage within him.

'And as for that bitch, the witch should burn in hell. Darkness has fallen over your wretched Empire since she arrived, you'd do better to drown her and toss her into the sea.'

Nathan didn't react, the ravings of a beaten man meant nothing to him, though he felt he had made a valid point about one thing.

'Darkness may have fallen Bales, but it has only been on you. Causing you to be blind to the chaos and destruction you have created.'

Bales eyed him sourly and said nothing, but with his body in chains it was impossible to fight back with all the hate and rage he felt inside. He resorted to the only act of contempt he had left; he spat at the man he refused to acknowledge as his Emperor anymore. Unfortunately, due to his injuries and being held in an iron grip by John, his aim fell short. It didn't stop John from yanking back on the chains hard to remind him of his lack of manners, he cried out in pain. Everyone ignored him.

Nathan resumed his questioning. 'Well, charming as this conversation is Bales, we have far more important things to get through before the end of the day, so let's get to the point shall we?' He inclined his head towards the killing fields piled high with the dead. 'How did you manage to bring an entire army from a dimension forbidden to the rest of the universe? I am of course flattering you to suggest that you would have the possible wherewithal to achieve such a thing, but I am willing to be surprised.'

Nathan caught Daci moving impatiently somewhere to his left, he silently hoped he would keep his mouth shut. Bales said nothing, but just glared sullenly until a familiar voice spoke up behind Nathan, the former General's features darkened considerably.

'I think I know what has happened here, and I can certainly say that *Bales* had very little to do with it other than be another's pawn.'

Nathan turned and looked at Jean enquiringly.

520

'What's your theory?'

Taking a moment to study Bales and then the three remaining Patrol members she paused before answering.

'As you know, Kyawann was formed when the Ti'akai was removed from the Seventh Sector, while the universe was still young and growing. The impact of that event significantly altered the way life was formed. Kyawann became the home for those that eventually became the Vaupír, Teiver, Spujki and Alyca.

'There are of course untold variations of lifeforms throughout the universe, and Kyawann is blessed with its own beautiful abundance of nature; even dragons have flourished in its creation. The barrier between the Seventh Sector and the rest of the universe was weak and susceptible at first, and the memory of encounters between the two dimensions has lived on through the genes of countless generations. While the nightmares of those within the universe have embellished in their imaginations, so too have the people of Kyawann; both consider the others as monsters. As the barriers between the dimensions became stronger and locked away the knowledge of their existence, some of those on Kyawann were stranded within the universe, and have since evolved amongst those who now live there.'

She looked hard at Bales again who refused to look away.

'And so we come to the present day. The barrier between Kyawann and the rest of the universe is now so strong, nothing can pass through it, only by opening a portal can passage be possible. And only one person has the capability to turn the key to that portal, the Keeper of Souls.'

Jean looked up at Nathan who met her gaze. 'Me.'

'But you didn't bring Bales' army through.'

She shook her head slowly. 'No, I didn't. For someone else to open that portal would require immense power and supreme sacrifice. They would have had to create a means with which to attract those within Kyawann out, as they would certainly not have been allowed to enter. That, I believe, is where Bales comes in, *and* our old friends Gellan and Duran, who have also played a big hand in this deadly game of deceit.

'Within Bales I sense not one, but several souls, while these other three are like empty vessels.' She grimaced. 'It's quite creepy really. Though I am assuming that some have been lost on the way, as there are definitely more souls trapped inside this pathetic excuse of a man.'

She couldn't help the sneer in her voice, and Nathan could only agree with her sentiments.

'Anyhow, a great catalyst would have had to have happened for the door to open, and the destruction of a few soulless humans would unlikely to have been sufficient. Bales would have been protected to make sure he survived, so it would be interesting to know what they used.'

'They got too close.'

Everyone looked sharply at one of Bales' Captains who stood with the others, he seemed lost and confused. He blinked when he realised that all eyes were now suddenly on him. Nathan approached him and spoke quietly.

'What do you mean? What happened?'

Nathan fought against the urge to recoil from the dead eyes of the man, he looked as if in pain, and Nathan couldn't help but pity him.

'The two that brought us to that awful place, they got too close, and when Andy died they seemed to get sucked into the light, though they were still there afterwards.' The man looked even more confused, and Nathan turned to Jean, he was shocked to see her trying to stifle a grin.

'Do you understand what he means?'

'Oh yes, and I can't help but smile at the irony. Gellan and Duran got their wish alright, but they may not have been willing to pay such a high price had they known what it would cost.'

She looked around her. 'I would suspect that somewhere out there, those two are desperately trying to find a way to turn themselves back into gods.'

Nathan almost spluttered. 'Are you saying that they are now human?'

Jean nodded, and even Nathan had to grin at the thought.

'Well, well, there's a thought to ponder.'

He turned back to Bales.

'But that doesn't matter to you anymore. Your fate has already been sealed.'

Bales looked at him and laughed. 'You think Belan frightens me?'

Nathan shook his head. 'You're not destined for the luxury of prison, your crimes have already afforded the fate of your future.'

As Bales looked on confused, and Daci watched with a questioning look on his face. Nathan approached Jean again, but this time he was close, he barely made a noise as he whispered.

'Do you have it?'

The humour of a moment ago was now lost, she closed her eyes and simply said, 'Yes.'

Without another word, he turned and faced Bales. Standing tall and resolute, Nathan's face had become a mask devoid of emotion.

'Victor Bales, I, Nathan, Guardian and Overlord of all creation, do stand before you in judgment. I find you guilty of the most heinous crimes that threaten the very fabric of existence. Your soul is without light and plunges to the depths of the deepest abyss. There are no measures that exist to cleanse its darkness, it festers in its own foul morass. And so, I condemn you and those souls of whom you use most vilely.'

By now Bales was visibly shaking, and Nathan felt sick to the stomach knowing the inevitable task that he had to perform. Turning back to Jean, he saw that she too understood. She placed her hands against her heart and closed her eyes in concentration. Then, within her grip a sword appeared. Unlike the swords that she and the Knights had taken up when they became Guardians, this was a thing she would rather never see again. Its blood red stone, that rested upon the pommel, had a glow that seemed unnatural. Holding it out to Nathan, he took it in his right hand and the ruby like stone grew in its brightness.

He nodded to John, who made a concerted effort to keep his gaze away from the sword before stepping away from his prisoner.

Bales now understood, the enormity of his fate at last weighed him down, and his legs gave way. He fell heavily to his knees, his face was stricken as he began to beg.

'No. Not this. I can change. I was a knight of the Order. You can't do this.'

Nathan's voice was without emotion as he faced him. 'Victor Bales, with the blade of H'ntei, I have made judgment and found you guilty. And by the gods may your souls at last be rid of the evil you have bestowed upon them.'

Tears ran down the face of Bales and he opened his mouth to beg once more, but his words were never heard. Nathan had thrust the blade of H'ntei into his heart, and all that could be heard was the anguished pain of a sudden gust of wind as the souls within him were released; perishing as they tried to flee their inevitable fate.

With a twist, Nathan released the blade, and as the body fell forward, he swung the sword up to cleave the head of Victor Bales from his shoulders.

Beside him, the bodies of his Captains slumped in the arms of their guards, succumbing to the fate of their General. The guards dropped the corpses to lay on the ground, moving away quickly, with the look of fear and nausea clear on their faces.

Nathan stepped back and fought down the revulsion that coursed through him, H'ntei seemed alive, he could feel a sick elation as it vibrated in his hands. If he didn't know better he would have said it was purring.

525

Bales' blood appeared to seep into the blade itself and Nathan just wanted to throw it from him, but he knew that would be impossible. Such was the nature of this awful weapon of destruction, it could only be held by two people in all of existence.

One to wield it, but to not keep it, and one to possess it, but never use it.

He turned back to Jean and she held out her hand to take the offending blade. With regret he passed it back, knowing how much it would hurt her to feel it in her grasp; but he had no choice. Once in her hands she closed her eyes again and H'ntei disappeared. Nathan could only hope it was to a place that Jean couldn't feel its vile presence.

A gasp of anguish caught both of their attentions and they turned in time to see Daci pushing the lifeless body of Kendon from his own sword. He looked at them in resignation.

'All judgement and execution has been passed.'

Nathan just nodded. Far too much blood had been needlessly spilt today, he just wanted to scour its filth from his body and sleep in welcome oblivion for a while. But first they needed to rid the killing fields of the dead. He turned and spoke to Daci.

'Do you not wish to remove your own dead and take them back to Kyawann with you?'

The Vaupír shook his head. 'To us, the soul is the life that resides within a temporary body. In death they move on and leave an empty husk behind that has no more purpose on this plane.'

'I understand.' He looked at Jean. 'We should clear this, though it may take some time.'

She inclined her head, but then spoke to Daci. 'I will send your army back to Kyawann, they have been here too long and no doubt want to return home.'

The vaupír agreed and gave orders for his soldiers to make ready to leave. Nathan heard Jean make the strange utterances again, before the army, that had come to rid the invaders from Kelan were gone. Only Daci and Mandril remained.

There was a sudden flurry of movement above them and the dragons, that had sat atop the cliffs, watching in silence until now, settled on the area between the palisades and the Imperial army that had gathered to watch their Emperor in stunned awe.

Again horses had to be settled, but by now they had either become used to the strange creatures that had visited their world, or were too tired to fight anymore.

The dragons sat on their haunches, resting winged elbows on the ground while wrapping their tails about themselves. Nathan looked questioningly at Jean and she gave him a tired smile.

'They're just curious.'

He shrugged and he raised his hand with Jean following, as the two of them released the blue flames that would engulf, at least in part, the piles of dead. But as the first flames licked at the bodies, another burst of fire joined them. Stunned, the two of them realised that the dragons had added their own fire. Concern crossed both their faces, neither knew exactly what this would do.

527

There was a moment where only the blue flames continued their cleansing of the dead, but then there was a huge blast, and at once there was an inferno ravaging the killing fields. The blaze spread like wild fire, burning with a blue intensity that they hadn't seen before. But then, even as it tore through the dead, it turned and headed for the ranks of those watching under the city walls.

Concern and confusion ran through those engulfed by the blaze, but no heat emanated from the flames. Instead, it remained cool and purifying. The inferno ran through the entire fields between the city and the forest. Until eventually, the flames were no more than a flicker amongst the dead, finally receding into piles of ashes left behind.

Nathan and Jean exchanged glances, before Nathan called out that everyone should cover their faces. Cloths were rapidly held over the heads of the horses and people turned away, some burying their faces into their animal's necks. Then, together, the two both raised their hands again, and with a simultaneous click of their fingers, the burnt remains were driven into the air, making the atmosphere thick with ash, before eventually disappearing into the ether.

Daci and Mandril watched in stunned silence. They had been told the stories that had passed down the centuries of the man who had the power of the universe in his hands. With the execution of the traitor, they had come to respect and, they would also admit, fear, the one Jean called Nathan. The soul's journey was intrinsic to Kyawann life, and to destroy it was both terrible and terrifying. As Nathan and Jean had joined with the dragon's fire, their reverence to him was complete.

The Vaupír approached them both, the Knights also joining them, ensuring Daci and Mandril understood the Guardians would protect them no matter what. Daci inclined his head to Damien in recognition of his loyalty, then turned his attention back to Jean and Nathan.

'Today has been a great day in the history of Kyawann. We have not only vanquished the rebels that have plagued our peace, but we have come to understand our cousins within the vast universe as allies; to be honoured, and not feared. We leave now, with light in our hearts and songs within our souls. There will be many stories and ballads sung to remember this day, rejoicing in the meeting of the Keeper of Souls and the Heart of Creation. May their Guardians remain strong and ardent in their duty.'

Nathan extended his hand to the two Vaupír, who received it gladly in turn.

'May the next time we meet be under more pleasant circumstances. The Empire owes you a great debt of gratitude. Both it, and I, hope a greater understanding of one another is possible in the future.'

Jean stepped forward to each of the Vaupír, and they lightly touched foreheads, where a brief moment of connection was made. She stood back, and with a final gesture of farewell, Jean opened a doorway for the Vaupír to return to Kyawann, then stepping through they were gone.

A deep throated cooing broke the ensuing silence, everyone turned to see the smallest of the dragons extending its head down in curiosity of the humans at its feet. The Knights stepped back at the sudden closeness and it snorted warm moist air at the abrupt movement.

They were all now drenched under their already hot armour, and sweat dripped down their faces. Wiping the moisture away they looked to Jean to ask what they should do next, the last thing they needed was to upset one of the beasts. Jean laughed and stepped up to the dragon, and like she did with the Vaupír, she touched her head to that of the dragon. More cooing followed and Jean was giggling as she pulled away, looking at Nathan.

'It appears she's taken quite a shine to you.'

Daniel grinned. 'Let's hope no male dragons get jealous then.'

Jean shook her head. 'Oh no, all dragons are female, they are created from a genetic defect that only affects the females.'

He cocked an eyebrow and looked at her curiously. 'So how do you get baby dragons then?'

She laughed. 'Ah well, that is from some very dedicated males that make the trek to seek out a dragon mate. The course of true love is a long and dangerous journey to their nests in the mountains, and most of the males don't make it. But basically, the creatures that dragons originally come from are really just what we would call dinosaurs.'

Daniel was by now openly laughing. 'So you are saying females are dragons?'

Jean rolled her eyes. 'Yes, that's right, but then I will also have to admit that all males are dinosaurs.'

Daniel stopped laughing and looked around for some help. Damien slapped him on the shoulder.

'You're on your own with that one.'

Jean turned back to Nathan and held out her hand for him to come forward. He figured the day couldn't possibly get any stranger, and made to join her. She then, urged him to touch the dragon's head as she had done, and tentatively he closed with the huge animal. As their heads touched, he was immediately immersed in sensations of clear, icy air, soaring mountains and open grassland. Seas rushed under him with the brilliance of a golden sun guiding his way. Experiences of ages past wrapped around him, and for a while he felt alive in such ancient knowledge. He realised that despite his own age, compared to these magnificent creatures, he was still a relatively young man.

With some reluctance he eventually moved away, seeing the great ancient intelligence within the dragon's eyes and understood that she had experienced his thoughts and feelings too. He felt awkward that he should be the one who had received the better of the experience. He watched the dragon glance at Jean with a look of love and respect, and thought that maybe his life was turning out to be not as bad as he at first believed.

Jean had placed a hand on Nathan's arm. 'They need to return home now.' And together they stepped back.

All five of the dragons then pushed off from the ground, flapping great wings that caused a fair bit of downdraft, then they swooped up unto the air.

At first, they flew out over the city towards the sea, climbing higher into the sky. Then, in an elegant, but breathtaking dive, then glided over the amazed humans below, before closing their wings and spinning their bodies in the air. Finally, swooping upwards, they made their way

531

towards the eastern horizon. The air seemed to crack as their bodies shimmered, and their dark iridescent skin became bright metallic colours. Below them, their audience gasped at the spectacle, as the air in the east, opened in a golden haze and the dragons were gone.

Jean shook her head. 'Show offs.'

Nathan glanced at her. 'Didn't you have to open the door for them to pass through?'

She shook her head. 'No, they can open the door themselves, but only after I have called them.'

A final look back at the spot where the dragons had disappeared, Nathan turned to the Knights and the army still standing behind them. A number of the scales had fallen from the dragons as they had performed their aerial tricks and some of the soldiers were picking them up.

Paul also held one in his hands. 'Amazing, they are not scales at all, but more like feathers made of a biological metal.'

He turned it over in his hands. On one side it was an iridescent black, and on the other, a pearlescent gold. He grinned at Jean as he tucked it gently away within the folds of his surcoat.

Later that afternoon, as the sun was beginning to set behind the wall of the city, Jean and the Knights returned to the room in the stable yard to remove their armour. They walked together in quiet contemplation, and Nathan assumed, that like him, they were reflecting on the events of the past few days and were trying to come to terms with everything they had discovered.

He watched Jean as she sat beside him while grooms helped to remove his armour. Once done, they left the Knights alone, taking the armour to be cleaned and stowed.

An unexpected shout rang out within the subdued atmosphere of the room. Damien was standing behind Stephen with a shocked look on his face, before rapidly removing the rest of his clothing and scrambling to look over his shoulder.

'Are they there? Have they gone?'

His excited face looked around at the startled and confused expressions around him.

'Are my scars gone?'

Everyone looked at him in shocked silence. Where only earlier that morning, Damien, along with the others had displayed their ravaged backs, his skin was now blemish free.

All of a sudden, the rest of the Knights followed his cue and stripped to stare in amazement at their own clear backs.

Jean had stood aside and was trying not to laugh at the spectacle of seven men throwing their clothes off around her. When they were all finally standing around in stunned silence, she spoke.

'The dragons, it must have been the dragon fire with the blue flames that has cleansed your wounds.' She thought for a moment, and opening the buttons of Nathan's borrowed shirt she was still wearing, she looked for her own familiar scar that had disfigured her body from breast to hip. But like the Knight she saw with delight that it was gone.

The Knights and Jean were grinning like children as they dressed, and Paul disappeared through a door to his office, carrying the precious dragon feather with him. With a great sense of relief, Nathan looked around the room and considered how much he depended on Jean and the Knights, people he loved and respected more than anything in the world; despite their differences. He couldn't contemplate being without any of them. Jean was right, he needed to be more open with them, share his thoughts and not hide them away. He knew he had to be honest with them as well as himself, he owned them that at least.

Jean caught him looking at her and moved to put her arms around him. Pulling her nearer to him he hugged her back, relishing in the intimacy without fear of rejection. He didn't think he had ever felt more content and happy.

Paul returned to the room with a wooden box that was making a lot of vibrating noises.

'John, someone desperately wants to speak to you.'

He held out the box that contained all of their mobile phones. John took out his violently trilling device.

'It's Christopher, probably wondering what all the garbled messages I left him, were all about.'

He answered the call and moved away from the group.

Nathan was about to give Jean a long awaited kiss, when he stopped, noticing that Jean had also sensed it.

Something was very wrong.

Pain coursed into the room and they looked about in time to see John crumple to his knees. His face stricken with grief and pain, while his voice cracked as he spoke.

'It's Christopher. He's dead.'

Printed in Great Britain
by Amazon